Don't tell the BRIDE

Wedding Party Collection

Wedding Party Collection

April 2017

May 2017

June 2017

July 2017

August 2017

September 2017

Don't tell the BRIDE

Wedding Party Collection

Kelly HUNTER

Tessa RADLEY

Cindy KIRK

MILLS & BOON

HarperCollins
PUBLISHERS
Since 1817

Published in Great Britain 2017
By Mills & Boon, an imprint of HarperCollins*Publishers*
1 London Bridge Street, London, SE1 9GF

ISBN: 9780263930894

09-0417

Our policy is to use papers that are natural, renewable and recyclable products and made from wood grown in sustainable forests.
The logging and manufacturing processes conform to the legal environmental regulations of the country of origin.

Printed and bound in Spain
by CPI, Barcelona

WHAT THE BRIDE DIDN'T KNOW

KELLY HUNTER

For my mother, grandmother, aunt, children, Anne, Trish, Carol, Fi, Meredith, Lissa, Linda, Barb, Rosie and Jo.

Thanks for all your support.

Accidentally educated in the sciences, **Kelly Hunter** has always had a weakness for fairy tales, fantasy worlds and losing herself in a good book. Husband…yes. Children…two boys. Cooking and cleaning…sigh. Sports…no, not really – in spite of the best efforts of her family. Gardening…yes. Roses, of course. Kelly was born in Australia and has traveled extensively. Although she enjoys living and working in different parts of the world, she still calls Australia home.

Kelly's novels *Sleeping Partner* and *Revealed: A Prince and a Pregnancy* were both finalists for a Romance Writers of America RITA® Award in the Best Contemporary Series Romance category!

Visit Kelly online at www.kellyhunter.net.

PROLOGUE

Seventeen-year-old Lena West didn't understand the question. It had something to do with Euler's formula and complex *z* but, beyond that, Lena had no clue. Groaning, she dropped her pen on top of her grid paper and put her palms to her eyes so that she couldn't see the sweep of ocean beyond the screen door. Summer and school work never mixed well. Not when there was a beach a few metres from the house and a swell that had seen her older brother take to the water the minute they'd arrived home from school.

It wasn't fair that Jared could do his maths homework in his head. It didn't help that her two *younger* siblings were bona-fide geniuses—one evil and one not—and could have answered question six in under ten seconds. Fourteen-year-old Poppy—who was not evil—would have helped her had she been around, but Poppy had been seconded to the University of Queensland's mathematical think tank and spent most of her time in Brisbane these days. Thirteen-year-old Damon wasn't around to ask either. He was pulling yet another after-school detention—his theory being that if he was unruly enough and sneaky enough, he might just manage to avoid the land of secret-squirrel think thanks altogether. Lena applauded Damon's initiative, even if she didn't like his chances.

When you were that bright, people noticed.

Not that Lena had anything to worry about there.

Sighing, Lena opened her eyes and picked up her pen. Question six. There it was. Mocking her. One simple little question that everybody else in her freaky family could do in their sleep.

'Moron,' she grumbled.

'Who is?' said a deliciously deep voice from behind her and Lena nearly slipped her skin because she hadn't heard anyone come in. She knew the voice though, and her scowl deepened as she turned to glare at Adrian Sinclair, their neighbour from two doors down and Jared's best friend since kindergarten. 'Don't you *knock?*' she asked grumpily and knew it for a stupid question even as it left her mouth. Adrian didn't have to knock—he practically lived here.

'Didn't want to interrupt your thought flow.'

'And yet, you did.'

Adrian's grin kicked sideways. 'You said "moron". I thought you were talking to me.'

'Moron.'

'See what I mean?'

Hard not to smile right along with Adrian's laughing brown eyes. 'Smiling crooked will get you nowhere.'

'That's not always true. Jared around?'

'Out there.' Lena nodded towards the Pacific. It was still blue. It still beckoned. Jared was heading out of the water, board in hand. 'Why aren't you out there with him?'

'Thinking about it,' said Adrian. 'Why aren't you?'

'I have a maths test tomorrow.' Lena eyed him speculatively. Adrian had chosen the same school subjects that Jared had. Same subjects she'd chosen, give or take a language or two. He and Jared were a year ahead of her in school. 'What do you know about Euler's formula and complex planes?'

Adrian moved closer, edging in over her shoulder. 'Which question's giving you trouble?'

'Six.'

'The bonus question? You know you can always leave it?'

'How about we pretend that's not an option?' It wasn't. Not in this household.

'All right.' Adrian reached for her textbook and started flipping through it as if he actually knew what he was looking for. Long wrists. Big hands like paddles. Thick, strong fingers with callouses that came of hours spent kite surfing. Lena had the insane urge to put her palm against his and take measure, note down exactly how warm and big and rough those hands of his were…

And then the textbook thunked down on the table beside her, and Adrian's chest brushed her shoulder as he pointed to a particular section of text, and…*damn* but it was getting hot in here.

'You want a chair?' she asked, the better to put some breathing distance between them.

'Been sitting all day. 'M good.'

Lena shifted restlessly and got a nose full of Adrian's body-scent for her trouble. He smelled spicy clean, tantalisingly fine—and this after an afternoon of school sport. As if he'd taken the time to shower before heading over here, which made no sense at all given his tendency to end up in the ocean regardless.

'So…' he prompted, his voice gruffer than usual. 'Question six.'

Right. Question six. Lena dragged her attention back

to the matter at hand. No! Not the hands! Question six. 'So I tried to find a—'

'What's going on?' said a voice from the patio doorway, and she knew every nuance of that voice too, no need to look up to know that Jared was standing in the doorway or that he'd be wearing a scowl.

She looked up anyway and met her brother's narrowed gaze with curiosity. He had unruly black hair—a trait they shared, although hers was considerably longer and considerably more unruly. He had bluer eyes than she did because hers often tended towards grey in the right kind of light. They both had athletic builds. Lena had a yearning for curves, but it wasn't going to happen. She had a scowl just like the one Jared was wearing. The family resemblance was strong.

'What's wrong with you? Not enough Jared West groupies on the beach?' Jared was a wanted man as far as the girls around here were concerned. Most of those girls made friends with Lena in order to get closer to him, which wasn't a problem except that Jared changed girlfriends with dazzling speed and not many of them stayed friends with Lena afterwards.

'Their loss,' Jared had told her when she'd complained about the defection of her friends, and, while his curt words had soothed her ego, the fact remained that Lena was still appallingly low on company because of him. Jared had been more inclined to let her tag around with him after that, probably out of pity.

Lena could have done without the pity, but beggars couldn't be choosers.

'I *said,* what are you doing?' repeated Jared, heavy on the ice.

'Trig,' said Lena, figuring a straight answer might appease him.

Jared's gaze shifted to Adrian. 'That what she's calling you these days?'

Adrian held Jared's bleak gaze with an enigmatic one of his own. 'If something's bothering you, J, spit it out.'

Jared's gaze shifted between her and Adrian once more. Adrian straightened slowly and some message flashed between him and her brother that Lena didn't have the cipher for.

'You know the rules,' said Jared curtly.

'Do I know the rules?' she asked. 'What rules?'

'He thought I was hitting on you,' said Adrian, after another long and loaded silence. 'It's not encouraged.'

'*Excuse* me?' said Lena. There were two issues buried in that simple little statement, and while her mind shied away from the implication that Adrian might actually *like* her enough to hit on her, it had no trouble whatsoever grappling with the second. 'Jared *West,* are you scaring away my potential boyfriends? Because if you are…and I find out you are…' Lena narrowed her gaze. 'Is this why Ty Chester didn't ask me to the year eleven dance? Because he was going to—I know he was. And then he *didn't*.'

'Nah, that one was all you,' said Jared. 'He probably thought you were going to ask him hang-gliding in return. I hear he's scared of heights.'

'And kittens,' added Adrian. 'Possibly his own shadow.'

'Maybe I was after a refreshing change,' she grumbled. 'Maybe I *wanted* to see how the quiet, handsome half lived.' Facts were facts. Ty Chester *was* uncommonly handsome. Nor would it have killed her to spend some time with people she *hadn't* hero-worshipped since birth.

'You'd have eaten him alive,' said Jared.

'Yes, that was the plan. Jared, I swear, if I ever catch you interfering in my love life I will make your love life a living hell. Yours too,' she told Adrian for good measure.

'Mine's already a living hell,' murmured Adrian and Jared snorted. More silent communication passed between them, effectively cutting her out of the loop. They did it all the time and mostly it didn't bother her. Today, it did.

'Lord, you two, get a room.'

'Yeah, *Trig,*' said Jared, darkly gleeful. 'Let's get a room.'

'If we go surfing this afternoon, I'm going to drown you,' said Trig, formerly known as Adrian.

Jared flipped him a friendly finger.

'Is this foreplay?' asked Lena. 'Because if it is, can it happen elsewhere? I'm trying to concentrate on my homework here.' A valid point as far as she was concerned. Unfortunately, it focused Jared's attention back on her books.

'Since when do you need help with maths homework?' he asked.

'Since it got hard. What kind of idiot question is that?'

'Seriously? You really can't do basic trigonometry?'

'This is why I don't think I'm fully related to any of them,' Lena told Adrian. 'I'm the milkman's baby.'

'Yeah, baby, but you've got a lot of grit,' offered Adrian. 'Who cares if it takes you a fraction longer than the rest of them to figure out a trigonometry proof? You'll still get there.'

'Yeah, but not fast enough. And then they'll disown me. That's what happens to people who can't keep up.'

'Since when have you ever not kept up?' This from

Jared who'd never had to work to keep up with anything. He was always out front; always the leader. And Lena had always worked her butt off to make sure that she wasn't that far behind.

It was costing her, though. More and more, she could feel the gap between what her siblings could do and what she could do widening. It was the curse of being an ordinary person in an extraordinary family.

'Would you disown me if I did fall behind?' she asked.

And shocked Jared speechless.

Adrian was looking at her funny—as if he'd known all along that her insecurities were there but he couldn't quite figure out why she was voicing them now. Lena didn't know why she was voicing them now either. It was just a maths question.

'Never mind,' she said awkwardly.

'You won't fall behind.' Jared had finally found his voice. 'I won't let you.'

He just didn't get it. 'But what if that's where I'm meant to be? Water finding its own level, and all that?'

'No,' said Jared grimly. 'The hell with that. That's just defeatist.'

'No one's leaving anyone behind,' said Adrian soothingly. 'No one here's defeated. Jared's never going to disown you, Lena. He's insanely protective of you. Did you not just see him go caveman on my arse for daring to look at you sideways?'

'Sure I did,' said Lena. 'But he's protecting *you,* not me.'

'Maybe I'm protecting you both,' said Jared. 'Anyone ever think of that?'

'Overachiever,' murmured Lena and Adrian nodded

his agreement, and it made Lena laugh and broke the tension and she was all for it staying broken.

'How about I start this conversation again?' she offered.

'Can you do it without the emo infusion?' asked Jared.

'You want the bare basics?' She could do that. She pointed the pen at her chest. 'Imbecile in need of a little help with her maths homework, before *she* can go surfing. I'm stuck on question six.'

Which was how Lena scored *two* maths tutors for the rest of the year and how Adrian Sinclair earned the nickname Trig.

Nothing to do with being trigger happy at all.

Even if he was.

CHAPTER ONE

IT WASN'T EASY being green. Green being the colour of envy. Envy being the emotion Lena owned when she saw others walking around effortlessly and without pain. She tried to keep her resentments in check, but envy had powerful friends like self-pity and unfocused anger and when *they* came to play, Lena's brightside surrendered with barely a murmur. Being gut shot nineteen months ago had brought out the worst in her rather than the best.

Focus on the positives, the overworked physio had told her briskly at the start of her rehabilitation.

You're alive.

You can walk.

The physio had tapped the side of Lena's skull next. You're really strong. Up here.

Lena had taken that last comment as a compliment. Right up until the physio had started telling her to back off on the exercises and let her body heal. Lena had ignored her, at which point the physio had started comparing Lena to someone's pet ox.

As in overly stubborn and none too bright.

It didn't help that the other woman might possibly have been right.

Still, stubbornness had got her to the airport this

morning, and through the airport, and if she sank down into the row of seats next to the boarding gate with a muffled curse and a certain amount of relief, so what?

She'd made it.

Another half an hour and she'd be on a plane bound for Istanbul and when she got there she was going to find Jared, her wayward brother, and haul him home in time for Christmas. She could do this. *Was* doing this.

Didn't matter that she was doing it one step at a time.

Lena closed her eyes and rubbed at her face, putting the heels of her hands to her eye sockets and rolling them in slow circles, and it was hell on mascara but she didn't wear any anyway—her lashes were black enough and thick enough to go without. Her hair was thick and black too, and straight these days, on account of a good cut and a run-in with a hair straightener this morning. The wave would come back next time she washed it, but for now she looked reasonably put together. Less like an invalid and more like a woman on a mission.

Someone took a seat beside her and Lena lowered her hands, cracked a glance and groaned at the sight of her nemesis, Adrian Sinclair, glaring back at her.

Trig was big. As in six feet five and perfectly proportioned. He'd grown into his hands. Grown into the coat-hanger shoulders he'd had at sixteen. Good for him.

Lena had stopped growing at a respectable five-eight. Nothing wrong with medium height. Nothing wrong with medium anything.

'Go away,' she said by way of greeting.

'No,' he said by way of hello. 'I heard you failed your physical.'

Way to rub it in. 'I'll take it again. I've put in for special consideration.'

'You won't get it.'

'You're blocking it?'

'You overestimate my influence,' rumbled Trig. 'Lena—'

'No,' she said, cutting him off fast. 'Whatever you're going to say about my current state of well-being, *don't.* I don't want to hear it.'

'I know you don't, but I am *done* talking around it.' Trig's jaw tightened. He had a nice jaw. Strong. Square. It provided a much-needed counterpoint to his meltingly pretty brown eyes. 'When are you going to get it through your thick head that you are never going to get your old job back?'

Lena said nothing. Not what she wanted to hear.

'Doesn't mean you can't be equally effective elsewhere,' continued Trig doggedly.

'Behind a *desk?*'

'Operations control. Halls of power. Could be fun.'

'If it's that much fun, why don't *you* do it?'

'What do you think I've been *doing* these past nineteen months? Besides dropping everything on a regular basis to come babysit you? Why do you think I took myself off rotation in the first place?'

Lena had the grace to flush. Like her and Jared, Trig had been part of an elite intelligence reconnaissance team once, and, just like her, Trig had loved his job. The extreme physicality of it. The danger and the excitement. The close calls and the adrenaline. Trig *had* to be missing all that. 'Why *did* you take yourself off rotation? They'd have assigned you to another team. No one asked you to sit at a desk. And I *don't* need a babysitter.'

'Yeah, I wish you'd prove it.' Trig eased his legs out in front of him and tried to make himself comfortable in the too-small airport seat. Big man, with a body honed for combat. The pretty face and the easy smile…those were just for disarmament purposes.

'Adrian, what are you doing here?' Adrian was his real name. Lena only ever used it when talk turned serious. 'How'd you even know I was here?'

'Damon called me. He had you flagged the minute you passed through Customs.'

'Man, I hate that.' Who'd have a computer hacker for a brother? 'No respect for privacy whatsoever.'

'Handy, though. Exactly what is it you plan to do in Istanbul, Lena?'

'Find Jared.'

'What makes you think he's still there?'

'I don't. But it's the only lead we've got. Nineteen months and not one word on his whereabouts until now. What if he needs our help?'

'If he needs our help he'll ask for it.'

'What if he can't? Jared's in over his head. I can feel it. He wouldn't go this long without finding a way to contact us. He just wouldn't.'

'He would if he thought the risk of blowing his cover was too great.'

'If it's that dangerous, maybe he shouldn't be there at all.'

Trig shrugged. 'Jared wants answers. He *needs* answers. Get in his way and he's not going to be happy.'

'I won't get in his way. You give me too little credit.'

'I have never given you too little credit. That's not a mistake I'm likely to make. Too much *leeway,* on the other hand…'

'Misogynist.'

'Not even close.'

'So you *don't* plan to sling me over your shoulder and forcibly remove me from the boarding area?'

'Too showy,' said Trig, pulling out his mobile phone and tapping the screen. A nerve twisted low in Lena's belly and she shifted restlessly in her seat and looked away. She'd always had a thing for Trig's hands. A little part of her had long wondered what they might wring from her if Trig ever put his mind to it.

Not that he ever did.

'We took a vote; me, Damon and Poppy,' Trig continued. 'In the event that I can't persuade you to stay here and be sensible, I get to go with you and be stupid. Damon's already got me a ticket. You can thank him later.'

'Thanking him isn't exactly what I have in mind.'

'Damon cares for you, Lena. He already has one sibling missing. He doesn't want another gone and I don't want to have to explain to Jared why the hell I let you go looking for him alone. It'll be bad enough trying to explain why I let you look for him at all.'

'You approve of what he's doing,' she said sourly. 'You don't want him safe. You want him to find out who sabotaged the East Timor run.'

'Damn right I do.'

'What'd you and Jared do? Toss a coin to see who went and who stayed to look after the invalid?'

'Didn't have to. He went. I stayed.' Trig eyed her flatly and Lena was the first to look away. She hadn't been the best of company these past nineteen months—too jacked up on painkillers and self-pity to take it easy on anyone. Too focused on getting through the day upright to worry about hurting anyone else's feelings along the way. Trig deserved better from her. Her family deserved better from her.

'Sorry,' she said and got a knee nudge from those long lanky legs in reply. 'I am sorry.'

'I know.'

But unless she actually *did* something about changing her mindset and her ways, sorry was just another empty word.

'You sitting next to me on this flight?' she asked.

Trig nodded, his eyes scanning the other passengers.

'Don't suppose Damon upgraded us to Business while he was deep in the bowels of the airline's supposedly secure system?'

'He did. Said we'd need the leg room. You need to check in with the boarding staff.'

Call it fate, intervention or the joys of having a computer-hacking genius for a brother, but the overhead speaker system chose that moment to request her presence at the boarding desk.

'You want me to get that?' Trig asked.

'No.' Lena made it to her feet. 'I can do it.'

It was to Trig's credit that he merely watched as she walked carefully to the service desk and exchanged her economy ticket for a business class one.

No credit to him at all when he sauntered over, face tight as he wrapped one arm around her waist and another beneath her knees and carried her silently back to her seat.

She wasn't grateful for his silence or his strength.

She wasn't.

They'd travelled together before. Eaten together, slept beside each other on beaches and in ditches. Lena knew Trig's scent, the long lines of his back and the breadth of his shoulders. Shoulders built to cry on, though she rarely had. Strength enough to carry others, though he'd never had to carry her.

Until she'd been shot.

A part of her hated that she couldn't match him any

more. Couldn't pit her speed and agility against his brute force and make a proper competition out of it. The rest of her just wanted to curl up against his strength and take shelter from the pain.

The boarding call for their flight came over the speaker system.

'Lena—' began Trig, and she knew what he was going to say before he said it. She stopped him because she didn't want to hear yet another round of how she was too frail for this and how she should leave well enough alone.

'Don't tell me to reconsider,' she said and knew the threadiness of her voice for desperation. 'Please. I have to find him. I have to see for myself that he's okay. As soon as I know that, I'll leave. I promise. But I have to know that he's okay. I need him to see that *I'm* okay.'

Trig said nothing, just reached for Lena's little travel backpack sitting on the seat beside her. Reached for it at the same time she did.

'I can—' she began.

'Lena, if you don't let me carry your bag, I'm probably going to shoot you myself,' he said with exaggerated mildness. 'I want to help. You might even say I *need* to help…same way you need to see your brother and fix things with him. So let go of the *goddamn bag*.'

She let go of the bag. Trig didn't really have a hair trigger. Not all of the time.

'I don't think you'd shoot me,' she murmured finally. 'Even if you did have your gun. I think you're all bluff.'

'Am not.' Trig fell into step beside her—no small feat for a man whose stride was a good foot longer than hers. 'I'm ruthless and menacing and perfectly capable of following through on my threats. I wish you'd remember that.'

Maybe if she didn't know him so well, she'd think him more menacing. Trouble was she knew how gentle those big hands could be when it came to wounded things. Knew that he'd cut his hands off before hurting her.

Enough with the fixation on his hands.

They boarded the plane and found their seats. Trig stowed their bags and watched her settle tentatively into the wide and comfy seat. Ten seconds later he dangled a little pillow in front of her nose. Lena took it and set it at the small of her back.

Better.

'You got a plan for when we get to Istanbul?' Trig gave her another pillow and she contemplated swatting him with it, but tucked it down the side of the seat instead. She could always smother him with it later.

'I have a plan,' she said. 'And a meeting with Amos Carter in two days' time.'

'Please tell me you're not basing this entire journey on Carter being able to tell you where Jared is,' said Trig. 'Because I've already shaken that tree. He *thought* he saw him in Bodrum but he didn't get close enough for a positive ID. That was six weeks ago.'

'I know that. And if Amos has nothing more to add I'm heading for Bodrum to play tourist and see what I can see. My eyes are better than his. I know Jared's habits. If he's there I'll find him. If he's been there, I'll find out where he's gone.'

She eyed Trig speculatively, trying to figure the best way to fit him into her plan. 'We could pretend to be holidaying together. We could be on our honeymoon. Good cover.'

Trig looked startled. And then he looked wary. 'Not necessarily. Bodrum's a tourist mecca. Boats. Parties.

Outdoor nightclubs. Vice. We're probably going to be exploring that vice. I don't think pretending to be married would help at all.'

'You're absolutely right,' said Lena, perfectly willing to improve on her current plan. 'I could be your pimp instead. You could be Igor The Masterful. There could be leather involved.'

'Yeah, let's not go there either.'

Lena smiled at the flight hostess standing right behind him. To the hostie's credit she didn't bat an eyelash at the wayward conversation, just took her tongs and handed Trig a steaming flannel. She handed one to Lena too. Lena thanked her sweetly and shook it out and wiped hands and arms all the way to the elbows.

Trig sat down and draped his over his face.

'I'm still here,' said Lena.

'Don't remind me.'

'At least it's not the belly of a Hercules,' she said. 'And your legs actually fit in the space they've been given. It's all win.'

'I'm over winning.' She could still make out the words, muffled as they were beneath the face cloth. 'These days I'm all about risk analysis and minimising collateral damage.'

Well, hell. 'When did you grow up?'

'Twenty-second of April, twenty eleven.'

The day she'd been shot.

CHAPTER TWO

TWENTY-SIX HOURS later Trig collected their bags and herded Lena out of Ataturk airport space and into a rusty, pale blue taxi. No fuss, no big deal made about Lena's slow and steady walking pace, and she was grateful for that. Grateful too that Trig had chosen to accompany her.

'Where to?' asked the driver in perfectly serviceable English as he opened the boot and swung their luggage into it, smoothly cataloguing them as foreigners and English-speaking ones at that. The street kids here could do much the same. Pick a German out of a crowd. An American. The English. Apparently it had something to do with shoes.

'The Best Southern Presidential Hotel near the Grand Bazaar,' Lena told the driver. 'And can you do something else for us? Can you take us past the Blue Mosque on the way there?'

'Madam, it would be my uttermost pleasure to do that for you,' announced the beaming driver. 'This is your first visit to our magnificent city, no? You and your husband must also journey to Topkapi Sarayi and Ayasofya. And the Bazaar of course. My cousin sells silk carpets there. I shall inform him of your imminent arrival and he shall treat you like family. Here.'

The driver turned towards them, waving a small cardboard square. 'My cousin's business card. His shop is situated along Sahaflar Caddesi. It is a street of many sharks. *Many* sharks, but not my cousin. Tell him Yasar Sahin sent you. This is me. I have written it on the card for you already.'

Trig took the card from the driver in silence, probably in the hope that the driver would turn around and drive. Lena grinned. Trig had a weakness for carpets and rugs and wall hangings and tapestries. She had no idea why.

'You know you want one,' she murmured.

'Don't you dare mention jewellery,' he murmured back, but Yasar Sahin heard him.

'Are you looking for gold?' Another card appeared in the driver's nimble fingers. 'Silver? This man is my *brother* and his jewellery will make your wife weep.'

'I don't want her to weep,' said Trig but he took that card too. He didn't mention that Lena wasn't his wife.

'Are you hungry?' asked the driver. 'On this road is my favourite kebab stand. Best in the city.'

'Another brother?' asked Lena.

'Twin,' said the driver and Lena laughed.

They didn't get the kebabs, they saw the Blue Mosque at dusk and they arrived at the hotel without mishap.

Trig tipped well because Lena was still smiling. He got Yasar's personal business card for his trouble. 'Because I am also a tour guide and fixer,' said Yasar.

'Fixer?'

'Problem solver.'

Of course he was.

The hotel Lena had chosen to stay in was mid-range and well located. She'd told the check-in clerk that Trig was her husband, who'd joined her on the trip unexpectedly, and the clerk had added Trig's details to the booking without so much as a murmur.

'You sure about this?' he murmured as the clerk went to fetch their door cards.

'Why? You want another room?'

He didn't know.

'It's a twin room. Two beds.'

Still one room though.

And boy were quarters snug.

Trig eyed the short distance between the two beds with misgivings. They'd weathered plenty, he and Lena. Sharing a hotel room was not on the list.

He put her bag on the rack at the end of the bed farthest away from the door. Lena inspected the bathroom and proclaimed it satisfactory, because she'd wanted one with a spa bath and got it. Next thing he knew, the bath taps were on and Lena was rummaging through her belongings for fresh clothes.

'You want to shower while the bath is running?' she asked him. 'Because—fair warning—when I get in the bath I am not going to want to get out.'

'You're sore?'

'I just want to work the kinks out.'

'Right.' Trig cleared his throat and opened his bag, staring down at the mess of clothes he hadn't bothered to fold, and tried not to think about Lena, naked in a bath not ten feet away from him. 'So...okay, yeah. I can shower now.' He grabbed at a faded pair of jeans and an equally well-worn T-shirt and then paused. 'Where do you want to go for dinner?' This could, conceivably, affect his choice of T-shirt.

'I'm all in favour of room service, provided the menu looks good. And it's not because I don't want to walk anywhere,' she added defensively. 'Room service for dinner this evening has always been part of the plan.'

Far be it from him to mess with the plan. He eyeballed the distance between the beds again. 'Is it just me or is this room kind of small?'

'Maybe if you'd stop *growing...*'

'I have.' Okay, so he was extra tall and his shoulders were broad. For the most part, he was good with it. 'You just think I should have stopped *sooner.*' He eyed his little double bed with misgivings. 'That's not a double bed. It's a miniature double bed.'

'Princess.'

'Are we bickering?' he asked. 'Because Poppy tells me she's heartily sick of our bickering. I thought I might give it up for Lent.'

'It's not Lent,' Lena informed him. 'Besides, I like bickering with you. Makes me feel all comfortable and peachy-normal.'

Trig snorted. At sixteen, bickering with Lena had been his first line of defence against anyone discovering just how infatuated he was with her. He was still gone on her, no question. But these days the bickering got old fast.

He found his toiletries bag and stalked into the bathroom, only to find that that room was the size of a bath *mat* and that the spa was filling ever so slowly—a sneaky deterrent to filling it at all. Instead of four walls, the bathroom had two walls, a side door and one of those shuttered, half-walls dividing it from the main room. Trig reached for the shutters.

She-who-bickered would of a certainty want them shut.

He eyed the bathroom door and the floor mat in its way. He could shut that at the last minute. Never let it be said that Adrian Sinclair had more than a regular dislike for small spaces. Just don't ever put him in a submarine.

'Hey, Trig.' Lena's voice floated through the door. 'Five things you never wanted to be. And don't say, "Your babysitter".'

Never wanted to be in love with my best friend's sister, he thought darkly. Especially since she'd never once given him the slightest encouragement.

'I never wanted to be a motor mechanic,' he said instead.

'Be serious.'

'I am serious.' He turned on the shower taps, hoping for a little pressure. Nope. Maybe if he turned the bath taps off. He shucked his clothes and dropped them on the floor. And Lena appeared in the doorway.

'Dammit, Lena! Close quarters!' But he didn't reach for a towel or turn to hide his body. Most of it she'd seen before, and as for the rest…well…nothing to be ashamed of there.

Lena dropped her gaze, but not to the floor. She swallowed hard. 'I, ah—'

'Yes?' he enquired silkily, half of him annoyed and half most emphatically not.

His brain thought she was objectifying him and he objected to that.

His body didn't give a damn whether she objectified him or not.

'I, ah—' Finally she dragged her gaze up and over the rest of him and then, with what seemed like a whole lot of effort, looked away. 'Sorry. Pretty sure I'll remember what I wanted to tell you sooner or later.'

'Size queen,' he challenged softly.

'Yeah, well. Who knew?' She did the quickest about-turn he'd seen from her in a long time and headed back into the other part of the room, the part he couldn't see. 'I mean, I'd heard rumours… Your old girlfriends aren't exactly discreet.'

'No?' He'd had girlfriends over the years—not plenty, but enough. He'd tried hard to fall for each and every one. 'What are they?'

'Grateful,' she said dryly. 'Now I know why.'

'You really don't,' he felt obliged to point out, and left the bathroom door open and turned back towards the shower. 'Who's to say it wasn't my winning personality?'

'You do like to win,' she said as he stepped beneath the spray and closed the shower door. Surely one closed door between them would be enough.

'You keep saying that.'

'Only because it's true.'

All throughout their teens and beyond, he, Lena and Jared had pushed each other to be faster, cannier, more fearless. It had got them into plenty of trouble. Got them into the Secret Intelligence Service too. Jared rising through the ranks because he was a leader born, Trig and Lena rising with him because they had skills too and the suits knew the makings of a crack infiltration team when they saw one.

No space between him and Lena at all when it came to what they knew about each other. No strength or flaw left unexamined. No shortage of loyalty or love. Lena loved him like a brother and like a comrade-in-arms, and that was worth something. It was.

But sometimes she saw the reckless boy he'd once been rather than the man he was now.

Sometimes she coaxed him into competitive games he no longer had the heart to play.

He raised his voice so that she'd hear him over the spray. 'Is there a burger on that menu?'

'Hang on…' She came back to the bathroom doorway, casual as you please now that a plate of frosted glass stood between her and his nakedness. 'Yes, there's a burger on the menu. Lamb burger on Turkish. Surprise. There's also meatballs and potatoes, salads, green beans, and lots of pastries.'

'Baklava?'

'Oodles of baklava. Walnut, pistachio, cashew, pine nuts… You want yours drizzled in rose water?'

'Rather have it in my mouth.' He squirted shampoo in his palm and raised his hands to his head.

'Are you posing on purpose?'

'Are you looking on purpose?' It seemed like a reasonable reply. 'Because I've no objection. You want a closer look, all you gotta do is say.' He reached for the shower door and smirked as Lena squeaked a protest and fled. 'Thought you were fearless.'

'That was before I got scarred for life. Now I'm wary. Don't want to get scarred for life twice.'

'Amen to that,' he muttered, all playfulness gone as he shoved his head beneath the spray again, the better to chase away the image of Lena on her back in the mud, her guts hot and slippery against his hands while the world around them exploded. Scrub that memory from his mind.

Good if he could.

'What kind of baklava did you want?' asked Lena.

'Is there a mixed plate?'

'I can ask.'

He heard Lena ordering the food.

He tried to think about the real reason they were in Turkey. Get Lena's eyes on Jared and Jared's on her.

Let them realise that everyone was okay and then get Lena the hell out of harm's way before Jared could tear him a new one.

Simple plan.

Didn't take a genius to know that the execution was going to be a bitch.

Trig emerged from the bathroom squeaky clean and somewhat calmer about sharing a hotel room with Lena. Lena had the television on and was standing to one side of it, flicking through the channels. She glanced at him, eyes wary. He thought she had relaxed a bit. Possibly because he had his clothes on.

'Food'll be here in an hour,' she said. 'I thought you'd take longer. I thought I might soak in the spa.'

Soak. Right. Lena was about to get naked and soapy not five steps from where he was standing, and he was going to ignore her and not even think about palming the bulge in his pants, not even just to rearrange it.

'I need a walk,' he muttered. And tried not to slam the door on his way out.

Lena sagged against the nearest wall the minute the door closed behind him. She didn't know what to make of Trig's moods these days—one minute teasing, short-tempered the next. That was *her* bailiwick, not Trig's. Trig was the even-tempered one, rock-steady in any crisis.

Calm, even when she'd been flat on her back in the sticky grey clay of East Timor and he'd been holding her guts in place with his hands. Calm when Jared had skidded in beside him and told him to get out of the way and Trig had said no, just no, but Jared had backed off, and gone and stolen transport and got them to safety while Trig kept Lena alive.

Trig, steady as you please, as the world around her had turned cold and grey.

'Don't you,' he'd said, his voice hard and implacable in her ear. '*Fight*, damn you. You always do.'

She'd fought.

She was still fighting.

Her injuries. Her reliance on others.

Her feelings for Trig and the memory of his cheek against hers and the gutted murmur of his voice when he'd thought her unconscious.

'Stay with me, Lena. Don't you *dare* go where I can't follow.'

Closest he'd ever come to saying he had feelings for her that weren't exactly brotherly.

Once upon a time, maybe, yeah, she'd have been all over that. All over *him* if he'd given her enough encouragement.

But now?

No way.

Because what could she offer him now? She who could barely hold herself together from one day to the next. She whose default setting ran more towards lashing out at people than to loving them.

And then there was the matter of her not so minor physical injuries. A body as beautiful as Trig's deserved a beautiful body beneath it, not one like hers, all scarred and barely working. No babies from this body, and Trig knew it. He'd been there when the doctor had broken *that* news, only it was hardly news to Lena because given the mess her body had been in at the time she'd already figured as much.

It had been news to Trig though, and she'd plucked

at a thread in the loose-woven hospital blanket and watched beneath lowered lashes as he'd dropped his head to the web of his hands and kept it there for the duration of the doctor's explanation. No comment from him at all when he'd finally lifted his head, just a stark, shattered glance in her direction before he'd swiftly looked away.

Not pity. He didn't do pity.

It had looked a lot like grief.

A bottle of red wine stood on the counter above the little hotel-room fridge. Lena cracked it and poured herself a generous glass full. She picked through her suitcase for a change of clothes and took those and the wine with her to the bathroom.

Water would help. Water always helped her relax and think clearly.

Find Jared. That was her goal.

Keep Lena out of trouble. She was pretty sure that was Trig's goal.

And then, once the world was set right, she and Trig could find a new way of communicating. One that didn't involve him being overprotective and her being defensive. One that involved more honesty and less bickering. Lena sipped at her wine and stared pensively at the slowly filling tub.

One that involved a little more wholly platonic appreciation for the person he was.

CHAPTER THREE

TRIG RETURNED JUST as their dinner arrived. He gave her a nod, tipped the man for his service and started moving dishes from the room-service cart to the little table for two over by the window.

Lena poured him a wine and another one for herself. She didn't ask him about his walk straight away. Given the tension that had followed him into the room, she figured she might hold that totally innocuous question in reserve.

'You taken any painkillers?' he asked, not an unreasonable question given how much of the wine she'd drunk. What could she say? It had been a long bath.

'Not yet. Tonight I'm rocking the red wine instead.'

'Any particular reason why?'

'Long day.' You. 'New city.' You. Never want to be on the wrong side of you.

She used to be able to read him just by looking at him. These days she'd have better luck reading Farsi.

Trig took a seat, lifted his burger and bit into it, chewing steadily.

Lena sat opposite, picked at her spicy chicken salad and drank some more wine.

'When are you meeting with Carter?'

'Tomorrow at two p.m. at the Nuruosmaniye Gate of the Grand Bazaar. You want to come?'

'I'll watch.'

'From afar?'

'Not that far.'

'Play your cards right and I might even buy you a silk scarf.'

Trig smiled. 'Not my thing.'

'How's the burger?'

Trig nodded and took another hefty bite.

The burger was fine.

He looked at her salad and kept on chewing, right up until he swallowed. 'Get your own,' he said darkly.

Mind reader. 'I'll have you know that this salad's delicious. Crisp little salad leaves and cucumber. Tasty tomato. All very healthy.' How was she to know that she'd take one look at Trig's burger and want something drippy too.

Trig's sigh was well practised as he broke what was left of his burger in two and held out one half to her.

She took it with a grin. 'My brothers aren't nearly such soft touches.'

'I'm not one of your brothers,' he said, and something about the way he said it shut her up completely.

Good thing she had the burger to concentrate on. And the wine. And those two little double beds that hovered in her view no matter where she looked.

'Adrian, is there a problem? Between you and me?' She hurried on, never mind his frown. 'Because we've been friends a long time and I know I've relied on you far more than I should these past couple of years. You've been more than patient with me, and I'm grateful, because I know damn well that I don't deserve anyone's patience a lot of the time. It's just…lately I get the feeling that you've had enough of me. And that would be perfectly understandable. *Is* perfectly understandable. And if that's the case, you need to stand back and let me take care of myself. I can, you know.'

'You sure about that?'

'Sure as I can be without actually having done it. I have this family who seem to think I'm fragile, you see. They baby me. They send you to handle me when they can't. I don't think that's fair on you. You don't have to do that. You have your own life to live.'

He thought on that, right through what was left of his burger, and then he drained his wine and turned his attention to the baklava.

'Tell me why I'm here,' he said finally.

That was easy. 'You're the family-appointed baby-sitter, sent to keep me out of trouble.'

'That's one reason. But it's not the main one.'

'Loyalty to Jared.'

'Has nothing to do with it.'

'You have a hankering for baklava?'

'Not enough to travel halfway round the world for it.' Trig eyed her steadily and no matter how much Lena ached to look away, she couldn't. She couldn't find her breath either.

'You're well enough to go chasing after Jared,' he said finally. 'I figure you're well enough to hear me out. Not going to jump you, Lena. Nothing you don't want. But you need to know that I'm here because I want to be here. With you. Because there's pretty much nowhere else I'd rather be than with you. You need to know that I have feelings for you that are in no way brotherly. You need to know that I both love and hate it when you treat me like family.'

He took a deep breath. 'You also need to know what

you do to me when you book us into a hotel as husband and wife. Because it gives me ideas.'

She didn't understand. He'd peppered her with too much information and not enough time to process any of it. 'I— Pardon?'

'I want you.'

'You—do?'

He looked at her as if she were a little bit dim. 'Yes.'

'But…you can't.'

'Pretty sure I can.'

'I'm broken.'

'Nah, just banged up.'

'I'm *me*.'

'Yes.' He was looking at her as if she were minus a few brain cells again. He was just so…calm.

And she wasn't. Somehow she had to bring this farce of a conversation under control. 'How's the baklava?'

'Tastes like dust.'

'More wine?' She poured him some anyway, whether he wanted it or not, and maybe that wasn't such a good idea because he drained it in one long swallow. 'You need to give me some time with this.'

'Little hint for you, Lena: this doesn't require much thinking. We've known each other a long time. I've been trying to impress you since primary school. You're either impressed or you're not. You either want me or you don't.'

'It's not that simple.'

'Yeah, it is.'

'I saw your body earlier.' She didn't know how to say what she wanted to say. 'It's perfect.'

'It's skin.'

'It's still perfect.'

'Still just skin. You think I can't see beneath yours?'

He eyed her steadily. 'You have flaws. So do I. No one's going into this blind.'

'Look at me, Adrian. Think of all the things you can do that I can't do any more. I'd hold you back and you'd come to hate me for it. *I'd* come to hate me for it. You'd have to be blind to want this.'

'I'm not blind,' he said grimly. 'This *can* work—you and me. You just have to want it to.' He sat back in his chair and pushed a hand through his dark shaggy curls. 'This isn't going well, is it? You don't think of me in that way at all.'

'I didn't say that! Don't put words in my mouth. God.' Trust her to push him away when she didn't mean to. She just didn't know how to *not* push him away now that he wanted to get closer. 'You're important to me, Adrian. You occupy a huge part of my life and always have done. Aren't you scared that if this doesn't work out, we'll lose everything else we *do* have?'

'Scared is watching you slide into unconsciousness for the sixth time in as many hours. Scared is thinking you're going to die in my arms. This doesn't even rate a mention on the fear scale.'

'Speak for yourself. I'm terrified here.' Lena reached over and circled his wrist with her fingers as best she could, one fingertip to his pulse point and her heart beating a rapid tattoo. His pulse skittered all over the place too. 'You're not that calm.'

'Could be I'm a *little* nervous. Doesn't mean I haven't thought it through,' he said stubbornly. He withdrew his hand from beneath her fingers and headed for the bed-side phone. He picked it up, pressed a button and waited.

'What are you doing?'

'You said you needed some time with this. I'm giv-ing you some.' He turned his head into the phone a little. 'This is Adrian Sinclair. I'm going to need a second room. King bed this time.' He listened a moment. 'No, it doesn't have to be connected to this one.' He waited another moment. 'Thanks.'

He put the phone down. 'A porter will be here for my bag in a few minutes.'

'You didn't have to do that.'

He didn't have to repack his bag. His stuff was good to go. She didn't want him to go. 'Adrian, I—'

'See you for breakfast, yeah?'

Hell. 'Yeah.' She tried again. 'It wasn't a no. I haven't said no to anything you've put forward. I *have* thought of you like that. From time to time. I'm female. You're you. Who wouldn't?'

She thought she saw a glimmer of a smile.

'But think about it, Adrian. Are you sure this is what you want? Because I really don't think you *have* thought this through.'

He frowned down at her, and then he leaned down and gently brushed his lips against the corner of her mouth. His lips were soft and warm. Lena felt her eyes flutter closed.

He drew back slowly and she wondered when his eyes had got so dark and hungry.

'I've thought it through. You need to do the same.'

He picked up his bag; he walked to the door.

And it clicked shut behind him.

As far as declarations of intent were concerned, that one could have gone better, decided Trig as he headed for the lifts. Lena had never handled romance well. In her teens she'd been too forward with boys, too fearless, too competitive, and she'd sent them running. Later on she'd got the hang of not scaring away potential suitors—she'd even taken a few of them to her bed, but for some reason known only to her none of them had ever measured up. Not in her eyes.

Not in Trig's or Jared's eyes either.

So she'd had standards that had suited them all.

Standards based around her father, the highly successful international banker. Around Damon, adrenaline junkie and hacker extraordinaire. Around Jared, who feared nothing and regularly achieved the impossible.

Standards that made her picky, and then, when she did break things off with the latest but not quite greatest, she'd start second-guessing herself and getting all despondent because the jerk she'd just let go had told her she wasn't feminine enough or that she needed to soften up a bit before any man would take her seriously. Sour grapes, a parting shot, but Lena had never seen it that way.

She'd mope for a few days and then Jared would tell her he was going skydiving on Friday and that he'd saved her a chute.

She'd try and be softer with other people for a bit and then Trig would turn up with his lightest kite-boarding rig, and there'd be a thirty-knot cross-shore wind blowing and he'd eyeball the conditions and they'd barely be manageable and he'd ask if she wanted to go break something.

The answer to that being, *'Hell, yes.'* Always yes.

Until she'd got shot and everything had changed for all of them.

These days no one challenged Lena to push harder or go faster, even though she still pushed herself.

These days he looked at her with concern in his eyes;

he knew he did. And she looked at him and told him to go away.

Rough couple of years.

But things were getting better now. Lena was getting better now and together they could find a new way of doing things and of being with each other if only she'd try.

The lift doors opened. A uniformed boy gave him an appraising stare. 'Mr Sinclair?'

Trig nodded.

'Let me take your luggage.' If the boy wondered why Mr Sinclair needed to change rooms, he was too discreet to ask. 'Room 406 for you, Mr Sinclair. I have your entry cards here.'

Trig stepped into the lift.

He just had to convince her to try.

CHAPTER FOUR

TRIG WOKE TO the sound of morning prayer at a nearby mosque. His bed had been big enough but his dreams had been chaotic. Loss, always loss. Lena walking away from him because he'd asked too much of her. Lena disappearing into the gluggy grey mud of East Timor. Slipping away from him, one way or another, with Trig powerless to prevent any of it.

The prayer song was hypnotic.

Trig closed his eyes and ran his hands through his hair and sent up a prayer of his own that this day would be a good day and that Lena wouldn't be freaking out about last night's declaration of undying devotion—or whatever it was that he'd declared.

She wouldn't run; she was smarter than that.

But she might feel uneasy with him and he wouldn't put it past her to have argued herself around to thinking that she wasn't good enough for him or that he'd be better off without her. For someone so magnificent, she had the lowest sense of self-worth he'd ever encountered.

She'd told him once that it came of being an ordinary person in an extraordinary family. She'd never seen herself as extraordinary too.

He reached for the hotel phone, tapped in the other room number and waited.

She wouldn't have done a runner. If nothing else, she knew he'd track her through Amos Carter if he had to. She might reschedule but she wouldn't blow that meeting off. Her need to find Jared was too strong.

'What?' she finally mumbled, once she'd picked up.

'You want to have breakfast at this little café I saw on my walk last night?'

'When?'

'Now.'

'What time is it?'

'Five-seventeen.'

Lena groaned, a sleepy, sexy sound that had him shifting restlessly. 'You want to have breakfast *now?*'

'I'm starving.'

'You're always starving.'

'Their breakfast special is lentil soup, a loaf of sourdough and a big chunk of cheese.'

'Go get 'em, Tiger. Bring me back a cup of tea,' she muttered and hung up.

Trig grinned and shoved the sheet aside, suddenly hungry to seize the day. She hadn't said no and she hadn't been wary. She hadn't said, 'Darling, come make me yours,' yet either, but that was pure fantasy anyway.

He got breakfast.

He went walking and found the gate where Lena would meet up with Carter and set about exploring exit options and observation points. By the time the seven a.m. prayer session sounded, he was back at the hotel and knocking on Lena's door, takeaway tea in one hand and a tub of yoghurt and honey in the other.

'Breakfast,' he said when she opened the door, and she let him through and closed the door behind him and yawned.

She looked like a waif. A little too slender, a halo of

tangled black hair and those startling bluish-grey eyes, smudged with black lashes. A modelling agency had offered to contract her once after seeing her on the beach. Surfing sponsors had come after her too. She'd turned down both offers with startled surprise. Couldn't see what they'd seen in her. Didn't want what they'd offered anyway.

'Is this the courting you?' she wanted to know as he set the tea and yoghurt on the table.

'This is the impatient me,' he said. 'You've seen this me before. I'm waiting to see if you want me to court you before I start that.'

'My mistake.' Lena smirked and carefully removed the lid on her tea. 'What's got you all pepped up?'

'You mean besides wanting to know if you'll go out with me?'

'Yeah, besides that. Because I'm not awake enough yet to make a definitive decision on that. I couldn't think clearly enough to make a decision on it last night either.'

'Red wine does that.'

'True.' She sipped at her tea and let out an appreciative sigh. 'So you're happy this morning because…'

'You have got to see this bazaar.'

'You're excited about *shopping*?'

'It's not shopping, it's haggling. It's a blood sport.'

'Is anything even open yet?'

'Couple of stalls are.'

'What did you buy?'

'Carpet. But I haven't bought it yet. I've just had it set aside so I can think about it.'

'Uh-huh. How much?'

'That's what we're negotiating.'

'Ballpark.'

'It's a really nice carpet. Silk.'

'Uh-huh.'

Seven thousand dollars *was* a lot to pay for a two metre by one point six metre bit of mat that people walked on. 'It's an investment piece.'

'Is it magic?'

'I didn't ask. Maybe you should come with me when I go back.'

'When are you going back?'

'After I've shopped around.'

'Who are you and what have you done with Trig?'

'Could be I'm nesting,' he said. Way to harp on a tricky subject. 'You all the way awake yet?'

'No.'

'Because if you are, now would be a good time to tell me if you're going to go out with me.'

'Still weighing the pros and cons.'

There was just no rushing her these days. 'I brought you breakfast. That would be a pro.'

'You also woke me up at five a.m.'

'You're welcome.'

He could make her snort. That had to count for something.

'How's the body this morning?'

'Functional,' she said around a mouthful of yoghurt. 'Stop fussing. Boyfriends don't fuss.'

'Now you're just making shit up.'

'No, I'm pretty sure it's true.'

He shook his head, slid her a sideways glance. 'Pursuit aside, how are we tracking with regards to our regular relationship? The one that *doesn't* have me in knots. We good?'

'Yeah.' She sounded a little uncertain. 'We're good.'

They made it through the morning, mostly because Trig headed back out again to look at carpets, and then it was time to meet Carter, with Lena taking point and Trig bleeding into the bustle at the gate. Another tourist, one of many, and maybe he was meeting someone or perhaps he was just taking a breather before diving into the next shop full of goodies. Either way, nothing untoward here.

He spotted Carter moments before the older man made him, but they didn't acknowledge each other. He and Carter had worked together before, albeit briefly, back in the days when Carter had worked for ASIS. Carter would know Trig was running surveillance on the meet. Carter probably had someone else doing the same.

Carter approached Lena and held out his hands and she took them and smiled as he kissed her on each cheek. Old acquaintances and all for show. Trig ground his teeth and watched some more as Carter and Lena strolled through the gate and into the bazaar, their pace leisurely and their conversation animated.

Trig made a process out of checking his phone as he waited to see who else might be headed that way before he too took a stroll. It was a busy gate. A lot of people followed Carter and Lena into the bazaar.

He kept them in sight while he browsed and they browsed and then five minutes later Carter bought Lena a scoop full of candied citrus, presented it to her with a smile, kissed her once again on each cheek and, between one blink and the next, disappeared into the ether.

Lena didn't look back at Trig; she knew this game too well for that. She bought three silk scarves and a handful of sugared almonds. She paused outside a shop filled with carpets and the vendor—and probably his brother—instantly tried to woo her in. She offered them almonds, which they refused. They offered her apple tea, and carpet viewing, which she refused. With a great deal of hand waving all round, everyone called it quits and Lena moved on.

No one but Trig followed her, and no one followed him, but he stayed on her tail just that little bit longer because they didn't know what Jared was into and because Carter was just that little bit unpredictable when it came to who he was working for at any one time.

Lena turned down a side lane of the bazaar, and then another. They'd reached a narrow walkway full of fabrics—an explosion of colour pinned to walls and strung across ceilings. Fabric everywhere and a group of youths with fierce eagle eyes coming towards them. They passed Lena, jostled her, and no one reached out to break her fall as she went down hard. She hit her head on the metal foot of a display rack. She didn't get up.

By the time Trig reached her, her wallet was gone and so were the youths. A few people yelled out. No one gave chase.

'Lena.' She looked so very small and crumpled. She wasn't conscious and he didn't want to move her. He reached for the pulse point at her wrist. *'Lena.'*

Other people had crouched down beside them. 'She's with you?' one man asked and Trig nodded. Hands reached out to gently shake her. He didn't know who they belonged to.

Don't,' he growled and pushed all those other hands away, dog with a bone and he didn't care who knew it. 'Don't touch her.'

Someone else tried to get the crowd around them to move back a step. Someone passed a cloth through to the man who'd spoken earlier and he handed it to Trig. 'For her head,' the man said and used gestures to suggest that Trig wipe her face.

The cloth was wet and smelled only of water. Trig drew it across Lena's forehead.

She didn't even flinch.

Trig looked for a bump on Lena's skull and found it towards the back of her head. Not that big, according to his fingers, but big enough to knock her unconscious nonetheless. 'Can you call me an ambulance?' he asked the man.

'Private or public?'

'Private.'

'Take taxi—is faster,' said a woman, but the man held up his finger and shook his head, and then started arguing with the woman, too fast for Trig to even try to understand. They weren't a threat. They were trying to help. He thought the man might be the proprietor of the nearby stall.

Lena stirred and Trig wiped the cloth across her forehead again. Her eyelashes fluttered.

'Lena?'

But she didn't come round fully.

Another person handed him an unopened bottle of water. 'Thank you,' he said as the crowd around them grew larger and talk turned to the pickpocket gangs and notifying the police that they were back in the area. Lena opened her eyes again and this time they stayed open while Trig checked her pupils for unevenness and then covered her eyes with his palm.

'Try and keep your eyes open and in a few more seconds I'll take my hand away,' he told her quietly, while his heart thundered and his mind flashed back to the ambush in East Timor. Some injuries were messy. This one was not. Didn't mean the outcome couldn't be catastrophic. 'I'm going to check your pupils for responsiveness to light.'

'You're a doctor?' asked Trig's new best friend, the one who'd called for an ambulance.

'Medic.' He had some combat first-aid training, that was all. 'Not a doctor.' Please don't let her pupils be blown.

He took his hand away from Lena's eyes and her pupils responded. Lena looked bewildered. Her eyes searched the crowd and finally came to rest back on him.

'Where am I?' she asked.

'The Grand Bazaar.' And when that didn't seem to ring any bells, 'Istanbul.'

'Oh.'

'You fell and hit your head. Pickpockets. They got your wallet.'

'Gonna be sick,' she said and rolled onto her side, but she wasn't sick, she just closed her eyes and put her cheek to the floor and slipped into a state of not-quite-thereness.

He tried not to let that worry him as he held the wet flannel to the bump on her head, and damn but it felt bigger.

She opened her eyes again a few minutes later. 'Just rest,' he told her. 'Don't need to move you yet. An ambulance is on its way.'

'Here's hoping I have insurance,' she murmured, and fixed him with a dazed gaze.

''Course you do.'

'Next question—'

He had to lean down to even hear her.

'—Who are you?'

She didn't like hospitals. She could barely remember her own name, but she knew with utter certainty that she did *not* like hospitals. And that she'd been in them a lot. Her body confirmed it when they sent her for the MRI and asked her to change into a gown. The scars on her lower belly and high on her leg told of a major collision between her body and…something. Car crash, maybe.

She couldn't quite remember.

'You have titanium pins and plates in your left leg and hip,' the big guy had said when he'd helped her fill out a medical history form, finally taking the clipboard and pen from her and filling out the information sheet himself. 'You've had several recent operations and intensive and ongoing physiotherapy.'

He knew her blood type and he knew her name.

Lena Sinclair.

She knew her name was Lena. Bits and pieces of her memory were starting to come back. The scarves hanging in the marketplace. The impression that someone, or several someones, had been following her. Her name was Lena, Lena Sinclair, and the big guy, who she couldn't quite remember…

He was her husband.

His name was Adrian. She'd read it on his credit cards and on the hospital forms. Adrian Sinclair. Husband. And he seemed so familiar, hauntingly familiar, and he made her feel safe, and he'd hovered while the doctors had seen to her, and if she couldn't quite remember much about him at the moment, well, there were a lot of things she couldn't quite remember at the moment.

He was the most beautiful man she'd ever seen.

'My name's Lena, Lena Sinclair,' she told the doctors. 'I'm Australian and I was shopping in the Grand Bazaar when thieves knocked me to the ground and took off with my wallet.'

There'd been mutterings then, about the crime rate

in the city. The police had been notified. Cards would be cancelled. Her husband would take care of it. 'Lena, relax,' he'd told her firmly. 'First things first. Just get the MRI done.'

Lena. Lena Sinclair.

She could remember pretty much everything that had happened since waking up in the bazaar. As for her life *before* then… She was Australian and she'd grown up on the beach with two brothers and a sister whose names she couldn't quite recall.

'Concussion,' the doctor told her. 'Minor head trauma.'

A cracking headache, nausea and, heavens, why did the lights have to be so bright?

'Temporary confusion and memory loss are both symptoms of concussion,' the doctor told her when Lena confessed to scrambled memories and a whole lot of fog. 'The painkillers I've given you won't have helped. You remember who you are?'

'Lena. Lena Sinclair.'

'You remember your family and your past?'

'Sort of.'

'It's common not to remember the events leading up to the knock on the head.'

Good to know she was common.

'Do you remember your husband?'

'Yes,' she said. She remembered that he made her feel safe. She remembered his hands.

'You need to rest your body and your brain,' the doctor told her. 'I've given you pain medication and something to minimise the swelling. I'm releasing you into the care of your husband, and if he hovers or wakes you several times through the night, it's because I've told him to. If you start to feel anxious, let him know. Should your headache or nausea worsen, should you become disoriented, should your co-ordination worsen…you let him know and he'll bring you back here.'

'Okay.'

'You already have co-ordination issues due to your previous injuries. I'm not talking about those. I'm talking about new limitations, just so we're clear.'

'Clear,' she said faintly. She just wanted to get out of the hospital.

She hated hospitals.

And then they *were* out of the hospital and the street was unfamiliar and the smell of the city invaded her nostrils and she immediately wanted away from there too.

A taxi stood waiting for them. Her husband must have arranged it because the driver seemed to know him. 'Your lady wife *must* stay close to you,' he kept telling her stony-faced husband. 'It's not always safe here. Where did you and your lady wife *go?*'

'Just take us back to the hotel.' He could sound menacing when he wanted to, this husband she couldn't quite recall. He could make talkative taxi drivers shut the hell up and drive.

The hotel was a pleasant, mid-range affair, with a buffet restaurant that her husband glanced at as they headed across the foyer towards the lifts.

'Are you hungry?' she asked him.

'I could eat.'

He'd been at her side all day. In waiting rooms and examination rooms. He'd been her voice when she couldn't remember what she'd done to her leg. There'd been no time for him to slip out and grab some food.

'We could eat at the buffet,' she said, and made it sound like a question.

'I was thinking room service.'

Which could take some time to arrive. 'Or we could eat now.'

'You're hungry?'

'No, but you are. You fill up. I'll pick and choose. Everyone's a winner.'

'I'd rather get you back to the room.'

'The head is woolly but I'm feeling no pain,' she assured him. 'The painkillers are good and the food is right there. How about I let you know the minute I've had enough?'

He didn't look convinced.

'Okay, how about you watch me intently all through dinner and *you* let me know when I've had enough?'

'You look like you've had enough already.' Blunt, this husband of hers.

'I think I can stretch it another twenty minutes. Or we could stand here arguing.'

He smiled at that, really smiled, and Lena watched, mesmerised, for it was a wicked, charming smile full of warmth and wide approval.

'It is you,' he murmured, and steered her towards the restaurant entrance. He gave the maître d' their room number and saw her seated, but he didn't sit.

'I'm going to go change our booking. Get us another couple of days here. You be okay here while I do that?'

'I'll be fine.'

She watched him go. Broad shoulders, slim hips, long legs and all gorgeous.

And then he disappeared from sight and it took all her effort to quell the panic that arrived with his disappearance. *Breathe, Lena.* Everything was fine. She was fine.

They were staying here, they had a room here, and

if she needed to get to it all she had to do was ask the front desk for a number and a key. Her memory would be back soon and her husband wasn't going anywhere. He'd be back soon too.

A waiter asked if she wanted anything to drink with dinner and she ordered fizzy water for them both. She had a feeling her husband drank beer, but she didn't know if he would want one with their meal. The waiter assured her that he would return once her husband did.

Five minutes later her husband returned.

'Done?' she queried.

'Done.'

'Where were we supposed to go after this?'

'You don't remember?'

'No.' No need to alarm him with how much she *didn't* remember. Yet. 'I'm a little fuzzy on the details.'

'We were going to Bodrum to find Jared.'

'Oh.' Was now a good time to tell him that she had no idea who Jared was? 'Right.'

Her husband, Adrian, was looking at her funny. And that name...her husband's name...didn't sit altogether right with her either. 'Do I call you something other than Adrian?'

'Trig,' he said gruffly. 'You call me Trig.'

'Okay.' She started to nod and then thought the better of it. 'Okay. Oh, and the waiter came by and I ordered you a soda water. I wasn't sure whether you'd want anything alcoholic.'

'Not tonight.' He followed her to the buffet. Stayed behind her while she browsed and added little spoonfuls of this and that to her plate. She waited for Trig to load up his plate, which he did—with generous helpings of pretty much everything.

Trig frowned at her half-filled plate.

'I'm probably going to have seconds,' she lied.

'You know I can tell when you're lying, right?'

She hadn't known that. She added a spoonful of what looked like sweet potato to her plate.

They returned to the table and sat. Trig ate, and Lena mostly watched. He took her close scrutiny in his stride.

'Why aren't we wearing our wedding rings?' she asked finally, and watched as her husband choked on his food.

He coughed, eyes watering, and reached for his water. 'What?' he croaked.

'At first I thought the thieves must have taken them too, but then I noticed that you're not wearing one either, and I'm pretty sure I gave you one.'

He blinked at that and took another great gulp of his water.

'Lena, exactly how much *do* you remember about your past?' Her husband's words came out measured and even but his gaze could probably have penetrated steel.

'Lots of bits and pieces,' she said. 'Lots. But I don't remember our wedding.'

'What's your maiden name?'

'Um—'

'Your brothers' names?'

'Dan. No, Damien.' One of them was called Damien.

'Damon.'

'Yes, Damon.' An image of a laughing, dark-haired boy on a surfboard came to her. 'He surfs. He loves the sea.' Trig remained stony-faced and Lena's confidence faltered. 'Doesn't he?'

'Yes.'

'See? Memory on the mend.'

But her husband didn't seem to think so. 'Lena, can you remember why we're even in Turkey?'

'Not really, no. Everything's foggy. But I do remember you. I know you. Feel safe with you. You're my husband.'

Trig.

A new and startling thought occurred to her—one that explained away her husband's grimness and their current lack of wedding rings. 'We're not *just*...just-married, are we? Were we going to buy rings here?' It made sense. It was almost coming back to her. 'Are we on our honeymoon?'

He didn't say anything for a very long time, and then he looked her dead in the eye and said, 'Yes.'

CHAPTER FIVE

SHE BARELY REMEMBERED HIM. Trig tried to conceal his growing panic beneath another mouthful of food. Lena really did think she was married to him. Because he'd told the hospital staff they were in order to get her the attention she'd needed.

'I'm so sorry,' she was saying. 'I've really screwed up, haven't I? I'm a little light on details but I do remember you. You like the ocean too. And we played together as children. You and me and another boy.'

'Jared.' She couldn't even remember Jared.

'Yes. Jared. Jared, my…'

Trig waited. Lena frowned.

'Brother,' he told her, because he couldn't stand the confusion in her eyes.

'Right. I'm pretty sure the concussion's screwing with my head.'

'You think?' Sarcasm didn't become him, given the circumstances, but it was that or outright panic. She'd barely touched her food. He'd hardly made a dent in his and he shovelled another load down, because he didn't rule out another trip to the hospital in the not too distant future.

'You should try and eat something,' he said gruffly, and she speared a small chunk of baked eggplanty stuff and ate it. Usually if he suggested she eat more, she'd tell him in no uncertain terms that she didn't tell him what to eat.

Lena's memory-lapse problem was worse than he thought.

He needed to get her upstairs and resting.

He needed to stop totally freaking out.

'We're after platinum rings,' she said suddenly. 'With a brushed finish.'

What did he even *say* to that?

'And carpet. I wanted one of those too.'

'A silk one,' he said, and condemned himself to hell for his sins.

'Expensive?'

'Oh, yes.'

'And you had a…problem with that?' she continued tentatively.

'Not at all. I'm thinking we need two.' And a brain transfusion. For him.

'Are we rich?' She wasn't even pretending to remember stuff any more.

'Between us, we have resources.' He thought that was a relatively fair call. 'And your father's a very rich man.'

'I don't sponge off him, do I?'

'No, but you're used to a certain way of life. You and your siblings all travel wherever you want, whenever you want to. You have several family houses and apartments at your disposal.'

'But the beach house is ours. I remember the beach house.'

'That's Damon's.'

'Oh.' Lena's face fell and she blinked back sudden tears. 'Could have sworn it was ours.'

'We've spent a lot of time there lately,' he offered gruffly. 'There's an indoor heated pool there that's good for rehab. You've done a lot of rehab on your leg.'

'Oh,' she said again.

Trig set his napkin on the table and pushed away abruptly. 'C'mon. I've had enough and you need to rest.'

She tried to follow swiftly. She caught her hip on the edge of the table and winced.

'Easy, though. There's no rush.'

'Nothing works,' she whispered.

'It works. It just works different from the way you expect it to.'

She clutched at his arm and together they headed slowly for the lifts. 'Do I have a crooked wooden walking stick?'

'Yes.'

'Did you give it to me for when you weren't around?'

'Yes.'

'Thought so.'

The lift door opened and they stepped in. Lena didn't release his arm when he thought she would. The old Lena wouldn't have taken his arm at all. He looked at the picture they made in the mirror, she was looking at the picture they made too, and her eyes were like bruises. He'd wanted this—them—for so long, but not like this. He needed the old Lena back before he pursued this.

'I must have a really excellent personality,' she said.

'Why's that?'

'Look at you.'

He eyed himself warily. Same oversized buffoon who'd failed to protect Lena. Again.

'You look like a Hollywood action hero.' She frowned when he didn't reply. 'You're not, are you?'

'Pass.'

'Professional athlete?'

'No.'

'Fireman? I hear those boys lift a lot of weights in their spare time?'

'Where'd you hear that?'

'So you *are* a fireman?'

'No.'

She stood there in silence, but not for long. 'So what *do* you do? A wife should probably know.'

'I work for Australia's Special Intelligence Service.'

'You're a spy? Are you *serious?*'

'You work for them too.'

The lift doors opened and before Lena could protest, Trig lifted her into his arms and headed for the room. She'd done enough walking for the day and maybe, just maybe, he needed to hold her for a little while and pretend that she was safe.

'Do you carry me often?' she asked as she wound her arms around his neck and relaxed into his arms.

'As often as I can.'

And then Lena pressed her face to the hollow of his neck and took a deep breath and her arms tightened around him.

'I remember this,' she murmured. 'I remember the way you smell.'

Trig didn't need to die and go to hell. Hell had come to him.

She pressed a tentative kiss to his neck and his arms tightened around her. 'Why do I call you Trig?'

'Because I tutored you in trigonometry back in high school.'

'So, I needed help. Meaning I'm not exactly a scholar.'

'Depends on the company. You topped your state in mathematics, which for most seventeen-year-old girls is an excellent result. You just happen to have a couple of geeky geniuses in the family. It skews your expectations.'

'I sound insecure.'

She *was* insecure. More so since East Timor. She just couldn't get it through her head that her family cherished her for who she was. That her common sense and iron will often carried *them.*

They'd reached the door and Trig set her down reluctantly and opened it. His bag stood just inside the door, he'd had the hotel staff shift it from last night's room back to this one. The doctor had said to monitor Lena through the night. He'd figured he could do that better from her room than from his. At that point he'd still been under the impression that Lena *knew* she wasn't his wife.

She looked at the two beds and slanted him a sideways glance. 'Not exactly the honeymoon suite. Or the Ritz.'

'Yeah, about that...' Was *now* the right time to tell her that they weren't married or would that news only confuse and alarm her more? Did he let her sleep on it and hope to hell she woke up with her memory back?

Who the hell knew?

'Sometimes your leg bothers you and you need the extra space to stretch out. And tonight, for example, what with your head and your leg and the fact that you really don't remember me...it's probably a relief to you that we have twin beds tonight, right?'

She didn't say 'right,' she said 'oh,' and for a moment looked utterly lost.

'So, your gear's all here,' he continued doggedly and

gestured towards the cupboard and her suitcase. 'I, ah, can run you a bath while I have a quick shower. The bath takes a while to fill.'

'No bath,' she said. 'I'll shower after you and then jump into bed. This bed.' She pointed to the one nearest the window. Trig nodded and slung his bag on the other one and rifled through it for clean underwear and a T-shirt and sweats. He needed a shower and a lot more distance from Lena than was currently available, but sometimes a man had to take what he could get.

He reached for the shutter divider between bathroom and bedroom.

'Can you not?' Lena asked hurriedly.

'What?'

'I mean, you can shut them, of course you can. But if you wanted to leave them open you could do that too. It's just…I feel better when I can see you.'

How could he possibly close them after that?

He left them open. He walked around the other side of that half wall and into the bathroom and shucked his clothes quickly, no showing off allowed. He didn't want Lena looking and wondering. He most emphatically didn't want her coming and touching.

Much.

He stepped into the shower before he'd even turned on the taps. He washed away the stench of fear and let icy resolve replace it. He could offer Lena comfort and reassurance tonight. He'd spent plenty of nights in the chair beside her hospital bed—tonight would be a lot like that, what with Lena wounded and aching and him half worried out of his brain. They'd done this before. Nothing to sweat about.

Except for the bit where *she thought he was her husband.*

Nothing to sweat about at all.

* * *

Lena opened her suitcase while her husband took the longest shower in the history of mankind. She really wanted to see him when he emerged, slick with water and minus a towel. She figured that particular image ought to be engraved on her brain, concussion or not, but unfortunately she had no memory of it.

She found her toiletries bag amongst her clothes and opened it up and found all sorts of yummy things. Lovely brand-name make-up. A travel-sized bottle of rose-scented perfume, and she popped the cap and lifted it to her nose with the thought that a familiar scent might jog a few memories back into place, and it did, for she had a brief flash of a laughing dark-haired woman wearing a totally awesome headband full of feathers.

'Do I know a Ruby?' she asked as she stoppered the perfume and returned it to the toiletries bag.

'Damon's wife,' came the rumble from the shower cubicle. 'Ruby's cool.'

'Does she buy me perfume?'

'She takes you frock shopping, for which I'm eternally grateful. She may have bought you perfume—I can't say for sure.'

'Why are you grateful?' Lena couldn't seem to find any frocks at all amongst the clothes she'd brought. These clothes ran more to casual trousers and tops that wouldn't need ironing.

'Ruby's totally committed to bringing sexy back. I heartily approve.'

Lena rifled through her clothes again and lifted out the plainest pair of white cotton panties that she'd ever seen. What kind of woman took *these* on her honeymoon? 'Maybe you should have married her.'

'Nah. She can't surf. Or hang-glide. Or put a bullet in a moving car wheel from half a kilometre away.'

'And I can?'

This time he hesitated before answering. 'You used to be able to. Little bit different now.'

She couldn't remember any of that, but the notion that she'd once done all that didn't particularly alarm her, so maybe it was true. 'So how did I get all the scars? And the bad leg?'

The water cut off abruptly. Moments later the top half of Trig appeared, framed in the cutaway wall. Water ran off him in rivulets and muscle played over bone as he reached for a towel and set it to his face and then scrubbed his hair with it. She couldn't see anything below mid waist, but even so…

All that sun-bronzed, spectacularly muscled glory and it was *hers*.

How in hell had she managed that?

'You don't remember what happened to your leg?' he said when his face re-emerged from beneath the towel and the towel drifted lower. Never had a woman been more resentful of a wall.

'No.'

'You got shot. On a mission. Nineteen months ago. You've made a spectacular recovery, given the prognosis.'

'What was the prognosis?'

'A wheelchair.'

Oh. Well, then… 'Good for me.'

'Good for us all.'

His clothes went on and she mourned the loss of skin. She wondered if he wore PJs to bed and hoped he did not.

'Shower's free,' he said on his way out and if that

wasn't a hint for her to wash away the smell of the street and the hospital, nothing was.

'I'm getting there.' She was. 'But I can't find my honeymoon nightie. Do you have it?'

Trig opened his mouth as if to speak and then shut it again with a snap. He shook his head. No.

She looked beneath the pillows. 'Did we rip it?'

Still no sound from Trig.

'Could be the cleaner mistook it for ribbon,' he said at last.

'Ribbon?'

'There wasn't much of it. But there were bows. Lots of bows. Made out of ribbon.'

'Oh.' Lena tried to reconcile ribbon nightwear with the rest of her clothing. 'I really should be able to remember that.'

She passed her husband on the way to the shower and when she stepped beneath the spray she could have sworn she heard him whimper. So she'd screwed up their honeymoon by falling prey to a gang of pickpockets. She couldn't have been much of an operative—they were probably glad to be rid of her.

She contemplated washing her hair and decided it could wait. Her hair took for ever to dry, the bump on her head was starting to ache and she wanted nothing more than to fall into bed in the arms of her husband and burrow into his warmth until she fell asleep. Tomorrow would be a better day. Tomorrow she'd have her memory back and they might even be able to continue on to wherever it was they were going.

It could have been worse. She might not have been married to a wonderful man who knew exactly how to take quiet control of hospital staff and taxi drivers and her.

She could have been alone.

* * *

Trig had set his laptop up at the table by the time Lena emerged from the shower, scrubbed pink and wrapped in a fluffy white towel. She rifled through her suitcase, but couldn't seem to find whatever she was looking for.

'What was I *thinking?*' she grumbled, and disappeared back into the bathroom with a little grey T-shirt and a pair of yellow-and-white-striped boy-leg panties in hand.

Trig sent up silent thanks for small mercies given that she hadn't dropped towel in front of him, and went back to surfing the net for local news, more specifically what had been happening in the port city of Bodrum on Turkey's southwest coast. It killed the time. It could prove useful. And it gave him something to do while Lena prepared for bed.

Because Lena preparing for bed involved her sitting on the bed and applying scented lotion to every millimetre of visible skin. It involved the brushing of hair—and working gently around the bump on her head and it involved the gentle lift and fall of her breasts and slender arms as she wove her hair into a long loose plait that he immediately wanted to undo, much like the imaginary ribbon nightgown that he also wanted to undo.

Eventually, Lena slid between the sheets, but she didn't lie down and the torture continued. She had pillows to divvy out and covers to turn down and Trig had no idea what was in the email he'd just read.

'Will you be much longer?' she asked, and he looked up to find her looking at him, her glorious grey-blue eyes full of silent entreaty.

He could be misreading her.

But he didn't think so.

'Why?' he croaked, and cleared his throat and tried

again. 'Is the light bothering you? I still have some work to get through, but I can turn off the room lights, no problem.' Maybe he wouldn't covet what he couldn't see. Worth a try. 'It's a backlit screen. I can keep working.'

'I know you said we sometimes sleep in different beds but could you come to this bed tonight when you're done?'

'Yeah,' he said. 'Sure.' And vowed to wait until she was asleep before going anywhere near that bed and the temptation within it.

She lay back against the pillows, with her head to one side, carefully avoiding the bump on the back of her head. She let out a little sigh that did nothing whatsoever for his calm. 'Good?' he asked gruffly.

'Heaven.'

'Close your eyes.'

'Why?'

'I have it on good authority that you'll sleep better if you do.'

'How about a trade? I'll close them if you come and hold me.'

What was a husband to do?

So he lay down atop the covers, on his side, and pushed her hair away from her face with fingers too big and clumsy for the job, but she smiled at him, so he stroked the pad of his thumb against her cheek bone, rough against silky soft and smooth, and she made a little hum of pleasure and tilted her face towards his touch.

'Pretty sure I need a good-night kiss,' she mumbled, her eyes at half-mast already. 'You should probably get onto that before I fall asleep.'

She was wounded. He could do this. He pressed an

almost-there kiss to the very corner of her mouth. The whole thing took maybe a couple of seconds.

'That's not a kiss.'

'Yeah, it is.'

'It's not a honeymoon kiss.'

'The honeymoon's on hiatus.'

'Seems a shame.'

'You need to get better first. Get your memory back.' And then, technically, they needed to get married.

'I can't remember your kisses.' She reached up and traced the curve of his lips with her fingertips. 'I want to.'

He'd never kissed her full on the mouth before. He'd always aimed for brotherly, and nailed it. Cheek kisses were good—they encouraged restraint. He and Lena had never practised anything *but* restraint when it came to kissing.

'Just one,' she murmured, her eyes grave on his.

'Lena—'

'It's not every day a woman gets to repeat her first kiss.'

'You can't remember *any* kisses?'

'Nope. First kiss. Going once… Going twice…'

Oh, hell.

He didn't wait to be asked a third time. He did try and do their first kiss justice—starting slow, keeping his hunger in check. No tongue, just the press of his lips against hers and those lips of hers were warmer and more willing than he'd ever imagined, and soft… so soft…

No tongue whatsoever until she flicked at the seam of his lips and tempted them open, and curled her tongue around his. And then he slanted his lips and deepened the kiss just a little. He tried to quieten her slick, darting tongue with the long slow slide of his as he learned her taste and committed it to memory. He tried to ignore just how well that smart mouth of hers matched his, but it fitted—it fitted so perfect and true that he lost himself for a moment, just surrendered all thought and took what he'd always wanted.

Lena couldn't believe she'd forgotten this man's kisses. Because they were everything she'd ever imagined kisses would be, from that first slow sweet slide to the all-consuming hunger that raced through her now. They'd done this before. How else could it be so perfect?

She'd known he was a big man—her memory might be faulty but there was nothing wrong with her eyes. What she hadn't understood was how much she gloried in his size and all that ruthlessly controlled strength looming over her. So much of him to explore and she wrenched her lips away from that too knowing mouth and set lips and teeth to his jaw instead.

A shudder swept through him and he groaned, more responsive than she could have ever dared wish for. She turned her lips to the strong cords of his neck and he cursed, even as he urged her closer.

'*Now* I remember why I married you,' she whispered against his skin and he trembled some more.

'Lena—'

'Mmm?'

'Lena, *please*.' Anyone would think she was torturing him. 'You have to stop. *I* have to stop. *Please*.'

Oh, he begged so *pretty*. A hot lick of power rushed over her, and she wondered what else he might beg for. What she might demand of him if she but had the courage to ask.

He kissed her again, hard and fast and ruthless, and

then he was off the bed with a speed that surprised her, looking everywhere but back at her as he found his phone and slid those giant feet into his shoes. 'You need to rest and recover,' he muttered and headed for the door. 'And I need to make a couple of calls.'

CHAPTER SIX

TRIG PACED THE length of the hall as he waited for Damon to pick up. He didn't want to talk to Damon, he wanted Damon's wife Ruby on the other end of the line, but there was a protocol involved when ringing up someone else's wife in the middle of the night and Trig wanted to observe it.

'This better be good,' said Damon when he finally picked up.

'It is. Put Ruby on. I need her advice.'

'About what?'

'You don't want to know.'

'I do want to know.'

'Your sister took a fall today and hit her head.'

'I'm putting you on speaker phone.' Nothing but tight concern in Damon's voice now.

'She's had an MRI and the doctors saw nothing to concern them. They've released her from the hospital, but she has concussion and some memory loss.' He paused and wondered how best to deliver this next bit. 'She thinks we're married.'

He thought he heard scuffling and Ruby's low laughter, and then Ruby's voice came through warm and smoothly amused. 'How did that happen?'

'Lena had no ID when we got to the hospital and I

had all mine. Easier to claim her and get her in front of a doctor and think about other consequences later. Ruby, she doesn't even remember Jared. She thinks we're on our honeymoon. She's back in the room. She thinks we share a bed! Do you have any idea how much I *want* to share that bed?' His voice had risen an octave or two.

'Touch my sister under those conditions and I will gut you,' said Damon.

'Don't threaten him,' muttered Ruby. 'How is that helpful?'

'He doesn't need to threaten me. If I take her now, I'll gut *myself.* She keeps getting me to hold her, Ruby. She wants the reassurance. She thinks she's my *wife.* You're a wife. What do I do?'

'You hold her, you moron.'

'Dead moron,' added Damon.

'What if she doesn't get her memory back? What if she wakes up in the morning and still thinks she's Mrs Lena Sinclair?'

'Got a nice ring to it,' said Ruby.

'Not helping.'

'Trig, sweetie. If Lena still thinks she's married to you in the morning, head on home to the beach house and we'll meet you there. Stay married, at least in Lena's eyes. Bring her home. That's my advice.'

'I can do that.'

'We know you can. That's why no one here is pacing around the room like a lunatic.' Ruby's voice had softened. 'Adrian, honey, give Lena a cuddle if she needs one—no one's going to castrate you for that, not even Lena when her memory returns. Just don't let the fairy tale get out of hand. Tell her you want to wait until she's fully recovered before you initiate marital relations.

That's the truth anyway, isn't it? There has to be *some* reason you haven't made your move yet.'

'Does fear of rejection count?'

'We all own that one,' said Ruby dryly. 'Don't go thinking you're special.'

'Not special,' he said.

'But very worthy,' said Ruby quickly. 'Just because you shouldn't be making your move on Lena *now,* doesn't mean you shouldn't be making one at all. Move, by all means. We all want to see that.'

'You do?' He'd never really broached the subject of his feelings for Lena with any of her siblings before, but he wanted their approval. Jared's most of all. 'You speaking for Damon now too?'

'Yes,' said Damon. 'And Damon's speaking for the family.'

'That include Jared?'

'Proxy vote,' said Damon. 'Jared's not here.'

'I suggest you let Lena deal with Jared in the unlikely event that he objects to you courting her,' said Ruby. 'The man owes her.'

'For what?'

'Disappearing. Putting vengeance before family.' Ruby's voice had cooled considerably, but Ruby's father had disappeared without a trace too. Ruby knew what it felt like to be one of the ones they left behind. 'Brother Jared needs to spend some time in the naughty corner when he finally reappears.'

The words *if he reappears* went unspoken but Trig heard them anyway. 'You could suggest it to him,' he muttered. 'Although, fair warning, Jared doesn't take too kindly to reprimand.'

'So I've heard,' said Ruby, and then she yawned.

Damn but she could make him grin. 'I want front-row tickets to your first meeting with Jared. And popcorn.'

'Get in line,' said Damon. 'Take care of my sister. You've got this. I trust you.'

A substantially calmer Trig returned to the room and closed the door quietly behind him. He took a deep breath and searched for some of that steely resolve that everyone else seemed to think he had an endless supply of. He headed for the beds and for Lena who was in one of those beds, hurt and confused and…

Fast asleep.

CHAPTER SEVEN

TUESDAY MORNING BROKE with the sound of the dawn prayer. Istanbul, thought Lena. I'm in Istanbul with its mosques and its rich cultural history and its slick market thieves. Her head throbbed when she moved it ever so slightly—time for more painkillers. There they were on the bedside table with a glass of water beside them, two of them, ready to go.

She eased up onto her elbow and reached for them with her spare hand, and then reached for the water to wash them down with. Give it five or ten minutes and the throbbing would stop and the fog would take over, fog being preferable to pain on most occasions, both of them preferable to being dead.

She rolled over, careful not to lie on the lump on her head, and there was Trig, next to her on the bed, faint shadows beneath his eyes and those long girly lashes. He looked younger in sleep and his body was even bigger up close.

He was still the most beautiful man she'd ever seen.

The urge to touch him became unbearable and she scooted closer and slid her hand across his chest. She'd have plastered herself against the rest of him only he'd slept on top of the covers rather than between them. Five more minutes, maybe ten, and the throbbing would stop and maybe she'd be able to do something about waking him in ways a man on his honeymoon might want to be woken, but for now just resting her cheek on his shoulder would do.

And then he rolled towards her and the covers got shoved to the bottom of the bed as he gathered her close and wrapped his arms around her. Target acquired, mission accomplished, and with the faintest rumbling sigh he slid straight back into sleep.

Five more minutes, she thought as she burrowed into his warmth. Five more minutes.

Or maybe an hour.

Trig woke slowly, with Lena wrapped around him like a limpet and strands of silky black hair tickling his jaw. She stirred as soon as he shifted, and snuggled in closer even as he tried to draw away.

'Lena—' Somehow, one of his hands had made its way to her waist. The other one had journeyed a little lower. Neither hand was in any hurry to let go. 'Lena, I need to get up.'

'No, you don't.'

'I really do.' He pressed a brief kiss to her shoulder and then peeled himself out of there, one reluctant limb at a time. 'What do you want for breakfast?'

'You.'

She still had her eyes closed. She'd rolled over into his warm spot, tucked her arms beneath his pillow and probably wasn't awake enough to know what she was saying.

'And some of that yoghurt you got me yesterday. And the tea,' she mumbled into the pillow.

'So you do remember.'

'It was good tea.'

'About the man and wife thing…'

'I know,' she murmured. 'Who wants a wife who gets beat up on the first day of their honeymoon? I'm a bad wife. Already. But I will make it up to you. Promise. Just as soon as I get up and go shopping.'

So much for Lena waking up this morning with her memories intact. 'I really think you should rest,' he said. And he'd book those flights. 'Shopping can wait.'

'Wrong.' She rolled onto her back and fixed him with a sleepy gaze. 'Have you *seen* the clothes in my suitcase? No. And you're not going to. They're funeral clothes. I brought the wrong suitcase.'

'You have a funeral suitcase?'

'I must have. There's no other explanation.'

'Pretty sure I can think of one. You want to hear it?'

'No, I want to shop. And eat yoghurt,' she pleaded wistfully. 'And pastry. Lots of flaky breakfast pastry. I'm starving.'

Now he was starving too.

'Lena, do you remember where you are?'

'Istanbul.'

'Do you know why you're here?'

'Honeymoon.'

Okeydokey, then. Time for another trip to the hospital. 'You want me to get you anything else while I'm out?'

'Yes,' she said. 'Champagne and strawberries.'

Five hours later, the doctor declared the swelling in Lena's head much reduced and Trig had declared her memory much improved. She could talk about Damon, Poppy and her father with assurance. She could talk about Jared and the things they'd done in the past. But she had no recollection of getting shot in East Timor, or of her long and arduous recovery, or of Jared going rogue in order to find out who'd betrayed them.

She still thought she was Mrs Lena Sinclair.

The doctor had nixed any long-haul flights for Lena for the next few days, but all was not lost.

The doctor had also banned sex.

'Got it,' he'd told the doctor swiftly. 'No sex. Plenty of rest. Doctor's orders.'

And then Lena had turned accusing eyes on him and it would have been flattering and funny if it hadn't been so tragic.

They'd returned to the hotel and Lena had obediently dozed for a couple of hours before declaring herself completely over the hotel-room experience and desperate to take a slow, relaxing walk through the hippodrome next to the Blue Mosque.

'Is this a honeymoon thing?' he asked suspiciously. Because it sounded like a honeymoon thing and he wanted to avoid those.

'It's a tourist thing.'

'The doctor said you had to rest.'

'And I have. Now I need to do something.'

'The walking will tire you.'

'How about a Turkish bath, then? Warm water. Relaxation. I hear they even throw in a massage.'

'Water baby.'

'I do recall a fondness for water. And doing a lot of leg rehab in it.' Lena frowned. 'You said I got shot in the line of duty. I still don't remember a thing.'

'Lucky you.'

'Can you describe it to me?'

'No.'

She looked at him with far too penetrating a gaze and he thought she would push the issue, but then she shrugged and rifled through her suitcase and held up a brightly coloured swimsuit. 'So…Turkish bath or unwanted interrogation? Which will it be?'

Which was how they ended up at a Turkish bath house, with him being shepherded through a door to the left labelled men and Lena being pointed to the one on the right that said women.

'Wait for me when you get out,' he commanded gruffly.

'Don't I always?'

Surprisingly, upon reflection, the answer was yes. He gave her a grin. 'Rest and relaxation,' he said. 'Don't forget.'

'I'm on it.'

Once through the man door, an attendant showed him to a shower cubicle and change room. 'You must shower first,' the attendant said. 'And then this door will take you into the bathing area.'

Trig nodded. There'd been pictures of the bath house on the waiting room walls. Rooms full of marble and cascading water. Huge stone slabs where bodies lay prone and masseuses worked their magic. Enough steam to make a belching dragon proud.

Lena's post-op physiotherapy programme had involved a lot of water-based stretching and exercises and whether she remembered those exercises or not, a warm bathing pool and massage would be good for her.

Trig showered and stowed his wallet and clothing in the locker provided. He picked up a tiny square face cloth from a carefully folded pile of them sitting at the door to the bathing area. No swimwear required, apparently. It said so, right there on the instructions plaque hanging on the wall.

The first thing his eyes were drawn to as he stepped

into the room was the high domed and tiled ceiling. The second thing he saw was Lena entering through a door on the other side of the room.

Why on earth would a bathing house have separate change-room areas when the bathing area was for males and females both?

Like him, Lena had only one cloth.

And she didn't seem to know where to put it.

Only half a dozen other people swam or lazed beneath the cascading water pouring from spouts in the wall. A few men. A few women. No one seemed to be paying much attention to anyone else.

Didn't matter. Lena stood butt naked with one tiny little cloth that she seemed to want to cover the worst of her scarring with. He crossed to her quickly and held out his cloth.

'Here. Use it. Cover yourself up.'

She seemed to find his glower amusing. 'Which bits? Because these wash cloths? Really not that big.'

'Get in the pool,' he ordered. The pool would provide at least some protection against prying eyes. And they *were* drawing attention. He could feel eyes boring into his back. 'You'd think they might have mentioned when we came in that this was a mixed bathing pool.'

Lena was making her way slowly down the steps, holding fast to the hand rail. 'Relax,' she said. 'This is working for me. Are you sure you don't want your flannel back? Or mine as well, for that matter. Because, frankly, most of the women and some of the men in here are staring at you and salivating.' Her lashes swept over her eyes and she scanned him from head to toe. 'And why wouldn't they? There's a lot to love.'

He followed her down into the water fast. He'd never

considered himself body shy, but still… 'Keep the flannels. *Use* the flannels. Why aren't you freaking out?'

'Too busy watching you,' she said with a grin, and then slid into the water and struck out for the far side of the pool. 'Oh, this is nice.'

'Wouldn't you be more comfortable if you were, oh, I don't know…not buck naked?'

'Adrian Sinclair.' Her voice floated warm and teasing across the water. 'Are you self-conscious?'

'Apparently.' The water was deliciously warm, bordering on hot. Lena would like it. 'I'm also possessive—particularly where you're concerned. And I'm on my honeymoon and all kinds of frustrated. You might want to keep this in mind should the masseur attempt to wash you down.' The masseur was washing someone down on the marble block now, and there were suds, lots of suds, and a wet white towel that the masseur was scouring the skin with. He wasn't being gentle. 'Maybe you should give that experience a miss, because if he scrubs too hard and antagonises your scars I'll have to relieve him of his arms.'

'I'm sure he'll adjust his ministrations accordingly.'

Trig watched as the masseur fisted half the towel around his hands and proceeded to bring the free end of the towel down hard on the person's back. He did it again and the towel landed lower this time. Again and again, all the way down to the toes. Every time the towel came down the body strung out on the slab twitched.

'I might give the flagellation a miss,' said Lena after a moment.

The masseur had downed the towel and picked up a huge bucket full of water. For someone so small and wiry, the man had some serious body strength. Next minute, he'd thrown the entire contents of the bucket at the person lying on the slab.

'Wasn't expecting that,' said Lena as the person sat up, a man, now that you could see past the suds. The front of him got slammed with another full bucket of water and then he stood up and headed towards a nearby waterfall of water and half disappeared under it. 'You reckon that was cold water?'

'Yes.'

'Me too.'

She had such a shameless grin. 'You going to tell me how I got these scars now? Because I think I'm ready to hear it. It bothers me that I can't remember if this happened because I did something wrong.'

'You did nothing wrong.'

'I don't suppose you could expand on that?'

'I don't want to discuss it.'

'Trig, I look at my body in the mirror and I see the scars and feel the aches but I don't know how they got there. It's really disconcerting, and I'd really like to know. I appreciate that it's probably not a memory that you want to revisit, but please...'

Trig scrubbed his hand over his face. He had no defences against a pleading Lena. None.

'So we were on a simple recon run in East Timor,' he began. 'There'd been a last-minute change of plans and we got asked to check out an old chemical weapons lab that had been reported abandoned about three years earlier. That's what the mission profile said. We came in careful, we always do, and found cobwebs and dust. No footprints. No sign of use. No equipment on the benches, nothing in the cupboards. The place had been picked clean and left to rot.

'We came back outside. Didn't figure we had a problem until semi-automatic fire came at us from the left flank and took you down. I don't know why, because there was nothing there to protect. Another two minutes and we'd have been out of there. No activity to report. Not coming back.'

'Did we catch the shooter?'

'No.'

'Do we have any idea who did the shooting?'

'No. And no rebel group put their hand up for it. The incident's been buried. No press coverage, nothing but an internal memo or two and a verdict of random opportunistic insurgence.'

'You don't sound convinced.'

'I'm not. There's something else going on. Jared's looking into it. Quietly.'

Lena nodded. Trig waited.

But no memories of Lena coming to Turkey specifically to find Jared were forthcoming.

Lena leaned her head back against the tiled lip of the pool and closed her eyes. 'Think I'm going to forget the scrub-down altogether and stay right here for at least an hour. The only thing I plan on opening my eyes for is to watch you get all sudsed up and sluiced back down. I could appreciate that show a lot.'

'Never going to happen.'

'Probably for the best. If it did, I'd want a way of showing ownership and you're not wearing a ring. By the way, when *are* we getting our rings? Because I have some more ideas on what I'd like.'

'You do?'

'I do. And I found a wad of cash and a couple of credit cards in my suitcase belonging to one Lena West. I can pay for rings.'

'Gentleman pays for the rings, Lena.'

'Since when?'

'Pretty sure it's a rule.'

'Do we follow rules? As a rule.'

'Always. What sort of wedding ring do you want?'

'Plain brushed platinum. Wide.'

'You want diamonds in it?'

'Meh.'

'What about a diamond engagement ring?'

'Shouldn't I already have one of those?' Lena frowned. 'I wish I could remember your proposal. I want to know how you got away with not giving me a ring.'

'It's possible I promised you the world instead.'

'Not the moon and the stars?'

'Those too. And Saturn's rings.'

'Classy,' she murmured. 'Were we beneath the stars at the time?'

Trig made an executive decision. 'We were on the beach, lying in the whitewash watching baby turtles hatch and return to the sea and it was a starry, starry night.'

'I can see how that would work. Where would you have even put a ring?'

'Exactly.'

'I could have a turtle engraved on the inside of mine,' she murmured.

Or not.

'Or the date.'

Or not.

'What *was* the date of our wedding?'

'November the twenty-eighth.'

'I've been married almost a week already? Doesn't feel like a week.' She favoured him with a sultry smile.

'You really are going to have to bed me soon. Because it's criminal that I can't remember any of that.'

'You can't help it. No need to dwell on it. I'm not dwelling on it.'

'I can't remember any of the sex we had before marriage, either. That's assuming we had it.'

'Lena, can we *not* talk about the sex we may or may not have had? I am stark naked in a public bathing pool and at some point I am going to have to get out of here without giving anyone here a heart attack.'

'You want your wash cloth back?'

'No! Keep the cloth. You need that cloth to cover *you* up when we get out of here.'

'This isn't working for you, is it? You're not relaxing.'

'Maybe if we stopped *talking*.'

She lasted less than five minutes. Five minutes during which he convinced himself that if he took nothing too seriously, he could probably get through another day of being married to Lena without losing his mind.

'So would *you* wear a brushed-platinum wedding band?' she asked.

'Yes.' Not a lie. More of a theoretical answer to a theoretical question.

'There could be a glossy strip running through it like a wave. And there could be diamonds, little ones, like a little wavy strip crosswise across the band. Or little sapphires the colour of the sea. But not the deep blue sea. The light blue sea.'

'I see.' And he did.

'Maybe we should consult a jewellery designer.'

'Maybe. Are you tired?' he asked. 'I'm tired.'

'Hot water does that. May I ask you another question that I can't remember the answer to?'

'Shoot.'

'It's December the fourth already and we're in Turkey on our honeymoon. How long is our honeymoon going to take and where are we going for Christmas?'

'That's two questions.' And he didn't know the answer to either. 'Two weeks for the honeymoon—though if your memory doesn't reappear in all its glory soon I want to cut this trip short and take you home.'

Lena said nothing.

'I mean it, Lena.'

'I know you do. I can hear it in your voice.' She brought her hands to the surface of the water and started churning slow circle patterns in the froth. 'I'm remembering more. I can tell you that. I remember tagging after you and Jared when I was a kid and resenting the hell out of you both for being stronger, faster and more fearless than me. I remember wanting to rip Jessica's eyes out because you took her to your year twelve formal.'

'Really? You remember that?'

'As if it were yesterday. First time I'd ever seen you wearing a suit and tie and the things it did for your shoulders and my libido. As for Jessica, she had an hourglass figure, waist-length auburn hair and a smile just for you. In another universe I might have even liked her. She didn't even look at Jared.'

'Yeah, that was always a good sign in a date. Jessica was a good sport.' Who'd known by the end of the night that Trig didn't want to take things any further. 'Probably still is.'

'Jealous wife here,' warned Lena.

'You're a good sport too,' he offered hastily.

'Are you sure? Because I seem to recall that I really, really like to win.'

'This is true.'

'I also have this niggling suspicion that I'm a bad loser.'

'Sometimes you react badly when you're forced to reveal weakness in front of others,' he offered carefully. 'You hate that.'

'Well, who wouldn't?'

'Borrowing strength from someone else when you need it doesn't make you weak. Makes you human.' He laid out his thoughts for her; honest in a way he'd never been before. 'Sometimes I wish you'd lean on others a little more.'

'Doesn't that make me needy?'

'Not saying I want to tie your shoelaces for you. But when you're railing against your body's limitations and when you're scared about being left out or left behind, would it kill you to say something?'

'Like what? Carry me?'

'Something like that.'

'You've carried me before.'

'I have.'

'Which must give you a certain sense of self-worth.'

'I'm usually more focused on staying alive at the time.'

'Can't you see that me borrowing strength from others gives me less self-worth? That the last thing I want is to be a burden to you?'

'It's not like that. That's not what offering and receiving help is all about.'

'I hear you,' she said solemnly. 'I do, but, Adrian, ask yourself this: when has anyone ever carried you?'

Lena couldn't quite pinpoint the exact moment in the bath house when the conversation had turned from teasing to her pleading with Trig to understand her thoughts and feelings when it came to relying on others for things she ought to be able to do for herself.

She *did* rely on him when she needed to.

She'd relied on him yesterday—for memories and form-filling-out, for safety, and she'd let him carry her and rejoiced in the act; she remembered that part quite well. She was relying on him now, for information and companionship. What more did he want from her? Did she really try to hide her weaknesses from *him?*

They lasted an hour in the hot pool and beneath the cascading falls of water. There was a ledge you could lie on beneath one of the cascades and let the water beat down on you, and it did it with exactly the right amount of pressure. She made Trig try it but he preferred the more directed pressure of a side spout. Neither of them took up the masseuse's offer to soap them up and wash them down.

Maybe next time.

An hour and twenty minutes after they'd entered the bath house, they stepped out onto the street, squeaky clean and smelling ever so faintly of roses. Lena liked smelling of roses. She liked Trig smelling of roses too.

She came down the bath-house steps, feeling freer in her gait than she had been in days.

'You're walking easier.' He didn't miss much, this husband of hers.

'I know. Turkish baths are my new favourite place. And I know I suggested we look for rings after this, but I'm having second thoughts.' Never let it be said that she couldn't admit to weakness. She could work on that. Work on it right now. 'I'm tired, my head's beginning to throb and all I want to do is curl up on that hotel bed with a plate of fruit and a movie.'

'Lena West, are you admitting that you're not up to shopping with me?'

'I am. And I hope you're impressed and it's not Lena West. The name's Lena Sinclair.'

She did love a man with a wide and blinding smile.

They hailed a taxi and when they reached the hotel foyer they dropped by the restaurant and ordered a plate of fresh fruit and pastries, and hot coffee and tea to be brought to the room. She was getting used to this hotel now. The foyer and the lifts, the long walk from the lifts to the room.

She got halfway down the corridor before deciding she could use some more help. Especially if it involved being up close and personal with a husband who smelled ever so faintly of roses.

'Ouch,' she said and stopped. Trig stopped too. 'Could be I need a little more help.'

'With what?'

'Walking. I have this burning need to be in our room right now, and we'd get there a whole lot faster if you carried me.'

'Burning need, huh?'

'Scorching.'

He swung her into his arms. Damn, but she loved his smile. 'You feeling any less worthy there, princess?'

'No, I'm feeling kind of smug.'

'I've unleashed a monster.'

'Pretty sure I'll get the asking-for-help balance right eventually. Right now I'm feeling so breathless all of a sudden. I may need mouth-to-mouth.'

He got her to the door and got her inside.

And kissed her senseless.

The food arrived ten minutes later. Ten minutes during which her husband had avoided being on the bed with her for all he was worth, offered to run her another bath, twice, opened his computer and scowled at his emails and generally set her on edge with his inability to settle. He downed two cups of thick, fragrant coffee in rapid succession and stared at the walls as if contemplating climbing them.

'Got an email in from your brother,' he said finally.

'Jared?'

'Damon. He's got us seats on a flight out of here in three days' time.'

Lena sat up straighter so she could look her take-charge husband in the eye. 'What happens if my memory comes back before then?'

'Then I guess we cancel and continue on to Bodrum.'

'What's in Bodrum?'

He hesitated, just for a second. 'Boats.'

For the first time since waking up on the floor of Istanbul's Grand Bazaar, she wondered if her husband was lying to her.

'Seems like a long way to come for something I know we have a lot of at home.'

'Diving's not bad either.'

'Maybe if we were talking about Sharm El Sheik, down the bottom of the Sinai. Which we're not. We're talking about the Bosphorus.'

'Your geography's improving,' he murmured. 'That's got to be a good sign.'

Her spidey-sense was twitching too. Lena didn't know if that was a good thing or not.

'You're awfully worried about when I get my memory back, aren't you?'

Her husband's eyes grew carefully guarded. 'Not really.'

'Did we have a fight?'

'We often fight. Usually for no good reason.'

'So we *did* have a fight.'

'I didn't say that.'

'There's something you're not telling me. What don't I know?'

Trig ran a frustrated hand through his already dishevelled hair. 'I don't *know* what you don't know. Right now, I don't think *either* of us have a handle on what you do and don't know. There's stuff you're repressing.'

'The bad stuff?'

'Yeah. And I don't know how much of that to tell you right now, so I'm hedging, and waiting to see what does come back to you, and I'm stalling, for very good reasons, and hoping to hell that you'll wake up tomorrow morning and try and break my jaw, because then I'll *know* you're back.'

'Must've been some fight.'

'We didn't fight.'

'Then why can't I remember our wedding day? Why am I repressing that?' She suddenly felt nervous. More than nervous. 'Was it bad? For you? Was our wedding night a disaster?'

'God help me.'

'Tell me!'

'No.'

'No you won't tell me or no it wasn't a disaster?'

'It wasn't a *disaster.*'

'Do we have pictures of our wedding day?' Because she hadn't seen any on his laptop.

'I don't know about any pictures. We left right after… the thing.'

'The wedding.'

Trig nodded jerkily. 'Lena, can't you let it go? Just for now?'

'I can't.' She couldn't look at him any more. 'I can't remember our wedding day, or when you proposed to me or what we're like when we're together. Nothing, not even a flash, and of all the things I want to remember, it's those. It feels…disrespectful that I can't. Who forgets their own wedding?'

'It's not disrespectful.' Her cool, calm husband was unravelling fast.

'And we really are okay? We're not on the verge of divorce after a week?'

'No,' he said gruffly. 'No. Lena, I gotta get out of here for a bit. I'm going mad.'

'Will you look for wedding rings while you're out?'

'What?' The poor man looked positively hunted.

'Wedding rings. You could go browsing. Haggling. Blood sport.'

'I, uh, wasn't planning to.'

'Could you?' Anxiousness made her fidget. 'I mean, I wouldn't mind.' He'd told her to be clear about her fears. 'It'd give me something solid to hold to when I can't remember. Something real.'

She couldn't read him, this husband of hers. His face was all shut down and he stood so very still.

'You sure you wouldn't rather wait until your memory comes back?' She could barely hear him.

'I don't want to wait. I'd come with you—we can do it tomorrow if you'd rather not choose them on your own—but I don't want to wait. I trust you to choose well.'

Trig ran a big hand over his face.

'Trust you full stop,' she said, hoping to reassure him.

And somehow made it worse.

'I'll look,' he said hoarsely and handed over his laptop for her entertainment and fled as if the hounds of hell were snapping at his heels.

Lena let out a breath when the door snicked closed behind her husband. *Damn,* but she wished she could remember what had gone wrong between them. Because *something* had and she needed to know what so that she could fix it.

Restless, she turned to his computer and trawled through his music file, trying to find something she *didn't* thoroughly approve of.

Maybe he'd downloaded his entire music collection from her.

She scrolled though the photo files next and found plenty of her and Trig or her and Jared, or Jared and Trig—most of them involving ropes and sails and water. She saw pictures of her and Poppy in an elegant apartment and felt relatively certain that the apartment in the picture belonged to her father. She saw a picture of Damon giving surfing lessons to a buxom redhead wearing a buzzy-bee headband and knew it had to be Ruby.

Her memory was returning. Maybe not all at once, maybe in fits and starts, but it *was* coming back.

She trolled through Trig's video collection next. A couple of V8 car races that didn't interest her at all. Some big wave surfing footage that did. The entire season three of a local cooking show. Huh. And a TV miniseries about a circus, a drifter and a whole bunch of supernatural goings-on.

The creepy circus show won hands down.

She was still watching it four hours later when Trig returned. Well, maybe not watching it intently. It was entirely possible that she'd drifted off to sleep at some point between the first episode and wherever they were up to now. Daylight had come and gone. Dusk ruled the sky now.

Trig looked at her, looked at the computer screen.

'Relaxing,' he said.

She did like a man with a crooked smile. 'Doctor's orders.'

'You do know you've seen this before.'

'As far as I'm concerned, it's all new. And if this is new, think what else could be an all-new experience. I've been re-virginised.'

'Don't even go there.' Trig pointed a warning finger at her.

'Think about it. I've barely been kissed. My breasts have never been tou—'

'Lena!'

'I love it when your voice gets all gruff and commanding.' She lay back on the bed, all biddable and boneless. 'Who knew?'

'No sex. Doctor's orders.'

'Honeymoon,' she reminded him.

'You're just bored.'

This was true. 'So entertain me. What's new in the land of out there?'

'Well, the shopping here is still an experience to remember and I still pray for my life whenever I get into a taxi. The taxi driver's name this time round was Boris.'

'Did he know where to find the best wedding rings?'

'Of course he did. What kind of question is that?'

'And did you find any *you* liked?'

'You want to see?'

Lena sat up fast. Of course she wanted to see. 'What kind of question is that?'

He put his hand in his jeans pocket, pulled out a little velvet pouch and tossed it onto the bed.

Lena eyed the little pouch with extreme anticipation. 'Not that I don't appreciate the right-to-my-fingertips delivery but shouldn't you be on bended knee?'

'Couldn't you just think of the turtles?'

'I would if I could remember them. Bend. And give me the proposal speech.'

And wonder of wonders he went down on one knee and made Lena breathless.

'Heaven help me,' he said.

'Keep talking.'

'Okay.' He cleared his throat and swallowed hard. 'Okay, I can do this.'

'Hang on.' She smoothed back her hair and straightened her top, sat up straight, shoulders back and an imaginary book sitting on her head. No need for complacence just because they'd done this before. 'Ready.'

'Glad one of us is.'

'Take your time.'

He took a deep breath instead. 'We've known each other a long time,' he began raggedly. 'I've loved you for a long time. You're it for me. For better and for ever, there's nowhere else I'd rather be than at your side, so… Lena Aurelia West, will you marry me?'

Those weren't tears in her eyes. They *weren't.*

'Yes,' she said simply. 'Yes. I love you too.'

Trig let out a breath and Lena realised, belatedly, that he was nervous. Really nervous.

'Why are you shaking? You knew I'd say yes.' She closed the laptop and pushed it away. She reached out to her husband and coaxed him up onto the bed. 'That was so beautiful. You should do it again.'

'Once was enough.'

'Twice.'

'Right.'

'You look pale.'

'Probably fear.' He picked up the little royal-blue velvet pouch. It had silver writing on it that she didn't understand, that she didn't need to understand as he pried loose the string, took her hand, turned it palm up, and tipped three rings into it, two of them significantly smaller and more ornate than the third.

She picked up the first of the smaller rings. The brushed platinum had a glossy wave running through it. The second of the smaller rings was identical, except that this time the wave was a string of vivid blue sapphires, running from small to large and back to small again. Separate, they were beautiful. Together, on her finger, they looked superb.

'Real enough for you?' he asked.

'Yes.' They must have cost him a fortune.

She looked to the third ring. Brushed platinum, same as hers, but no wave ran through the thick plain band. She picked it up and studied the finish before reaching for his hand and pushing it onto his finger.

'Suits you,' she murmured. 'I'd have got you one with a wave as well. And I'd have been wrong. Have I mentioned lately, just how much I love your hands?'

'What?'

'Hands. Yours. I have a total fetish for them. Goes back years.'

'How many years?'

'You remember that kitten we found stuck in the drainpipe?'

'Yeah, but I remember the kitten's mother that found us two minutes later more. She *bit* me.'

'She did.' Lena grinned at the memory, for it was vivid, bright and *there.* 'You have a gentle touch, big guy. Even when under attack. That's when I fell for your hands.'

Her husband blushed, and Lena grinned some more. 'Truly, you're such a beautiful man, inside and out. I just wish I could remember what I did to deserve you. Because looking at you and then looking at me… Adrian, can I ask another question that you're not going to want to answer? Because it's a big one, and it's bugging me.'

'Can I reserve the right to not answer?'

'Where I got shot—there's so much scarring, so many hollows. Am I still able to have children?'

He didn't have to say a word; his eyes answered for him. Lena nodded and bit down hard on her lower lip. 'Okay.' She drew a ragged breath. 'Okay. *God.* I don't know what you see in me.'

'Don't you say that,' he said fiercely. 'Why do you *say* stuff like that? You're it for me. You always have been, and if you still want children, well, maybe we can't make one but we can care for one that needs caring for. Whatever you want to do, I'm in. All in. Promise me you'll remember that and that you'll remember this. Us. The way we are now.'

She straddled him because he was looking down at his wedding ring and she thought that he might bolt; she wrapped her arms around his neck and took his mouth with hers, gentle and coaxing at first, and then more languidly when he responded.

'Make love to me,' she whispered. She wanted that, wanted him inside her so damn much. 'We can go slow. Easy as breathing. The doctor couldn't possibly object to that.'

'We can't.' His hands were at her back and his lips were at her neck. '*I* can't. You need to get your memory back first.'

'For this?' His lips skated across her breastbone and sent a shaft of pure pleasure straight through her. 'Pretty sure I don't. I'm all for making new memories.'

'Lena, the doctor said no. You have a habit of ignoring doctor's orders.'

'Sounds about right.'

'It has a habit of backfiring.'

'Oh.'

He sat back against the headboard with Lena still on top of him. She leaned into him and he started drawing lazy lines across her back. Nice. As was the firmness still tightly lodged against her thighs. She rocked against him ever so gently. 'You going to take care of that?'

'It can wait. Tortured denial's my thing.'

'Really?'

'Apparently.' Those clever hands of his scratched at a spot behind her ear and almost set her to purring. 'Tomorrow,' he said, and it sounded like a prayer for salvation. 'Let's see how you're tracking tomorrow.'

He couldn't sleep. How was a man supposed to sleep when his head was full of the scent of the woman he loved and his heart was fair breaking under the weight of all the lies he'd just fed her. Not all of it lies: his proposal had been true. Lay his soul bare and hope Lena remembered in the morning.

See where this road led them and hopefully stumble across Jared along the way.

He still hadn't forgotten the real reason Lena was here, even if she had.

Because he could take Lena home the minute she was cleared to fly, and wait for her full memory to return, but the minute it did she'd be back out looking for her missing brother again.

He had half a mind to try and find Jared over the next couple of days, get Lena and her brother to sight each other and *then* take Lena home.

Trig slipped from the bed and reached for his T-shirt. He left the room with a mobile phone and minimum fanfare. The phone had come from Damon. Not government issue, nothing that could be traced back to him.

He punched in a number he knew off by heart and waited to see if a message bank would pick up the call. The message bank wasn't full and it should have been by now. Someone was clearing those calls. Hopefully it was Jared.

'Hey, man.' Jared would know who it was by the sound of his voice. If someone else had Jared's phone, Trig didn't plan on making it any easier for them to identify him. 'Haven't seen you for a while and we're in the area so we're going to drop in. You owe me, big time. And you need to be there.'

CHAPTER EIGHT

LENA WOKE THE next morning feeling clearer-headed than she had in days. Trig wasn't there—she remembered him rolling over and gathering her close and kissing her temple and then telling her he was heading out to get breakfast. She'd told him she'd come too, but she hadn't opened her eyes or properly woken up, and when she'd murmured something along the lines of five more minutes he'd told her it was five in the morning and to go back to sleep.

A command she'd been only too happy to follow.

So her husband was an early riser. She'd been an early riser too, back in the day when surfing had been an option, or sea kayaking had been an option. Kayaking might still be an option, come to think of it. Plenty of backwaters not too far away from Damon's beach house.

Or maybe it was time to get a pretty little cottage of her own, somewhere on the river. A cottage with panelled half-walls, high ceilings and bay windows. A yesteryear cottage that cried out for Persian carpet runners and wide verandahs. Her family would think she'd gone nuts—but she could put an indoor bathing pool in one of the rooms if she got creative enough. She could fit it out like a Turkish spa.

She was still in that lovely dream place where anything was possible when Trig came back with breakfast. Strawberry yoghurt today, and mixed nuts and flaky pastry and some kind of spicy scrambled egg.

She sat up and pushed her tangle of hair away from her face. Every night she plaited it and tied it off with a hairband. Every morning the hairband had disappeared and the plait was a tangle. She hoped Trig liked the dishevelled look.

She should probably let him in on the granny cottage idea as well. 'Do you think any shops here sell marble water-spouts and feature walls? And tiles like the ones in the pool yesterday?'

'Why?' He handed her a cup of tea and bent down to place a fleeting kiss on the very edge of her lips.

'I want a Turkish bathing room in the cottage we're buying on the banks of a lazy river.'

'We're buying a cottage?'

'On the banks of a lazy river. So that I can get up and go kayaking and you can get up to no good with a tool belt.' Trig's father was a carpenter-builder. His older brother was a builder as well and Trig had spent many a school holiday with a tool belt strapped to his waist. Lena had the niggling suspicion that Trig's father resented the hell out of the Wests for leading Trig away from the family business.

'You want me to put on a tool belt?'

'Only when you're not out protecting national secrets. And if it's hot on the banks of that lazy river you can lose the shirt. I might even make a calendar of you looking like that. You could be Mr January all the way through to December.'

'Don't you dare.'

'Oh, I dare. You should know that by now.'

Her husband smiled his wide, happy smile. 'I've missed you,' he said, and then his gaze slid to the rings on her wedding finger and his smile dimmed. 'How's the head?'

'The bump is on its way down.' She took his hand and slid it through her hair. 'Feel.'

He did. Damn but he had a nice touch. She closed her eyes, tilted her head back and let him cradle the weight of it in that big hand of his. 'Mmm.'

He let her go in a hurry and retreated to the other side of the table.

'You are the shyest person I know when it comes to physical affection,' she told him grumpily.

'Doctor's orders.'

'I'm going back there today, just to get that particular directive lifted.'

'You still can't remember squat.'

'I'm remembering a little more each day. I'm on disability leave from work. And I just failed my physical.'

Trig grunted.

'I was a slow waddling duck for those pickpockets. ASIS isn't going to put me back in the field. Not sure I *want* to go back in the field if all I'm going to be is a liability. I need a new focus. Maybe a whole new career.' She eyed him curiously. 'Have you ever thought of quitting the business?'

'Not yet.'

'But you took a desk job.'

'You remember that?'

'Didn't you?'

'Yeah.' He rubbed at his temple.

'What's it like?'

'Lot of analysis.'

'Frustrating?'

Trig gave a reluctant nod.

'You could return to fieldwork.'

'What? And leave you all alone in the little house on the river? Who'd put the Christmas decorations on the roof?'

So he *had* altered his work focus because she'd been forced to alter hers. The confirmation gave her mixed feelings. On the one hand Lena was grateful that she was so well loved. On the other hand she was dismayed that he'd chosen to limit himself in order to be there for her. She wasn't that needy. Was she? 'You want to put Christmas decorations on the roof?' she asked lightly.

'I want Christmas decorations everywhere.'

Maybe it was time she expanded her earlier dream. 'I'm having second thoughts about the little house on the river. I think we need a big old farmhouse instead, with sheds to house all the toys and decorations when they're not being used. And if we're living on the river, I want a powerboat. A really fast one. I could take up speedboat racing.'

'Yeah, that's really going to encourage me to leave you there by yourself.'

'You could take up speedboat racing as well. I seem to recall having a quarter share in a plane that I could sell.'

'Handy,' he said dryly.

'Isn't it? I thought I might ring Jared today. Or Poppy. And I got a phone message in from someone only the name's not ringing any bells. Amos Carter.'

Trig frowned. 'Let me see it.'

She handed over her phone and Trig found the message and frowned some more.

'Who is he?'

'An old work contact.'

'Jericho3, Milta Bodrum Marina,' she said next. 'Is it a boat or a missile?'

'Don't know.'

'Are we curious?'

'I'm curious. Leave it with me. You're concussed.'

Lena sipped her tea. 'I still can't remember getting married.'

Trig eyed her sharply. Lena dropped her gaze. She wanted to. She was *trying* to.

'I guess what I'm saying is that if that particular memory stays elusive, I'd kind of like to do it all over again. The ceremony. Do you think the families would go for that?'

'I think your family would do anything for you. And mine could be persuaded along.'

'Would *you* do anything for me?'

'You really need to ask?' He held her gaze. Lena was the first to look away.

'So, yeah. That could happen,' he said gruffly. 'Get well and anything could happen.'

'You mean my leg.'

'Your leg is as good as it's ever likely to get. The kayaking and the speedboat racing are good options for you. I like that you're talking about them.'

'Promise me something. Promise you'll race me.'

Trig grinned and placed his hand to his mighty heart. 'Don't expect any quarter.'

'I'd take it as a grave insult if you gave me any. So what's the plan for today? I know you said we should go home if my memory stays faulty, but it *is* improving. I remembered that your father's a builder this morning. I remember you working his jobs in order to get the money to buy your surf kites. True or not true?'

'True.'

'So I'd like to stay. Maybe we could continue on with our honeymoon plans. Make the most of this time together, regardless.'

Trig looked to be on the verge of protest.

'After I've seen the doctor today and been given the all-clear, of course.'

'You're so amenable.'

'Aren't I always?'

Trig almost choked on his coffee. 'Yeah, no. I'm thinking it's a concussion side effect that has to do with a whole bunch of bad feelings that you can't remember.'

'But you prefer me amenable? You like this me better than you like the old me.'

Trig took his time answering. 'There's a few old yous. You as a kid. You as a comrade-in-arms. You trying to make your body work the way it did before, scared as hell that it wouldn't and even more scared of being cast aside by the people you love because of it. I had trouble getting that through to you. Fell in love with you even more because of it though. And then there's this you who's a whole lot like the old you—before the shooting—only softer somehow, and more assured. I could get used to this you too.'

'But which me do you love?'

'All of them.'

Good answer. 'So, assuming the doctor gives me the okay, where to next on the honeymoon trip?'

'Bodrum.'

'So you *do* know what Jericho3 is?'

'No,' he muttered. 'But I aim to.'

Lena got the all-clear to travel from the doctor and permission to back off on the medications. The doctor made a more thorough examination of the bruises on her hip this time around and made her show him what leg movement she had and asked her whether the pain there was any worse than before.

'No,' she assured him. 'That's about as good as it gets.'

The doctor nodded. 'You're on pain medication?'

'And anti-inflammatories. The leg has improved a lot. It's been nineteen months. I'm off the painkillers for the most part. I'll take them occasionally and the anti-inflammatories too if I have a big day of movement coming up.'

'I didn't know you were off the painkillers,' said Trig.

'Not completely. But on a good day I can get by without. Doctor, what about the sex with my husband? Am I cleared to do that? Because we're on our honeymoon.'

'Ah.' The doctor slid Trig a sideways glance. 'Again, if you're sensible and don't indulge in anything too rigorous you should be fine.'

Lena beamed. Trig frowned.

For a man on his honeymoon he didn't look altogether pleased about the lifting of the no-sex ban.

'You want us on the next flight home, don't you?' Lena accused as they left the doctor's rooms.

'The thought had crossed my mind.'

'Why?'

'Because your memory's still impaired.'

'It's not that impaired.'

'That's one opinion.'

'Aren't we meant to be meeting up with Jared while we're here? When's that scheduled for?'

'It's not. I haven't heard from him.' Trig nodded towards a dark grey saloon that was fast approaching. 'There's our driver.' The vehicle slid to a halt and Trig opened the rear door for her. Traffic backed up behind the vehicle but both Trig and the driver seemed unconcerned. 'I'm tossing up whether we should go to Bodrum or not,' Trig said as they got under way.

'Bodrum is indeed a most pleasant holiday destination,' offered the taxi driver. The driver's name was Yasar. Yasar was a cheerful man with many relatives.

'I promise to rest,' Lena said. Hopefully this would reassure him.

'And do exactly what I say,' Trig said.

'Was that in our marriage vows? I don't think it was.'

Trig sighed. 'You could at least pretend obedience. How else am I going to pretend that taking you to Bodrum is even a halfway good idea? Because it's not. It's the worst idea I've ever had, with the exception of one or two others.'

'What were the others?'

'Imbecilic.'

Lena grinned at him. 'I'd like to go to Bodrum. It sounds relaxing. I'll stay out of your way if there's work there for you that you want to chase up. I'm okay with you multitasking. We could fly there this afternoon after we shop.'

'Shop for what?'

'Clothes.' Lena leaned forward towards the driver. 'Yasar, are there any big department stores nearby?'

'Indeed, there are,' Yasar offered in a voice filled with deep despair. 'Although why anyone would want to shop there, when for marginally more effort I can take you to any number of specialty stores that also offer discretionary discounting—'

'Not today, Yasar,' Trig cut in firmly. 'Just find us a department store.'

Ten minutes later, Yasar slowed the car to a halt in front of a huge department store.

'How long are we going to be?' Trig asked her.

'Half an hour.'

'Half an hour,' said Yasar, looking to Trig. 'I shall be back in this very spot at exactly ten fifty. Shall I be bearing kebabs and cold beverages for you and your lady wife?'

'Yes,' said Trig. 'Yasar, what are you like at booking flights?'

'I have a gift for it,' said Yasar. 'I also have a cousin who is a travel agent.'

'See if your cousin can book us on a flight to Bodrum later this afternoon.'

Yasar nodded sagely.

'Handy guy,' she murmured as Yasar drove away.

'He's a fixer.'

They entered the store and headed past the perfume counters and towards the escalators, where a giant sign told them what items would be on what floor. 'I propose we divide and conquer,' she told him briskly. 'Second floor for you.'

'Second floor is women's evening wear.'

'Exactly. I need a dress to go dancing in. Don't bring too much sexy back and I don't do baby pink or ruffles.'

'But you could.'

'Yes, and you could do purple spandex but I don't buy it for you.'

'Good point. Where are you going while I'm on level two?'

'Level four.' She smiled angelically. 'Lingerie and nightwear.'

Trig peeled off onto the second floor of the department store with fear in his heart and lust in his soul. When Lena wanted something she had a frightening habit of getting it. Lena was buying lingerie and he'd been sent off to buy her a dress. If Trig wasn't mistaken, she was gearing up for the full wedding night experience.

With him.

A shop assistant hovered; one with Bambi eyes and more curves than a roller coaster. She looked him up and down, her eyes approving until she saw the wedding ring on his finger and then they turned assessing. 'May I assist you?' she said.

'I need a gown for my wife. She wants to go dancing.'

Twenty-five minutes later, he and Lena met at the entrance doors to the store. Yasar and his taxi stood waiting, two take-away coffee cups in hand. Lena had a wide and wicked smile on her face and carried three shopping bags.

Trig had one bag and a headache.

'Yasar, did you know that this is our honeymoon?' said Lena when she got back into the taxi and accepted the hot tea and kebab that the driver handed her.

'But, *no*.'

'Yes, and I don't know anything about Bodrum but I do know that I want to stay somewhere magical and luxurious tonight. Somewhere with billowing gauze curtains and velvet pillows. A truly grand establishment where bite-sized delicacies are delivered to the room on a silver platter. It could even be a bridal suite in a fancy hotel.'

Trig stifled a groan. This was going nowhere good.

'Lady wife of Gentleman Sinclair, I do know of such a place in Bodrum. It is quite famous.'

'I have a credit card,' said Lena.

'Payment at this most exquisite abode may *only* be made by credit card,' said Yasar. 'Indeed, it is not for the financially challenged. I myself have never been there.' Yasar met Trig's gaze in the rear-view mirror. 'There are other options.'

Trig was all for exploring other options.

'What's it called?' Lena asked.

'Saul's Caravan. Though it is not a caravan, you understand. It is an old stone residence overlooking the city. It is thought to have once housed a King's concubine.'

'Do we have anywhere booked?' Lena turned to him, her eyes imploring.

'No. But…'

'But what?'

'I think I have a headache. I could be coming down with something. I'm probably not going to be of much use to you tonight, romance-wise, that's all. We could save ourselves for another time.'

Lena eyed him thoughtfully before turning her attention to Yasar. 'Yasar, what do you have for headaches?'

'There is a drink,' began Yasar, above the wailing of the radio.

Of course there was.

Lena went ahead and organised a two-night stay at Saul's Caravan. The hotel accommodation to date had been fine but nothing special, and her encounter with the pickpockets and subsequent visits to the doctor had left her feeling as if they needed some place special in order to get this honeymoon back on track.

A driver from Saul's Caravan collected them from the airport, his immaculate dark grey suit and the brand-new Mercedes he led them to an indication of what they might expect. The hotel stood high on a cliff face, grim, grey and surrounded by high stone walls half smothered in jasmine.

'Look.' Lena leaned across Trig to get a better look as they passed the entry gates. 'It has a turret. I've always wanted a turret.'

'I've always wanted a puppy,' said Trig, but he smiled as they came to a stop at the hotel entrance.

The carved double entrance doors could have graced the Versailles palace. The mosaic tiles that covered the ground looked as if they belonged in a museum. A staggeringly beautiful woman greeted them and introduced herself as Aylin, the proprietor of Saul's Caravan. She didn't bother with check-in, but led them to their suite and showed them inside.

It felt a lot like stepping into Aladdin's cave. Silver candlesticks and burnished pewter ware glowed atop burnished wooden dressers and sideboards. Gauze drapes hung from the roof above the huge four-poster bed and there was enough exquisite linen draping the bed itself to open a linen store. Old tapestries hung on the walls, half a dozen Persian carpets scattered the floor.

Because why have just one?

The suite had a tiny courtyard garden and sweeping views of Bodrum and the Aegean.

There was an outdoor eating area and a small indoor sunken pool, half hidden behind a carved wooden partition. A life-sized marble lion stretched out next to the partition. He appeared to be protecting a sleeping cherub. A life-sized painted plaster Virgin Mary graced one corner of the room, a jade Buddha sat in the opposite corner, and a trompe l'oeil of what Lena suspected was a Muslim prayer covered an entire wall. The room also contained a harp, a pianola, fairy lights and a gong.

'Oh, yes,' murmured Lena.

'Are we still on the planet?' Trig clearly doubted it.

Lena headed for the en suite—which was not to be confused with the other bathing pool. 'Hey, Trig. There's a surfboard-shaped mirror right here in the dressing room, next to the Tinkerbell lamp. Do you feel at home yet? Tell me you do, because there are costumes here too—that or someone's left their clothes behind.' She reappeared. 'I love this place.'

'I think it's mental.'

'Yeah, but I'm not in my right mind now either and you won't be once I'm through with you. This place works on so many levels.'

Aylin smiled softly. 'This room is strategically lit of an evening,' she offered. 'There are lights, for example, beneath the bed.'

'Electrocution as well.' Trig nodded sagely. 'Tell me that doesn't cost extra.'

'It doesn't cost extra,' said Aylin.

Lena liked this woman already. 'See? What's not to love?'

Lena was on for the ride, the adventure, the unexpected.

'One night,' Trig said.

'I booked us in for two.'

'There's half a winged cherub sticking out of the ceiling.'

Lena looked up. Indeed there was. And it wasn't his upper half. She chewed on her lip and stifled another smile. 'Definitely two.'

Trig rolled his eyes, but Lena knew she had him.

'Two nights,' she told Aylin sweetly and the woman nodded and stepped aside so that their driver could enter with their bags. A young woman followed in his wake, carrying a silver tray bearing refreshments. Another woman entered with a tray of fresh fruit.

'You feeling indulged enough yet, princess?' Trig wanted to know.

'Is the bed big enough for you?' she shot back. Because it was the biggest bed she'd ever seen. Antique. Custom made. Ever so slightly daunting. But Trig would fit on it and so would she.

'We're on our honeymoon,' Lena murmured and Aylin looked first at Lena and then at Trig in clear assessment of what he might bring to the honeymoon party. And smiled.

If there was ever a place for a scarred and insecure woman to seduce a man, this was it, decided Lena as the staff left and she started exploring her surroundings in earnest. The furniture choices and combinations had a whimsy about them—they celebrated the absurd and the unexpected, the ridiculous and the frayed. The blue and white tiled mosaic on the bathroom floor had a jagged crack running through one corner but still dared the viewer to gaze on it and call it anything but magnificent. You could find beauty in imperfection here. An imperfect woman might find courage here and the boldness to seduce a wary man.

Because her husband? Whatever else he was, he was also a wary man. Especially when it came to being physically intimate with her. Kisses, he delivered with impressive thoroughness and abandon. Hugs, touches and full body contact, he could do that too, provided everyone was wearing clothes.

Jump into bed and the man had a habit of leaving the room.

And maybe that had been on account of the doctor's orders, but Lena didn't entirely buy into that scenario.

Trig wasn't pushing the physical intimacy at all.

Take now, for example. They had everything they could possibly need when it came to an afternoon of seduction. They had water and wine, a tray full of finger-food delicacies and even a little hookah with a selection of flavoured tobaccos. And he stood there as if uncomfortable in his own skin, hunching slightly as he looked towards Bodrum with a brooding expression on his face.

He'd been brooding ever since he'd checked his phone—correction, one of his phones, because he had at least two that she'd seen.

He held it in his hand now, big thumb stroking absently over the screen. Whatever his mind was on, it wasn't on her.

And Lena did most firmly want it on her.

She came to stand beside him, freshly showered and wrapped in an emerald silk robe that she'd found hanging on the back of the bathroom door. 'That a work phone?'

'No. It's one of Damon's. His are less traceable than the ones from work.'

'There's a disturbing thought,' she said dryly.

'Yeah.' He finally turned to look at her and his expression turned even more brooding. 'Not that I have any objection to what you're wearing but what happened to your clothes?'

'They're coming up. You might have wanted me to take them back off.' There was that hunted look again. 'Guess not.'

'Well, not *immediately*. I figured you might like to try the food first. And the wine.' He headed for the table and put it between them. 'Champagne?' The champagne cork popped and Trig poured bubbly yellow liquid into delicate crystal flutes engraved with grape leaves and clusters. He poured himself one and drained it in one swift swallow.

Lena sipped at hers. 'I've never seen anyone do champagne flute shots before.'

'First time for everything,' he murmured, looking anywhere but at her. 'And I need to shower now. Right now. A lot. Really not clean.' He nodded far too enthusiastically and disappeared back inside.

Lena watched him go and sighed. Cleanliness was indeed a virtue, but still…

She found the shopping bag with the dress Trig had chosen for her and peeked inside. She put her hand in and pulled out a mass of cobalt-blue chiffon.

The dress had a fitted strapless bodice and layers of gauzy skirt that flared out gently from the waist and ended in a mass of ruffles.

'Do I do ruffles?' she murmured. ''I don't recall that I do.'

She ditched the robe, slipped into the lilac strapless bra and matching panties that she'd bought earlier, and then slipped the dress over her head. The bodice fitted neatly once she'd found the zip. The skirt fell in soft waves to mid-calf and she grabbed onto a bedpost and swooshed her leg up through the layers, pointed toe and all. It was an altogether feminine creation and gloriously light and soft against her skin.

She *did* do ruffles.

But she'd forgotten to ask for shoes.

Never mind; they didn't *have* to go out dancing tonight. Nothing wrong with dancing barefoot here.

Her body felt good—as good as it was going to get.

She reached for her make-up bag and painted her face in a tiny mirror pinned to the wall above three flying plaster ducks. Crowded, this room full of curiosities.

If her husband ran out of things to do to her and wanted to go exploring, he could always start opening drawers. He'd probably fall down a rabbit hole.

Twenty minutes later, Lena had done all the primping she could think of to do and her husband *still* hadn't emerged from the bathroom. Lena pounded on the door. 'Adrian, honey. You'd better not be in there taking the edge off. I have plans for that.'

Trig groaned.

'Really not reassuring,' she offered next. 'Is anything wrong?'

'Lena, I know what you want.' He had a great voice and he knew just how to drop it an octave and make it all husky and awkward. 'I just don't know that I can deliver the magical wedding-night experience you're after.'

Lena leaned her shoulder against the door and her hip soon followed. 'Why not?'

'Performance pressure,' came the husky reply.

'Seriously? You? I mean—you're the biggest show-off I know and you're not exactly inexperienced.' Or underendowed. She looked down at her rings and damned if they didn't start blurring on account of unshed tears. 'Didn't see that coming.'

Trig said nothing.

'If it helps any, I'm hardly Little Miss Confident when it comes to that area of our relationship,' she offered haltingly. 'I have body parts that aren't all that flexible any more. Not sure how that works when you get thrown into the mix. I mean… It *does* work between us, doesn't it? Sexually? *You* know this, even if I don't?'

'Yeah.' Inside the bathroom Trig stared at his reflection in the mirror and prayed for mercy. 'Works fine.'

What the hell else could he say? Tell her he had no idea and let her worry about that too?

'So, are you nearly done in there?'

'Yeah.' He'd been staring blankly at the mosaic on the floor for the last ten minutes, with the water beating down on his back and no idea how he was going to get through this night. 'I'll be out in a minute, and there'll be dancing and, y'know, amazing conversation and food and stuff. But not bed stuff. Not yet. I want to woo you first.' Woo? *Woo?* Who in this day and age said woo? He was losing his mind.

'You want another champagne?' she asked.

'That'd be good.' Maybe he could drink his way out of this. Or drink Lena under the table. No sex after that, just hangovers from hell and a Lena who'd *know* he'd sabotaged the evening deliberately. That was assuming that he could get Lena to drink heavily in the first place.

Bad idea. 'Actually, I don't want another drink right now. Maybe later.'

He heard her sigh, clear through the door.

He could always say he'd come down with a contagious social disease. Trig shuddered and thunked his head gently against the mirror. Not sure he really wanted to explore that one.

An argument, then. A rip-roaring quarrel that ended with Lena relegating him to the doghouse. He and Lena had argument down to a fine art. There'd be muscle memory, and synapse memory and maybe she'd *regain* her memory and then it'd really be on.

But he didn't want to argue with her either.

'We should go out tonight,' he said. 'We should go out right now and see the sights. You could seduce me while we're doing that. Or you could, y'know, get interested in the sights and leave the seduction for later. We could dine out, go dancing. Make it like a date. I bet you don't remember any of our dates.'

Mainly because they'd never been on one.

'I remember the first time you took me kite surfing,' she offered.

'It doesn't count if your brother was there. Bodrum has a castle. They turned it into a maritime museum. Don't you want to go and see the castle? I bet it has turrets.' Lena liked turrets.

'Would it make you lose the performance anxiety?'

'Couldn't hurt. It'd also help if you didn't *mention* the performance anxiety.'

'Oh,' she said. 'Got it. So…sightseeing and then a dinner date?'

'Yes.' Maybe he could tire her out completely. Now there was a thought.

'Should I wear my dress?'

'Not for the sightseeing part.'

'So, we're coming back here before we go for dinner?'

'Not sure.'

'I'm taking that as a yes. We could have dinner here if we didn't feel like going out again.'

Or not. He could arrange it so that they didn't come back here. Avoiding that would mean avoiding the problem of Lena's near nakedness while she got changed, not to mention the wearing of that frothy blue dress the saleswoman had persuaded him to buy this morning.

Lena in that dress in this place was just courting trouble. He eyed his reflection in the mirror and took a deep breath. 'I'll be out in a minute. And then we'll go.'

'There's no hurry.' She sounded a little bit wistful. 'I still have to get changed.'

So it took her husband half an hour to shower, shave and throw on a T-shirt and a pair of faded jeans. So she'd changed out of the pretty blue dress and thrown on a pair of grey shorts and another one of those simple cotton T-shirts that her suitcase seemed to be full of, and then she'd helped herself to more nibbles and poured herself another champagne by the time he appeared.

Adrian Sinclair was worth the wait.

Lena watched from the hanging love seat in the courtyard garden as he padded through the room, his bare feet making no sound as he stepped out onto the tiles. She knew those feet, from surfboards of old, and she knew those big hands for she'd grasped them often enough as he'd reached down to haul her into a boat or up a cliff face. She knew what his hair looked like wet because she'd seen it wet a thousand times. She knew this man and loved him. And she knew he loved her.

He didn't need to have performance anxiety. Not around her. She honestly had no idea why he would.

'Ready to go?' he asked, and she nodded.

'We have a driver,' she told him. 'He'll drop us off and pick us up wherever we want.'

Trig nodded.

'Did you know that this place is still family-owned? About fifty years ago, the upkeep was sending the family broke and a terrace wall fell down, fortunately not on any guests, but they did find an iron strongbox buried in the footings. It was full of jewellery.'

'Jewellery fit for a princess?'

'Better.' Lena grinned. 'Jewels designed to placate a royal concubine. They sold three pieces, kept the rest, and it was enough to fully restore this place and run it as a luxury hotel until the hotel became profitable in its own right. Did you know that there are only ten guests here at any one time and eighteen permanent staff?'

'I do now.'

'And that they'll shop for us if we tell them what we want?'

'What do you want?'

'Shoes. To go with the dress you bought me earlier. Which is glorious, by the way. I tried it on.'

'Does it fit?'

'To perfection.'

'Not sure I got the colour right.'

'I love it. It makes me feel like a dancer and I almost have curves.' She'd never had curves. 'Do you remember that dress you, Jared and Poppy helped me pick out when I was in year twelve?'

In the absence of a mother's guidance, Lena had done her best with buying things like make-up and clothes, but the sheer choice that her father's bankcard had provided had always overwhelmed her, and when it had come to choosing a dress for the school formal, Jared and Trig had just kept saying no. No to the little black dress because she didn't have enough curves to pull it off. No to the A-line silk tunic with the psychedelic purple swirls because it was far too short and altogether too easy for someone to get their hands beneath it. And she'd been adamantly against any of the more feminine creations Poppy had urged her towards. Hard to embrace feminine clothing when she'd been so set on being one of the boys. She'd finally settled on a glittery red flapper creation with enough crystal beading hanging off it to sink a boat. 'That dress was so wrong.'

'That dress did not get my vote,' said Trig as he

slipped on a pair of shoes and pocketed his wallet. 'It looked like a lampshade and weighed a ton. You could have worn it as a weight belt while diving.'

He did remember it. 'Did I ever tell you that when I danced in it the beaded fringe flew out and started smacking people?'

'Maybe you were dancing too close to them.'

'Nope. Those fringes were really long. People got whacked from half a metre away. I didn't get up close and personal with anyone at that dance.'

'Probably because of the dress.'

'Pretty sure it was because of me.' Lena smoothed her fingers down the front of her serviceable shorts. 'No date. No dance partners other than whoever was dancing in the group.' Lena *knew* she pursued things too aggressively at times. Sports, adrenaline highs, men… boy, could she scare men away when she wanted to. And Trig and Jared had encouraged it.

Maybe she *had* been too focused on sex these past few days.

Maybe she needed to cut her husband a break.

'I remember wanting to ask you to be my partner for that night,' she said. 'It would have made it bearable.'

'Why didn't you?'

'You were twelve hundred kilometres away. And Jared said you were busy.'

'Not that busy,' her husband said, after a pause.

'I also wasn't sure whether I wanted to mess with the status quo between you, me and Jared. I didn't want you to get the wrong idea—or possibly the same ideas that I had. You and Jared were my friendship group, my safety net, and I didn't fit anywhere else. If I stuffed that up I'd have no one.'

Trig had his hands in his pockets and a frown on

his face but he nodded as if he understood. 'Weigh your risks.'

'Exactly.'

He nodded again, his eyes dark with some unidentifiable emotion. 'So about this date. You ready to go?'

She most certainly was.

Trig had more than one ulterior motive for having the driver drop them at the marina rather than the castle. This was the marina that Amos Carter had steered them towards. Jericho3 could be the name of a boat. It sounded too easy, but Trig didn't mind easy. Right now he craved it. His other reason was nastier, because it involved making Lena walk to the castle from the marina—a distance she could have covered with ease two years ago, but this was now and he knew that she'd have trouble even making it to the castle from here, no matter how often she stopped for a breather along the way.

'Are we looking for anything in particular?' Lena asked, with her gaze firmly fixed on the half a dozen sturdy wooden tourist yachts bobbing up and down in their moorings. The sterns of the boats were loaded with cushions and lounges. The undercover bow areas contained dining tables and chairs. The boats were manned by young men with flashing white smiles and darkly suntanned skin. 'Jericho3 perhaps?'

'Yes.'

'I *knew* it.' Lena slid her hand in the crook of his elbow. 'I knew you had an ulterior motive for dragging us down here this afternoon. You think it's the name of a boat?'

'No harm in looking.' Trig eyed the people on the nearby tourist yachts.

'No women,' said Lena.

'Maybe they're below.'

'Maybe we could do a trip on one of them. Good way to look around, make some enquiries.'

'You don't want to go out on those boats.' The girl who sidled up to them had a bright smile, copper-coloured hair and enough confidence for a dozen street touts. 'Come back tomorrow morning before ten if you want a day tour.'

'Maybe we want a night tour,' said Lena.

'You might,' said the girl. 'But not on those boats. See all the pretty boys? You pay them and they serve you. The bedrooms are below. Sometimes they don't even bother with bedrooms. These are the night *pleasure* boats.'

'Oh.' Lena coloured.

Trig grinned. 'We're not interested.'

'I know,' said the girl. 'You want *my* boat. Taxi service only. Take you around the castle and then on a tour of the bay. Drop you back here or at the castle marina if you'd rather. Twenty-five lira.'

'Seems a little steep,' said Trig.

'I also saved you from the night boats.'

'What if we *had* wanted the night boats?' Trig asked curiously.

'Then I would have recommended my friend Akbar's fine vessel. It is the most orderly of all the pleasure yachts because he does not allow drug taking or unruly behaviour on board. Nor does he drug your drinks and steal all your money, unlike some.'

'What a gentleman,' said Lena. 'And your taxi is where?'

'Down here.'

The girl's water taxi was in fact a decent-sized cruiser. 'I have lifejackets,' she told them as she hopped nimbly into it, grabbed at a rope and started manoeuvring the cruiser towards a nearby ladder, attached to the wharf. 'My pilot's licence is legitimate. Twenty lira, because I like you. And I'll tell you stories about Bodrum night life along the way.'

Lena glanced at Trig. 'Means I don't have to walk to the castle. I'm good with this.'

'How are you going to get into the boat?'

'Slowly. Possibly with your help. As in you go first and then when I look like I'm going to fall, you catch me. It's all part of my asking-for-help-if-I-need-it plan. You like this plan, I hasten to add.'

'How do you know?'

'Because you said so.'

'You remember that?'

Lena frowned. 'Not as a specific memory. More of a general knowledge thing. Why? Am I wrong? Are you on a quest to make me more independent?'

'No.' The girl bumped the boat against the ladder. Trig climbed down and drew Lena down after him, hands to her waist as he lifted her from the ladder into the cruiser. 'You want help, I'm your man.'

'Nice,' said the girl approvingly, and winked at Lena. 'What'd you do to your leg?'

'Stuffed it,' Lena said. 'And the hip. And parts of the spine.'

The girl started the motor. 'You should sit. I'll go slow. Even when I'm out of the marina.'

'Do me a favour, and don't,' said Lena, coming to stand by the girl. 'I'm thinking of buying a speedboat. I want to feel how my body holds up to a bit of speed.'

'You got it,' said the girl, and when they cleared the marina and turned towards Bodrum castle she gunned it. Lena stood beside her, one hand on the back of the pilot's seat and the other on the top of the windscreen.

She wasn't even *trying* to seduce him, decided Trig darkly. She was simply being her old self—the one who saw opportunity at every turn and seized it. The one who only had to look at him and smile in order to seduce him.

She was looking back at him now, her hair whipping across her face. That smile. That one right there.

'I can do this,' she said.

'See how you pull up tomorrow.'

Her eyes dimmed but her chin came up and he loved that about her too. Never tell Lena she couldn't do something, because she'd do it just to prove you wrong.

'This is the castle,' said the girl over the roar of the engines. 'It was built by the Knights Hospitaller, otherwise known as The Knights of the Order of St John. They called it St Peter's Castle and it served as a refuge and stronghold for all the Christians in the land and beyond. Later, the castle was surrendered to Sultan Suleiman and became a mosque. *That* got destroyed by the French in World War One, and then it became a museum. Take a tour. Very special.'

'What about the things you don't learn on castle tours?' Trig asked. 'There's a lot of money floating in this bay. Where does it all come from?'

The girl shot him a sharp glance. Trig did his best to look harmless.

'Tourists,' she said finally. 'Hedonists. The pleasure seekers of Eastern Europe. You can indulge in anything here, for a price. Many people come to do just that.'

'Is the crime organised?'

'Very.'

'Who are the main players?'

'Turks. Russians.'

'Any Asians?'

'No.'

'Ever heard of a boat called the *Jericho3?*'

'I got no business with anyone connected to the *Jericho3,*' their copper-haired pilot offered grimly. 'I like to keep it that way.'

'Know where we can find it?'

'No.'

'Wouldn't be asking if I didn't need to know.'

'I can't help you, man. Little matter of staying alive.'

'No problem.' Trig smiled easily. Harmless. See? 'Tell us about the night life. Tourist stuff only.'

The girl told them about open-air night clubs that backed onto the sea. She told them about the live music and the bars, the street parties and light shows. She dropped them off at the wharf below the castle's eastern walls and Trig paid her and tipped well, and told her she didn't need to take them any further and her sunny smile reappeared.

'You had me worried, big guy.'

'Don't be.'

Her eyes narrowed. 'That vessel you mentioned. How much do you know about it?'

'I have a name. I have a friend who might be on it.'

'By choice?'

Trig shrugged.

The girl shook her head. 'It's a mega yacht, with helicopters, a defence system, and a seventy-strong crew, most of them Russian. Thirty or so guest rooms. Not everyone's a guest.'

'I don't see anything like that here.'

'It stays offshore. Nice and private out there.'

'How does it refuel?'

'Tanker.'

'Anyone ever come in off it?'

'A woman and a kid. They go to the hospital here once a week, regular as clockwork.'

'Which day?'

'Tomorrow. Look for a power cruiser coming in to this wharf around ten a.m.'

'Thanks.'

'You seem nice,' she said. 'Don't be a dead man.' And then she got under way.

'Guess that saves us walking past a thousand small sailing yachts,' said Lena. 'Really wasn't looking forward to that.'

Trig snorted. 'I can't believe you just admitted that.'

'What? That walking more than a mile or so wears me out?'

'Yes.'

'It's hardly a secret.'

'I know. But you usually don't like admitting it.'

'I'm older and wiser now. I also don't mind admitting complete ignorance as to why we're here. You do realise that I can't remember *anything* about why that yacht is so important? Or who you think might be on it.'

'I realise.'

'Care to share?'

'Not really. Honeymoon, remember?'

'I do remember.' Lena stared up at the towering castle. 'That is a big castle.'

'I know. The view from the top of that turret is going to be *great*.'

'Maybe if I had a *week*,' she joked dryly. 'I used to have a healthy relationship with steps. Now they just send me weak in the knees.'

'I'll carry you,' he heard himself suggest.

'That'll wear *you* out,' she said. 'Let's just see a bit of the museum.'

They managed to get through half of one wing of the museum before closing time. They took it easy and avoided steps.

And Lena wore herself out anyway.

'Aches don't count if you had fun getting them,' she told him as they waited for their ride back to the hotel. 'It also makes relaxing at the end of the day *so good.* Please tell me it's the end of the day.'

'There's still dinner and dancing to go.'

'Oh.' Lena visibly wilted. 'Right.'

'Aches don't count if you have fun getting them.' Trig grinned. Lena thumped him and for a split second all was well with his world.

The sun had slid low in the sky by the time they arrived back at the hotel. Lena had stiffened up during the drive and Trig watched her take her time getting out of the car. He didn't miss a wince. Neither did the driver.

'We have a heated bathing pool that is very relaxing,' the driver told them as he escorted them to the front of the house.

'You mean the one in the room?' asked Lena.

'In addition to the one in the room.'

'I love Turkey,' murmured Lena.

'Also an in-house masseuse.'

'Perfect. What's the dress code for this bathing pool?'

'Swimwear is, of course, required. But the bathing caps need not be worn. The hair need not need be covered.'

'That's a requirement in some places?'

'In some places it is so. For cultural reasons, you understand. The bathing in such establishments is also segregated. But not here.' The driver glanced at Trig. 'Shall I arrange beverages for two out by the pool?'

'Not for me. I have some calls to make,' said Trig. 'But Lena might like something.'

'What would you suggest?' Lena asked the driver.

'For the thirsty I might suggest susurluk ayrani. It is a chilled drink made from yoghurt and garnished with mint. Very refreshing.'

'I would like to feel refreshed,' said Lena.

'You want me to bring your swimmers out to the pool?' Trig had guilt now. Lots and lots of guilt on account of all the walking he'd encouraged Lena to do today.

'No, I'll change in the room. I want to do it in front of the mirror next to the Tinkerbell lamp, just in case the mirror tells me I'm the fairest of them all.'

'I wouldn't discount it.'

'And I wouldn't want to miss it. You don't mind me taking a dip and leaving you to your own devices for a while?' she asked.

'Not at all. Take your time. Relax.'

'You know what would make that sentence perfect? If you added, "I'll order dinner for us and I'll get them to set it up in our little courtyard garden."'

'You don't want to go back into Bodrum?'

'I *really* don't want to go back into Bodrum. We could dine and dance here. You could put me straight to bed when I fall asleep with my head on your shoulder, having mistaken you for a gently swaying mountain.'

'Tempting.'

'I knew you'd see it my way.'

'Go and bathe. I'll have a menu sent to you out by the pool. You do realise that I'm indulging you completely?'

'You're a good man.'

'I'll see what the mirror says.' He was pretty sure the mirror would call him a fool.

Lena headed towards the suite. Trig headed back out through those massive entrance doors and decided to investigate the hotel perimeter. He was nosey that way, and he needed privacy in order to make a call.

He pulled out Damon's phone and checked for messages. From Jared. From Damon. From anyone.

Nothing.

He put a call through to Damon next.

'I'm in Bodrum in a concubine's lair overlooking the castle of St Peter,' he said, when Damon picked up.

'Amen,' said Damon.

'That all you got?'

'I can always put Ruby on. She might have more.'

'Do that.'

'No. How's Lena?'

'She still thinks we're on our honeymoon.'

'Then why aren't you on a plane?'

'Because I'm following a lead on Jared. There's a mega yacht hereabouts called the *Jericho3.* I need to know more about it. Ownership. Specs. Whatever you can find within the next eight hours.'

'You thinking of paying it a visit?'

'No. I'm thinking that would be suicide. My best hope is that Jared's worked his way onto it. Worst-case scenario—he's a prisoner on it.'

'How are you going to find out which?'

'Hopefully, Jared's going to show himself.'

'Assuming he can.'

'Yeah,' muttered Trig. 'Let's assume that for now.'

'Are you letting Lena in on any of this?'

'I'm about to.'

'Is that wise? She's not exactly operational.'

'I can protect her. She's only after a glimpse of Jared. Proof that he's alive. We'll keep our distance.'

'Does she *remember* wanting to see him?'

'She will. And when she does, she'll have already seen him and won't feel inclined to go tearing after Jared again. Or would you rather I brought her home and we end up back here in another week's time doing exactly the same thing?'

Damon sighed.

'It's under control. I'll bring her home as soon as she's seen Jared. How soon can you and Ruby get to the beach house?'

'About that. Are you sure you're going to need us there?'

'Your sister thinks I married her. You want me to repeat that?'

'No, I got it.' Damon's voice was droll, very droll.

'I would love to marry Lena, I would. But I haven't married her yet and she is going to have my balls when she finds out. She's going to need someone to scream at. That would be me. Then she's going to need someone to argue with some more, once she's calmed down. That would be you. And then someone needs to argue my case. That's where Ruby comes in.'

'Does Ruby know that she's arguing your case?'

'Not yet. Put her on.'

'No can do. Ruby's asleep and I'm not waking her up. She's sleeping for three.'

'What?'

'Twins.'

'God help us.'

'Your congratulations are most heartily accepted.'

'Congratulations,' Trig said quickly. 'I mean…yeah. Congratulations. Twice.'

Did it make him a bad person that his first thought was not for Ruby and Damon's happiness but that he was never going to have that? That Lena was never going to know babies the way Ruby would know them. 'Is everything okay? With Ruby and the babies?'

'Everything's good. There's no real reason Ruby can't travel. I'm just…'

'I get it.' He got it.

'Lena can come to Hong Kong. You can both come, and we'll do the not-exactly-married debrief here.'

'Sold.' What else could he say? The only reason he'd chosen Damon's beach house as the debrief venue in the first place was because Lena had spent so much time there and the surroundings would be familiar. They could work around that. Lena's father lived in Hong Kong. He had a penthouse there. Maybe that would count as home ground too.

'Better get you that information,' Damon said. 'Stay safe.' And then he was gone.

Trig scrolled through the pictures he'd taken of the castle and picked one that he'd taken from the wharf. He sent it to Jared's number. He didn't add words, but he thought them.

We're here, man. And if we can't get to you you're going to have to come to us.

If you can.

CHAPTER NINE

THE MEAL LENA ordered for them turned out to be a feast. Saul's Caravan set a lavish table, and not just in terms of the food. Lena discovered that fine china did not have to match when each piece was exquisite. She discovered that solid silver water pitchers and solid silver serving trays were mighty heavy, and that meze dishes were only the precursor to the main meal and that maybe she shouldn't have tried a little bit of everything, because when the spicy lamb dish arrived, Lena had barely any room left in her stomach.

'How much did you order?' Trig had partaken heartily of the meze too.

'I ordered the traditional feast for two, and Aylin mentioned something about five courses.' They'd started with dips and bread and then moved on to the meze. 'I'm thinking we're up to course three and I'm pretty sure the last course involves coffee.'

Lena served a small portion of the lamb onto her heavily patterned blue and white plate and avoided the rice altogether. She indicated that she would serve Trig too, and he held out his plate while she spooned lamb onto it. 'Enough?'

'Thanks.'

He'd been on his best gentlemanly behaviour all evening. Keeping her wine glass topped up, saying he liked the dress and ignoring the fact that she wasn't wearing any shoes and that her hair was still half damp from her swim and the shower she'd taken afterwards.

She'd made some effort—she had make-up and perfume on. Trig had made an effort too, for he'd dug a white collared shirt out of his bag and had it ironed before putting it on over jeans.

He'd never blended into the background easily, Trig Sinclair. His size had always made people look twice and the reckless glint in his eyes had usually kept their attention. Put him and Jared together, turn them loose on a party or a bar and chaos ensued. Women wanted to bed them, men wanted to challenge them and Lena often wanted to knock their heads together and tell them to grow up.

Looking at Trig tonight, his face smiling but his eyes guarded, Lena thought that maybe he *had* grown up. And that Lena had somehow missed it.

'Five things you never wanted to be,' she said. It was an old game, this one. A way of filling in conversation and acquiring information that you might not already know.

'Conflicted,' he said.

'About what?'

'You. Your past and my part in it. I always assumed that by letting you tag along with us whenever we went windsurfing or hang-gliding or whatever fool adrenaline rush we were on that week, that Jared and I were giving you options. It never occurred to me that we were limiting them. You followed us into covert operations without even thinking about the consequences. None of us did, but you're the one who got busted up. That weighs on me a lot.'

'Where's this coming from?'

'I spoke to Damon earlier. We talked about you. About your limitations.'

'Thanks for nothing.'

'Ruby's pregnant.'

'Oh.' She refused to feel envy. She refused to feel longing. Those emotions had no place in the presence of Ruby's good news. 'That's good, isn't it? I get to be an auntie. Ruby gets to buy headbands for a baby. You can't tell me you're not looking forward to that.'

Trig's eyes warmed ever so slightly. 'Maybe. And it's babies. Plural. She's having twins.'

'Seriously?' Lena laughed. 'That is awesome. You think they'd let us borrow them?'

'I want children, Lena.'

Lena's laughter stuck in her throat. They hadn't talked about this; she knew it instinctively. Why hadn't they ever talked about this?

'No can do. I do know my limitations in that regard. You'll get no biological children from me.'

'We could adopt,' her husband said gruffly.

'We could.' That was one option. 'Or you could have a biological child with someone else. We could explore surrogacy.'

'You'd consider that?'

'You might have to get me a good shrink, but, yes. I could get on board with that. Could you?'

'I'd probably have to share your shrink for a while.'

'I could probably be your shrink for a while. These past couple of years I've become intimately acquainted with helplessness, hopelessness, anger, envy and old-fashioned irrational behaviour. I can show you round.'

Trig smiled at that and she reached forward and covered his hand with her own. 'Don't give up on me.'

'Never.'

This was why she'd married this man.

'I feel as if I'm in a place where I don't have to run to keep up any more,' she confessed. 'I *can't* run any more. Best I can do is hold my ground and stumble along, and you know what? You're still there for me, and my family is still there, because it was never about me keeping up. It was about me believing that I belonged and I *do* believe that now. I'm happy now. I married you, which I have to say is probably the smartest thing I've ever done.'

'About that…' His gaze flickered to the bed.

'Yes, about that. No pressure.'

'Right,' said Trig faintly and Lena smiled and cut him a break.

'How's your food?'

'Good.' Trig loaded up his fork and looked at it as if he couldn't quite remember where it should go.

Lena smiled and took a quick bite of the fragrant lamb stew. Tasty.

'Forget the bed,' she said, although she hadn't. 'We still have several more courses to get through, and dancing still to go. I have my dancing frock on and everything.'

'But no shoes.'

'I don't need shoes. You're not wearing any either,' she felt obliged to point out.

'There's no music.'

'I found some pianola rolls. I put one in. Want to see if it plays?'

'You love this room,' he said with a crooked smile as she rose from the table, caught hold of his hand and tugged him towards the pianola.

'I really do. It's a little bit beautiful, a whole lot fascinating, and kind of cracked when you look up close. I'm hoping it might be the way you see me. Because, newfound sense of belonging or not, I'm *still* trying to figure out what you see in me.'

She fiddled with the pianola settings and the machine began to play a bright and jazzy tune that put her in mind of Gershwin and New York.

'I should have packed the red lampshade dress.'

'Or you could sit this one out.'

'Good idea.' She reached for another of the scrolls crammed into the shelving beside the pianola. 'Hey, I remember this one from my mother's jewellery box! Open the lid and music played and the little ballerina went round and round and round.'

'I don't want to go round and round,' said Trig.

She pulled out another roll. 'ABBA?'

'Don't make me shoot you.'

'You do realise you're not going to be able to threaten our children or our nephews and nieces with a shotgun every time they don't share your taste?'

'I'll figure something out.'

'What about this one?' she said, holding up a pianola roll for his inspection. 'I think it's French.' It was also something she could sway to—her dancing skills hadn't exactly improved with age. 'Bear with me,' she said as she went to swap the rolls, only now Trig had decided to figure out how pianolas worked too. 'Focus.'

'I am focused.'

'On me.'

He poked his head back out of the old machine's innards. 'But I can focus on you any time.'

He looked sincere. He sounded sincere. He set the pianola roll to rolling and the first few notes of gentle piano music flowed into the room.

'Seems a little slow,' he murmured.

'It's perfect. Which carpet would you like to dance on?'

He smiled at that. 'The blue one by the end of the bed.'

'That's your favourite? Because I'm thinking of buying one just like it for the farmhouse on the banks of the lazy river.'

'I do like the idea of a farmhouse on the banks of a lazy river,' he admitted. Moments later he surrendered a wry smile and held out his hand for hers. When they reached the blue carpet he swung her gently around and into his arms and she put her hand to his chest, deeply satisfied when he drew a swift breath. His nipples had tightened and wasn't that a pretty sight against the cotton of his shirt? She swiped her thumb across one well-defined little bump and he bit back a whimper. 'You like that?'

He nodded.

She pressed a gentle kiss to his jaw next. 'And that?'

'Not complaining.'

'Not encouraging me either.'

'About that—'

She kissed his throat next and slid her hands beneath his shirt as he stood there and trembled beneath her touch. Heady business, seducing this husband of hers.

'We should dance,' he muttered.

'To do that I'm pretty sure someone has to move.'

So he stepped in closer, wrapped his hands around her waist and began to move. He'd always been athletic. Occasionally, in the midst of one of his teenage growth spurts, he'd get a little clumsy until he figured out the workings of his bigger, broader body.

He wasn't clumsy now.

Lena let her body follow where he led, and revelled in the brush of her chest against his, of her hips against his. Trig's eyes darkened as he pushed her hair back off her face with his fingertips.

'You do that a lot,' she murmured.

'Been wanting to do it for years.'

'What stopped you?'

'I wasn't sure if it was what you wanted. Still not sure.'

'I'm sure,' she said, but he was already turning away.

'C'mon, let's finish the feast,' he said and drew her back towards the table. They finished their main course and then smiling people cleared the table and dessert and coffee arrived.

Lena looked at the table laden with sweet delicacies and groaned. 'I can't.' There was simply no room left in her stomach.

Trig grinned and popped a baklava into his mouth.

'Oh, stuff it,' she said and reached for a baklava too.

Trig began to laugh, a sound that was front and centre of so many of her memories. He hadn't laughed much on this trip. For a man on his honeymoon he seemed to have a hell of a lot on his mind.

'Are you really worried about having sex with me?' she asked and Trig promptly swallowed down hard on his baklava. 'Because I truly don't understand why.'

'I just want you to have all your memories back first.'

'I don't understand that either. What's wrong with making new memories? I'm loving these new memories.'

Trig sat back and began to fiddle with the stem of his wine glass. 'Me too.'

'Is it the room? Is it too weird? Because, I have to say… I really like this place. I could get naked here and my scars wouldn't look that out of place amongst the freaky furnishings. They fit. I fit. Being here with you in this place, it's like a gift. Makes me want to check my inhibitions at the door.'

Trig pinned her with an intent gaze. 'What inhibitions?'

'Well, there's the scars… I saw the way people stared at me in the bath house. I know the marks aren't pretty, they're never going to be pretty but they're mine and the getting of them wasn't without honour. You told me that.'

'Lena—'

'We don't have to have the lights on. They can be off.'

'I thought you said you were checking your inhibitions at the door?'

'I'm just thinking about ways to make it better for you. You said you had performance pressure. I wondered if maybe you had trouble staying interested because of the scars.'

'I don't need the lights off,' he said flatly.

'Because you wouldn't have to touch them. The scars, I mean. I don't know what we usually do, but I do know that they wouldn't be a turn-on for you. You probably just…skim.'

'Lena, you have no idea what you're talking about,' he said icily. 'I love you. Every contrary bit of you. Why the *hell* would I want to skim?'

He moved fast when he wanted to. He swept her off her feet and the next thing she knew she was on the bed and Trig was sinking down next to her, sending pillows tumbling to the floor. No weight on her at all but for the pressure of his hands curling around her wrists as he pinned her arms above her head.

'I don't skim,' he rasped, and dragged his lips from her temple to the edge of her mouth. 'Not with you. How the hell can you not know that?'

And then his lips were on hers and she opened for him and tasted champagne and cinnamon and the truth of his desire for her and it lit her blood faster than anything else ever could.

He didn't rush. He kissed her for a good long while before moving on to her shoulders and her throat. By the time his lips skated the bodice of her dress, Lena was writhing against him, impatient for more. He found the zipper on her dress and it slid down easy and then his lips were on her again, his tongue curling around her nipple, flicking over it and then sucking softly, testing to see which one she liked best and hands down the sucking won. Hands in his hair she told him that, with her head flung back and her breath gone ragged.

He began to edge her dress down further but she stopped him with her hands. 'Lights off,' she whispered.

'No.'

He shed his shirt, he got all the way undressed, not a shy bone in his body, and she loved that about him, even as she struggled with shedding her dress. He let her keep her panties on as he pressed open-mouthed kisses to the underside of her breasts and then her ribs and then his fingers touched the scar tissue that ran all the way from hip to groin. He pushed her legs apart and licked a stripe straight up the worst of the scars and she shuddered beneath the onslaught.

'Don't,' she whimpered. She didn't need this. He didn't need to do this.

But he pressed soft kisses into the rest of her scars next and then set his mouth to the centre of her panties and started drawing circles with his tongue. Ever smaller circles until she was pushing those panties down herself and the minute she had them off one leg he got one arm beneath her buttocks and set his mouth to her again.

She couldn't stop watching him and he kept his eyes on her, right up until his fingers joined the party and exposed her even more.

And then his lips were back on her scars and his cheek felt soft against them as he explored them with exactly the same attention as he'd given to the rest of her.

'You don't ever need to hide these from me,' he muttered, while his fingers continued to work their magic, rendering her slick and ready for him. 'I've seen them. I've watched you fight against them, get angry at them, despair of them but those are your emotions, not mine. These marks on your skin are a part of you now and I love them. I love you.'

He eased back up the bed until they were face-to-face again.

'Say it,' he demanded softly. 'Say, "Trig loves all of me and always will and I will never doubt it".'

'Trig loves me,' she whispered.

'Louder.'

'Trig loves me,' she said more firmly.

'Again.'

'You love me. Now would you mind *showing* me?'

'Been showing you for years.'

He eased onto his back, his gaze intent, willing her to follow, and she went with him, hands to his chest as she straddled him. Damn but he was built. She wasn't going to break him, that was for sure. She wondered how careful he had to be when it came to not breaking her.

'Take your time,' he muttered. 'There's no rush.'

'That's good.' Because she wasn't in any hurry.

She started at his shoulders, touching and tasting, not skimming as she moved down his torso and learned the way his muscles ran and bunched. She put her hand over his and learned the rhythms he liked, the little flick of his thumb at the top of each stroke, and eventually she wet her lips and took him in her mouth, just the tip and took his curse as a benediction.

His hand fell away and she took him in deeper, feeling the stretch in her lips because he was beautifully proportioned all over and wasn't exactly small. She tried to take a little more but ended up pulling off him with a loud pop. 'Damn but you'd think I'd remember that,' she offered. 'Not to mention what I used to do with it because right now I'm guessing that deep throating you is out unless I'm a hell of a lot more practised at this than I appear to be.'

Trig groaned and hooked his hands beneath her armpits and the next minute he was kissing her again and surging against her, not inside her, not yet, but doing a mighty fine job of jutting up against her sweet spot regardless.

He had a thing about her hair, winding his hands in it as he grasped her head and deepened the kiss. He had a thing for wrapping his arms around her, one hand between her shoulder blades and the other palming her buttocks. He had a thing about kisses, deep and dirty.

Finally, she sat up and took him in hand and positioned him at her entrance. He put his hands to her hips and bit his lower lip, his eyes a hot glitter as he gave a little push.

Lena gasped. Trig stopped, closed his eyes and breathed.

She pitched forward, skin against skin, as much as

she could. 'Kiss me through it,' she whispered against his lips, and he did, until he was embedded all the way inside her.

'You okay?' he asked.

'I will be.'

'You sure?'

'You know me. I love a good challenge.'

'You're not exactly reassuring me here, Lena.'

'You don't need reassuring—we've done this before.' She moved, a slow slide, a little pitch from side to side. He controlled her with his hands at her waist, lifting until she was almost off him, before sliding slowly back into her.

This time they both groaned.

He kept the pace slow and the rhythm easy. 'You're holding back on me, aren't you?' she whispered. 'I thought you said you were all in?'

'I *am* all in. Which is why I'm holding back on you.'

The man had a point. 'Doesn't seem exactly fair.'

'I'm good,' he said. 'Any gooder and I'll be gone.'

'Still—'

'Why are you even thinking?' he said, and flipped her over and kissed her, probably just to shut her up, but the kiss turned sweet and tender somewhere along the way, and his hands were so very gentle as he slid between her legs and began to move.

She stopped thinking around about the time he tilted her hips just so and rocked against her. Every muscle in her stomach and below tightened in response.

'You like that?' he murmured against her lips.

'Just like that.'

So he gave it to her exactly like that and shot her up to a place where she didn't have to think at all.

Just feel.

* * *

Trig woke well before the dawn, pretending sleep, watching Lena sleep until he couldn't stay there a moment longer. Regret rode him hard and shame followed suit. He hadn't meant to lie beyond the hospital emergency rooms. He'd never meant to lie to Lena at all, but the lies had just kept coming and there'd never been a time to tell her straight that they weren't married.

Except maybe last night.

Or the one before that.

Rolling from the bed, he groped around on the floor for his sweat pants and pulled them on. He headed for the courtyard and some air, looking out over the low stone fence at the lights of the city below. A party city, some said. A reckless place where people left their inhibitions behind and went after what they truly wanted.

Last night he'd taken what he'd wanted and to hell with the consequences.

This morning he wouldn't be able to look at himself in the mirror.

He heard the rustle of bedcovers followed by a barely there groan. He turned and watched as Lena slipped from the bed and limped over to her suitcase. She drew out a white baby-doll nightie and slipped it on, lifting her hair out from underneath it. She tried to finger-comb her hair, caught him looking at her and stopped and shot him a rueful smile.

What was she thinking? What was her brain *doing* when it buried some memories and made a meal out of others? Why had she found it so easy to believe that they were married?

She walked up to his side and turned her back on the city lights in favour of leaning back against the wall and looking at him.

He couldn't hold her gaze.

He leaned forward, hands to the wall and kept his eyes on the city. He shouldn't have given in. Nobody was perfect, he knew that, but *hell.* His abuse of Lena's trust was staggering.

'Couldn't sleep?'

'No.'

'Anything to do with me?'

'No.'

'Pretty sure you're lying.'

'Yeah, well. I do that.'

Lena wrapped her arms around her waist as if cold. 'Why?'

Trig closed his eyes. 'Just one bad call leading to the next, I guess. I got no excuses for you, Lena.'

She stayed silent for a while after that and Trig willed her to go away, go back to bed, anywhere as long as it was away from him. But she didn't go anywhere, just ducked her head and bumped her shoulder against his. Wanting body contact, more body contact, and he flinched beneath the weight of her need and his guilt.

'What else have you lied about?' she asked raggedly.

Where did he even start?

'Do you love me?' she whispered and he closed his eyes and told her the one truth that had never wavered.

'So much.'

'Then it's the job you're lying about. You keep checking your phone. Something's up. Is it a job? For ASIS?'

'There is a job here,' he offered, and cursed himself for taking the coward's way out. 'And you do need to know the basics of it, because it involves Jared, and because before you got concussed you were spearheading it.'

Lena blinked and then put the heels of her hands to her eyes in a gesture he knew of old.

'I don't remember,' she whispered.

'I know.'

'Then isn't it time you told me why we're here?'

'We're here to find Jared.'

'And then what?'

'And then we leave.'

'Doesn't sound like much of a job.'

'Finding him's the catch.'

'*Jericho3,*' she murmured.

'I had Damon do some digging. The owner's a billionaire arms dealer. Russian.'

'Specialising in what?'

'Everything.'

'And that's where you think Jared is?'

'Best guess. Truth is, I don't know. He could be undercover. He might not want to break cover. He might not be able to break cover.'

'If Jared's undercover, why does he want to see us at all?'

'Didn't say he did. We're the ones pushing for contact.'

'But why?'

'The old you is concerned for Jared's safety. He hasn't been in contact for a while.'

'Are you concerned for his safety?' Lena asked bluntly.

'Not as concerned as you.'

'Are ASIS concerned for his safety?' Trig hesitated, and Lena drew a ragged breath. 'Trig? Tell me Jared's not working off the grid.'

'Can't tell you that.'

She put her hand to her head. 'But he *is* reporting to someone. To you.'

'No.'

'How long since anyone's seen him?'

'It's been a while.'

'Trig, how *long?*'

'Nineteen months.'

'What?' She didn't understand. Her confusion was visible, palpable, and so was her anxiety. He reached for her and she went to him, still trusting him as he wrapped his arms around her.

'How could we get married without him being there?' Her words were muffled by his chest but Trig heard them anyway. He could have come clean then. We're not married, he could have said.

But he didn't.

'Copper-haired girl said a woman and kid come in off that floating fortress once a week to attend a hospital appointment, regular as clockwork. They're due in today. Copper-haired girl said they come with bodyguards. There'll be someone to pilot the cruiser. I've tried to let Jared know we're here. Someone's clearing his phone messages. Might not be Jared, but if it is, he knows we're here and he'll do what he can to contact us.'

'You think he'll be part of the crew that's coming in today?'

'If he can be.'

'And if he's not?'

'I take you home. Come back alone. Try and get an invite aboard *Jericho3.*'

'No!' Lena's arms tightened around his waist. 'I'm not losing you too.'

'Lena—'

'*No.* If Jared can't get off that boat we put someone on watch here and we go home and pull Poppy and Damon into the picture and plan from there. You don't get to be the idiot my brother is. I won't let you.'

'God, I love the new you.' Trig lifted her and set her gently on the stone wall and she wrapped her legs around him and her arms around him as if she'd never let him go.

'Good, because I'm beginning to think that the old me was a fool.' Her eyes were grey this morning, a clear and guileless grey. 'I love you. These secrets you keep from me, they don't change that.'

He kissed her so that he wouldn't have to speak.

Because the secret he still held… The one that sat like acid in his gut…

That little revelation was primed to destroy both their worlds and he had no one to blame but himself.

CHAPTER TEN

'I DON'T LIKE IT,' Lena said at nine forty-five a.m. as they stood at the base of the eastern wall of Bodrum castle. Beyond the wall, a wharf teemed with tourists. Beyond that, a dozen tourist boats bobbed gently on the water.

'Plenty of cover,' said Trig. 'Lots of exits.'

'Lots of women and kids,' countered Lena grumpily. 'We don't know what kind of watercraft they'll be coming in on or when. What if we miss them?'

'The craft is going to be ocean-going, expensive, and the woman and kid have bodyguards. They won't be hard to spot, Lena. They're just not here yet.'

'I hate waiting,' she muttered. 'What time is it?'

'Nine-fifty.'

They'd been there since seven thirty, playing tourists, finding seats, taking pictures of the castle. The wharf was a beautiful, bustling place to have breakfast, but breakfast was long gone and nervousness was taking hold. 'I have a bad feeling about this,' she said. 'And I don't even know why. Something's off.' She looked up at Trig and didn't miss the swift flash of humour in his eyes. 'And don't say I don't have enough gut left to have gut instincts, because you're wrong. Half the touts here haven't taken their eyes off us for at least half an hour. They can ID us.'

'Why would they need to? We haven't done anything,' said Trig, and pulled her to her feet and slung his arm around her shoulder and guided her towards the tourist day boats—the ones that went out at ten and returned late in the afternoon. 'We're not *going* to do anything.'

Ten minutes later they'd reached the end of the wharf and there was still no sign of Jared. They stopped and looked out over the water. 'How's your leg?' asked Trig.

'Aches like a bitch.'

'And the rest of you?' Trig had a hand to the back of his neck and he would not meet her gaze. 'Does that ache too?'

'You mean from the sex?'

Trig cleared his throat and a slow flush crept up his neck. 'Yeah.'

'Those particular aches and pains were hard earned and I'm savouring every one of them,' she murmured. 'I can't believe I forgot how truly talented you are. Or how responsive.'

Trig looked as if he wanted to disappear. 'Hey,' she cajoled softly. 'I'm really sorry I couldn't remember any of it. I should have been able to, because it was mind-blowing. I'm saying this just in case you happen to have any performance anxiety left and in case it was connected to me not remembering our lovemaking. Trust me, your lovemaking is *not* something a woman would ever strive to forget.'

He laughed at that. A curt, embarrassed bark, cut short when his attention snagged on something out in the bay.

'What is it? Is it Jared?' Nineteen months since they'd last seen Jared, Trig had said, and all of a sudden Lena fiercely needed to see him and know that he was alive.

'Three hundred metres to the left of the tall ship,' murmured Trig. 'Six-seater orange power racer. Huge.'

Lena scanned the water for the vessel Trig had described and found it. 'Whoa. Not exactly hiding its light under a bushel, is it?'

'Please don't tell me you want one.'

'Couldn't afford it,' she said simply, for that was a billionaire's toy, no question. 'There's a kid in one of those seats.'

Trig nodded.

'I can't make out any faces.'

'Yet,' he said, and all of a sudden Lena desperately wanted one of those faces to belong to Jared. She wanted it with a ferocity that surprised her.

'Looks like it's heading for the far berths.' Lena wanted to hurry, but Trig was having none of it. He took her hand in his and swung her round to face him and waited until he had her full attention.

'Lena, you gave me your word that you only wanted to sight Jared and let him sight you. You promised me that you'd stay the hell out of whatever he's into.'

'I can't even remember that promise,' she snapped back.

'Then it's lucky I can.'

'Can we at least get a little closer?'

'Yes, but you need to stay close.'

'Done! Don't make me bruise you. C'mon.'

She pulled him forward and he came reluctantly. The powerboat drew closer. Four men, a woman and a kid.

'Pilot,' said Trig and the pilot was Jared, as darkly tanned and sinewy as she'd ever seen him. Lena stumbled and Trig shot out his hand to steady her.

'I'm okay,' she said faintly, but she didn't feel okay. Jared seemed to be aiming the boat for a berth at the very end of the wharf, a berth with a pier and a steel gate where the pier met the wharf. Trig made her stop short of it, still well within the tourist throng. Lena turned back towards the castle as Jared manoeuvred the cruiser closer, her eyes suddenly filled with tears. She couldn't even see Jared any more.

She wanted to scream at him, shake him for worrying them the way he had. For disappearing so completely. For blaming himself for her injuries.

Damn but her head hurt.

'Lena?' Trig said gruffly.

'I'm okay. Headache.' Every muscle in her body wanted to turn around so that her eyes could drink in the sight of Jared. It wasn't as if the boat wasn't stare worthy. Plenty of others would be looking at that beautiful superfast boat. She'd turn and look too. Soon. As soon as her tears went away. Damned if she'd let Jared see her crying. 'What are they doing?'

'Docking.'

'Who's getting off?'

'The woman and the kid. Two security types.'

'Not Jared?'

'No.'

'Has he seen you?' Trig was the most obvious one that Jared would look for. His size made him stand out.

'Yes.'

Lena turned, ignoring the stabbing pain behind one eye. She perused the boat, taking care to look impressed. It wasn't hard. And then she let her hungry gaze rest on Jared. He'd taken his sunglasses off and was using the hem of his T-shirt to clean them. He was looking straight at her.

'Go toss your water bottle in the bin over there,' Trig ordered gruffly. 'You wanted Jared to see you walking, so walk. Make sure he can see you.'

The words rang true. So true. Lena straightened and started towards the bin, smoothing out her gait as she went, trying to make walking seem effortless. 'Standing,' she wanted to say to her brother. 'Walking, you moron.' She tossed the empty bottle in the bin and turned so that the boat would come into view. Jared was watching her, a tiny smile tilting his lips. 'See? I've done my part,' she wanted to say to him. 'Don't kill yourself doing yours. Matter of fact how about you get yourself home and give up this business of…this business of…'

Revenge.

Memory tugged at her, sharp and piercing, maddeningly out of reach. What the hell did any of this have to do with revenge?

Jared's passengers were just passing by, the security types lazily alert and carrying concealed, the woman digging in her purse and never breaking stride. The little boy looked straight at her, smiled and bent down to tie his shoelace. He didn't look sick. The woman stopped and looked back as if she'd sensed the disruption. 'Celik!' she said sharply, a name and a reprimand all tied up in a bow.

Celik stood and hurried to catch up to the woman. He didn't look back.

Neither of them looked back.

Lena looked to Jared and the other man in the boat. They were pulling away from the wharf, leaving, and she felt a swift tug of regret. She wanted her brother back within reach. Finding out who was responsible for her getting shot was all well and good, but not if it cost him his life and not if it meant him staying undercover for years.

'Let someone else go save the world,' she muttered and knew in that moment that she was done with ASIS, even if Jared wasn't. Even if Trig wasn't. She'd had enough.

Pain struck her just behind the eye again and she stopped and swayed and brought her fingers up to her forehead to try and chase it away. Blackness began to close in on her as her vision narrowed down to tunnels, the kind of tunnels that came with migraines, and all she wanted to do was get back to Trig and borrow some of his strength. Trig, who was her best friend and lover and…

Husband.

'God damn son of a bitch,' she muttered as knowledge slammed into her like a sucker punch.

Adrian Sinclair was many things to Lena but he wasn't her husband.

The proposal she hadn't been able to remember.

No wedding pictures to remind her of the big day.

The sex…

The sex.

She had barely enough time to glare at him; he'd barely taken half a dozen steps towards her before the world around her turned black.

Lena came to in Trig's arms, cradled to his chest. He was sitting on one of the benches scattered along the wharf. No humongous crowd surrounded them, and for that she was inordinately grateful.

She struggled up, out of his arms, and he let her go, but only as far as the space next to him on the seat. She smoothed back her hair and tried to make sense out of the jumble of memories crashing over her. 'I just—'

'Fainted,' said Trig, and handed her his half-full water bottle.

'For how long?'

'Couple of minutes.'

'Did Jared see?'

'Don't know, but he's gone. I caught you. There wasn't much fuss. Need to get you to the hospital here, though.'

'You planning on telling them you're my husband too?'

'You remember,' he said flatly.

Lena nodded slowly. 'Just then. Funny thing, memory loss. Bits and pieces kept coming back but not everything, not until I saw Jared and then they rushed back in like a tsunami. I remembered getting shot. I remembered you telling me to hold on. I remember waking up in the hospital in Darwin and everything else that came after… All the missing pieces, they slotted in as if they'd never been gone.'

'That's good,' he said.

'I still don't remember marrying you.'

Trig said nothing.

'We're not married, are we?'

'No.'

She nodded and twisted at her rings with clumsy fingers. She ducked her head because she didn't want him to see her cry. 'Why'd you let me believe that?'

'Your wallet was gone, you had no ID. I became your spouse at the hospital to get you treated faster. I didn't realise you actually believed we were married until we got back to the hotel.'

'Why didn't you tell me then?'

'I didn't want to worry you. I wanted to protect you. I also thought that you'd most likely wake up the next morning and remember everything.'

'You lied to me.'

Trig nodded.

'I *trusted* you.'

'You still can.'

'*How?* You let me make a fool of myself with you! You *encouraged* it.'

'Is that what you think?'

'What else am I supposed to think?' She wrenched the rings off her finger and they sat there in her palm, shining dully. 'You let me believe in these.'

'You said you wanted them.'

'I was delusional. How could you let me believe in something that wasn't real?'

'It wasn't like that.'

'I was there. It was exactly like that.' The rings sat in her hand, softly gleaming. All she had to do was tilt her hand and they'd fall to the ground, but he wrapped his big hand around hers and gently closed her fingers over the rings.

'I'm sorry,' he said.

'You should be.' She wrenched her hand away. 'I trusted you. I *bedded* you. And you *let* me!'

'You made it difficult for me not to.'

'Oh, so it's *my* fault.'

'No. The fault's all mine.' He ran his hand over his face. 'I know I should have put you on a plane back to Australia the minute the doctor declared you fit to fly. I didn't. I brought you here instead in the hope that you could have a moment with your brother and see for yourself that he was okay. It's why you came to Turkey. It's the only reason you came here. I know that some of the decisions I've made over these past few days haven't been good ones, but I made that decision for you. I knew it would mean another night with you, but I honestly thought I could handle it.'

'Handle me.'

'I should have known better.' Trig's eyes beseeched her to listen. 'It wasn't all lies, Lena. I *want* that kind of relationship with you. My ring on your finger. You taking life in both hands and racing speedboats because it excites you and because you can. The farmhouse on the banks of the lazy river. The whole damn fantasy.'

'Maybe you do.' Lena's eyes began to fill with tears again. 'Doesn't give you the right to just reach out and *take* it.'

'Or we could dial it back a notch or two and you could agree to go out with me.'

She laughed at that. A bubbling, stumbling hiccough at his audacity. 'I *trusted* you.'

'You still can.'

'No.' She took his hand in hers and tipped the rings into his palm. She carefully closed his fingers around them and then withdrew from him altogether. She brought her knees to her chest and put her head to her knees, blocking out the world around them but the pain of betrayal stayed with her. 'I can't.'

On the subject of Lena going to the hospital, Trig stood unmoveable. Upon hearing of her recent concussion, the medical staff decided to monitor her overnight. Trig brought in clothes and toiletries. He called her family and gave them the happenings of the day. He changed their flights and had the Istanbul doctor forward her medical records on to this new hospital. He took control. Quietly. Efficiently. He didn't pretend to be her husband.

'I'm feeling okay,' Lena told him when the nurse came in to tell him that visiting hours were over and that Lena needed her rest. 'I honestly think I'm fine now. He's leaving.

'No lie. I'm feeling okay,' Lena repeated as the nurse withdrew from the room. Tension hung there between them, a tension built on all the things they hadn't said these past few hours. He'd helped her find Jared, and that was worth something. But he'd betrayed her trust too, and that hurt; God, it hurt. A nameless stranger had put a spray of bullets in her gut and almost destroyed her. This man had put a bullet straight through her heart.

'I want to thank you for today,' she began. 'Jared's alive and I know that now. I've seen him and he's seen me. Whatever he's doing… I can't stop him from doing it. He wants to save the world, one bad guy at a time, and that's a noble ambition. It's just not my ambition any more. Mine are smaller now. Right now I just want to get through the day without falling apart emotionally. I always have had an emo streak.'

'You're doing fine,' he said gruffly.

'No. I'm not. I need you to not be here any more. I need you to hear what I'm saying. You should go home.'

When visiting hours came around the next morning, Poppy was there for her.

And Trig was not.

CHAPTER ELEVEN

FIVE DAYS LATER, Lena was back at Damon's beach house by the sea and Poppy—who'd escorted her there—had headed back to Darwin and the delicious Sebastian who'd claimed Poppy's heart. Poppy hadn't pried, when it came to what had happened between Lena and Trig in Turkey. Poppy had been relieved to know that Jared was alive, and more relieved still when the doctor had discharged Lena and given her the all-clear to travel. Jared was busy doing whatever it was he was doing, and that was his idiot decision and no one else's, as far as Poppy was concerned.

'*Now* will you let it go and concentrate on living your life?' Poppy had said as they'd packed their bags for home. 'Because it's right there in front of you and it's ready when you are.'

Five days since Lena had told Trig to go.

And the loneliness and sense of *wrong* ate away at her soul.

She had everything she needed here at Damon's house. Comfort and space and a gorgeous indoor pool. So many pools in her life, only now she remembered why. The countless hours of water-based rehab. The agonising stretches as she regained the use of her left leg, one millimetre at a time, refusing to admit defeat.

Damon had practically given over this house to her—no wonder she'd thought of it as hers. Hers and Trig's, because he'd spent almost as much time here as she had these past nineteen months. Babysitting her, she'd always thought. Encouraging her with his silence when others had told her to stop. Adding his strength of will to hers. Sometimes he'd even gone away when she'd yelled at him to leave her alone, but he'd never stayed gone for long. It wasn't his way. This time, though…

All bets were off.

Her mobile rang and Lena found it on the little table beside Damon's front door and looked at the screen in sudden trepidation, swiftly followed by a stab of disappointment. Not Trig. Ruby. Lena tapped the screen to answer the call and stood a little straighter because Ruby had that effect on people.

'I hear congratulations are in order,' she said lightly, for she hadn't yet congratulated Ruby on her pregnancy, and that was an oversight she wanted to fix. 'Congratulations.'

'Thank you. I told Damon I wanted to tell you in person but boys will be boys. Apparently he and Trig had nothing else to talk about on the phone the other day besides the fact that Trig was setting up a meeting with your brother and that somewhere along the line he'd fake married you. Which is, in fact, why I'm calling you. I hear you're still at odds with my second favourite man on the planet.'

'Ruby, are you cross examining me?'

'Would you like me to rephrase the question? What's going on, Lena? It's not like you to hold a grudge.'

'He let me think that we were on our honeymoon, Ruby. He lied to me. Over and over again. Who *does* that? To someone they supposedly care about?'

'You need to examine the event carefully,' said Ruby. 'Did he at any time *tell* you that you were on your honeymoon? Or did you assume it? Because maybe what happened was that you assumed it and Trig simply failed to correct you. Maybe the doctor had ordered rest for you. No strenuous activity or thinking too hard. Maybe Trig thought you'd sleep on it and wake up the next morning with your memories intact.'

'You're his defence lawyer, aren't you?'

'If I was I wouldn't be calling you. Your partial memory loss placed Trig in an extremely awkward situation. He did his best. He always does his best for you.'

'He lied to me. He let me make a fool out of myself. Ruby…' Lena bit back a sob '…I was so happy. I was planning all sorts of rubbish.'

'Like what?'

'A big old house for us to live in. Christmas decorations. Kids. I can't have kids. Didn't stop me saying yes to them. Adopted kids. Surrogate kids. I'm pretty sure we made plans to borrow your kids every now and again. We had it all worked out. I thought it was *real*. I bedded him. I thought it was real.'

'Trig *slept* with you?'

'Yes.'

'Poor Trig.'

'Poor *Trig?* What about poor me?'

'He knew you'd find out that you weren't married to him sooner or later. He figured that as long as the marriage sham didn't go too far and that you got to see Jared, everything would work out for the best in the long run. Your needs before his, and all that. How *did* you get him to bed you, by the way? Because the last time I spoke to him that was definitely not part of the plan. On pain of death not part of the plan.'

'Oh, you know me.' Lena closed her eyes and rubbed at her temple. 'I badger and bully and prey on people's weaknesses and generally don't take no for an answer.'

'I'm relatively sure that's not true,' said Ruby carefully.

'You weren't there.'

'So you're *not* blaming Trig for that part of the mess.'

'Oh, no. I still am. He's a great target for anger. I think it's those broad shoulders. It's just…maybe I'm okay with blaming me too. Doesn't make anything *right.*'

'No, but it's a start,' Ruby offered gently. 'Here's what you're going to do. You're going to make a coffee or a tea, and then you're going to sit down and draw up two columns. The first column is what happened in Turkey. Stick to the facts. The second column is what you want to happen now.'

'What about what Trig wants to happen?'

'Add another column. Get him to fill it out. You *do* know that he's stupidly in love with you? You're not second-guessing that?'

'I am second-guessing that. I look in the mirror and there's so much of me there that's not pretty. Inside and out. I don't know what he sees in me.'

'Soul mate, kindred spirit, partner in crime…'

'I can't do those things that we used to do.'

'May I draw your attention back to column two?' Ruby said patiently. 'In it you put all the things that you can do, want to do and dream of doing with the man you call Trig.'

'That's another three columns.'

'Have it your way. Call me tomorrow if you get stuck. Call Trig tomorrow too. Don't blame yourself, or him, for a situation that neither of you had much control over. Do take control of the situation you're in now.'

'Are you sure you're a lawyer and not a psychotherapist?'

'Sometimes you have to be both.'

Lena paused. Ruby was part of this family now. A strong and savvy woman with a lot of good times and bad behind her. The kind of woman a person could rely on. 'May I really call you if I need more help with this?'

'Any time.'

'Thanks. Tell Damon hello.'

'Will do.' Ruby hung up. Lena put her phone back on the table. Weariness washed over her as she made her way to the couch. Being off her feet and horizontal beckoned. Memories of Trig beckoned too. Of him in a Turkish bath house, valiantly trying to preserve her modesty. Of him talking starry nights and turtles. Of Lena dancing in his arms while a pianola played softly in the background. Of Trig stripped naked and loving her.

Say it.

Trig loves me.

Again.

You do know that he's stupidly in love with you.

Trig loves me.

Again.

Two minutes later, she was asleep.

Adrian Sinclair had never been one for inactivity. Waiting drove him crazy. Waiting for word from a woman who'd already driven him crazy merely doubled the crazy. He couldn't sit still. He couldn't sleep. Work didn't hold his interest. Physical activity leading to exhaustion couldn't stem his agitation. For the last three nights he'd gone to bed exhausted and woken up dreaming of Lena. Replaying in his head what he should have done or could have done.

And hadn't.

He knew Lena was home now. She'd arrived home with Poppy the day before yesterday. Poppy had called. Lena hadn't. Ruby had called. Lena hadn't. Trig's father had called, and Trig had asked him what kind of price old farmhouses on the banks of a lazy river were going for.

His father had asked him what he'd been drinking, but he'd been drinking nothing, nothing at all.

And Lena still hadn't called.

Adrian Sinclair had always gone after what he wanted, sometimes with excruciating single-mindedness. Unless one was talking about the indomitable Lena West. Trig had barely gone after Lena at all. He'd been waiting for the right time, the right place, the right blasted moon in the sky.

He was done waiting. He needed a plan of attack, a plan to make Lena respond to him again the way she'd responded to him in Turkey. She'd been happy with him once. All he had to do was make that happen again. He could fight dirty. He could fight hard. Why wait?

He hated waiting.

By the time Trig arrived home from work that afternoon he had a plan. By the time he'd opened his emails and seen the picture of the old homestead that his father had sent him, he had a better plan. He dialled Lena's number but she didn't pick up. Half an hour later he dialled it again. This time she must have had it with her, because she answered on the third ring.

'Do you remember what I made you repeat back to

me when we were making love in the crazy room?' he began without preamble.

'What?'

'Say it. Say Trig loves me and always will.'

'I'm not a parrot.'

She sounded frustrated. He could handle a frustrated Lena. He'd been doing so for the past two years. It wasn't as if he'd been expecting a declaration of undying devotion from her or even a simple 'I've missed you'. But she *had* told him she'd loved him not so long ago, and he held to that the way a free soloing climber so often held to a rock face.

By his fingertips.

'Okay, so I lied to you about us being married. I should have come clean and I didn't and I ended up with one foot in heaven and the other one in hell. You gave me a glimpse of what we *could* have if we dropped the barriers and simply let ourselves be what we wanted to be. Like married, for example. We could make that happen. Everything we talked about we could make happen if we wanted it to.'

She had no comeback for him beyond a strangled sound that he hoped to hell wasn't a sob.

'I love you, Lena. I always will. Check your emails.'

He hung up on her after that. He sent her the picture of the old homestead his father had sent him and the links to the 'For Sale' information. He attached his father's rough estimate of what it would cost to make it habitable.

'Where's the river?' she emailed back, some ten minutes later.

He didn't wait ten minutes to reply. 'Below the hill.

It's a mostly lazy river prone to brief yet frenzied flooding. That's why the house is on the hill.'

She didn't write back.

Trig decided not to think of her lack of response as defeat. She'd answered his call and she'd answered his email and it was a start. He'd never thought that winning Lena's forgiveness was going to be easy. He didn't want easy. He'd never courted that.

He wanted Lena.

The next morning, before work, he emailed her links to a bunch of mosaic tile manufacturers. For the bathhouse floor, he wrote. And left it at that.

She called him that evening when he was on his way home from work.

'I need help filling out a form,' she said.

'What kind of form?'

'There's three columns. Column one is what happened to us in Turkey, otherwise known as "The Facts" column. Column two is what I want to happen from here on in. Column three is what you want to happen. It was Ruby's idea.'

'I love that woman.'

'You say that a lot. You can understand my confusion.'

'I love you more.'

Lena sighed. 'May I send you the form?'

'Have you filled out your column yet?'

'I filled out the first two columns. It took me two days.'

'What if I don't agree with The Facts?'

'Feel free to amend them. Ruby said you might want to. Something about reframing.'

'Smart woman.'

Silence filled the car.

'You're smart too,' he added hastily. 'I know that.'

'It's probably better if you don't talk,' she said, and hung up.

Trig made it home in record time and only marginally exceeded the speed limit. He grabbed his personal laptop from the floor beside the couch, carried it through to the kitchen and sat it next to last night's empty pizza box. He opened it up and switched it on. He grabbed a cola from the fridge and waited for his computer to wake up completely. He grabbed a stool, sat on it and started jiggling his leg. He vowed to get a faster computer along with a speedier Internet service. He hated waiting. Finally, he found Lena's email and opened it up. She hadn't bothered with an introduction. She'd started with column one.

The Facts:

1)Lena loves Trig (and not like a brother). Romantically. Inescapably. No one else has ever measured up to him. Not even close.

Trig hadn't been aware of this fact until now and snorted cola up his nose and then all over the counter on account of it. But he was totally on board with this fact. He read it again, just to make sure he'd read it right before moving on to fact number two.

2)Trig loves Lena.

No surprises there.

3)Everyone but Lena and Trig knows that Lena loves Trig and that Trig loves Lena (this fact has been substantiated by Ruby, Poppy, Poppy's Seb, Damon and Damon on Jared's behalf).

Some people were so smug.

4)Lena and Trig went to Istanbul to find Jared. They found him.

Nothing but the facts.

5)Lena fell and hit her head, lost her memory and thought she was married to Trig.

True.

6)Trig let her believe that she was married to him.

Loaded word, 'let'. It implied some semblance of control.

7)Lena wanted to bed Trig.

Trig grinned in spite of himself and downed half a can of cola, this time without getting it up his nose.

8)Trig resisted.

'Yes, I did. And it wasn't exactly easy.'

9)Lena still wanted to bed Trig.

Trig *liked* these facts.

10) Trig resisted. Some might call that chivalrous. Lena found it frustrating.

'Try being me.'

11)Lena seduced Trig.

That was one interpretation.

12)Trig let her.

He really thought she was misusing the word 'let'. He wanted a new word. One that described active participation.

13)Lena saw Jared, regained her memory, realised she wasn't married to Trig and got confused and angry.

Succinct.

14)Lena thought she might have coerced Trig into something he didn't want.

'What?' When had he *ever* given her the impression that he didn't know exactly what he wanted? Namely her. Unless she was talking about those times during those first few nights when she'd wanted him to be cosy with her and he hadn't…and then later when she'd wanted a wedding night to remember and he'd developed a fondness for long showers and a predilection for performance anxiety… Okay, so maybe she had a point.

But surely proclaiming his love for her before, during and *after* her memory loss had to count for something?

15)Lena thought Trig might have coerced her into something she didn't want. She didn't know what to think and she didn't know what was real.

'Figure it out,' he begged her. 'Believe.'

16)Lena temporarily ignored the fact that she loves Trig and Trig loves her and that they could probably work something out.

That was the end of The Facts according to Lena. Trig ran a shaky hand across his face. There were some high points, sure. The first two points and the last. Love. Remarkable things could happen in the presence of love. But there'd been some low points too. Sighing, Trig moved on to the next column.

What Lena Wants:
1)Lena has never really thought about what she wants.

Not helpful, Lena.

2)She followed Trig and Jared into the special intelligence service because it seemed like a good fit for her and because she wanted to maintain her connection with them. Her heart wasn't always in the job but she was with Jared and Trig so she was mostly happy.

Trig frowned. Thinking that Lena needed to reconsider her options on account of her recent physical limitations was one thing. Having Lena admit that she'd never been completely on board with a career in special intelligence was quite another. Sure, it was good news in the overall scheme of things *now,* but you'd think he might have noticed. Or that Jared might have noticed. Why the hell hadn't anyone noticed that her heart wasn't in it? *Mostly happy.* What the hell was that?

3)Working for ASIS doesn't seem like such a good fit for Lena any more.

Trig agreed. She could do a lot better than mostly happy.

4)Lena needs a new career. She's considering becoming a physiotherapist to people with mobility issues, or a psychotherapist to people with mobility issues, or both.

He could see her doing that.

5)She has the money to go back to school and study. Lena likes study, even if study doesn't always like her.

Lena was smart. Maybe not as smart as her siblings, Jared excluded, but few people were. Trig had no doubt that Lena would accomplish whatever she set out to do. She never gave up. Even when the odds were stacked against her. He loved that about her. He always had.

6)In her spare time, Lena will race speedboats. Should Lena and Trig acquire two speedboats, Lena will race the red one.

Trig laughed.

7)Lena wants to marry Trig.

Trig's heart kicked hard against his chest.

8)And live in a farmhouse high on a hill above the banks of a lazy and occasionally crazy river. And help raise his babies, adopted babies and possibly a couple of puppies. Lena wants the children to call her Mum and the dogs to think she's the boss.

Trig ran a rough hand across his face. Everything he'd ever wanted was right here in column two. Mainly because everything he'd ever wanted had always led back to Lena.

9)She also wants a Turkish bathing pool built somewhere inside the farmhouse. This pool will have water spouts, waterfalls and marble ledges to lie on.

Fortunately she didn't want a eunuch with that.

10)Lena still wants Jared home so that she can kick his arse for not keeping in touch—but that can wait.
11)Lena wants to work around her physical limitations rather than resent them. She may need to be reminded of this from time to time.

Damn, but he loved this woman.

12)Lena wants Trig. Repeat: Lena wants Trig and wants to know what he wants so that she can ad-

just her plans accordingly. Compromise is *in her vocabulary. She looked it up in the Wiktionary.*

The third column, 'What Trig Wants', stood ominously blank. The cut and paste option had never been more tempting. Instead, Trig opened up a new file and prepared to give his future some serious thought.

Half an hour and half a dozen words later, Trig decided that he was a man of action rather than words. Fifteen minutes after that he was in the car, heading for Damon's beach house and Lena.

Lena woke to the sound of someone pounding impatiently on Damon's front door. She squinted at the bedside clock and groaned. Five twenty-two a.m. She'd waited up last night until almost one a.m. Waiting for a reply from Trig that had never come. He hadn't emailed or called. She'd finally caved and called him, only to find that his phone was out of range or turned off. Why hadn't he called? Because he wasn't mean like that. Thoughtless on occasion, yes, but never mean. Lena's eyes drifted closed.

And the pounding started again and this time her brain kicked into gear and she sat bolt upright. Who *else* would be at her door at five-something a.m.?

Her body didn't want to hurry down Damon's long hallway but where there was a will there was a way and Lena made it to the door in record time. She unbolted it and opened it and there stood Trig, his smile brighter than the sun. The dark stubble on his face and the rumpled business shirt minus tie only added to his appeal.

'I brought croissants,' he said. 'They're still hot.'

Lena had to move to see past him, but eventually she spotted his car. 'You drove here overnight?'

'It's not that far.'

'How much coffee did you have?'

'I lost count,' he murmured and dropped a kiss on her unprotesting lips as he sailed past her. 'Consider me wide awake.'

He headed for the kitchen, Lena followed. 'You drove here,' she said again.

'The planes were too slow.'

'So you drove here.'

'You're not quite as awake as me, are you?'

Guess not.

'You said you loved me. In an *email*,' he continued as if she'd just shredded his favourite kite sail. 'I've decided to forgive you for that, by the way, but I needed to be here in person to give you my reply. Because that's how it's done. *In person.*'

'Oh.' Lena tried to hide her smile. She leaned against the kitchen counter with her hands trapped between her back and the counter, because if she reached for him they wouldn't talk and he sounded like he needed to talk. 'I thought I'd *already* told you that I loved you in person,' she offered dulcetly. 'I remember it distinctly. It was right after you proposed the second time. Or was it the first? Or does that time not count because I thought we were already married and you knew we weren't.'

'It counts.' Trig scowled.

Lena smiled.

'For someone who looks so angelic, you're really good at torture,' he muttered.

'You love it,' she said. 'You love me.'

'I do.' Trig reached behind him and pulled from his pocket a crumpled sheet of paper. He unfolded it and it turned into two crumpled sheets of paper. 'It's your list of what you want.'

'Where's yours?'

In my head. He scanned the paper. Nodded a couple of times.

'I don't want to quit ASIS,' he said. 'I may even want to take the occasional field job. When the kids arrive I aim to retire from fieldwork and carve out a place for myself in operations review. Turns out I'm good at it. That okay by you?'

'Yes.' Just because she didn't want a man as careless with his life as Jared was, didn't mean she wanted a placid man who played everything safe. 'That'll work.'

'Good.' He returned his attention to the paper in his hand. 'I have a couple of adjustments to make to the poolside plans. I want Turkish tile trim, a retractable roof and a marble mermaid on the steps. And fairy lights.'

'Because, why not?' she murmured.

'Exactly. And much as I want Jared at my wedding, I'm not going to wait another nineteen months for him to come home. I say we send him an invite to our June wedding and see if he turns up.'

'June, you say. Okay.' She could be a winter bride. 'Give him an exit date to aspire to.'

'Puppies,' Trig said next, and Lena smiled at his priorities. 'I want to get them from the pound and they must, when grown, stand at least knee high. I will train the puppies not to crush the children. All children and puppies will think I'm the boss.'

'You always did like a challenge.'

'So true. I want to honeymoon at Saul's Caravan, and this time we'll do it right.'

'Perfect,' said Lena.

Trig tossed the paper on the counter and stepped in close, his hands either side of her, his eyes smiling as he pressed his lips to the curve of her mouth. 'Do I need to propose to you again?'

'I think you do.'

'You want the moon and the stars again?'

'And the turtles. And Saturn's rings.'

'I knew you liked that one best.'

'Well, you always remember your first.'

She wound her arms around his neck and kissed him, then. Savouring him. Loving him. She reached for the topmost button of his shirt and undid it. She undid the second button for him too.

'I love you, Lena.'

'I know,' she whispered and brought her hands up to frame his face. 'And you're right. Saying it to the person in person is better, so… Adrian Trig Sinclair, I love you too.'

CHAPTER TWELVE

Six months later...

LENA COULDN'T REACH the zip on her dress. Fortunately, that was what bridesmaids were for. Poppy and Ruby fussed and tweaked until the silk and tulle sweetheart gown sat perfectly on Lena's skin, unashamedly romantic with its fitted beaded bodice and floor-length tulle skirt. Lena had chosen the gown, with Poppy and Ruby's full approval. Ruby had chosen the shoes and the hair accessories, because, frankly, when you had an expert in the family it paid to stand back and let them do what they did best.

The wedding shoes were amber-whorled white sling-backs. Thc headband involved an elegant sufficiency of tiny gumnuts and delicate white flannel flowers, perfect for an outdoor wedding that would shortly take place beneath a towering redgum on the banks of a lazy river.

Ruby and her baby belly glowed in a moss-green full-length gown with an empire waist. Poppy's dress ran along similar lines except that hers was a pale sky-blue. The old farmhouse bedroom that currently doubled as the dressing room had been finished and furnished last week—an early wedding gift from Lena's soon-to-be father-in-law. The bed was custom made and enormous.

The freshly waxed floorboards had come from fallen timber, sourced on the farm. The silk carpets that covered large sections of floorboards had come from Persia. Lena had bought them at auction three weeks earlier and hiding them from Trig had required great stealth and the assistance of a recently rebuilt chimney.

Trig had wanted to light a fire in the fireplace last night.

Yeah, no.

Not until Damon and Seb had dragged Trig to the other end of the property to cut firewood, leaving Lena, Ruby and Poppy to shift the damn things.

Ruby was six months pregnant with twins, Lena had a gammy leg and Poppy had been too busy laughing to be of much help at all, but between the three of them they'd hauled the carpets into one of the shower stalls in an unfinished bathroom, and Trig's brother and father had laid them out in the master bedroom this morning.

Lena hoped Trig loved them.

If he didn't, she could always send him out shopping for more.

'Half an hour until go time,' said Poppy, and Lena looked out of the big bay window towards the lawn where the after-the-ceremony celebrations would take place. A marquee had been set up on the garden lawn. Inside, a trio of waiters offered liquid refreshments to arriving guests. Parasols, picnic rugs and fluffy beach towels had been made available for the more intrepid guests who wanted to explore the river banks or the river itself. Caterers had taken over the kitchen. Long trestle tables had appeared on the lawn, covered in white linen tablecloths, shiny silverware and white accompaniments. The florist and her assistants were putting the final touches to the table arrangements. The bridal bouquets waited on the sideboard, a romantic mass of flannel flowers, gumnuts and soft green leaves.

A pair of vintage Aston Martin DB9s stood waiting in the circular driveway, ready to take first Ruby and Poppy and then Lena and her father down the freshly levelled track from the house to the redgum by the river where the wedding would take place. One of the Astons was silver, the other a British racing green. Together, they put Lena in mind of fast men and reckless women. They were a gift to her and Trig from her father.

Trig didn't know they owned the Astons yet, or that twice a year at a racetrack in Brisbane enthusiasts still raced the things. Good times ahead.

The photographer tried to be unobtrusive as she took stills of them getting ready. The photographer had already been out and taken photos of the cars.

'What have I forgotten?' Lena knew she was almost ready, but not quite.

'Jewellery,' said Poppy, with the click of her fingers, and reached for a tired velvet case that she nonetheless treated with reverence. They'd belonged to their mother.

Gently, Poppy helped her put them on.

'Beautiful,' said Ruby, suddenly misty eyed.

'Perfect,' said Poppy.

Lena's wedding planner stuck her head around the door, her eyes bright and her smile reassuring. 'How are we going?'

'She's ready,' said Poppy.

'Good. The musicians are here and they're all set up, the caterer wants to take your kitchen with him wherever he goes and the groom and his party have been spotted. They're down by the river.'

'Hopefully not getting wet,' Ruby muttered.

'There was some mention of a speedboat,' the wedding planner replied carefully. 'A very fast speedboat. Apparently they arrived in one.'

'Fancy that.' Lena grinned. She hadn't had time to go speedboat shopping, what with finding and buying the farm and getting it restored and enrolling in university and planning a wedding. Perhaps Trig had.

The only blight on her otherwise perfect day was the absence of Jared. By all accounts he was still on the floating fortress belonging to the billionaire arms dealer. 'I wish Jared was here.' There, she'd said it.

'His loss,' said Ruby gently.

'Damn right it is.' But it still stung and not just on her account. She hurt on Trig's behalf too.

'He'd have been here if he could have,' Poppy said defensively.

Or if he'd wanted to. But Lena kept that thought to herself. No point focusing on the negatives. She'd stopped doing that, for the most part. Joy ruled her now, along with gratitude for what was. Happiness did that. And love. Love made so many things possible.

The wedding planner checked her phone and smiled some more. 'Your father's here. He's out by the cars. We've scheduled ten minutes for photos. Twenty minutes until we leave for the river bank.'

It wasn't that far. Most of the guests had opted to walk down the hill from the homestead to the river bank.

The photographer nodded and made her exit. Poppy handed Lena the bridal bouquet.

Together, Ruby and Poppy floated the bridal veil over Lena's head.

'You look so beautiful,' said Poppy.

'You do.' Ruby nodded. 'Hope suits you. Happiness suits you.'

'Are you ready?' asked Poppy and Lena nodded.

Yes, she was.

Trig hated waiting. He especially hated waiting in front of three hundred or so guests for his bride to turn up, but he made the most of it and greeted people, right up until Damon's phone buzzed and a text message from Ruby told them Lena was on her way.

Damon herded him and Trig's brother Matthew, his best man, beneath the redgum, where they waited some more.

A dark green Aston Martin appeared on the track down to the river. A silver one followed.

'Nice,' said Matthew.

'Very nice,' agreed Damon, and turned to Trig and straightened the little white flannel flower on his lapel. 'Also a wedding gift. My father said to tell you that one of them's yours and that the green one's marginally faster. Welcome to the family.'

'Thanks. I think.' Trig could barely breathe as Poppy and Ruby emerged from the first car and then helped Lena and her father exit the second. They fussed and they fiddled and generally took for ever.

'Something's wrong,' he said.

'No, I'm pretty sure it's normal,' said Matthew.

'It's normal,' said the celebrant. 'They're waiting for the music.'

Right. The music.

Solo guitar, and it started right on cue.

Poppy lined up in the walkway between the ancient fallen gums that doubled as pews. Ruby moved into place behind her. Then Lena and her father began to head his way. Lena looked so beautiful, so fragile, but she wasn't fragile at all. She was the keeper of his heart and she held it with the same strength and determination that she brought to everything else.

'Breathe,' prompted his brother and Trig remembered to breathe.

And then Lena was upon him, with Poppy and Ruby beside her as her father moved away.

'Dearly beloved,' began the celebrant, and Trig felt himself relax a fraction. This was real. It was really happening.

The thrum of a fast-moving speedboat reached his ears. A really fast-moving speedboat. The celebrant frowned and glanced towards the river.

'Dearly beloved,' he said again, only now just about everyone's attention was turned towards the river, including Lena's. Trig looked too as the speedboat came into view from around the bend. He narrowed his eyes, because the boat looked strangely familiar. As in almost exactly the same as the one he'd arrived in except that the one he'd arrived in was black and this one was red.

'Trig,' said Lena, in a voice that was nowhere near calm. 'Is that maniac driving the boat *Jared*? Because it sure as hell looks like Jared.'

It *was* Jared, Trig decided. And Trig was going to kill him. 'Did you know about this?' he barked at Damon. 'Did you know he was on his way? And you didn't tell us?'

'No!' Damon held up his hands. 'No. Not my fault. Or my doing. You were the one who texted him the invitation.'

'Did *any* of you know?' Trig's voice was dangerously calm.

But the answers all came back no.

'Could be his evil twin,' said Damon helpfully.

'You wished him here,' Poppy told Lena solemnly, right before she dissolved into helpless giggles.

Matthew turned to the crowd and held up his hands. 'We're taking a five-minute break, people.'

Lena's father came to stand with them and so did Seb. Trig drew a steadying breath. Five minutes wasn't so long. And then he'd be married. He watched in tight-lipped silence as Jared kept that boat at full throttle until cutting the engine at the very last minute and swinging the craft in behind Trig's. Jared missed the other boat by at least an inch.

'And you wanted him here why?' murmured Ruby.

Excellent question.

And then Jared climbed from the boat and strode confidently towards them. Only his eyes gave him away, because they were pleading and wary and long past exhausted. An angry graze ran the length of his face. The less said about his jeans and filthy T-shirt, the better.

'You didn't RSVP,' said Lena tightly. Lena looked as if she was about to cry.

'But I did get here.' Jared silently pleaded with her for understanding before turning his battered face towards Trig. 'Honoured to be your groomsman, man. Did you really think I was going to miss this one?'

'You stole my boat. My *other* boat. Lena's boat.'

'Pity he couldn't have stolen a suit to go with it,' muttered Ruby.

'I don't believe we've met,' said Jared, straightening fast, his eyes straying to Ruby's big belly.

Damon stepped up and offered the introductions. 'Ruby, Jared. Jared, Ruby. Ruby's my wife.'

'You did manage to miss that one,' offered Ruby.

'I'm Seb,' said Sebastian, shrugging out of his jacket and handing it to Jared, who got with the programme fast and slipped it on. 'I'm here with Poppy. We're not married. Yet.'

Jared's eyes grew sharp fast. He held out his hand and Seb shook it. Hand crushing ensued.

'This isn't at all how I imagined this would go,' said Poppy, leaning forward and frowning at both Jared and Seb.

'Never assume,' offered Jared.

'Trig?' Lena's voice wobbled, he could hear it wobbling and the notion that she might be having second thoughts focused him the way nothing else could.

'What do you need?' Behind him, Seb and Lena's father melted away and his groomsmen fell silently into line, first his brother then Jared and then Damon.

'Can we ignore them and get married now?' Her voice still wobbled.

'I'm ignoring them. I can't even see them. There's only you.' He closed his fingers over hers and brought her fingers up to his lips.

The celebrant smiled and started again. 'Dearly beloved…'

Five minutes later, the friends and families that had gathered beneath a big old redgum tree by the banks of a lazy river cheered, clapped, whistled and hollered with delight.

As first the bride and then the groom said I Do.

* * * * *

BLACK WIDOW BRIDE

TESSA RADLEY

For my mother, grandmother, aunt, children,
Anne, Trish, Carol, Fi, Meredith, Lissa,
Linda, Barb, Rosie and Jo.

Thanks for all your support.

Tessa Radley loves travelling, reading and watching the world around her. As a teen Tessa wanted to be an intrepid foreign correspondent. But after completing a Bachelor of Arts degree and marrying her sweetheart, she became fascinated by law and ended up studying further and practicing as a lawyer in a city firm.

A six-month break spent travelling through Australia with her family re-awoke the yen to write. And life as a writer suits her perfectly—travelling and reading count as research, and as for analysing the world...well, she can think "what if?" all day long. When she's not reading, travelling or thinking about writing, she's spending time with her husband, her two sons or her zany and wonderful friends. You can contact Tessa through her website, www.tessaradley.com.

One

How had it all gone so horribly wrong?

Rebecca Grainger wrapped her arms around her stomach, nausea welling up. If she could only stop thinking about it, then maybe the sick feeling in the pit of her stomach would subside. The wedding was her priority, Rebecca told herself. Focus on that. She'd already been paid for arranging it—in full—the cheque flung at her last night.

Last night. That kiss. No, don't think about last night.

Concentrate on the wedding. An Asteriades event. A desperate glance swept the tables laden with glittering silver cutlery and Baccarat glasses, the slim crystal vases each bearing six glorious long-stemmed white roses on the tables.

Naturally she'd had unlimited resources at her disposal, and no expense had been spared for Damon Asteriades's wedding. The vaulted ballroom ceiling of Auckland's San Lorenzo Hotel had been draped in soft white folds of fabric to give the dreamy, romantic mood of a bower. Garlands of ivy and hothouse white roses festooned the walls, filling the ballroom with heady scent.

Brass wall-mounted sconces held torches that added an intimate glow, while the vast room had been heated to allow women to show off an astonishing array of flimsy designer gowns even though the winter air blew cold outside.

In the centre of the otherwise empty dance floor, Damon Asteriades performed a graceful manoeuvre, twirling his new bride to the melodious strains of the "Blue Danube" waltz, his dark head close to her pale blond hair. He was one hundred per cent gorgeous Greek male from the top of his overlong jet-black hair to the tips of his tanned fingers, with a Greek male's hotheaded certainty that he was always right. And right now Rebecca wished he were a million light-years away.

"My son is a fool."

At the voice of Soula Asteriades—Damon's mother and widow of the powerful Ari Asteriades—Rebecca smiled and said, "Damon wouldn't care for that description."

"And look at you, Rebecca! My dear, did you have to wear scarlet? Like a red flag to a bull?" Soula sighed. "That wicked dress will only fuel the tales that grow in each retelling."

Rebecca laughed and glanced down at the extravagant Vera Wang dress she wore. "Let them gossip. I don't care. At least I'm not stealing the bride's thunder and wearing white."

"But you should've been. You would've made a beautiful bride. If only Ari had been here—he might have knocked some sense into the boy's head."

Shocked, Rebecca stared at the older woman. *"Soula?"*

"This wedding is a mistake, but now it's too late. My son has made his choice and he must live with it. That's my last word." Soula disappeared into the throng surrounding them.

Disconcerted, Rebecca turned her attention to the dance floor. Damon chose that moment for an uncharacteristic display of public affection—brushing a kiss across the top of his bride's head. The bride tilted her face up, revealing astonishment but none of the sparkling joy expected. Rebecca couldn't help wishing that Damon was where she was right now—in hell.

She couldn't bear to watch. She closed her eyes. Her head ached with a combination of inner tension, the strain of the day and the residue of last night's wine. She wanted the wedding over. Done. So that she could rid her mouth of the bitter taste of betrayal.

"Come. Time for us to join them."

Rebecca's painful thoughts were jogged by a touch on her cold, clammy arm, and she became abruptly aware that the music from the stylish ensemble on the raised dais was fading. Savvas, the bridegroom's brother and best man, stared at her expectantly.

She forced a smile. "Sorry, Savvas. I was miles away." He gave her a wide grin. "Stop worrying, everything's magnificent. The flowers, the menu, the cake, the dress. Women will be queuing for you to organise their perfect day."

Rebecca blinked at Savvas's enthusiasm. Organising yet another Auckland high-society wedding was the last thing she wanted; yet she was thankful that he'd put her distraction down to anxiety about the success of the function. No one—not Savvas, nor anyone else—knew why she had fretted all day. Or why the memory of these particular nuptials would cast a pall over every wedding for years to come.

Oh, God, how could she have been so stupid last night!

"Come." Savvas tugged her hand insistently.

She dug her sandal-clad toes in, not budging. "I don't dance at weddings I've organised." Over Savvas's shoulder she met the bridegroom's narrow-eyed gaze, read the disdain.

It hurt.

More fool her. She dragged her attention back to Savvas.

He chuckled, oblivious to the tension that strung her tighter than the violinist's bowstring, his blue eyes lighting up with merriment, eyes so like his brother's that her heart jolted. No, she reprimanded herself, don't go there!

"No excuses. You're not working tonight, you must dance.

Come. It's traditional, the maid of honor and best man join in next. Look, everyone's waiting."

A rapid glance around told Rebecca he was right. Hordes of exquisitely dressed couples had flocked to the edge of the dance floor and stood waiting for them. Even Damon's mother was there, her eyes sympathetic. Rebecca raised her chin. Instinctively she touched the opal pendant that rested just above her breasts.

And then her gaze collided with blue. A cold, icy blue. Damon Asteriades was glaring now, disapproval evident in the hard slash of his mouth, his bride clamped in his arms.

His bride.

Fliss.

Her best friend.

Rebecca tossed her head, slid her chilled hand into the crook of the arm Savvas offered and, forcing a parody of a smile onto her lips, allowed him to lead her onto the floor, the flouncy skirt of her scarlet dress swirling around her legs.

She would dance. Damn Damon Asteriades! She would laugh, too, wouldn't let Damon glimpse the misery in her heart, the emptiness in her soul. Damon would never know what it had cost her to organise his wedding to Fliss, to help Fliss with the myriad choices of music, flowers, fabrics, or how sick and despondent she had felt trudging up the aisle behind the pair of them.

Nor would he ever know of her quiet desperation when the white-and-gold-robed priest had pronounced them man and wife. Of the ache that had sharpened as the bridal couple had turned to face the congregation. Fliss had been pale, but she'd managed to give Damon a flirtatious glance from under her lashes. And Damon had sought Rebecca's gaze, his eyes blazing with triumph, as if to say, Nothing you can do now.

Oh, yes, she'd dance. She'd be as outrageous as ever, and not a soul would guess at the agony hidden beneath the brittle facade. They'd see what they always saw: brazen, independent Rebecca.

Never again would she allow herself to become vulnerable to this raw, consuming emotion. It hurt too much.

She smiled determinedly up at Savvas as he put an arm around her shoulder and ignored the glower from the midst of the dance floor.

"Hey, brother, my turn to dance with the bride."

Startled by Savvas's words, Rebecca surfaced from the numb place to which she'd retreated, a place where she felt nothing. No pain, no emotion. The sudden stop brought her back to the present, back to the ballroom. Savvas stepped away as the romantic melody faded.

In front of her stood her nemesis, the man she knew she would never escape.

Even in this dim light his blue gaze glittered. Only the bent blade of a nose that had clearly been broken more than once saved his face from the classic beauty his full mouth and impossibly high cheekbones promised. Instead it created a face filled with danger, utterly compelling and ruthlessly sensual. A modern-day pirate.

Hastily she looked away, grabbing for her departing dance partner.

"Savvas?"

But Savvas was gone, spinning Fliss away, Fliss's wedding dress fanning out against his legs. Feeling utterly alone, Rebecca waited, heart thudding with apprehension, refusing to look at Damon.

"So, you are now trying to seduce my brother? Another crack at the Asteriades fortune, hmm?" Her head shot back at the cynical words. There was something dark and tumultuous in his eyes.

He was angry?

What about *her?*

What gave him the right to judge her? He didn't even know her—hadn't had the slightest inclination to get to know her.

"Go to hell," she muttered through grimly smiling teeth and swung away.

"Oh, no, Rebecca." A hard hand caught her elbow. "It's not going to be that easy. I'm not going to allow you to cause a scene and leave me standing alone on the dance floor. You're not making a fool of me."

Rebecca tried to wrench free. The grip tightened. Big. Strong. Powerful. She didn't have a hope of escaping Damon Asteriades. But the last thing in the world she wanted today was to be held in his arms, to dance with him.

No.

She must have said it aloud, because his mouth flattened as he twirled her around to face him.

"Yes," he hissed. His eyes had turned to flat, unforgiving cobalt chips. "You will dance with me." His right hand moved to rest on her waist as the joyous bars of the next waltz struck up. "For once in your selfish life you will do something for someone else. I will not allow you to destroy Felicity's day."

As he'd already destroyed her.

Rebecca wanted to laugh hysterically. Damon had no idea…no idea that he would destroy Fliss, too. Dear, beloved Fliss, the closest thing she had to a sister. Her best friend. Her business partner. Or at least she had been until last night when, after the final wedding rehearsal, Fliss had signed her share in Dream Occasions over to Rebecca.

And why? Because Damon had demanded it.

The lord and master had made it clear he wanted all ties to Rebecca severed, and Fliss had obeyed. Rebecca had been hotly, impulsively furious. Yet under the fury there had simmered the unspeakable pain of betrayal. Rebecca knew why Fliss had capitulated. Hell, she even understood why her friend was so desperate to marry a man to whom she was so totally unsuited.

But Fliss should've known better, should *never* have agreed to marry him. Yet how could Fliss refuse? Because Fliss craved security—as Rebecca once had. Unlike a heroine tied to the train tracks in one of those ancient black-and-white movies, Fliss didn't see the danger. She saw only Damon's solid strength. His power and wealth.

Damon was too strong. He'd dominate her. Fliss would never stand up to him. Rebecca feared Fliss would wither and die. So last night Rebecca had decided to take matters into her own hands.

A cold line of goose bumps swept her spine. Rebecca gave a convulsive shiver at the memory of what had happened next.

And afterward…

God! She would *never* forget the thrust of Damon's anger, his contempt…or his furious passion…as long as she lived. Not even the gallons of red wine she'd consumed later had dimmed the pain, the knowledge of what that one last desperate shot had cost.

"Fliss," she said gently as Damon's hand enfolded hers—trapping her—as he led her into the waltz.

Damon glared down at her, uncomprehending.

"She likes to be called Fliss. Or hasn't she told you that yet?"

His black eyebrows drew together, and she was terribly aware of the heat of his hand on her waist, of the intimate pressure of his palm against hers, of his hot, sexy scent.

"Her name is Felicity," he said repressively. "It's beautiful. A happy name. The other sounds insubstantial, like fairy floss."

"But she hates it. Or don't her wishes matter to you?"

The name reminded Fliss of less happy times, of a childhood where she'd been shy, small for her age—of the bullying she'd endured at school as the child of a foster home, of the stark discipline meted out by foster parents who had their own two daughters to love. Rebecca knew because she'd been there, raised by the same distant but well-meaning couple. How could she explain it to Damon? She couldn't! Rebecca reminded herself she was no longer the rock in Fliss's life. It was up to Fliss to tell her husband what she chose.

Momentarily Damon looked taken aback, but already his face was hardening. "It has nothing to do with you what I call my wife. All I ask is that you refrain from ruining this day."

My wife.

Again the agonising sharpness pierced her heart. Rebecca pushed the pain away. She'd deal with it later, much later, when this appalling day was over and she was alone.

"And how would I do that?" She raised a brow, pretending an insouciance she was far from feeling, here, trapped within the heat of his arms, mindless of the other dancing couples surrounding them. "Savvas told me that everything is stunning—the flowers…the wedding dress…the wedding cake—that it's a Dream Occasion. How could I possibly *ruin* it?" Each word she uttered was another blow to her already battered heart.

But he didn't smile at her intentional pun on her business's name. Instead his glower darkened. "Don't be obtuse. I'm not doubting your professional ability, it's your penchant for stirring up trouble that has me worried."

If only she could hate him.

Damon despised her. And, at this moment, she didn't like him much either. To be quite honest, more than anything in the world she wanted to kill Damon Asteriades, business tycoon, billionaire…and the blindest, most stubborn, most controlling man she'd ever met. If he'd been more attuned to her, he would've known that Fliss would be safe, that there'd be no catfight on the dance floor tonight. Rebellion stirred within Rebecca. Perhaps she should give him cause to worry. Punish him a little.

She gave her slowest, most sultry smile. "Trouble? People say that's my middle name."

"You are trouble." His lips barely moved. His eyes were harder than the diamonds that graced Fliss's neck. "I don't want you talking to Savvas. Leave him alone. You're not getting your talons into my brother."

Her defiance wavered. Damon's brutal reaction was predictable. Before she'd met him, she'd heard tales about him.

Of his business successes, his clever, decisive mind, his devastating good looks. But she'd never expected the raw, primal emotion he'd aroused in her. They'd met at a wedding she and Fliss had organised for a business colleague of his. She'd taken one look at the gorgeous guy with the dark, brooding magnetism and fallen. Hard.

He'd been charming, attentive, interested—she'd thought. Until he'd learned her name, figured out that she was Aaron Grainger's scandalous widow. In an instant he'd changed. Withdrawn. Become distant and, worse, disinterested. She'd watched his eyes narrow, and with one raking glance he'd stripped her to the soul, then he'd dismissed her and stepped past her to congratulate the groom. But it had been far too late for caution. She'd been lost.

Caught up in her thoughts, Rebecca let her hips move fluidly to the rhythm of the music. For a moment his body responded and they moved as one, dipping and swaying. But an instant later he tensed and moved away.

Always it had been so.

After that first encounter, she'd searched him out shamelessly, using business acquaintances and her connections as Aaron Grainger's widow to secure invitations to places he frequented, inexorably driven by a raw attraction that had gone to the heart of her. How hard she'd tried to recapture that magical moment. Always she imagined a moment of softening, a flash of heat, then it was gone—and the man of steel returned. Until finally she'd realised the overwhelming attraction existed only in her own mind.

Damon hadn't seemed to feel anything.

The discovery crushed her.

Even now, as they danced, his body was rigid, unbending, his gaze fixed on something over her shoulder. Totally removed from her. Her mouth twisted. So much for fate. Nothing in her life had ever been easy, so why should falling in love be any different?

But she'd *never* expected fate's final cruel twist: that Damon would take one look at Fliss's sweet blond gentleness and want it for himself. Or how much that would devastate her.

And there was nothing she could do about it.

Last night had proved that.

Oh, God, last night…

She stared at his mouth pressed into a hard line, remembered the hard, seeking pressure against her lips, remembered how…

No, no, don't think about it!

So Rebecca said the first thing that came into her head. "Both you and Savvas dance well. Did you attend lessons?"

"Forget about how well Savvas dances, you little troublemaker," he ground out. "I want you to stay away from him, he's too young."

Troublemaker?

Why the hell not. What did she have to lose? Rebecca blocked out his disparaging voice and, humming the refrain of the waltz, let her body brush his, heard his breath catch and repeated the fleeting brush of body against body.

"*Theos*. Stop it!" The hand on her waist moved to her shoulder, a manacle, holding her at bay.

She resisted the urge to sag in his arms as despair overwhelmed her. Forced herself not to crumple, to stay tall and straight and move lightly, with grace, on feet that felt leaden. She gave him a mocking little smile. He glared back, more than angry now.

His disgust, his distrust, seared her.

What was she doing? She sagged against him, the struggle going out of her. His body tightened, then firm hands pushed her away, holding her at a distance. The ache inside intensified. What was she trying to prove? Damon was right. *This was wrong*. However much he'd hurt her, however much she felt he deserved her bad behaviour, Fliss's wedding was not the place for it. Nor was it worth losing the only thing she had left—her self-respect.

But there was no reason she shouldn't needle him just a teeny-weeny little bit.

Her spine stiffened. She shot him a swift upward glance. "Savvas told me he's twenty-seven. That's three years older than me. I'd say he's the perfect age for me."

"Listen to me!" Damon sounded at the end of his tether. "My brother is light-years younger in experience. No match for a woman like you."

The words stung.

"A woman like me?"

Anger swirled through her at the injustice of it all.

Damon Asteriades didn't even know what kind of woman she was. How could he be so blind? How *dare* he fail to recognise—*refuse* to recognise—what lay between them? He should not be marrying Fliss today—or any other woman for that matter. Damn him, there was only one woman on earth he should ever have contemplated marrying. *Her*.

There. She'd admitted it.

Admitted what lay at the heart of her pain. What he'd always refused to recognise. And now it was too late.

He was married.

To her best friend.

Yet still this *thing*…this force…burned with a life of its own, bigger than both of them. And sometimes, like now, she almost convinced herself he was aware of it—even feared it. Experimentally Rebecca let her fingers slide along the shoulder of his wedding suit, over the fine fabric of his white shirt collar, until she touched the bare skin of his neck. She thought—dreamed—she detected the smallest of shudders.

"Shame on you! You know nothing about me," she whispered and blew gently into the soft hollow beside his clenched jaw. "You never chose to find out anything about me."

He started. "For God's sake! What's to find out? I know more than I ever wanted." Bitterness spilled from him. "You're a black widow. You grasp and demand and devour and leave nothing behind."

"That's a—"

"Lie? *Is it?* But there's nothing to disprove my words, is there? You married Aaron Grainger for his fortune, and when everything was gone you drove him to suicide."

She gasped. "You know, no one has *ever* dared say that to my face before." Helplessly she flapped the hand that a moment ago had stroked his neck. "I heard the rumours existed, but I never thought anyone of substance believed them. I certainly never thought *you* the type to believe gossip."

The hand on her waist tightened. The tempo of the music quickened. The dancing speeded up, building to the finale.

"Yes, but I've got more than gossip to go on, haven't I? *Haven't I?*" His face was pressed up against hers now. She could see her reflection glittering in his eyes, could smell the heat of his fury. "I know exactly the kind of woman you are. The kind that kisses her best friend's man, begs him to—"

"Shut up!"

He spun her around, pulled her close to avoid another couple. "You promise sin and desire and deliver nothing but carnal delight. I know the temptation you are. Only last night—"

She froze in his arms and came to a sudden jarring halt.

"I said shut up," she huffed. "Or do you want me to cause that scene you're so terrified of? Here, on Fliss's big day?" Standing dead still on the dance floor, no longer able to move, she watched the realisation dawn as he became aware of where they both stood, of what calamity had nearly befallen them, and watched the mantle of iron control drop into place as the next melody began.

"I must be mad," he bit out, his voice full of self-disgust, and he reared back as though he feared she might contaminate him.

The sheer force of his words released Rebecca from the insanity that held her rooted to the ground. If he was mad, then she must be trapped in the same madness.

Damon was married. Untouchable. Better she remember that.

Shrugging out of his arms, she spun around and stalked away.

He let her go.

And she didn't dare look back.

Two

Almost four years later

Tuesday morning started badly. Rebecca overslept, and by the time T.J. managed to wake her, his insistent little fingers squeezing her cheeks, the dazzling almost-summer sun was already well up in the cloudless Northland sky.

T.J. was querulous as she hurriedly dressed him. Guilt took over. Yesterday she'd stayed home, taken him to the doctor for the earache that had plagued him over the weekend. Last night he'd cried a little before finally dropping off to sleep, leaving Rebecca to toss and turn for most of the night listening out for him. But he'd slept through.

Promising herself that she'd cut her workday short and spend the afternoon with him, Rebecca rushed him out the door and strapped him into the car seat, while he grumbled incessantly.

The whole drive over, Rebecca tried telling herself that

Dorothy—T.J.'s caregiver and a former hospice nurse—was far better qualified to look after T.J., that she wasn't deserting her baby when he needed her most. To no avail.

Dorothy, bless her kind heart, took one look at T.J.'s mutinous expression and opened her arms wide, promising he could watch a *Thomas the Tank Engine* DVD so long as he drank some juice and ate sliced mango and apple first. T.J.'s face brightened instantly and Rebecca heaved a giant sigh of relief.

After Rebecca handed over T.J.'s medication, Dorothy fixed her with a sharp glance. "Don't you worry yourself about this young man. He'll be fine. You stayed with him yesterday when he needed you most. Today you can fix your attention on Chocolatique."

The understanding beneath the brisk words made Rebecca's throat tighten.

As if sensing her volatile, emotive state, Dorothy murmured, "Now, now, Rebecca, off with you, and don't forget to bring me those almond truffles I'm so addicted to when you collect our boy."

"Do I ever forget?" Rebecca gave the older woman a fond smile.

The glow of good humour that Dorothy generated stayed with Rebecca all the way to Chocolatique. There, on the threshold of her business, all remnants of pleasure evaporated and she came to a shocked, gut-wrenching halt.

Him.

Damon Asteriades sprawled across the wing armchair nearest the door, showing total disregard for the designer suit that he wore with the casual abandon of the very wealthy. In a flash, Rebecca took in the highly polished handmade leather shoes, the open jacket and loosened tie, incongruous in Tohunga. At this time of year the town was populated by European backpackers in T-shirts, shorts and sandals. Up, up went her eyes over the finely carved mouth…up…until his chilling narrowed gaze propelled her into action.

She crossed the threshold, apprehension parching her mouth, and croaked, "What are *you* doing here?"

"The one good thing I remember about you, Rebecca, was your polish, your semblance of manners. Has living up here in the back-of-the-beyond stripped the last veneer of civilisation from you?"

Rebecca stared into the brutally handsome face, at a total loss for words.

He straightened. "I have a matter I need to discuss with you."

"With me?" Rebecca's heart lurched. What was he doing up here in Tohunga, hundreds of kilometres north of Auckland? Had the day of reckoning, the day she'd been dreading for more than three years, finally arrived?

Damon gestured to the empty chair across from him. "Do you see anyone else?" His dangerous pirate face was unreadable, harder than ever, new lines bracketing his full mouth, but it lacked the killing anger she'd expected.

"What do you want with me?" And immediately wished the tense, hasty words unsaid. Don't panic, she told herself. Keep it calm, polite. Don't let him see the dread.

He didn't answer. Instead his unnerving gaze swept her from head to toe.

"You haven't changed."

It didn't sound like a compliment.

Rebecca knew she shouldn't allow him to rattle her. There was nothing wrong with her appearance. The sundress was well cut and appropriate to the warm October spring morning, her long ebony hair secured in a neat French twist. Unless her emotions gave her away, he would see only a well-groomed woman in total command of herself and her surroundings.

She took her time returning the inspection. The suit would be Italian. Armani perhaps. The unbuttoned jacket revealed a white shirt. It would be made of the finest silk, she remembered, hand tailored for him. Fitting the muscled body beneath to perfection.

Wrenching her gaze away, she stared into cool blue eyes. "So what do you want?" Certainly not her. He'd never wanted her. But T.J.…well, T.J. was another story.

Rebecca swallowed the bitter, coppery taste of pure terror.

Chocolatique was *her* business, she reminded herself, coming closer.

And *he* was the interloper.

Yet Chocolatique, with its familiar comforting fragrance of chocolate, the warm red and amber tones of the cosy, elegant decor she had spent days selecting, failed to dispel Rebecca's fear.

Vaguely she registered that the shop was humming. With the exception of the one empty armchair opposite Damon, every seat in the shop was taken. Even the booths, carefully divided by screens and lush palms in pots to maximise privacy, were full. Yet the rise and fall of busy chatter failed to muffle Rebecca's unwanted awareness of the man who watched her as though he expected her to turn tail and run.

Oblivious to the tension, Miranda, her assistant, smiled a greeting from behind the spotless glass counter where dozens of delicacies containing chocolate in some form or another were displayed on hand-painted ceramic platters. It was still too early for the busloads of tourists who stopped in on their route to Cape Reinga for refreshments and to sample and purchase the delicately decorated chocolates several local women produced. For the sake of her regular customers who came each morning for cups of rich chocolate or mochaccino, Rebecca forced a smile.

"Rebecca…"

The rich, rough velvet of his voice caused tingles to vibrate up her spine. She shivered as every muscle in her body tightened. How did he do it? One word, and she reacted like a cat to its master's touch.

But she was no pet.

She was a woman. Her own woman. Damon Asteriades no

longer held any power over her. She no longer fancied herself in love with him. So she flashed him a careless smile. With deliberation, she folded her arms across the high back of the empty armchair opposite him, determined to show herself—*him*—that he had no longer had any effect on her. "Good morning, Damon. I would recommend—"

"I am done." He cut her off, and the newspaper across his knee rustled as he set it aside and leaned across the coffee table toward her. From her vantage point Rebecca couldn't help noticing the thickness of his silky black hair, the breadth of his shoulders under the fine fabric of his superbly fitting suit.

Then his fingers brushed hers and she gave a tiny, breathless gasp.

Before she could snatch her fingers away, he slid a rectangular piece of paper into her hand. Automatically she took it, then glanced down.

Instant déjà vu.

It was a cheque issued from a premier account, the bold gold print signifying that the bank deemed the signatory to be of great importance. Closer investigation revealed an obscene number of zeros, an amount far in excess of—she glanced at the empty coffee cup and crumbs and smudges that were all that remained of a slice of chocolate cheesecake—what he'd ordered.

"You appear to have overpaid," she said drily.

"For breakfast? Perhaps."

"For whatever," she retorted, his confident, lazy tone making her hackles rise. But she couldn't stop herself from glancing back at the plate in front of him. Chocolate cheesecake for *breakfast?* Her mouth twitched. But then, Damon had always had a sweet tooth.

"Ah, but that is not payment for 'whatever' as you so colloquially put it."

His words wiped away all residue of humour. Something in the way he watched her, the unwavering concentration, caused blood to rush to her face and her heart to start hammering. His full, gorgeous mouth twisted, and she tensed.

"No. The cheque is not for services rendered. At least not the kind that you clearly have in mind, *koukla*, if your flushed cheeks and bright eyes are anything to go by. Avaricious women never were much of a turn-on for me."

Humiliation scorched her. The worst of it was the knowledge that his words held more than a grain of truth. Clever, astute Damon had read the hope that had flooded her as her heart thudded—the hope that for once he'd experienced the same intense, hot flaring awareness she had.

Naturally the coldhearted bastard didn't feel a thing, while she trembled from the aftershock of the raw want that blasted through her, leaving her nipples tight and her body weak.

Damn him to the fires of hell.

She wasn't going to cower behind an armchair, she decided. She wasn't scared of Damon Asteriades. Nor did she fear the effect he had on her. That was nothing more than lust. Her heart was safe.

Stepping around the chair, she thrust the cheque back at him. "Take this and shove it!"

She told herself she could withstand his powerful magnetism. Because lust without love meant nothing—except bitter emptiness.

Instead of taking the cheque and ripping it up, he laid it very deliberately, faceup, on the small round table between them in a gesture loaded with challenge. "Now the negotiations start." He gave her a hard smile, but his glittering eyes held no humour. "Don't forget—I know that women like you are always on the lookout for easy money, for a wealthy benefactor."

Oh, how the barb hurt. "Get out of Chocolatique," she whispered, her lips tight. "I am not for sale. Ever."

He stared at her without blinking, then said very calmly, "You are overreacting. Whatever made you assume I'd *want* to buy you?"

How could she ever have loved this man? Believed that he might learn to love her back if he only knew her? Beyond speech, Rebecca glared at him, anger chopping through her, churning in her stomach. His gaze dropped and her breath caught in her throat.

The formfitting sundress splashed with red-and-white hibiscus flowers on a black background had seemed such a good idea earlier this morning, cool in the humid Northland climate. Yet now she felt exposed, naked. She refused to fold her arms and hide the puckered nipples that still pressed against the cotton fabric.

Her body switched treacherously to slow burn as those eyes traced the curve of her breasts, then lowered to the indent at her waist, making her feel like some concubine on the auction block. Except there was nothing sexual in his carefully calculated assessment.

Damon was putting her down, she told herself fiercely. This was his way of underscoring the fact that while she still desired him beyond reason, he detested her absolutely. She spun away and retreated so the high back of the empty armchair once again formed a solid barrier between them.

Had anyone else noticed the humiliating interaction? A glance toward the counter showed that Miranda was handing a customer a large box of truffles tied with a red organza bow, while one of the full-time waitresses Rebecca employed carried a tray laden with steaming cups and muffins to a secluded booth on the other side of the shop. No, she concluded, no one in the room was aware of how she felt—no one except Damon.

Resentment and desire smelted together, twisting tighter and tighter inside her until she wanted nothing more than to swing around and let rip and rage at him. But she refused to grant him that satisfaction. She would far rather see *him* flip, lose all control and go up in flames.

Her lips pursed at the wishful image. Little chance of that

happening. Damon was a total control freak. But she needed to find out what he wanted, what had brought him and his chequebook here. And the best way to find out was to provoke him. Carefully.

She swivelled to face him. "So what are you doing in Tohunga?" And raised an inquiring eyebrow. "Slumming?"

With some satisfaction, Rebecca heard the impatient breath he blew out.

"You are not going to get under my skin, woman. I promised my mother…"

"Promised your mother what?" She pounced on his words, the fear she'd refused to recognise easing.

He gave her a resentful look. "My mother, for some reason, holds you in high regard."

"I've always liked her, too. Soula has style, good taste and isn't as prejudiced as some." And she smiled demurely as fury flashed in his vivid blue eyes.

Through gritted teeth he said, "Savvas is to be married. My mother wants you to arrange the wedding."

"I'm sorry, I don't do weddings anymore," Rebecca replied without a hint of apology, her confidence returning at his bald request.

The blue eyes spat sparks and an almost-forgotten exhilaration filled her. For the first time since she'd known him she had the upper hand, and she relished it.

"No, you don't plan elaborate occasions anymore, you run a little sweetshop." He made it sound as if she'd come down in the world.

Rebecca ignored the taunt. "Did Soula tell you that she called me a fortnight ago to ask me to do the wedding?"

He inclined his head a small degree.

"And I told her that I had a business to tend, the 'little sweetshop', as so you quaintly put it. I can't up and leave—even if I wanted to." By the curl of her lip she hoped he got the message that she intended to do nothing of the sort. Never again would she put herself in Damon's range. "I'm sure your mother is more than capable of putting together and organising a wedding. She's a resourceful woman."

"Things are not as you remember. My mother…"

"What?" Rebecca prompted, something in his lowered voice, his taut expression, causing unease to curl inside her. She let go of the back of the armchair that she'd been clutching onto for support and stepped forward into the secluded circle that the seating created.

He hesitated. "My mother suffered a heart attack."

"When? Is she all right?"

Damon's face hardened. "The urgency of your concern does you credit—even if it is two years too late."

"Two years? I didn't know!"

"And why should you?" A red flush of anger flared across his outrageously angled cheekbones. "You are not among our family's intimates. I never wanted to see you, speak to you, again. You got what you wanted. You destroyed—"

He broke off and looked away.

Anguish slashed at her. Rebecca bit her lip to stop the hasty, impetuous words of explanation from escaping. "Damon…" she murmured at last.

He turned back, and Rebecca looked into the impassive, tightly controlled face of a stranger.

"*Then pirazi.*" He shrugged. "What the hell does it matter? The past is gone." He spoke in a flat, final tone from which all emotion had been leached. "All that counts is the present. My mother thinks arranging the wedding will be too much for her, given the state of her health."

"Why doesn't the bride's family assist?"

"Demetra came out on a visit from Greece and met Savvas here. She doesn't have the contacts—nor the inclination—to organise a function of this magnitude. As for her family—they live in Greece and will be flying out to New Zealand shortly before the celebrations, by which time it will be far too late."

Rebecca met his eyes. The restless force that lay behind the Aegean-blue irises still tugged at her.

Oh, God.

How could he still have this effect on her? Hadn't she learned a thing in the past four years? Apparently not. But she knew that to give in to his demand would be folly. The risks were too high.

She shook her head. "I'm sorry…"

His eyes sparked again. "Spare me the polite niceties. You're not sorry at all! But consider this—I'll make it well worth your while, pay you more than that." He gestured to the cheque on the table. "Then you can get someone in to run your little sweetshop."

He was throwing cash at her. Rebecca wanted to laugh in his face. Money didn't motivate her, whatever Damon thought.

"I don't think you could pay me enough to—"

"No need to bank my cheques any longer? Got another rich fool at your beck and call?"

The fury was back in full force.

This time Rebecca did laugh.

Damon bulleted to his feet and grasped her shoulders. "Damn you!"

His aftershave surrounded her, hauntingly familiar, a spicy mix of lemon and heat, mingling with the sexy scent of his skin. Then, just as suddenly as he had grabbed her, he dropped his hands from her shoulders as if he couldn't bear to touch her and swore softly, a string of Greek words, the meaning evident from his intensity. "I must be mad."

Resentment smouldered in his eyes as he sank back into the armchair and raked both hands through his rumpled hair.

And suddenly all the triumph Rebecca had expected to feel fell flat. She gave a quick glance around the shop. Still they had excited no attention. Unnerved by the powerful undercurrents swirling between them, Rebecca plopped into the armchair opposite him.

Hidden now by the high wingback armchair and the shielding palms in tall urns, she felt as if they'd been transported to another world that contained just the two of them…and the uncomfortable tension that lay like a tangled thread between them.

Damon sat forward, breathing hard. "Rebecca, my mother needs your help. I am asking you, *please?*"

He hated begging—she could see it in the tight whiteness of his clenched fists. Strangely she didn't enjoy seeing him in this position. She imagined Soula's strength diluted by physical weakness, knew what it must have taken the proud woman to ask for help a second time.

Then she thought of T.J., of everything that could go wrong.

There was no choice. "Damon…I…I can't."

"Can't?" Now the contempt was palpable. "Won't, I think. I don't remember you being vindictive, Rebecca. Strange, because I thought that in this cat-and-mouse game between us vengeance was *my* move."

Her heart stopped at the brooding darkness that shadowed his face. "Is that a threat? Because if it is, you can go," she said, her voice low, her spine stiff. "And when you leave, please don't slam the door behind you. Now get out."

There was a long, tense silence.

Damon didn't move.

Rebecca's nerves screamed with tension as she held his fathomless gaze. When she decided she'd finally gone too far, speaking to wealthy, powerful Damon Asteriades as though he were nothing but a hooligan, he spoke at last.

"Is that my cue to say 'Make me'?" he asked gently, then leaned back in *her* armchair in *her* shop.

If she hadn't known better, she'd have thought him completely at ease. The act was so good, in fact, that when his gaze swept from her face, over her body, down the length of her legs, discomfiture followed.

"You couldn't evict me—even if you wanted to," he continued, his gaze minutely examining her slim frame.

"Oh, for heaven's sake, stop playing games, Damon." Weariness infused Rebecca, followed quickly by impatience. "And lay off the long, lingering looks. I'm aware that you wouldn't want me if I was the last woman on Earth—"

"If you were the last woman on Earth, I'd say the men remaining would face a fate worse than death."

"Oh…" Her growl of frustration made him give that cold smile she hated. She loved seeing him laugh properly, his teeth flashing white against his tanned skin, revealing the sensual curve of his mouth. But this travesty of a smile never touched his watchful eyes.

"You'll have to learn to master that short fuse one of these days, Rebecca. Your eyes are flashing, your cheeks are scarlet. Again. At a guess, I'd say you're angry enough to…bite."

A further flush of heat swept her at his soft, suggestive words. "Bite?" she retorted. "Ha, you should be so lucky."

The smile stretched, revealing even white teeth. "I have no idea what any man would see in you. You are a vixen, a hellcat."

At least that made a change from the tired old labels of "black widow," "money-grubber"…

"Of course you wouldn't recognise my worth! You go for passive women you can dominate, force your will on."

"We will leave Felicity out of this." His voice was icy, his smile gone.

She widened her eyes. "Now why would you assume I was speaking of Fliss? She finally found the courage to stand up to you, to do what *she* wanted—"

"Be quiet." The whisper was a warning.

But Rebecca paid no heed. "No, I'm referring to the women you've been seeing for the past two years. Dolls, all of them."

"Ah, Rebecca, you disappoint me! You've been reading cheap gossip rags. I can assure you, the magazines got it wrong. They are not dolls," he purred, his mouth softening in a way that revealed masculine satisfaction and made her hands ball into fists.

"You're right, they're not even dolls. They're no more than cardboard cutouts. All identical. Skinny and blond and—"

"Jealous, Rebecca?"

Anguish exploded within her. Beyond thought, she drew back her right arm. His cool, narrowed gaze acted like a dash of freezing water and halted her intention to land the blow.

Coming rapidly to her senses, Rebecca peered around the edge of the armchair. Still no one watching. Thank God. Peace of mind, serenity and respect had been hard-earned in this small town. She wasn't going to let them be ripped away by one tempestuous public outburst.

Grimacing, she turned back to glare at him. "One day…" she muttered.

"You're not the first person to contemplate my untimely demise with great pleasure," he drawled.

She stared at him, shaken by the shock wave that went through her at the thought of a world without him in it. Reluctant to examine the implications of that realization, she hurriedly stood and scooped up his empty plate and cup and saucer with shaking hands.

He was on his feet instantly. "Retreating, Rebecca?"

I have to. But she remained mute, averting her face.

The sudden grasp on her elbow was firm but not painful. "Sit."

"No." She shook off his hold, frantically blinking away the sting of anger and hurt that she refused to let him see. Before she'd realised his intent, he'd taken the crockery from her hands and set it back on the table.

"Sit," he said again.

"I can't." She met his gaze, determined to appear cool and composed. "I've got work to do, orders to courier out." It wasn't a lie. Chocolatique was a successful operation. In addition to tourists who stopped to taste and buy, she had plenty of customers in Auckland who regularly ordered boxes of handmade chocolates by e-mail and phone.

"Rebecca, I am a busy man." He sank back into the

armchair, crossing his ankle over his knee. The cuffs of his fine silk shirt shot back, and he glanced impatiently at the Rolex on his wrist. "Right now I should be in Auckland finalising a sensitive business deal, not cooling my heels here. But my mother's health and happiness are more important than anything else in the world. So I ask you one final time to reconsider your position—it will be worth your while."

Despite his obvious impatience, his tone had changed, the offensiveness now gone, his jaw tight and his lean body coiled and utterly still as he waited for her reply.

It maddened Rebecca that he still thought he had only to wave a leather-bound chequebook and she'd fall into line. Like everyone else did. But not her. Tossing her head back, she gave him a withering look. "You've used that line to death, Damon. Four years ago you offered me money to stay away from Fliss—"

"But you couldn't, could you?" he growled. "Couldn't bear for her to find happiness, not when you wanted her man."

"No!" She covered her ears. "I'm not listening to this."

He came out of the armchair like a spring unwinding, fast and furious. Grabbing her wrists, he thrust her hands away from her ears. "Yes, admit it, Rebecca. Six weeks you let her have. Six weeks before you enticed her away. You were desperate for—"

"No," she repeated more loudly now that the offensiveness was back in full force. She glared at him. "It wasn't like that."

He bent toward her until his nose almost touched hers and his glittering blue eyes filled her vision. "God knows how you convinced Fliss to go with you in the end."

Perhaps the time had come to stop worrying about his reaction and to tell him the bald, tragic truth. That should stop him in his tracks.

She drew a deep, shuddering breath, and courage came in a rush. "She came of her own accord. I didn't force her. I told Fliss about my b—"

"Stop! I don't want to hear your lies. You stole my wife after only six weeks of marriage, and that is something I will never forgive! I will not listen to your lies." Damon was breathing hard, his eyes dark with anger. "But for you, my wife would still be alive."

He released her abruptly and she reeled away, realising with shock and horror that whatever she told him, he was not going to believe a word she said. She closed her mouth, rubbing her wrist absently. Rebecca heard his breath catch and his hand shot out.

"Let me see." The fingers that closed around her wrist were gentle. There was silence. She stood still, tense under his touch as his thumb massaged the spot where he'd held her. Then he said tonelessly, "I am sorry."

Rebecca stared at his long, tanned fingers resting against her wrist. "It's okay. There's not even a mark."

His voice rose. "It is *not* okay. I hurt you." Her head shot up. His beautiful full lips were drawn in a tight line, white and bloodless.

Rebecca bit back a hysterical giggle. He'd hurt her far worse in the past by refusing to believe in her integrity. He hadn't even liked her. *That* had hurt. Withdrawing her arm from his grasp, she smiled sadly. "You didn't—and it doesn't matter. Really."

His eyes were a brilliant, unfathomable blue. "So what do you say, Rebecca? Arrange Savvas's wedding and let's put the past behind us. Call it quits, hmm?"

She flicked him a glance.

Damon was prepared to bury the old resentments and bad feelings—perhaps there was a chance they could reach a truce. So that one day she would be able to tell him about T.J. And then there was that other temptation…

If she helped with the wedding—not for payment, of course, she couldn't do that—but to achieve a truce—then Damon might get to know her, might even discover what she'd always known, that they were bound by invisible ties too powerful to ignore. But…

Doubt assailed her.

Damon was a wealthy, powerful man. What if he found out the truth about T.J.? She simply couldn't risk T.J.'s security to chase a pitiful fantasy that she might—might—change Damon's poor opinion of her.

She sighed. "Look, I told you—I don't do weddings any more." Defeat weighed her down. Whatever she'd once felt for him he'd trampled into the dust, making it clear that he despised her. She waved a dismissive hand at the cheque on the table. "Not even for that ridiculously large amount of money."

"But my mother—"

"Your mother knows I can't do the wedding. I told her myself!" Soula had sounded fine on the telephone two weeks ago and the heart attack had taken place two years ago. This helpless sense of letting Soula down was just Damon's manipulation. In his world the end always justified the means. "If you want, I'll call her and tell her again that I can't do it."

Alarm lit his eyes. "I don't want you—"

"Talking to your mother. I know, I know!" Because he didn't want her finding out that he'd lied about his mother's health? Or because he didn't want Rebecca Grainger, a woman he utterly despised, having anything to do with his beloved mother?

He tried to say something, but she held up a hand, a new burn of hurt searing her at his appallingly low opinion of her, until all she wanted to do was hit back. "So please tell her not to call me again. And I don't want you bothering me, either. My answer stands."

His mouth snapped shut, an uncompromising line in that hard, wildly handsome face, while his eyes glittered with menace.

Yes, it was past time she accepted that there was nothing that she could salvage from the past, nothing that would make Damon look at her through kinder eyes.

"Now, you say you're such a busy, important man—you'd better get back to Auckland."

Rebecca didn't wait for his reply. One last reproachful look, then she whirled and bolted through her shop, ignoring the turning heads, until she reached the safety of her rabbit hole of an office behind the large workmanlike kitchen, shaken to the core by their bitter exchange.

Hours after their confrontation, Damon strode across the forecourt of the chain hotel of which he'd just checked out. Long shadows cast by the row of cypress trees edging the boundary crept like dark fingers across the cobbled pavers, reminding Damon that the afternoon was waning.

Had he heeded Rebecca's parting shot this morning, he'd already have been back in Auckland, closing the Rangiwhau deal. The CEO had demanded a face-to-face meeting this afternoon. Damon had stalled. Instead of concluding a lucrative deal that would make his shareholders a killing, he'd spent the afternoon closeted in a hotel room, juggling conference calls, working like a demon…all the while plotting how to get Rebecca to change her mind. And trying to rid himself of the ridiculous notion that he'd wounded her.

Impossible. The woman ate men for breakfast.

Damon had a fleeting memory of Aaron Grainger.

A good man. A shrewd banker who'd advanced Damon a hefty, much-needed loan in the nightmarish period after his father's death. Ari Asteriades had believed himself invincible. He'd made no provision for key personnel insurance, left no liquid funds available. Because of Aaron, Damon had managed to fight off the circling sharks and save Stellar International, keeping control in the family, keeping his tattered pride intact.

Aaron Grainger certainly hadn't deserved to die broken and bankrupt. Damon had heard the tales about Rebecca's profligacy. The fabulous designer wardrobe she'd ordered after her honeymoon, the jewels she'd demanded, the expensive flutters at the bookies on the racecourse, the overseas trips she'd insisted on. How she'd convinced a besotted Aaron to support her impulsive business schemes, all of which had demanded huge resources.

And then there had been the story about her lover. A handsome drug addict she'd begged Aaron to bail out of trouble. Rumour had it that Aaron had put his foot down that time. The lover had been history—but only after Aaron had paid off his horrendous debts.

Damon's jaw tightened. Reaching the Mercedes, Damon opened the trunk and tossed in his overnight bag and laptop case. Aaron should have put a stop to it sooner, before his beautiful wife had driven him to death—and dishonour.

No doubt about it, Rebecca deserved whatever she got.

He slammed the driver's door harder than he'd intended and stuck the key in the ignition. The ring of his cell phone interrupted his angry musings, and he jabbed a button on the cell phone where he'd just secured it against the dashboard. "Yes?" he demanded.

"Will she do it?" Savvas asked.

There was no need to ask to whom Savvas was referring. Reluctant to report his failure, Damon responded, "How is Mama?"

"Feeling dizzy again. The doctor is concerned about her. He says she worries too much, that she must take things easy."

"Or?" Damon knew there had to be a consequence. Dr. Campbell was not given to fussing unnecessarily.

"Or she could have another heart attack, and this time…" Savvas's voice trailed away.

"And this time it might prove fatal," Damon finished grimly.

"Don't talk like that!"

"It's the reality." Damon could almost see his brother crossing himself superstitiously at his words.

"You know, Damon, sometimes I wish I'd never asked Demetra to marry me. This damn wedding—"

"This from the man who preaches true love?" Damon cut in mockingly, disturbed more than he cared to admit by the idea that Savvas might be having second thoughts.

"No, no. I don't mean that I would forgo having met Demetra or falling in love with her. She's the best thing that ever happened to me. I meant I should have moved her in with me."

"*Vre*, the family would never have stood for it. Thea Iphegenia would've fainted in horror."

"Yet they turn a blind eye to the women you escort, Damon. They don't accuse you of sinning." Savvas's complaint filled the car's interior.

"That's different. I'm a widower. And anyway, I choose women of the world, not maidens with *marriage* written all over them, like your Demetra," he told his brother, his mouth twisting. He stared unseeingly through the windscreen into the golden glow of the late Northland afternoon. Felicity had been his last foray into respectability. It would be a cold day in hell before he tried it again.

"Maybe it would've been better to marry in court, present Mama and the family with a fait accompli. But now it's too late—the big Greek wedding is already in production. Damon, I fear it might kill Mama."

"Savvas, Mama wants this wedding. Desperately. Can you deprive her of it?"

His mother asked for so little. And gave them so much. Instead of retreating into tears and grief after his father's unexpected and devastating death, she had battled beside him as he'd wrestled for control of Stellar International. She deserved happiness, contentment.

Stupidly he'd thought his marriage would secure that.

He twisted the key. The Mercedes roared to life.

"Mama says she wants to hold a grandchild in her arms before she dies," Savvas was saying. "Demetra wants to start trying for a family as soon as the honeymoon's over. But first we need to arrange the wedding."

His mother lived for her family. *Family looked out for family*. That was his mother's creed. Cold, bitter rage twisted inside Damon's heart. All his mother wanted was to see Savvas wed. Rebecca could pull it off. Easily.

But Rebecca had already refused his mother's direct request—and now she'd refused him. He wasn't a man accustomed to refusal. Rebecca *would* help his mother and organise his brother's wedding. He'd make sure of it.

With slow deliberation he put the gear into reverse.

"It cannot be easy asking *her* for help. You hate her. I mean, not that I blame you or anything." Savvas faltered, then sighed. "Look, there's something I must tell you. After the wedding I saw her a couple of times and she seemed…quiet. I didn't see anything of the wild, wicked woman people talk about—"

"Hang on, are you telling me you *dated* Rebecca while I was on my honeymoon?" The car idled. Damon felt an almost forgotten red tide of rage boil up within him. *Hell.* He'd told her to stay away from Savvas.

"She's a very beautiful woman." His brother sounded sheepish.

"Beautiful?" Damon snorted. "If you like black widows. She's as dangerous as sin to the unwary."

"But, Damon, she wasn't like that!" Then, after a taut pause, Savvas amended hastily, "At least I could've sworn she wasn't like that. She was kind to me. We had some good times."

Good times? He didn't like that one little bit. Damon found he didn't even want to contemplate the implications. Reversing the car out of the parking bay in one smooth manoeuvre, he swung the steering wheel and headed smoothly for the exit. "No, of course she wasn't *like that*," Damon said bitingly. "That's her game. She spins her web, and the victim steps in."

There was a long silence. "Well, it's past." Savvas sighed more heavily this time. "After what she did, I didn't contact her again. You're my brother—how could I?"

Inside the suddenly silent Mercedes, Damon was fiercely

glad that Savvas had proved loyal to him and hoped it had cut Rebecca to the quick when Savvas had failed to call her again.

Savvas was speaking again and Damon forced himself to concentrate. "To see her, it must be hard for you. If she comes back to Auckland, it's going to cost—"

Damon cut him short. "Whatever the cost, I will do it. For Mama."

He clicked off the phone and swung the Mercedes into the main street of Tohunga. This time he'd do what he should've done from the outset: use charm. Rebecca had never made any bones about the attraction he'd held for her in the past. A little flirting, add a couple of handsome cheques and she'd be putty in his hands.

The empty parking space right outside Chocolatique gave him considerable satisfaction. It was all working out. As he entered Rebecca's shop, Damon straightened his tie, squared his shoulders and pasted a breathtaking smile to his face—one that guaranteed women would fall at his feet.

But Rebecca was not there. Gone for the day, he was advised by her blushing assistant, who kept sneaking him little looks from under her lashes.

Five minutes later, his smile gone, seething with impatience, Damon gunned his Mercedes down the road to Rebecca's home, determined to be out of this parochial town within an hour. And equally determined that when he left, Rebecca would be sitting beside him—whether she liked it or not.

Whatever the cost.

Three

Rebecca nosed the little yellow hatchback into the drive of the neat compact unit that had been her home since she'd sold Dream Occasions almost four years ago and relocated north.

In the small front garden the cheerful daffodils had finished flowering. The petunias and calendulas she and T.J. had planted were starting to bud. Soon the garden would be awash with colour and summer would be here in full swing. A large pohutukawa tree shaded the grassy spot where she and T.J. often played during the day. By the time Christmas came the massive tree would be covered with showers of flame-red flowers.

She switched the engine off and, turning, saw that T.J. had fallen asleep cradled in the car seat in the rear. His dark curly head drooped sideways and his mouth parted in an O.

Tenderness expanded inside her until she felt she would explode with emotion.

How dearly she loved him.

They were a family. No, more than family. In a relatively short time he'd become her whole world. All her reservations about what a poor mother she'd make given her lack of loving example had long since evaporated. She loved T.J. with all the fierce adoration of a lioness. He was hers. All hers. For once in her life she had someone that nothing and no one could take from her. Today she'd kept her silent promise and had rushed through her tasks at Chocolatique to spend some quality time with T.J. this afternoon. Except for dark shadows beneath his eyes, little sign remained of yesterday's illness.

With a still-sleeping T.J. bundled in her arms, Rebecca made for the unit, her stride quickening under his leaden weight. As she stepped onto the deck, a tall man straightened from where he'd been leaning against the wisteria-covered pergola that shaded the deck. Rebecca froze.

"You have a child!" Damon's voice was accusing, his face blank with shock.

Her grip on T.J. tightened. "Yes," she bit out and, radiating defiance, she faced him down over T.J.'s head.

A muscle worked in Damon's jaw. He looked odd, shaken. She frowned. If he suspected…

No. It wasn't possible. She'd taken such care.

She swivelled away, keeping T.J. screened from his line of sight.

Damon stepped out of the shadows formed by the tangle of ivy and wisteria. "I didn't know."

"And why should you? I don't count you among my intimates."

His head snapped back as she parroted his response from this morning back at him, and Rebecca watched over her shoulder with feline satisfaction as his pupils flared at her sharp tone.

Good! Let him know what rejection felt like.

Her gaze swept the street. "I don't see your car." The sleek silver Mercedes would've been difficult to miss in the empty street.

"I parked around the corner."

"Oh?" Had he suspected she might run if she knew he was lying in wait for her? Had he already known about T.J.? Was this a trap? But then, why play out the shocked charade pretending that he didn't know the child existed? Thoughts whipped back and forth until her head started to ache.

"T.J. hasn't been well. He needs rest. So you'll have to excuse me." Rebecca hitched T.J. higher, measuring the distance to her front door, anxious to escape.

"Wait a minute." Before she could reach the wooden door, Damon barred the entrance and took the keys from her nerveless fingers.

"What's the matter with him? And what the hell kind of name is T.J.?"

"What's wrong with T.J. need not concern you."

Ignoring the second part of the question, she shouldered her way past Damon and made for the carpeted stairs, determined to evade him. But the sound of his footsteps hard at her heels told her she'd failed.

Rebecca halted in the doorway of T.J.'s bedroom, keeping her back firmly to Damon. "You don't need to come in. You can wait downstairs."

He ignored the obstruction she'd attempted to create and stepped past her, his gaze roaming the room, taking in the sunny yellow walls, the mound of soft toys at the foot of the bed, the wooden tracks and brightly coloured trains in the corner.

The room shrank, Damon's powerful presence reducing it to the size of a closet. Rebecca was uncomfortably aware of his unwelcome proximity…of her rapid, shallow breathing.

Why couldn't he have stayed downstairs? And why did her body still respond to him with such irrational intensity? Rebecca ground her teeth with frustration. "Look, T.J. needs his sleep. The last thing I want is for him to awaken and find some strange man in his room."

Damon swung his attention away from the train-station mural she'd painted in bold colours on the wall above the bed, his gaze clashing with hers, his sensuous mouth askew with mockery. "He's not accustomed to waking to find strange men in his house? Now that amazes me, Rebecca."

The inference took her breath away.

"Now listen to me," she huffed. "I don't give a f…fluff what you think of me. But in my house, around my son, you will address me with respect. Right now I'm tired and T.J.'s been unwell. I need to put him to bed."

All at once the tension that had been throbbing inside her became too much. She bit her lip and looked away, blinking furiously, determined not to let the unaccustomed prick of tears show.

"I'm sorry."

For some reason, his unexpected apology was the last straw. Her throat thickened unbearably. She swallowed and shot him a desperate look. "Please…"

"Just go?" he finished, giving her a strange, whimsical smile, and crossing to the bed, he pulled the *Thomas the Tank Engine* cover back. "That's not the first time I've heard that today."

She moved closer, T.J. heavy as a block of lead in her arms. "Then I'm sorry to bore you," she said in a thin, high voice that sounded totally foreign compared to her usual husky tones.

"Bore me?" His mouth dropped open, his eyes glinting with something she didn't quite recognise. *"Bore me?"*

The sudden silence rang in her ears. Damon was standing so close she was conscious of his height, of the solid breadth of him. If she stretched her hand out around T.J.'s sleeping body, she could touch Damon's chest, feel the strong, vibrant beat of his heart.

"I think boring is one thing you could never be guilty of, Rebecca." He blew out hard, muttered something softly in Greek, then said with a touch of roughness, "Here, let me take the boy."

She jerked away as his fingers brushed her arm.

At once, the hands reaching for T.J. pulled back and

Damon spread his palms. "Okay, okay, I get the message! I'll wait downstairs." He threw her a hard, glittering look. "Never give an inch, never show any weakness, hmm?"

Rebecca ducked her head, refusing to meet his angry eyes, reluctant to reveal how much the electrical charge of the accidental touch had unnerved her. After a moment Damon's footsteps retreated, and for a wild instant she felt a sudden stupid sense of loss. Shaking, she hugged T.J. tightly against her breasts and inhaled his special baby smell until her turmoil calmed.

Then she gently deposited T.J. onto the royal-blue sheet and held her breath as he rolled over and gave a short grunt. He didn't waken. Instead his breathing steadied into the deep rhythm of sleep.

For a minute Rebecca stared at his sleeping face, the soft baby skin, the tousled dark curls, and pride and love stretched her heart to a tender pain.

T.J.

T.J. was her priority now.

Not her career. Not Damon. Not the wild, all-consuming attraction that had once upon a time nearly destroyed her. The most important thing in her life was T.J. And he rewarded her devotion with an uncritical, unconditional love that she would never, ever consider trading for the ferocious and destructive passion Damon had once stirred.

Damon's narrowed gaze and the sheer, untrammelled intensity emanating from him as he stood legs apart, arms folded, caused Rebecca's nerve endings to prickle warningly as she entered the living room.

"The boy is sleeping, yes?"

"Yes," she replied, pausing inside the doorway, more unsettled by his speculative stare than she cared to admit. Her gaze slid away. Took in the tailored suit that accentuated the hard, sleek lines of his body. His trademark white silk shirt was open at the neck, tie gone, the top button undone to reveal a glimpse of his tanned throat. She yanked her gaze back up to his face.

"I'm sorry he is not well. Is it something serious?"

The genuine concern in those devastating eyes forced Rebecca to say, "Just a routine ear infection."

He frowned. "I understand ear infections can be dangerous—that they can lead to permanent hearing loss."

Damon was vocalising her worst fears. Only yesterday she'd expressed the very same concerns to T.J.'s doctor—not that she'd ever admit that to Damon. Instead she tossed her head and said casually, "The doctor assured me a course of antibiotics will do the trick."

"So where is the child's father?"

The indolent question fell like a heavy rock into a tranquil pool, destroying any pretense of neutrality.

Rebecca stiffened.

"No longer in my life," she said, deliberately vague, avoiding the blue eyes that she was certain would be blazing with disapproval. The pause that followed stretched until her palms started to sweat. Fighting the urge to steal a fleeting glance at him, she kept her gaze lowered, uneasy with the turn the conversation had taken.

"Do you even *know* who his father is?"

Her head shot up, her affronted gaze colliding with his, and all at once she was too angry to fret about what she might give away. "What the hell kind of question is that? Of course I know who T.J.'s father is!"

She forced her expression into impassivity. Keep your cool, she counselled herself and then said aloud, "This is my home. I'd thank you to keep your…observations…to yourself. Now what can I do for you?"

"I ask no more than that you arrange Savvas's wedding," he replied, echoing her studied civility.

"I've already told you—I can't!"

"Rebecca," he said through gritted teeth, the false courtesy vanishing, his face darkening. "You know I'm a very wealthy man—"

Rolling her eyes, she interrupted him. "I already told you this morning I can't do the wedding and I'm not going to accept payment. You've done the bribery and corruption thing to death. Cutting the insults would be a good move, too." She held her breath and waited for him to explode.

His eyes flashed. His chest rose and fell under his crossed arms as he sucked in a deep breath. Then he sighed heavily. Unfolding his arms, he spread them wide. "Okay, whatever it takes to get you to do this damned wedding thing, I'll do it. So I can get back to Auckland and put my mother's mind at rest."

Rebecca blinked, stunned by his sudden capitulation. Damon did not negotiate, he issued ultimatums—and expected them to be met. A fresh wave of guilt rolled over her. Soula had always been kind to her. But helping Soula with the wedding was out of the question.

"What? No clever comeback?" Damon stared at her, his jaw clenched.

All at once, Rebecca recognised the truth of what he'd just said. Years ago, when they first met, she might have reacted to his statement that he'd do whatever it took with a risqué taunt like *Kiss me and I might consider it*. Comments that had drawn derision, followed by a closed, cold expression that shut her out. Totally.

Contrarily, it had been his very lack of response that had egged her on, demanding his attention by whatever means she could. And then had come the dawning realisation that he was interested in Fliss. While Rebecca burned anything she touched, Fliss cooked like a dream—a legacy of her Cordon Bleu training—and Damon had savoured rich slices of Sachertorte with half-closed eyes, his face alive with pleasure. Her heart breaking, Rebecca had watched him smile at Fliss with warm approval, his face reflecting an intent admiration he'd never shown toward her. Pretty, sweet Fliss, who was as different from Rebecca as a rabbit from a lioness.

Rebecca had backed off, waiting for Fliss to spurn him. But she hadn't. Fliss had had no right—

Stupid! Why did she keep getting tangled in the web of the past? She shook her head wildly, trying to dislodge the memories that still tortured her. No. That was all old history. Fliss was dead.

Instantly the urge to provoke Damon withered. Inside she felt flat and empty, worn out by the toll the emotional day had taken.

"Don't shake your head. Think about it. You can use the money for your business...for the boy." His gaze roved pointedly around the room, highlighting the tired carpets that needed replacing, the lounge suite that was showing signs of wear. "Surely money won't come amiss in jazzing up your lifestyle in this dull town. I can't see why you stay."

Rebecca stared expressionlessly at him. Going back to Auckland would simply reopen the old wounds. But for a lingering instant she considered the cheque Damon had dangled in front of her this morning. Now he was making it clear that the sky was the limit.

She *couldn't* accept payment to arrange Savvas's wedding. It wouldn't be right.

But, said a little evil, tempting voice at the back of her head, what might it mean to T.J.?

Although Chocolatique made them a fair living, it was a relatively new business that demanded time and all her resources. And, yes, she had a reasonable lump sum squirreled away in T.J.'s name that she intended to release to him on his twenty-fifth birthday. But what Damon was offering would eliminate years of worrying....

No! Rebecca thrust the temptation away. She couldn't accept his money, not for arranging an exclusive Auckland wedding. And she certainly had no intention of being in Damon's debt. Ever.

"My place is here," she said firmly. "I have T.J. to look after."

Damon looked flummoxed. It was obvious he hadn't factored a child into his calculations. But the confusion that clouded his brilliant blue eyes cleared almost immediately. "No problem. Bring the boy, too."

Rebecca laughed, a light, tinkling social laugh that carefully hid the sudden tightening around her heart. Bring T.J.? That was the last thing in the world she wanted!

"Get real, Damon. What would a child do in the Asteriades household? Destroy the antiques? Wreck the formal borders in the garden?"

Damon stared down his battered nose at her. "Demetra happens to like children. I'm sure she'll give you a hand if you ask nicely."

Demetra? His obvious fondness for the woman struck a raw nerve.

"And exactly who is Demetra?"

"I told you." He sounded impatient. "She is Savvas's fiancée."

"I'd forgotten her name was Demetra." Rebecca tried to ignore the relief that scalded her. And then annoyance kicked in. What did it matter who Damon's latest lover was?

Damon gave her a level stare. "Demetra is perfect for Savvas. She's kind, respectable, well brought up…."

Everything she wasn't. Each word landed like a well-placed barb. Recklessness flooded Rebecca. "Does she know what she's letting herself in for, marrying into the Asteriades clan?" she lashed out. "At least she's clever enough to realise what a bigot you are and how much nicer Savvas is."

"Ah, and you would know, wouldn't you?" He drilled her with narrowed, bitter eyes. "Savvas told me that the two of you dated after the wedding. How…*nice*—" he sneered "—were you to my brother, hmm?"

She flashed a wide white smile that didn't reveal any of the mix of emotions churning within her.

Anger.

Excitement.

And the thrill of danger that sparring with Damon always brought.

Softly, provocatively, she said, "You warned me to stay away from him, but Savvas called, said he wanted to see me. Your little brother liked me for myself. After the way you'd humiliated me, that was...*nice*." Staring through her eyelashes at him, she held her breath and waited for his response to the pointed mockery.

He didn't disappoint her.

His eyes flared brighter. "You little tramp..." He stepped abruptly closer. "You slept with my brother to get revenge on me. Because I married your best friend!"

Pain blossomed, but Rebecca refused to let him intimidate her. "Perhaps you place too much importance on yourself, your effect on the behaviour of others. Savvas lacks your arrogance—another reason why he is worth a million of you."

"Your mouth drips poison." He stalked closer still, his eyes blazing. "But I will deal with that."

The air had become electric, pulsing. Rebecca stood her ground. "Why the double standard? You can insult me with impunity, but when I retaliate..."

After a humming moment that pulsed with old resentments, latent attraction and myriad unspoken emotions, Damon spun on his heel, strode across the worn carpet and dropped down onto the homely sofa. For a long moment Rebecca stared at large, tanned hands clenching and unclenching between his thighs. Hands that could touch with the softness of silk or the cruelty of steel. Hands that made her shiver...and burn.

She forced her gaze back to his masklike face. He'd withdrawn. How she hated that.

"Forget it. I am not coming to Auckland." Rebecca spoke with finality, and when a sense of calm filled her, she knew she had made the right decision.

Turning away so she didn't need to see his expression when he realised that he had failed his mother, she closed off her mind to guilt. Damon had a dangerous effect on her. He aroused such reckless cravings she dared not risk being close to him.

"Look, I'm sorry."

She jumped as he spoke behind her; she hadn't heard him rise, or cross the room. She swung around. A dark lock had fallen onto his forehead. He brushed it back and sighed. More guilt stirred when she took in the unaccustomed tiredness in his eyes, the deep lines scored beside his mouth.

"I don't know what came over me. I swore I wouldn't let—" he shot her a hooded glance "—what happened in the past affect my dealings with you. I meant to be amenable." He flashed her a smile that might've been described as irresistible if it hadn't been directed at her.

Rebecca's mind started to click over. "You intended—" her breath caught "—to be *nice* to me."

His eyes flickered and a dull, red flush spread across his high cheekbones.

Bingo! Fury rose within her. "How far were you prepared to go, damn you?"

"Wait." He drew a breath. "Right now Mama is my only concern. She needs—"

She cut across before he could defend himself with clever words. "So you would've done *anything*," she said in a bitter little voice. "Used charm, seduced silly Rebecca?"

"No," he burst out. "I wouldn't have taken it that far."

Of course not. Sleeping with her was beneath the powerful, oh-so-perfect Damon Asteriades. "Well, fortunately for you it won't be necessary to go to such extremes. I can give you the name of someone who will plan a wonderful wedding for Savvas. Two someones, in fact. I'm sure the sisters who bought Dream Occasions would love the chance—"

"No!" The look he gave her burned with frustration. "I tried all that, but Mama insists on you. She trusts you and she's too on edge for me to risk arguing with her." He raked long fingers through his hair, but the recalcitrant locks fell forward again, dispelling the powerful-billionaire image.

Rebecca closed her mind to his boyish vulnerability and focused instead on the fact that Damon had tried to argue Soula out of asking for her help, on the fact that he truly seemed to believe his mother couldn't cope.

The trap was closing around her.

"Please help Mama. The child won't be a problem," he was saying. "We can work something out."

He was desperate.

As much as she wanted to slap him, punish him, Rebecca felt increasingly guilty that she had refused. Soula must be very unwell for him to go to such extremes. But how *could* she help? She had to put T.J.—and herself—first.

He's seen T.J., a little evil voice whispered. He hasn't put it together.

Dared she risk it? Rebecca chewed her bottom lip, thinking furiously. "It's not only a case of T.J. What will happen to my business while I'm away?"

Sensing her weakening, his blue eyes sharpened. "Surely your business can survive your absence for a couple of weeks? Later on, a lot of the wedding arrangements could be made from here. The move to Auckland won't be permanent."

"I don't know…." For a thread of time she wavered, and then all her misgivings crashed back. *What would happen if the truth came out?*

"Look, I'll double the amount of that cheque I offered this morn—" The jangle of Damon's cell phone caused him to break off.

The interruption made her hiss with relief. What was she thinking? She was mad even to consider it. Nothing, not even obscene amounts of money, would make her go back.

* * *

Almost. He'd almost had her!

Damon snarled a string of curses in Greek as he checked the caller ID. At the familiar number, a cold frisson ran down his spine and he stopped cursing abruptly. He rose, tension coiling in his gut, and stalked away from Rebecca, toward the blankness of the dark window.

"Mama? What is it?"

"Damon, I've been having pains in my chest. Savvas and Demetra are taking me to the hospital."

"Has Savvas called the doctor?"

"He's meeting us at the hospital. He says I'm going to have to stay there for a couple of days. My son, what am I to do?"

"Rest," Damon responded succinctly and stared out the window into the darkening night. Through the gloom he could barely make out the shape of the large tree rustling in the front garden.

"But what about the wedding? What about—"

"Don't give it another thought. I've got it all under control." Over his shoulder he shot the stubborn, maddening woman on the other side of the room a smouldering glance.

"Rebecca's going to do it? Oh, that's wonderful! I can't tell you how much peace of mind that brings me! Bring her to the hospital—I need to tell her what I've done, who I've spoken to, the venues I've considered."

He couldn't admit to his mother that he had failed. She had to believe he'd succeeded. For the sake of her heart. He'd handle what he'd tell her when he arrived back in Auckland, without Rebecca, later. Damon wondered for the thousandth time why his mother was so fixated on Rebecca. The women who had bought Dream Occasions from Rebecca would have leaped at the chance to arrange an Asteriades wedding.

It burned him that out of all the women in the world, his mother had to choose the one who had killed his marriage. Yet his mother refused to accept that Rebecca was to blame—

had always insisted that Fliss must have left of her own accord. Damon didn't—couldn't—accept that. But how could he refute it? He'd never told anyone, least of all his mother, about what had happened on the eve of his wedding....

All he could do now was murmur, "I will bring her. Hush now. I want you to relax. Do not worry about anything, I will take care of everything."

Rebecca found herself holding her breath as she listened to the one-sided conversation. With every sentence Damon's cheekbones stood out more starkly under tightly stretched skin, his tan draining to an unflattering putty shade.

Something twisted deep inside her as those rough fingers raked back the dark spikes of hair that had fallen forward over his eyes. And when he stared so helplessly into the night, his shoulders hunched, she had to force herself to be still, not to rush to his side, not to rest her hand on his arm, touch him...anything to banish the stark shock and bewilderment as he uttered frantic words of comfort.

"Mama? Mama..." He now called with desperation. "Can you hear me?" A shaking hand jabbed through his hair. "No, no, don't answer. Just get to the hospital. I will meet you there."

He cnded the call and turned to Rebecca, his eyes dark sunken pits in his bleak face.

"I have to go back to Auckland. My mother—" He wheeled away, placing a fisted hand against his temple.

Rebecca felt terrible. He hadn't lied. All the time he'd wasted trying to convince her, time he should have spent in Auckland, near his mother.

What if Soula died? What if Damon didn't make it in time, never saw his mother again?

She would never forgive herself! And if Soula died, who would take the hurt from Damon's eyes? Damon always looked after his family—who would be there for him?

Full of remorse, she hurried toward him and touched his sleeve. He started. "Damon, I'll come with you. I'll take care of…of…Savvas's wedding."

At the back of her mind lurked the awful thought that if Soula died, there would be no wedding, at least not until the mourning period was over. *Please,* Rebecca prayed, *please let Soula live to celebrate a wedding.*

The Asteriades mansion hadn't changed one iota, Rebecca saw as Damon swept into the formal curved driveway four hours later. The beam from the headlights illuminated neatly trimmed box hedges and large pots planted with bay trees that flanked the front door.

Back in Tohunga, a frantic rush had ensued before they'd left. In a matter of minutes Rebecca had made several necessarily brief phone calls. Miranda—with the help of her sister—would take care of Chocolatique until Rebecca returned. A call to her doctor assured her that T.J. was fit to travel, so all that was left was for Rebecca to arrange for the local handyman to mow her lawn and to pack.

During the journey Damon had made countless calls to Savvas and the doctors to check on his mother's progress. And although Savvas had repeatedly assured him that Soula was in good hands, that the heart attack had been arrested, under Damon's tightly leashed control Rebecca sensed his terror. That he might lose Soula, as he had already lost his father.

Oh, God, how well she understood his fear of loss. For once in his life Damon faced something he couldn't control. And she had no defence against his anguish. She could no more turn her back on him than she could cut off her arm.

Now, facing the imposing Georgian-style facade that loomed against the night sky, Rebecca shivered. It wasn't only Auckland's cooler night air that caused the ripples of gooseflesh. This house held memories she desperately wanted to forget. For a short time Fliss had lived here with Damon.

Even the elderly man who removed her suitcases from the trunk was familiar. Johnny, Damon's live-in butler.

"This way."

Rebecca turned at Damon's voice. T.J. was slung across his shoulder, fast asleep. She rushed over. "I'll take him. You go to the hospital."

But Damon carried on up the wide stairs lit by brass lamps to the front door. "Never fear, mama bear, I won't drop your baby. I'll show you your rooms, then I will go to the hospital. Savvas says Mama is sleeping peacefully."

Inside, Rebecca saw that the passage of time had wrought changes. She halted and stared with confusion at the three corridors that led from the spacious double-height lobby with its pale, glossy marble floor. Ahead, she recognised the stairs that led to Soula's rooms, but the red carpet had been pulled out and replaced with pale wool carpeting in an elegant oyster shade.

"I converted the wing Savvas and I shared on the ground floor into a suite of rooms for my mother after her heart attack. It made things easier—she didn't have to worry about the stairs."

That strong streak of protectiveness, Rebecca recognised. Damon took care of his own.

He headed for the staircase. "Demetra is staying in Mama's suite until the wedding."

Her heart fluttering, Rebecca asked, "And T.J. and me? Where will we be staying?"

"In my quarters."

Rebecca faltered. "Your quarters?"

Ahead of her, Damon paused on a landing. "Savvas and I had Mama's old suite extended and refurbished. But now Savvas has moved out—he bought a house where he and Demetra will live after the wedding—so it is mine alone."

Rebecca forced herself to follow him down a well-lit corridor glassed from floor to ceiling on the left. Through vast sheets of glass she could see a darkened courtyard where the flat gleam of water glittered blackly below.

He caught her sideways glance. "I replaced the old pool. The new one is more practical."

She remembered the fussy, elaborate pool with pockets of frothing water connected by artificial waterfalls and fountains decorated with fawning statues. A previous owner had possessed terrible taste. "You swim laps?"

"Every morning."

Rebecca made a mental note to keep away at that time. Then she thought of T.J.'s fascination with water. "Is the pool fenced?"

"The only access is through the house—and a gate in the garden which stays locked. I will give instructions to the staff to secure the ranch sliders at all times."

"Thank you."

"This will be your room." He opened a door to a room decorated in restful shades of cream. Curtains of heavy damask complemented a bedcover fashioned of rich ivory silk. On the wall hung a Monet print—or it might even be an original—the pale water lilies drifting on a pond adding to the restful mood of the room.

"And T.J.? Where will he sleep?"

"Through here."

She followed Damon into the adjoining room. It was smaller, clearly intended to be a dressing room, but a bed had been set up with bright, crisp new linen, while a selection of brand-new toys crowded the floor.

She pulled back the covers and he lowered T.J. so gently that her baby didn't even sigh. Deciding that T.J. could sleep in his clothes on this one occasion, Rebecca pulled his sandals off and fussed with the covers.

"There are bigger rooms, but I thought you would want the boy near you."

"Thank you." His thoughtfulness surprised her. Her gaze lingered on the array of toys. "But you didn't need to go to so much trouble—or expense."

"There wasn't much time. Johnny had a little over an hour

before the stores closed this evening. But I wanted your son to be settled, happy, while you are in Auckland. I don't want you fretting. If a few toys make the adjustment a little easier, then so be it." He gave a shrug.

Rebecca's heart contracted. That shrug—it was so intrinsically Damon.

She straightened, desperate to escape the sudden claustrophobia that cocooned them in the small, cosy room. Rapidly she made her way across the bigger bedroom to the large curtained windows. Pulling the heavy drapes aside, she stared out into the night.

In the courtyard below, the long, narrow pool mirrored the ripe moon, and through the open side windows Rebecca detected the scent of orange blossom and a whiff of jasmine on the night air.

"I need to go to the hospital. I'll leave you to settle in." Damon's voice sounded husky.

"Thank you."

But she heard no sound of footsteps, no thud of the door shutting behind him.

Driven by curiosity, she turned. He was watching her, an unreadable expression on his dark pirate face. The intense blue eyes were full of shadows, caused by the anxiety and concern for his mother, no doubt. But despite his uncharacteristic vulnerability she could still feel the pull that he'd always exerted.

She swung back to the window and stared blindly out, her back as tense as steel wire, her pulse hammering.

"It is too dark now to see how much better the courtyard looks with the lap pool and the landscaping I had done." His voice was low.

She wished he'd leave. Before she made a fool of herself. All over again.

"You always had a good eye," she admitted, her spine stiff. Old memories stirred. He'd picked out the wedding dress he'd wanted Fliss to wear. It had been perfect, enhancing her prettiness to almost become beauty—a far cry from the girlish flounces Fliss would have chosen.

"I'm honoured that you recognise my redeeming qualities." Irony tinged his voice.

Rebecca didn't respond.

A rough sigh came from behind her. "Again I must apologise. That was not necessary. You agreed to come, to help my mother with this infernal wedding that has her so worked up for some reason. Enough, it appears, to put her in hospital. The least I can do is extend true Greek hospitality."

"It's all right, Damon." She spoke to her faint reflection in the dark window. "I don't expect anything from you. Your feelings for me have always been plain."

He shifted behind her. "Have I been that bad?"

Rebecca drew a quivering breath, fortifying herself against the almost playful note in his voice. The last thing she needed was Damon extending false friendship because he felt obligated. Where would that leave her?

Head over heels in love?

God, no! Honest dislike was far, far better than false hopes.

"No reply? Not what I'd expect from you, Rebecca. What are you thinking, standing there so silent?"

That was a first. Damon had never been interested in her views, her thoughts. Too often he'd stifled her opinions with a harsh look, his mouth drawn into a sneer.

"Lost for words, hmm?" Again that hint of playfulness. "Or too polite to tell me that you think I've been worse than I suggest?"

She lifted a negligent shoulder and dropped it, refusing to be drawn…or charmed.

The silence stretched. She inhaled and became sharply aware of the heady fragrance of the orange blossom—and her awareness of the man behind her soared. She heard the soft rustle of silk as he shifted, heard the tempo of his breathing change. The tension started to wind tighter until Rebecca could stand it no longer and swung around.

He was standing much closer than she'd anticipated. The thick carpet must have muffled his approach. And there was something in his eyes—something elemental, something that she recognised.

Her heart leaped, and speeded to a gallop.

The air sizzled, charged. Rebecca wanted to fling her arms around him, pull him to her, feel his lips on hers. She tried to remember all the reasons it would be a bad idea.

He hated her. He was overwrought, worried by his mother's collapse. He'd been her best friend's husband.

It would be dangerous to T.J.—heck, it would be dangerous for *her.* There was no chance of a happy ending. Only heartbreak would come from this.

Yet none of it mattered. She didn't care. About any of it.

If only he would touch her. Kiss her. Set her on fire.

And when he moved, she closed the rest of the space between them. Breathing his name, she met his gaze, saw the flare of emotion, felt his response leap through her.

Then, as she stretched out her hand and her fingertips touched the firm muscle of his upper arm, he cursed, loudly, violently, and reeled away. But not before she'd glimpsed confusion in his eyes.

A stark, tormented uncertainty.

Rebecca held her breath as he stumbled to the door, and she did not release it until the door slammed shut behind him louder than a crack of thunder.

Four

Damn her!

Damon stepped up to the pool's edge. It was late, well past midnight. But he was too charged to sleep. Rebecca. The child. And the worry of visiting his mother in hospital and demanding answers from the physician on duty. All the events of the day had knotted the tension so tight that now his head threatened to explode. The water lay like a sheet of blackened silver under the moonlight. A moist sea breeze swept his torso and whispered across his thighs but failed to cool the heat that coursed through his naked body.

Upstairs, when Rebecca had tilted up her face, breathed his name…he'd almost drowned in the spell of her beauty. Then she'd touched him….

Tingles bolted through him as he recalled how her electrifying sensuality had wrapped around him. He stared into the flat water and decided she was definitely a witch.

A beautiful, seductive-as-sin witch.

And an avaricious one. For all her talk that she didn't do

weddings anymore, couldn't leave her business, in those moments before his mother called, money *had* finally swayed Rebecca, negating her lofty claim that she was immune to bribery. He snorted in disgust, the sound rupturing the silence of the night.

He was now committed to paying *double* what he'd planned. But what did it matter? The relief that flooded his mother's face at the news that Rebecca was in Auckland made it worth every dollar Rebecca was going screw out of him. Worth even the temporary loss of his own equanimity.

Damon launched himself into space and hit the dark water in a perfect arc, cutting through the silken chill with barely a splash. He surfaced halfway down the length of the black pool and started the long strokes to take him to the other end. Yet, instead of subsiding with each pull of his arms, the seething heat inside him grew.

He should never have asked her to come back.

Rebecca was trouble.

Years ago, from the first time he'd sensed her black, gleaming eyes on him and turned to see her glowing face, incandescent with desire, his interest had been snared. Discovering her name—that she was Grainger's widow—he'd known he was cursed.

It would have been so easy to succumb to the temptation in her beckoning eyes. But he would've despised himself. Instead he'd followed the dictates of his brain, turned his back on Rebecca's highly tempting but indisputably tarnished charms and chosen Felicity, never expecting a day's trouble.

Damon executed a tight racing turn and drove his body faster through the water. What foolishness had caused this ravaging attraction to reignite inside him? The child? Had it been the unexpected shock of discovering that wild, outrageous Rebecca had a child? The first time he'd seen her cradling the boy he'd felt hot and tense and…betrayed.

Mother of God! Rebecca must never discover she'd

breached his defences. A gasping breath and he dived down, down, plunging to the depths of the pool, streaking along the bottom, where the moonbeams were dim, to escape the fear that he would get no rest until he held her lush body naked against his.

Through the window Rebecca stared at the dark, churning water, the image of Damon's naked beauty imprinted on her mind. Every arch of muscle, every hollow of his body had been floodlit by the ghostly moon. She closed her eyes to block out the startling, stomach-tightening images. Desire twisted inside her.

No other man had ever affected her in this way.

Not even Aaron, whom she'd loved for his nurturing succour. Aaron, who'd given her the strength and courage to live her dreams, the support and know-how to start Dream Occasions—and later Chocolatique. But he'd never stirred a fraction of the emotion that Damon did merely by existing.

Oh, God.

Her soul recognised something elemental in Damon. Something that until tonight she'd thought wholly unrequited. Until she'd heard his ragged breathing, seen the shocked realisation, the unwanted knowledge in his eyes and known that he felt it, too. In a flash the future was alight with hope. Then he'd turned away, broken the golden thread of awareness that bound them. Leaving her trapped in the fire of desire.

Rebecca slept badly, and by the time she and T.J. came down to breakfast the following morning, Damon was already eating, engrossed in the business section of the morning paper lying open beside him. Clad in Armani corporate armour, his impressive nakedness hidden, he was every inch the powerful, remote billionaire Rebecca all too often scoured the country's top financial magazines to find. No hint remained of the primal, naked man from last night.

She hurtled into speech. "I'm sorry, we overslept. Are we very late?"

"No. I told Johnny to wait until you arrived so that you could have a hot breakfast." Damon's glance was cool, but he flashed a smile at T.J. before returning to his paper.

Suppressing her hurt at his offhand attitude, Rebecca busied herself with stacking two cushions onto a chair and helped T.J. to clamber up before seating herself beside him.

"I don't want to put your staff to any trouble," she said flatly.

Damon's face was wiped clean of all expression when he finally looked up. "Feeding the boy won't be any trouble."

Rebecca noted wryly that he didn't include her in the assessment. Her mouth slanting, she said, "Well, I don't want to be any trouble. A little fruit, sliced apple perhaps, and coffee would be fine for m—"

"The boy will require more sustenance than that," he interrupted.

A humiliating flush heated her cheeks at the rebuke. "Of course I wouldn't expect T.J. to eat only that. But he doesn't need a cooked breakfast either. Fruit and cereal will be fine."

T.J. chose that moment to utter hopefully, "Sc'ambed eggs, Mum? On toast?"

The look Damon gave her spoke volumes.

She ignored it and said firmly to T.J., "*And* apple slices."

"Okay." T.J. gave her a sunny smile, aware of his small victory.

Little monkey! She ruffled his curls. When she looked up, Damon was staring at her, a strange expression on his face. Before she could break the volatile silence, the door burst open and a petite wiry-haired brunette clad in jeans and a floral shirt rushed into the room.

"You must be…Rebecca?" The newcomer's English was accented, overlaid with an American drawl.

With a shock Rebecca realised this had to be Demetra. She'd expected someone more restrained—more obviously

Greek—than the young woman whose freckled, makeup-free face shone with good health. Rebecca smiled at her and got an answering grin. Then Demetra said, “And who is this handsome guy?”

“My son, T.J.” Tensely Rebecca waited for the inevitable questions to follow.

None did. Instead Demetra bolted around the table and sank down beside T.J. “What do you like doing most in the whole wide world?”

“Playing trains.” T.J. gave her a euphoric smile and started making *chuff-chuff* sounds.

“Uh, I don’t know that much about trains, but I betcha I’ll learn. I like digging in the garden more than anything else in the world.”

“I like digging in the garden, also. But I like trains more.”

Demetra laughed. “You’ll have to help me dig sometime. What kind of trains do you like?”

“Thomas and Gordon are bestest—they’re blue.”

“And blue is your favourite colour, right?”

T.J. nodded.

“You’ll have to introduce me to Thomas and Gordon right after you’ve had breakfast. For now, I’ll go chase Jane up.”

“Jane?” Rebecca queried.

“Damon’s chef. She comes in daily and cooks like a dream. Wait until you try—”

“Sc’ambled eggs?” T.J. interrupted worriedly.

“You want scrambled eggs, honey?”

T.J. nodded emphatically. “An’ toast.”

“Done!”

Demetra rose and was already halfway to the door when Damon called her back. “Better ask Jane for some apple slices for the boy, as well,” he said drily. “And Rebecca would like coffee with her fruit.”

“Okay.”

Then she was gone.

Rebecca blinked. That vital, vivacious creature was Demetra? Her heart lifted. She could see exactly why Savvas had fallen for her verve and warmth. She smiled at Damon—the first real smile since he'd erupted back into her life. "Demetra seems very nice."

"Nice?" Damon raised an eyebrow. "How you like that word."

Rebecca coloured and decided to ignore him. She stayed silent until Demetra returned at whirlwind speed, her arms piled high with plates for herself, Rebecca and T.J.

By the time T.J. licked the last morsel of scrambled egg off his spoon, Rebecca was ready to explode at Damon's rudeness. He'd barely uttered a word, answering only when spoken to and leaving the conversation to herself and Demetra to carry. Not that it had been a hardship; Demetra was a delight. Already she'd offered to look after T.J. while Rebecca visited Soula in hospital later in the morning. Demetra had also confided sotto voce that she viewed the approaching wedding with dread.

"Big, splashy functions are not me. But Savvas says his family expects it—and I know mine will, too, once they get here. So I'm relying on you, Rebecca, to make it a wonderful occasion for the parents. I don't need to know about the choices you make. All I want to see beforehand is the final venue you choose and I'd like to help choose the cake and I want your advice with my dress. Nothing too grand. The rest is up to you!"

"I'll do my best to make it a wedding that you and Savvas will enjoy, as well," Rebecca said, bemused by Demetra's quicksilver personality.

"All I want is Savvas—I love him!" Sincerity radiated from Demetra, and Rebecca wished she'd been blessed with the same love that Demetra shared with Savvas. "Okay," Demetra said more loudly. "Enough of this bride stuff, I'm off for a quick workout in the downstairs gym." And she vanished out the door.

A silence descended in her wake.

Rebecca started to segment the orange she had peeled, an orange she was already too full to eat. She placed two pieces in front of T.J., who attacked them with relish, juice dribbling down his chin.

With a brooding glance in T.J.'s direction, Damon said, "The boy may be excused if he wants."

"T.J. His name is T.J.," Rebecca said impatiently.

"It's a ridiculous name, for God's sake."

"It's his name," she rebuked, dropping her voice. "And he can be excused after he's finished the orange—I'll take him up with me."

Damon leaned back, his eyes narrowing. "What I call him, it upsets you?"

He hadn't taken her advice about Fliss's name preferences on board, so she shrugged. "He's a person, an individual with a name chosen just for him. He's not 'the boy.'"

She put another two segments on T.J.'s plate. He shoved one into his mouth with sticky fingers and picked up the remaining sliver. With a tiny-toothed grin at her, he slid from the chair before she could stop him and was around the table in a trice.

Rebecca watched, frozen, as T.J. offered Damon his last segment of orange. There was a moment of utter silence, then T.J. pushed the messy bit of orange at Damon, insistent now. Rebecca unfroze and leaped to her feet, hurrying toward them, aware that any moment the juice would land on Damon's expensive suit, aware that Damon was not accustomed to three-year-olds and sticky hands and that T.J. was likely to suffer the consequences of his impatience.

Damon's next act stunned her.

Taking the orange, he popped the sodden mass into his mouth. Then he gave T.J. a beaming smile. "Delicious, thank you, T.J."

T.J. squealed with pleasure. He battered his juice-stained fists against Damon's trousers and cackled, "Dee'icious, dee'icious."

Rebecca swept him up into her arms before he could do any more damage. Taking in the wet patches on Damon's thighs with a harassed glance, she said, "I'm so sorry."

Damon shrugged. "No matter. The suit will clean."

He was still smiling at T.J., and Rebecca went utterly still, staring at him. When his head turned, she tore her gaze away. "Excuse us, please." Without waiting for a response, she snatched a paper napkin from the table, flashed him a meaningless smile and made for the door.

"I'll collect you to visit my mother at noon. Be ready." Damon's command followed them out the room.

As she bolted through the doorway, T.J. reached over her shoulder to wave at Damon before whispering in her ear, "I like the man."

It was a shock to see Soula lying so frail and passive in the high hospital bed. Rebecca didn't dare look at Damon. Not that it would've helped. On the drive to the hospital, he'd continued the cold and remote treatment he'd started at breakfast, the silence building a wall of ice between them.

Far better to think about poor Soula, whose chalky pallor was barely distinguishable from the white sheets enveloping her, and whose eyes were closed despite the wide-screen plasma television blaring across a room that looked more like a luxurious hotel suite than a hospital ward.

As the ward door clicked shut, Soula's eyes opened and lit up. "Rebecca, how good to see you! Damon, you're back!" She struggled to sit up, paying scant attention to the drip secured to the back of her hand—or the wiring that protruded from under the bedclothes.

"Mama!" Damon crossed the private ward in two hasty strides. "No, Mama. Lie still."

"Don't be silly. I'm not yet dead, my son. Switch the television off." Damon complied. "Now raise the back of the bed."

While Damon was adjusting the bed-frame setting,

Rebecca approached the high bed, deeply shaken by Damon's mother's appearance. Only the dark, indomitable eyes showed a shred of the proud woman Rebecca remembered.

"I must look a wreck, hmm?"

Rebecca forced a smile, aware that Soula must have read the shock in her eyes but unable for the life of her to think of any platitude that would sound sincere.

"What? No answer, Rebecca?" The older woman gave a wan smile. "Better that than the lies the rest of the family feed me. This morning my eldest sister, Iphigenia, said I still put women of half my age to shame. Pah! All lies!" She rolled her eyes to the ceiling. "But I have to admit it's not as bad as it looks. White is a terrible colour. Look—" she flung an arm out "—white nightdress, white sheets, white blankets. So bad for an older woman—it simply doesn't do a thing for my complexion."

Affection for the acerbic woman overwhelming her, Rebecca bent to plant an impulsive kiss on the cheek that wore a few more wrinkles than it had in the past. "Nonsense," she whispered into Soula's ear. "True beauty comes from within. Hasn't anyone ever told you that?"

They exchanged a long look, then Soula's arms crept around Rebecca's neck and pulled her close. "It's so good to have you here, child. I was starting to despair."

The note of very real desperation in Soula's voice and the unexpected warmth of her hug caused something to splinter deep inside Rebecca and she hugged Soula back fiercely. Swallowing the burgeoning lump in her throat, she glanced up at the bank of equipment above the bed and said in a choked-up voice, "I have to admit I don't like seeing you tied to these machines. When will you be out and about?"

Damon reared up on the other side of the bed, outrage in his eyes. "*Out and about?* My mother needs—"

"Soon!" Soula interrupted her son." I will not stay in this place *ena lepto*—" she held up a thin forefinger "—longer than I need. Not one minute. Look at me! My hair needs attention, my nails need a manicure…." She held out elegant hands spoiled only by chipped nails.

"You should've told me. I would've organised a beautician, a hairdresser—" Damon waved a hand at her nails "—whoever you needed to fix that."

"How can I expect you and Savvas to understand? You are men! Look, I'm wearing nightclothes in the middle of the day. *And* I reek of antibacterial soap." She paused for breath. "I can't bear the smell of the antiseptic."

"Neither can I," said Rebecca with heartfelt fervour. Memories haunted her of the hospital her brother, James, had been in and out of before his death.

Soula gave her a sharp glance. "Only the experiences of the old and sick bring on such strong dislike."

"Perhaps." Rebecca kept her reply noncommittal, aware that she'd already given away more than she'd intended—especially with Damon hovering so close.

Soula patted Rebecca's hand. "One day you will tell me more, *pethi*."

Rebecca looked away. Not likely. It hurt too much.

Every single person she'd loved in her life had been ripped away.

Her parents.

James.

Aaron.

Fliss.

And with Damon she hadn't even got started before it had all come crashing down on her. All she had left was T.J. whom she loved more than life itself.

She blinked. Soula's hand was warm on hers and the weight of it resting there made her feel like the worst kind of fraud.

"Rebecca, *pethi*, I didn't mean to upset you."

Rebecca forced herself to snap out of the black grief that smothered her. Soula should be the focus of her concern now.

"Come, child, let's talk about other things." Soula glanced meaningfully over at her silent son. "Damon, stop glowering and make yourself useful. See if you can find coffee for yourself and Rebecca."

Rebecca winced, waiting for the inevitable explosion to follow the barrage of orders, then relaxed when Damon simply shot her a hooded look, his mouth slanted.

As soon as the two women were alone, Soula patted the bed invitingly, "*Kathiste,* come sit. Tell me what you think about this wedding that has me in such a state."

Not for the first time suspicion rose inside Rebecca and she pinned Soula with a thoughtful look, but the other woman simply smiled and looked angelic.

Raising one speaking eyebrow, Rebecca sat. "And while we talk I'll tend to some of those things that are bothering you so much. Where can I find your vanity case?"

Twenty minutes later Damon padded silently back into the ward. His mother and Rebecca were chatting softly—too softly for him to hear what they were saying—while Rebecca repainted his mother's nails. His mother's crow-black hair had been brushed and secured into a stylish knot that made her look more like her usual immaculate self. Her cheeks held a slight blush, and her lips were coloured with the shade she'd worn as long as he could remember.

Without warning, Soula laughed, and the dull helplessness that had cloaked him since receiving her call started to lift. All at once things seemed brighter. Happier.

His mother was going to be fine. She was not going to die. And he had Rebecca to thank for the transformation. He stepped forward and with his right foot pushed the door shut behind him. The thud caused both women's heads to shoot around.

Rebecca looked instantly wary, but his mother beamed. "Ah, coffee. Rebecca will enjoy that. Won't you, dear?" And without waiting for an answer, she continued. "Put it on the trolley where Rebecca can reach it."

"Two sugars, right?" he asked, unable to help noticing the easy relationship his mother and Rebecca shared. How had he failed to notice the strength of the bond between the two women in the past? Always he'd seen only the differences: one a proud Greek matriarch, widow of one of the richest men in the southern hemisphere, the other born and raised in a series of Auckland foster homes, a woman of questionable morals. One reluctant to succumb to the tyranny of age, the other young and lushly beautiful. Never before had he noticed the common bonds they shared: the strength of will, the burning determination, the stubborn tilt of the chin.

Both were staring at him now, waiting for a response to something he had not heard. He looked from one to the other. "I'm sorry?" he said in his most distant tone, not wanting either woman to conclude that he'd been in dreamland.

"I was commenting on the fact that you remembered that Rebecca takes two teaspoons of sugar in her coffee." For some reason his mother was smiling beatifically at him.

His brows drew together. "She must have told me." But he knew she hadn't. His internal radar had always been attuned to Rebecca's every action. He'd hated it, resented it fiercely. But there hadn't been a thing he could do about it. Except pretend it didn't exist.

And treat her as if she barely existed.

"No, she didn't," his mother said triumphantly. "You remembered from all those years ago."

Backed into a corner, he made the grudging admission. "Perhaps I did."

To his surprise, it was Rebecca who rescued him. "But then, how many women take two spoons of sugar? Not easy to forget. It's something that often makes me self-conscious, my addiction to sugar."

"It shouldn't," he said without thinking. "You can afford to eat whatever you like." And could've kicked himself at her startled expression…and his mother's smug one.

To his relief, his mother didn't comment. Instead she steered the conversation back to Demetra and Savvas's wedding and Damon started to relax.

"I can't help worrying about Demetra. About how she will cope with the strain of a high-profile marriage. She's very…" His mother paused searching for a word.

"Vivacious?" Rebecca inserted with a smile. "But, Soula, that's part of her charm. And don't you worry—as long as Savvas loves her, she'll be fine."

"I hope so." Despite the doubt in the words, his mother looked happier. "But she's not interested in the arrangements at all. The only thing that matters to her is the home Savvas has bought—and more than the house, the garden."

"Some women aren't into the whole wedding spectacle." Rebecca shrugged. "It doesn't mean a thing."

"She has other strengths. She's a landscaper," Damon said.

"Oh, yes, and she's very good with children, too." Soula's eyes lit up. "I can't wait to hold my first grandchild. Damon was very remiss."

Damon felt the explosive reply rising, bit it back and glared at Rebecca. How dare his mother bring this up? To her credit, Rebecca looked extremely uncomfortable.

Even as he glowered, Rebecca rose to her feet. "Speaking of children, I need to get back to the house. T.J. will be wondering where I am."

"I can't wait to meet your son, Rebecca. Does he take after you?"

Rebecca looked flustered. "Not really, although there is some family resemblance. His eyes are just like—" She broke off, blood draining from her face.

Damon took pity on her and said, "He has your dark hair."

"What?" Her face blanked out all emotion. A second later

he watched her snap out of the hell she'd retreated to and reply, "Yes, yes, of course he does."

Damon froze at the undiluted anguish he'd glimpsed in her dark eyes. Eyes so unlike T.J.'s that he concluded that T.J.'s must resemble his father's. A fleeting image of round blue eyes. Again he found himself wondering about the boy's—T.J's, he amended—father.

Then he forced himself to dismiss the speculation.

It was not his concern.

Yet there was something about the boy's features that was intensely familiar, but he could not put his finger on what it was. *Then pirazi*—it mattered not. It would come to him.

Rebecca had turned away and was shrugging on her jacket and collecting her bag. Something had stirred up old hurts for her, judging by the speed she made for the door.

"I can't wait to meet the little one," Soula said.

"Soon," Rebecca promised. From the doorway she gave Soula a little wave and bolted.

"You'll have to wait until you get home," Damon said firmly to his mother before kissing her cheek and hurrying after Rebecca.

"Come on, *come on*."

Shifting from foot to foot, Rebecca stabbed the button again, impatient for the elevator to arrive. Hearing Damon's distinctive tread behind her, she shoved her hands into her pockets and hunched into her jacket.

"What's the hurry?" His dark, fluid voice sent shivers that she didn't need down her spine.

"I need to get to T.J. I don't usually leave him for such long stretches of time."

"What about while you work?"

"That's different. He's known Dorothy, his caregiver, since birth. Demetra is a stranger, and the surroundings are alien, too." But even more than getting back to T.J. she wanted to escape. Away from the well-meaning questions, away from Damon and away from the hospital and the memories of awful helplessness it evoked.

An elevator arrived at last, already occupied by a nurse fussing over a hospital gurney. The patient was a young man in his early to mid twenties, Rebecca guessed. One arm was in plaster. What she could see of his face was covered in lacerations, the rest hidden beneath dressings and tape. He looked as though he'd been in a particularly nasty car smash. She stepped inside, transfixed, barely aware of Damon following behind. The patient groaned and turned his head. Rebecca jerked her horrified stare away.

The elevator sank and stopped at another floor. A beeper sounded. The doors slid open again, and the nurse and her patient were gone, the castors rattling against the endless corridor. Rebecca watched the disappearing gurney and prayed fiercely that the young man's prognosis was better than James's had been.

Desperation clawed at her throat. She felt sick, light-headed. "I need to get out of here."

"It's the hospital, isn't it?"

"I hate these places," Rebecca said with feeling, bile burning the back of her throat.

"Thank you for staying…for helping my mother. It made a great difference."

"It was nothing."

"Hardly nothing. She's afraid." He shot her a searching glance. "Was T.J.'s birth difficult?"

She swallowed hard, disconcerted by the sudden change of subject. His conclusion was not unreasonable in the circumstances. But what to say? "All births are difficult, but the reward is immeasurable. T.J. is a blessing."

"He's a son to be proud of. You've done well, raising him alone."

"Thank you." Her mouth tasted bitter.

If he only knew.

"You had a short stay in hospital after—" He broke off.

"After Fliss died. It was one night." Rebecca kept her tone flat as the elevator jarred to a stop. The doors shuddered open to reveal a well-lit underground car park. Rebecca hurried out.

Damon followed. "Was that when the dislike of hospitals began?"

"It didn't help," she said honestly, stopping and facing him. "But the phobia was already there." James, she couldn't stop thinking of James. The hospitals visits, the hopeless tests, the sudden brutal end. In a sudden blur of pain she remembered the night Fliss died, how she'd cried as Fliss had slipped away. She blinked and forced herself to look up at Damon instead.

His eyes were hooded, but there was none of the tightness in his jaw that she'd half expected. It was the first time Fliss had been mentioned without Damon going up in flames. That had to be progress. Rebecca sighed. She didn't want to fight anymore. She'd had enough.

Seeing Soula weak, ill and older had shaken her. And Rebecca had suddenly been struck by her own mortality. If anything happened to her, what would become of T.J.? She felt a disorientating sense of panic and sagged back against the wall. This was ridiculous! This place must be getting to her. The horrid memories.

Yet deep down she knew it was more than the starkness of the hospital, the haunting memories that called to her from the past. The man standing in front of her—the emotions he aroused—was part of it, too. A sharp ache shot through her head. Dizziness. All at once wide white space closed in on her.

"Hey, are you all right?"

With a sense of shock she became aware of Damon's hands on her shoulders, shaking her gently. For a moment she contemplated leaning forward, resting her head on his chest and releasing the tears she'd held in check for far too long.

But she didn't want to reveal any weakness to him. So she

lifted her head and gave him a wan smile. "I'm fine. Or at least I will be as soon as I get out of this place."

"Let's get you out then."

But he didn't move.

The expression on Rebecca's face caused something to shift in Damon's chest. There was a sadness on the exquisite features, a vulnerability he'd never seen before.

Or had he simply never wanted to see the loneliness?

With a spontaneity that was foreign to him, he leaned forward intending to brush a brief, comforting kiss across her lips. But that all changed the moment his lips touched hers. Instantly he was aware of the softness blooming beneath his. He felt the surprised hiss of her breath against his mouth, and a torrent of desire flooded him.

A primitive male urge rose within him to grind his lips on hers, push her up against the wall, feel her body against his and immerse himself in her heat. To take her and never let her go. Only the confusion in her eyes, the unexpected fragility she'd revealed, halted him.

No.

She had been through enough.

Instead he drew away and cupped her cheek with a gentle hand, heard her breath catch. Her dark eyes were wide and dazed, her lips parted, tempting him. She smelled of flowers, sweet and fragrant. For an instant his mind flashed to that moment in her bedroom when tension and something much more had buzzed between them. That time he'd escaped to the cold, dark water of the pool. But this time…this time he didn't want to stop. Didn't want to be sensible.

He wanted to drop his head, slant his mouth across hers and feel the wildness rock him.

It took everything he had, all his magnificent self-restraint, to leash the passion surging inside him. With careful control he leaned forward and dropped the lightest touch across her nose.

"That tickles." She gave him a small smile and wrinkled her nose at him.

"Does it?" Inside him, something melted. Today he'd seen another, softer side of Rebecca. So very different from the selfish, self-centred woman he'd known before. How patient, loving, she was with her son, how deftly she'd cheered his mother up, easing her fears.

"Yes," she murmured, her lashes fluttering against her cheeks.

A fierce pang of desire pierced him, and he fought to control the need to crush this wild, delicate woman against him. Inexplicably he ached to possess both sides of her—the caring woman and the sexy vamp. He stroked his fingers along her jaw, savouring the soft skin.

Was it the flashes of tender caring that Savvas had seen in her and liked? No doubt her body was another thing his brother had appreciated. Had his brother felt branded by her kisses? The way he did? Damon brooded over the notion and his hand dropped away from her face. Had Rebecca ever aroused this fearful sense of confusion in Savvas?

"Can you stand?" he bit out, then regretted his harshness.

She nodded, visibly pulling herself together, her eyes large liquid pools in her pale face.

Damon stepped back, his reason at war with his body. Fighting the urge to take her into his arms, to surround her with the warmth of his body, to taste her mouth and brand himself with her taste forever. To take her to his bed and keep her there until he discovered every fantasy she craved, stripped away every secret she possessed.

Hell!

His lack of discrimination stunned him. He swung away, disgusted by the insane surge of desire for a woman so many others had possessed. His own brother, Aaron Grainger, other men who watched her salaciously and spoke of her as "hot, hot, hot" and "great in the sack."

"Let's go," he said curtly. "T.J. is waiting."

Then he told himself to stop being stupid. What did he expect? Few women of Rebecca's age had only one lover. Wanting her, bedding her, didn't mean a thing. After all, it wasn't as if wanting equated to marrying the woman.

And he *was* going to have her. *Soon,* Damon vowed bleakly as they crossed the car park, Rebecca silent and withdrawn beside him. It was time to stop fighting the staggering attraction she held for him. And when he'd purged himself, he would walk away, leaving Rebecca and the past behind.

There'd be no loss of control, no emotion.

Only passion.

Five

Rebecca groaned and suppressed the urge to bang her head against the steering wheel at the labouring whine of the car's motor.

What a way to start a Friday morning. For nearly two days she'd successfully avoided Damon, ruthlessly using the wedding as an excuse to spend as much time away from his home as possible. She'd taken advantage of T.J.'s fascination with Demetra—and taken advantage of Demetra's kindhearted offer to babysit T.J.—to get as much organised as she could.

Even though her purpose had been to avoid Damon, Rebecca had been busy. She'd been back to the hospital to check the names of all the guests with Soula and had confirmed late additions with Demetra. A large number would be flying out from Greece, so she'd obtained quotes for their accommodation for Damon to approve. She'd visited the printers, where she'd been given samples of cards, colours and fonts for the embossing on the wedding invitations.

For today she'd lined up appointments to view several

venues for the wedding. But now the battery of the little run-around that Damon had organised for her to drive was flatter than a flopped soufflé. Her fault, of course. She'd failed to close the trunk properly yesterday when she'd returned from the hospital, which meant that the trunk's interior light had been on all night.

She dragged herself out the car and considered her options. Less than ten minutes ago Demetra had waved and driven away with T.J. safely strapped in the back of her sporty little SUV. Demetra planned to take T.J. to feed ducks in a park near her new home. On hearing about the pond, Rebecca had issued a dark warning about T.J.'s fondness of water. Demetra had promised to watch him like a hawk. Afterward she was taking T.J. to her new home for a light lunch and planned to keep him amused planting herbaceous borders in her fledgling garden.

As much as she hated taking advantage of Demetra's sweet nature, she could call and throw herself on Demetra's mercy and beg a ride to town.

Briefly Rebecca considered the other, less appealing option—cancelling her meetings.

"Is there a problem?" The dark velvet voice caused her to stiffen.

Damon.

It would be, of course. After successfully avoiding him, he had to find her beside a car with a flat battery. She'd been rattled by how nearly she'd fallen apart in front of him outside the elevator at the hospital, had intended to be cool, composed, elegant the next time she saw him. More than ever she wanted to kick the capricious car.

Heart sinking, she turned to face him. He looked fantastic in a dark, stylish suit with his usual white shirt and conservative narrow tie below that inscrutable face. Rebecca drew a steadying breath and tried to look more together than the jumble of chaotic emotions inside her allowed. If she told him what was wrong, perhaps he'd lend her another car—Soula's even.

A quick glance at her watch revealed that if she left now, she could still make her first appointment. So she told him. And waited for derisive male condemnation to follow.

"I'll take you," he said abruptly. With a click the electronic-controlled garage door behind her started to rise, revealing his silver Mercedes.

"No, no. That's not necessary."

"Come. Or you will be late." He already had his cell phone in his hand, and Rebecca could hear him instructing his PA to reschedule his appointments and organise someone to recharge Rebecca's car battery as he shepherded her toward the Mercedes.

When he asked where she was going, she told him in a small voice. Rebecca had expected Damon to leave her at the San Lorenzo hotel, but he stayed, striding tight-lipped into the lobby at her side. Rebecca found herself tensing. Of all the places in Auckland, this was the one that held the most painful memories. But it had the grandest ballroom in town. Her own distress was no reason to exclude it from the list of venues.

Andre, a slim, dapper Frenchman who was made for the role of events manager, welcomed Rebecca like a long-lost friend. "You're back in the business?"

With a strained smile Rebecca replied that she was simply doing a favour for a friend. She heard Damon mutter something barely audible about favours being expensive these days. Her brows jerked together in puzzlement. A sideways glance revealed that his mouth was compressed into a hard, tight line.

Rebecca was aware of the precise instant Andre recognised her companion, saw his visible double take. "*Monsieur* Asteriades, it is an honour to have you in our establishment. We are pleased to be of any service we can." The Frenchman quivered like a delighted whippet.

Not for the first time Rebecca's stomach curdled at the ingratiating treatment Damon received wherever he went. He was just a man, for goodness' sake, albeit a gorgeous, sexy man. Andre's deference increased as they walked around the function rooms, the ballroom, until Rebecca wanted to scream.

The tour wasn't made any easier by the gut-churning knowledge that the last time she'd been here had been on the night of Damon's wedding. She couldn't help wondering how often Damon had been here since.

Often, she concluded. What did he care? Of course Damon wouldn't share her despairing memories of the place. He'd only remember Fliss, their wedding.

What the hell did it matter? What she felt about the place was insignificant. Everything had happened nearly four years ago. It no longer had any bearing on the present. Even the decor had changed. Yet the ballroom still retained that rich ambience she remembered, making it the perfect place for a high-society wedding.

"You're not seriously considering this place, are you?" Damon muttered through gritted teeth when Andre whisked away to fetch some sample wine lists.

One look into his stormy eyes and Rebecca knew he hadn't forgotten one minute of that night. She stopped. This was about where she and Damon had parted company after that abortive dance. Even now, a lifetime later, she could recall the burning hurt, the utter misery that had filled her.

But she didn't allow any of the old turmoil to show. Keeping her voice absolutely composed, she said, "It's Auckland's premier venue, the ballroom holds a thousand guests comfortably."

"No."

"No?" She raised an eyebrow at his abrupt refusal, some unkind part of her wanting to make him sweat.

"Absolutely not. While the guests might be comfortable, I most certainly will not." A muscle flexed in his jaw, and his eyes glinted with something that looked like pain.

Perhaps the memory of Fliss, of the happiness they'd

shared that night, was too much? A terrible thought struck her. Had she been wrong all those years ago? Had Damon loved Fliss?

Madly?

Deeply?

Eternally?

And if he had, then he would never accept that she'd simply done what she'd had to the night before his wedding. What she'd believed was right.

"I think you're right," Rebecca conceded, hating the grey tinge that had crept in under his olive tan and hating herself for contributing to it. "It's huge and may be too overwhelming for Demetra. She told me she doesn't want anything too grand."

"Then let's get out of here," Damon said tersely.

Rebecca's second choice of venue was an old, established yacht club that fronted onto the Waitemata Harbour. It was far less imposing, the ballroom more intimate, the view of the water and Auckland's famous Harbour Bridge simply stunning. As the club's function manager guided them around, Damon unclenched his fisted hands and slowly started to relax.

He'd been appalled by the emotion that had smothered him at the San Lorenzo. His towering anger at Rebecca the night of his wedding had come blasting back, an unwelcome reminder of the friction that had existed between them.

Why?

Why had they fought all the time? Why had she insisted on challenging him? Telling him that he couldn't marry Fliss? Provoking him by flaunting her body at him, demanding that he kiss her…and more? And why had he been unable to let the smallest challenge pass?

He could remember wishing Rebecca would behave like Felicity, shy and in awe of him. Felicity had made a lovely bride. But even that memory was tarnished. Somehow he'd failed Felicity. She'd chosen to desert him. Had she known he'd failed her? That he'd betrayed her the night before he spoke his wedding vows?

He'd expected Rebecca to put up a fight against his high-handed veto of the San Lorenzo. Or at least to argue. She'd clearly established a good business relationship with Andre in the past. Yet she'd given in to his demand with barely a murmur. He'd been grateful, silently grateful. How could he, Damon Asteriades, confess that he couldn't bear the idea of celebrating his brother's wedding on the site where his own disastrous marriage had been sealed? Of dancing amidst too many damned ghosts?

Damon told himself he was tagging along to make sure she was fulfilling his mother's brief for the wedding. But he knew it was more than that.

The wanting, the dark desire, had him tied up in knots. And when he'd seen her struggling with the car, the opportunity had been too good to pass up. But he'd also been consumed by curiosity. He'd seen Rebecca the successful chocolate boutique owner, Rebecca the mother and Rebecca the kind friend to an ill older woman. He'd wanted to see more, to see all the facets that made up the enigmatic women who roused such strong responses in him.

As he followed in her wake, Damon had to admit Rebecca was good at what she'd once earned a living doing. Never would he have thought of asking a tenth of the questions listed on her clipboard. Once, she pulled out her cell phone, rang his mother to check whether any wheelchair facilities would be needed and conveyed the negative reply back to their guide. She questioned. She smiled. And each time she laughed, the heat inside Damon grew and he wanted to taste that lush, laughing mouth. *His*. He pushed the disturbing thought aside and watched her jot a note down on a pad. She was focused, professional and totally in charge.

The promise he'd made himself in the hospital car park reared up in his mind. He wanted her. All of her. And there was nothing to stop him having her.

Rebecca finished off, arranging to come back to meet the chef who handled the catering, and Damon reached in his pocket for his car keys. "Well, that's all for now," she told the function manager. "When I return, I will bring the bride to see if the venue fits with her plans."

Rebecca was deep in thought when they returned to the Mercedes. Something bothered her about the yacht club. Something that she couldn't quite put her finger on.

"Time for lunch, I think." Damon's voice interrupted her thoughts.

"Oh, I can't keep you any longer."

"We both need to eat. And there is something I've been wanting to discuss with you. You've been very hard to find, Rebecca, these past couple of days. I might almost think you've been avoiding me."

"Avoiding you?" Her voice was high-pitched. "Why would I do that?"

"If I knew, I wouldn't have had to tag along all morning to get a chance to see you alone."

So he'd stayed because he had an agenda of his own. Rebecca's pulse started to pound. "I don't think—"

"Don't." He held up a hand. "Don't think. Just come and share a meal with me. One of my favourite restaurants is not very far from here. I'll talk. You can listen and savour the food." He gave a slight smile that relieved his usually harsh features.

There'd be more to it than him talking, Rebecca suspected. A frisson slithered down her spine. Yet she was intrigued enough to want to see what kind of establishment he favoured. Even though she knew it was risky. Every minute she spent with him increased the attraction he held. Brought her closer to falling back into the dangerous quagmire of emotions she'd once before barely survived.

Slowly Rebecca nodded her assent.

Not far turned out to be a twenty-minute drive into the country, where Damon finally nosed the Mercedes into a long pohutukawa-lined avenue. The large hand-carved wooden letters against a schist wall announced simply Lakeland Lodge. Through the trees Rebecca caught a glimpse of a large country house and a vast silver sheet of water glittering beyond.

Her breath caught. "How lovely," she breathed.

The lodge radiated serenity. Informal arrangements of country flowers decorated the foyer, and Rebecca paused at a large picture window at the sight of the colourful gardens leading down to the lake.

"What magnificent gardens," she murmured.

Damon smiled. "I thought you'd like it here."

After a moment she took the arm he offered and they made their way to the restaurant, where Damon was greeted with enthusiasm and shown to a table with a fine view of the gardens.

"How on earth did you discover this place?" Rebecca asked after they'd perused the menu and placed their orders.

"In the way one finds out about all best-kept secrets—by word of mouth. I came here to celebrate the silver wedding anniversary of a business acquaintance."

"I never even knew it existed."

"Then I have achieved something. I didn't think there was an establishment in Auckland you didn't know." He gave her a narrow smile. Before Rebecca could retort, their smoked salmon starters arrived and a companionable silence fell between them.

"That was heavenly." She laid her fork down. Taking a deep breath she decided to get whatever he'd brought her here to discuss out of the way. "There is something you wanted to talk about?"

His eyes became serious, intent. His mouth flattened into a grim line. Apprehension flooded Rebecca. She hoped it wasn't what she'd been dreading. Did he suspect…?

Had he worked it out? No, he couldn't have. He'd have given some sign surely. But the gravity of his expression worried her as the seconds dragged past and still he didn't answer.

Just when her nerves reached breaking point, he sighed. "It's something I don't want to admit. Something I've been fighting for longer than I care to think about."

"What is it?" she asked in a rush.

He didn't reply.

The taut pallor of his face scared her. She pinned on a bright smile. "Come on, fess up. It can't be that bad."

Or could it? Was something wrong with Soula? But, no, she'd spoken to Soula only half an hour ago, and the older woman had sounded upbeat, joking that she would be dancing soon, that certainly she would not need a wheelchair.

Could it be…? Was something wrong with Damon? Horror swept her. She thought wildly of James, of the shock after his diagnosis.

"Are you ill?" She blurted it out and could have kicked herself when his eyes widened.

"No, no. Nothing like that. I want you, Rebecca." He blurted thc words out and a blaze of colour stained his angled cheekbones. Her knees went weak at the sight of the naked emotion that flamed in his eyes. Then the controlled mask dropped back into place and she thought she'd hallucinated.

She blinked. Once. Twice. But the remote, powerful businessman remained. Unshakable, hardly the kind of man who would utter such a stark statement with so much haunting desperation.

"What did you say?" she whispered at last as the seconds stretched and the silence grew more strained.

"I want to make love to you." His voice was flat, his face expressionless. He could've been talking about something mundane, something he didn't particularly care much about.

Except she'd seen that hectic, passionate flash of emotion. And a telltale flame of fire still seared his cheeks.

Disbelief floored her. "You can't."

"I'm a man, you're a woman. Why not?" A hint of amusement warmed his eyes, softening his impassive face.

"No." She shook her head wildly.

"Yes."

Spreading her hands apart, she shrugged helplessly. "We can't."

"Why not?" He challenged. "And don't think you can come up with a reason I haven't already thought of and dismissed."

"But—" What was she supposed to say? He'd caught her so off guard she couldn't even think straight. "You don't even *like* me."

He met her eyes levelly. "You're quite right. I didn't think I did."

She flinched, his honesty stinging. "So how can you even contemplate sleeping with me?" There was confusion. Yet somewhere in a deep, hidden part of her, she felt the first hint of rising excitement.

Damon wanted *her*.

"I'm beginning to accept that I must like *something* about you to want you." A ghost of a smile lit his eyes.

Outrage replaced euphoria. "Well, tough! You'll just have to live with the wanting, because nothing is going to happen between us. *It can't*." Did he honestly think she was going to take the scraps that he was throwing to her? Did he think she was that desperate?

Probably.

And he was right. Because she had no pride where Damon Asteriades was concerned. All he had to do was snap his fingers and she came running. Just witness her presence here in Auckland. Witness her presence here in this restaurant today. She'd known it would be a bad idea to spend time with him. But had that stopped her accepting his invitation to lunch?

No. Of course not.

Where Damon Asteriades was concerned, she had the survival instincts of a moth circling a bright flame. But she wasn't ready to be burned alive by him quite yet. No, he was going to have to work a hell of a lot harder. After all, she'd been waiting for him for what seemed like a lifetime. He wasn't going to knock her feet out from under her with a stark statement that he wanted to make love to her. She wanted more. Much, much more.

"Rebecca, stop resisting. I want you and I'm going to have you—the sooner you accept it, the better."

God, but he could be arrogant! "No way. I've been to hell and back because of you before and it's not a place I'm in a hurry to visit again."

He snorted. "You've got that wrong, *koukla. You* almost sent *me* to eternal damnation. You did everything you could to cause upheaval in my life. I meant nothing to you—I don't believe that for a second—it was the challenge that I represented."

You meant everything to me. You were my world, my universe, and you didn't give a damn about me! But she didn't say it aloud.

Instead she shook her head and laughed disbelievingly. "I'm not falling for this."

What was she supposed to say? What was she supposed to think? The man who stirred more emotion within her than she'd known existed *wanted her*. But he fiercely resented the need for her. She'd have to be stupid to take him up on it.

But she was incredibly tempted.

Fool!

Turning him down was going to be the hardest thing she'd ever done. She cast around, struggling to find the words that would drive him away forever.

He reached over the table, covering her hand with his. "Would it help if I told you that over the past few days I've grown to admire you immensely? That I think you have courage and tenacity and a compassion that I am only starting to discover? That I've seen a caring side of you I never knew existed? That I'm starting to think that I may have judged you too harshly sometimes and that I'm sorry for that."

His eyes glowed with sincerity and a warmth she'd never seen before. Underneath his hand, hers felt safe, protected.

Oh, God.

"That I'm starting to like you very much indeed. And that I'd like to get to know you better. Much, much better."

Inside she'd turned to mush. His words pooled in the empty hole below her breastbone and created a warm glow. A hesitant joy started to blossom. She turned her hand upward and threaded her fingers through his.

"Yes," she said slowly. "I rather think it would." And she was half relieved, half frustrated when the waitress arrived at that moment with their main course.

They spent the balance of the meal exploring common interests, neither alluding to the bombshell Damon had dropped. Yet the knowledge of his declaration lay behind every glance, every exchange, and the air between them simmered.

He made her feel like a starry-eyed teenager on her first date. Ridiculous. She had to stop this. If Damon realised how bad she had it…

Rebecca laid her fork down with a clatter, glancing around to avoid meeting Damon's eyes until she'd managed to mask the elated anticipation in hers.

The windows were covered with heavy navy drapes printed with pale flowers that should have looked awful but instead echoed the gardens outside. In the corner stood a grand piano, and along the walls hung exquisite paintings of country scenes. The high ceiling gave a light, airy feel to the place.

"You know," she said suddenly, "this place would be perfect for the wedding."

Damon looked around. A quick dismissive glance. Then she felt the heat as his gaze returned to her face. "You are probably right."

She tried to ignore the pull of his attraction, focused on the idea she'd had.

"No *probably* about it. It *is* perfect!" Rebecca felt the familiar rising excitement which signified that a plan was coming together. "It would mean a smaller guest list than what your mother has planned. But it could work. This room would easily hold four hundred, and the covered veranda could seat another two hundred at least. The gardens are magnificent—Demetra would be in rhapsodies."

She turned to Damon. The instant their eyes met, a shock of awareness arced between them. He gave a slow smile that made her heart turn over. "I can see why you were so good at this business. You have a knack for matching people to places."

"No." She brushed his praise aside, tried to still the thumping of her heart. "It's just listening and observation." But the way he was looking at her intensified, until heat crept into her cheeks.

"You must know all the places, so where would you choose to get married?"

"I didn't know this one," she pointed out. "I have you to thank for that."

His smile stretched, lighting his eyes with a warm, intimate glow. "I cheated. It's only been open for a couple of years. Before that it was a private estate. You couldn't have known about it. You were up in Northland when it opened. Now tell me about your dream wedding."

"My dream wedding?" She stared at him, bemused.

"You used to successfully plan everyone else's—" he grinned "—dream occasions. What would you do for yourself?"

She laughed. "I blew it. Aaron and I had a civil wedding. No big deal." Aaron had wanted to get married the instant she'd said yes. There hadn't even been time to think, much less plan an elaborate A-list wedding.

Something moved in his blue eyes. "Okay, then fantasize. Tell me what you wish you'd done."

"My fantasy wedding..." Rebecca paused a moment, looking away from the beautiful blue gaze to gather her thoughts. "Well, for starters, I wouldn't need all this." She gestured to the high sash windows, the rich country-house decor. "I'd want something simple, just a ceremony and some time afterward with the man I married—the man I loved." She threw him a quick glance. "Too often weddings are tense occasions, and the bride is stressed half to death. I'd want time with the man I love to reflect on the solemn importance of the vows we'd just taken. I'd want them to be very, very permanent."

She could see she'd surprised him with her outburst. He looked startled. She'd revealed more about herself than she'd ever intended. For a moment she thought he was about to argue with her. To lighten the mood, she gave a light laugh and a shrug. "A fantasy is all it is. I won't be getting married."

"Why not?" He was frowning now, his eyes a clear, cool blue.

"I've already been married."

The blue clouded over. "That's a good reason not to marry again?"

She didn't want to talk about her marriage. Not to Damon. She shrugged again. "So what other reason is there? Children, I suppose. I've already got T.J."

"That's not the only reason people marry. There are things like companionship, understanding, love—"

"Oh, don't tell me you believe in all that fairy-tale stuff, Damon?" Rebecca interrupted, her smile sharp as she struggled not to let irony creep through.

"That's why Savvas and Demetra are getting married." He sat back, stirring his coffee.

"Yes, but they aren't like us. We're realists. We've seen the grittier side of life. Marriage is a financial deal, exchanging wealth for fidelity, the promise of children, isn't it?" It hurt to play devil's advocate, but it was nothing more than what Damon believed.

"God, you are cynical." He glared at her. "But even if you believe that, there's still sex. That's another reason people like *you* and *me*—" he drawled the words "—marry."

"Sex?" That one word was all it took. Her heartbeat took off, thundering inside her rib cage, her breathing shallow.

"Yes, hot sweaty sex. Body rubbing against body—"

"Oh, that kind of sex," she interrupted with a dismissive flutter of her hand, determined to put a stop to this before she started to pant, before he saw what he was doing to her. "But, Damon, I don't need to marry, I simply need to take a lover for that kind of sex."

Damon went rigid, his face a tight mask.

"And there have been many lovers?"

If he only knew!

She fluttered her eyelashes. "I *never* kiss and tell."

"No, of course you don't!" Disbelief underscored his derogatory words. "But you do kiss?"

"Oh, yes," she said breathlessly. "I can kiss."

The next thing she knew, he was out of his chair, beside her, leaning over. And then his mouth slanted across hers.

And she went up in flames.

There was no tenderness. It was a kiss that burned with hunger, desperation and need. He tasted of coffee, of cream, of everything she'd ever desired.

When he finally pulled away, he said slowly, "Oh, yes, you can kiss, all right."

There were betraying flags of heat across his cheekbones, his breath came in rapid bursts and his eyes glittered.

"Perhaps it *is* time you took a lover," he said darkly.

"Perhaps," she replied, bravely holding his gaze. "I'll need to start looking around."

"Oh no!" He was shaking his head, his teeth bared in a feral grin. "No, *koukla*, you will look no farther than me. I am going to be your lover."

Six

Hours later Rebecca still couldn't believe that she hadn't told Damon to go to blazes. Instead she'd retreated into a dazed silence, illicit excitement fluttering deep inside her belly. On the way home, Rebecca sank back into the rich butter-coloured leather seat and closed her eyes. She felt the touch of Damon's glance from time to time, but he didn't speak. An oppressive, sweltering awareness filled the Mercedes.

The moment the car swept into the drive of the Asteriades mansion, Rebecca sat up, muttered her thanks and, before they'd come to a standstill, bolted from the car. Hurrying to her room, she spent the next couple of hours—until Demetra and T.J. came home—making lists of what would be needed for the wedding, calls that needed to be made about brides-maids' dresses, flowers, catering. Anything to keep busy and stop herself thinking about Damon's outrageous proposition. Anything to keep her as far away from him as possible.

I am going to be your lover.

The arrogant statement still rang in her ears that evening as she helped T.J. into the bath. Contrarily, she was almost disappointed that Damon hadn't followed up, hadn't battered down the door to find out where she'd hidden herself all afternoon.

He was messing with her head. Why hadn't he sought her out?

Why had he made such a passionate proclamation in the first place?

He hated her.

But he'd said he'd actually come to like her. Rebecca closed her eyes to block out the confusion that whirled round and round inside her head. Without end. When she opened them again, T.J. was staring at her, holding out a soapy sponge. She took it and started to wash him.

"Mummy," T.J.'s piping voice cut into her dilemma. "Demetra's going to get big, fat fish with shiny—" he hesitated "—skin."

"Scales," Rebecca corrected automatically. T.J. had returned from his day with Demetra happy, tired and covered in mud, showing no sign that he'd missed her at all. Rebecca had heard all about the ducks in the park pond and about the fishpond he'd helped the workmen dig out at Demetra's soon-to-be home.

Her mind slid back into the rut it couldn't get out of. How could Damon change from hate to something as insipid as *like?* And how dare she be so grateful that he actually liked her, that he wanted to get to know her better. How could she be tempted to settle for that?

Damon said he wanted to be her lover. *Why?*

Yet, deep in the throbbing darkness of her womb, she knew. Chemistry. This thing between them that would never rest until it was sated. Liking her, getting to know her, was nothing more than a line.

A line to get her into his bed. Somehow he'd fathomed what she wanted more than anything in the world—his respect, his admiration…to be *liked* by him.

Pathetic.

A splash of water brought her back to reality. T.J. giggled.

She gave a mock growl and pulled his wet, wriggling body toward her. With one hand she reached for a towel and swaddled T.J., patting him dry.

What on earth was she going to do?

"And Demetra's got a net to the pond so the birds can't eat the fish."

She dragged her attention back to T.J. "No, if a heron took them, that would not be good." She started to towel T.J.'s hair.

"We fed ducks at the park. Very greedy ducks," he said reprovingly. "Demetra said next time we'll take two breads."

Just a few days and already T.J. was at home here in the bosom of Damon's family. It would be a wrench when the time came to go back home. He would feel bereft. Rebecca pressed a hasty kiss to the top of his head as misgivings quaked through her.

"Mummy, can we make a fishpond? Get some fish? And ducks? Please?"

"We'll see." Rebecca tried to smile. Perhaps a pond would help him adjust to the separation. T.J. was at that age where creatures and water fascinated him. He kept her on her toes during excursions, feeding ducks in the park ponds and peering into rock pools at the sea's edge. In a couple of years she'd have to buy him a fishing rod.

That was when he was going to miss having a father. What did she know about fishing, about hooks and sinkers and bait, after all? Rebecca sighed and hung up the towel. When she turned around, she saw T.J. had put on his pyjama bottoms back to front. She moved to help him.

"No, me do it," he said with a three-year-old's fierce determination.

She shook her head. Her baby was growing up—too fast—with no father figure to give him guidance. But he had her. He didn't need anyone else. And, as she had told Damon earlier, she had no reason for marrying. Ever. Especially not for sex.

And she was *not* going to be Damon's lover.

* * *

The weekend passed in a rush. On Saturday, Rebecca ushered T.J. into the dining room to find Damon had discarded his corporate attire and was wearing a pair of faded Levi's, a Ralph Lauren T-shirt in plain white…and a devastating smile aimed right at her.

Her stomach started doing somersaults.

"On Monday, I fly to L.A. on business, so I thought we might go for a picnic today."

Her heart sank. "But I wanted to spend time with T.J. I've barely seen—"

"Of course T.J. will come, too." Damon gestured to a wicker hamper she hadn't noticed. "Jane has already filled that with treats."

"Picnic, picnic," T.J. chanted, jumping up and down.

"He'll love that," Rebecca said, wondering why Damon was doing this.

They spent the day at Goat Island, a marine reserve an hour's drive out of Auckland. The sun was hot enough to prickle, and the sea frothed onto the curve of beach below the pohutukawa trees.

"It's hard to believe the city is so near," Rebecca commented as she and Damon stood in the shallows, the sea sand squishing through her toes and T.J. squealing with delight when blue mau-mau flashed between his ankles.

"When he is older, he can snorkel to the island." Damon pointed at the rocky outcrop that gave the reserve its name and sheltered the bay from the open sea.

Rebecca laughed. "He'll love that. He's a real water baby."

At noon they ate the delicious fare Jane had prepared, and afterward Rebecca lazed on a towel, her head propped against a beach bag, watching Damon and T.J. build sand castles. T.J. bubbled with joy and Damon, well, Damon took her breath away. From behind the protective cover of her sunshades she eyed the hard curves of his chest muscles, the flat abs and the muscled thighs kneeling in the sand. Her breathing picked up. She couldn't deny the effect he had on her.

Finally she admitted the truth to herself: she wanted him. She glanced away and focused on the waves licking the beach and struggled to remind herself that Damon was downright *dangerous.* She'd drowned in his attraction before. Why should it be any different this time?

Yet later, when he invited her out to dinner, she called herself all kinds of fool and accepted with a flush of pleasure. That night, after T.J. had been put to bed, they paid a short visit to Soula, leaving Demetra and Savvas to babysit. Soula took one look at the layered gypsy-style skirt and off-the-shoulder top that Rebecca wore and her gaze sharpened.

"You two going out?" she asked coyly.

"We have reservations at Shipwrecks. I promised Rebecca seafood tonight—"

"We took T.J. to Goat Island for the day," Rebecca said hastily, before Soula got the wrong idea. "I bewailed the fact that we could not fish in the reserve. So Damon insisted on taking me out for dinner."

"I see," Soula smiled sphinxlike, leaving Rebecca to wonder what she did indeed see.

Dinner passed in a haze. Damon was wonderful company. His eyes gleamed with appreciation when she spoke and he laughed often, his lips curving into that smile that made her knees go weak.

Rebecca had to remind herself that she had no intention of being charmed, of allowing Damon Asteriades to become her lover. Yet she didn't want the evening to end. But she knew it would and she rather suspected she knew how he intended it to end. So she was more than a little disconcerted when he said good-night to her outside her bedroom door without even brushing his lips across her cheek.

On Sunday morning he was waiting, a trip to the zoo planned this time. T.J. was in his element. He ran around, his eyes wide as he gazed at lions, elephants, rhinos, while Rebecca spent the day trying to keep her eyes off Damon. He appeared unaware of her growing tension, laughing with T.J. at the antics of the spider monkeys and the otters, oblivious of her acute sensitivity to the lightest brush of his hand.

That evening, after T.J. fell into bed, sun-flushed and tired, Rebecca couldn't help wondering where it was all going to end…and what on earth had happened to Damon's declaration that he wanted her.

After a hectic day escorting Demetra to half a dozen dress designers, Rebecca was surprised to find Damon at the dinner table on Monday night. Demetra was regaling Savvas and Damon with stories about how terrible the day had been, how she'd been tangled in yards of fabric and had pins stuck into her. Rebecca started to laugh.

"It's all your fault," Demetra accused, her eyes sparkling.

"Admit it—you enjoyed yourself." Rebecca sat down between Savvas and Damon. T.J. was already in bed, fast asleep.

"Much more than I thought I would," Demetra conceded. "You knew what I would like."

"That's my job." Rebecca grinned at Demetra. Then to Damon, she said, "I thought you were flying out on a business trip today." She glanced down at the slice of melon on her plate. The last thing she wanted was Damon cottoning on to the fact that his every movement obsessed her.

"He was supposed to go to the States," Savvas responded. "But he's delayed it. He's got everyone in a flap about it because he needs to meet one of our American stakeholders."

"Next week." Damon's voice was short. "I told you I'll go next week."

"I can't understand what's so important that you have to be in Auckland this week."

"Don't worry yourself about it," Damon said in a peculiar tone.

Rebecca shot him a casual glance and froze. He was staring at her, his eyes burning. Her breath caught. Her pulse started to hammer. And she knew.

She was the reason he'd postponed his trip. Disjointed thoughts whirred round in her brain. So why hadn't he made a move on her? Why the outings with T.J. on the weekend and the dinner out if all he wanted was hot, sweaty sex?

She wished she could see inside his head, fathom what he was thinking.

But his intentions became no clearer with each day that followed. Each evening Damon would come home, play a little with her and T.J. and Demetra—sometimes Savvas would be there, too—and afterward he'd take her out. Once it was to see a movie she'd idly mentioned wanting to see, a couple of times he took her to dinner and on Thursday night he took her to a jazz concert. He was attentive, amusing and charming—a far cry from the hostile, critical man of the past. Rebecca was discovering a side of him that she'd never known existed. A side of him that made her crave more time in his company.

This was what she'd wanted—Damon to like her. For herself.

So that she could tell him the truth, so that he would believe she'd done what she had for the best reasons in the world, a little mischievous voice whispered. Because she'd wanted to spare him. But the man staring at her oozed confidence and power and far too much sex appeal for his own good. Her heart jolted. The blue eyes seared her, making her burn up inside and convincing her to push aside the little voice. Just a few days longer, she told herself, then she'd tell him. A few precious days to treasure this connection between them.

Because she knew it wouldn't last.

By Friday night Rebecca was ready to crack. It had been a busy week and she'd gotten lots done on the wedding. But it wasn't the wedding that had her in a tizz, it was Damon. Aside from the occasional hand under her elbow, he hadn't touched her, hadn't kissed her, and it was driving her mad.

She was confused. Out of her depth.

And she suspected he knew it.

They were meeting at seven on the deck for a drink. She'd forgotten to ask what they were doing tonight, forgotten to check if Demetra and Savvas could babysit T.J. No doubt Damon had it all under control. Like everything else in his life—including her.

Rebecca wasn't sure if she could endure another night out with the perfect escort…leaving her uncertain and yearning for more afterward.

It was seven o'clock on the dot when Rebecca stepped out through the ranch sliders onto the spacious raised deck overlooking the long sunken pool that reflected the crimson rays of the sinking sun.

Something tightened in Damon's chest as she paused, stilling for an instant before she stepped forward. A pair of black pants in a soft fabric swirled around her legs, and she wore high strappy sandals that made her look tall and lithe and incredibly sexy. His gazed moved up to the peacock-blue shirt that hugged her lush breasts, lingering briefly at the unbuttoned vee neckline where a blue opal set in gold dangled against her creamy skin. His brows contracted at the sight of the expensive pendant. *Soon she would be his.* She would wear jewellery he bought for her, not baubles from other men.

He leashed the primal wave of possessiveness that flooded him and jerked his eyes back to her face. "A punctual woman," he drawled. "A pearl beyond price."

She looked unsettled. Then she smiled her slow, sexy smile and heat kicked through him. He forgot about the opal, about the man who'd bought it for her.

"Old habits die hard," she said, sitting down on the chair he'd drawn up for her and taking the glass of white wine he held out with a smile of thanks.

"Yes, I remember that about you. You always had a reputation for being professional in your business dealings." He frowned. Her private reputation had been very different indeed.

A shadow fell across her face.

"What are you thinking?" He couldn't rid himself of this compulsion to delve into her thoughts, crawl under her skin to find out what made her tick.

"Nothing," she said. She touched the opal at her neck.

"Tell me."

She drew a breath. "It was Aaron who drilled the importance of punctuality into me. Your comment made me remember how much he taught me."

Damon forced himself not to glance at the pendant. He didn't want to think about her dead husband any more than he wanted to think about his dead wife. He didn't want the past or the future intruding. All he wanted was tonight—and the intriguing woman sitting beside him.

His woman. From tonight.

Until he tired of her. As he knew he would. It couldn't be otherwise.

He moved his chair closer and changed the subject. "What do you think of the wine?"

Rebecca lifted the glass to her lips. "Mmm. Buttery. Like a good Chardonnay should be." She held the glass up against the last rays of the evening light. The liquid turned to pure gold. "Good colour, too." Another sip. "Chilled. There's a hint of something else there…something slightly sweet."

"Melon? Pineapple?" Damon found he enjoyed teasing her.

She slanted him a wry look. "Honey, I think."

"Honey?"

Honey reminded him of that too-brief kiss they'd shared

at lunch the other day. She had tasted of honey. Sweet. Addictive. He could feel his eyes darkening, could feel the heavy languor in his limbs as he remembered the desire that had forked through him.

Rebecca had gone utterly still, caught in the same intense thrall that ensnared him. She gave a shiver and rubbed her arms.

"Cold?" he asked softly. But he knew it wasn't cold that had caused the rows of goose bumps that disappeared under the sleeves of her shirt. It was excitement. The same raw excitement that writhed within him.

She shook her head.

"Rebecca—"

"Where's Demetra?" she interrupted. "Where's Savvas?"

He sat back, forced himself to relax, to take it slowly. One step at a time. "Demetra said she wanted to see glowworms, so Savvas whipped her away to Waitomo. They plan to go blackwater rafting as well. They won't be back until Sunday afternoon at the earliest." He grinned wickedly. "There's no need to wait up for them."

"What about Jane? I'd hate to think she's waiting for us to eat." Rebecca sounded rattled. She took another quick sip of wine, leaned forward to set her glass down on the patio table.

He moved closer, enjoying her loss of composure. He wanted to see her abandon her cool, her poise. "Jane left about half an hour ago for the weekend. She prepared a cold spread. We'll eat when you're ready. The night is still young."

"And Johnny?"

"Johnny's gone to tea at his daughter's—he is a grandfather twice over now. He'll be back tomorrow."

He waited.

She didn't disappoint him. Her eyes widened, darkening as the import of his words struck her. "That means..." Her voice became husky, trailed off.

"That we are alone."

She stared wordlessly at him, her eyes huge, dark and velvety.

He placed a hand over hers. Her fingers were icy. "Except for T.J.—"

"He's…he's sleeping," she stuttered.

"Then, yes, we are alone."

She shuddered convulsively.

He let his fingers stroke over the back of her hand, softly, over her pale bare wrists, up her arm. The sleek, silky material of her sleeve clung to his fingers. His hand rested against the soft skin of her throat and then he placed his index finger under her chin. Her head tilted up.

Her lovely eyes were wary, but beneath the uncertainty there was a flare of fire.

"You know what I plan to do, don't you?"

"Yes." A whisper.

But it was enough for Damon. He bent forward until only an infinitesimal space separated them. "I'm going to kiss you," he murmured.

He brushed her lips.

Lightly.

It was a kiss meant to tease. Except it backfired on him. Instead of teasing her, it made him want more. Much, much more.

When Rebecca sighed, her lips parting, Damon could wait no longer. With a hungry groan he took her mouth, possessing it. He forgot to take it slowly, he forgot to be patient, he forgot about courting her. His tongue swept in to taste her sweetness. Like honey, wild and golden. And then he forgot everything as the hot fury of passion rushed over him.

He pulled her toward him, onto his lap.

Her body was soft, feminine against the hard planes of his, he was aware that she was moaning, and the sound spurred him on. To taste deeper. To kiss wilder.

After a while—he didn't know how long—he lifted his

head. His hands were shaking. He struggled with the button at her neckline. It gave. He slid his hand in and cupped her breast. Heard her breath catch.

The tip was hard against his fingers. He caught it between his fingertips, caressed it softly, circling the sensitive bud.

She gasped again. He covered her mouth. Devoured her. This time her tongue was wild against his, rubbing, playing, arousing.

He touched her, working the nipple, feeling the frantic bursts of shivers that ripped through her. He was hard under his jeans. Every time she wriggled her bottom in his lap he moaned, growing hotter and hotter.

His breathing was ragged when he forced himself to pull back.

Unbelievable. The desire that surged made him feel like a boy. Hasty. Impulsive. Out of control.

"Come." He rose to his feet, letting her slide down the length of his chest, aware of every soft curve of her pliant body. Taking her hand, he led her toward the open ranch sliders, where voile curtains billowed.

"Where—?"

"It will be warmer inside, the sea breeze is rising."

"What—"

Her eyes were wild, blind with passion.

"Tonight…I'm going to become your lover."

She gaped at him.

He wanted her to know, to know who he was and what was going to happen between. "Your lover, Rebecca."

"Yes."

That was what he'd been waiting for. Her capitulation. Her total commitment. He wanted her willing, he wanted her wanton. Because he intended to make her lose every vestige of control, he wanted to see the woman under the facade. The woman none of her other lovers had seen.

He wanted her as far out of control as he was.

* * *

"Your skin is so soft." His touch was surprisingly tender as he parted the final buttons of her shirt. He drew an exploratory finger across her torso, under her breasts, and a line of fire followed.

Rebecca lay on his bed fully clothed, only her sandals kicked off…and the necklace that Damon had removed with impatient, shaking fingers. Her head spun from the kisses he'd pressed on her mouth, her cheeks, her neck. Yet nothing had prepared her for this…

His touch.

The fire.

She caught her lip between her teeth, fought the wild sensation that arced through her.

"Tell me what you like, what turns you on. I want to know everything about you." His hand slid under her bra, brushed across the nipple. She stopped breathing.

"You like that?" Something akin to triumph glittered in his eyes.

She suppressed the urge to nod and stared at him, hoping her eyes didn't reveal what he was doing to her or how much she'd craved his touch.

But her body gave her away.

"You love it!" He drew that teasing finger back over the dark tip, and the nipple tightened, bringing a prickle close to pain. Rebecca groaned.

Damon pushed her shirt aside, off her shoulders, slid his hand behind her and then her breasts were free. "Beautiful. Such fullness, such softness." He touched the curves with strong hands that were oddly gentle.

Against her will, her back arched, pushing her breasts into his hands. Damon stared as if transfixed, then his head dropped and his mouth closed over the peak.

The sensation that exploded within Rebecca was like nothing she'd ever felt before. It flashed through her belly, between her legs, heating her, setting her on fire.

A groan burst from her as his tongue flicked. Another flick. Another flash of fire.

A groan tore from her throat.

He lifted his head, and the expression on his face caused her mouth to dry. Desire stretched his face into a pagan mask. His eyes gleamed and the curve of his mouth was softened by passion. His whole attention focused on her.

Nothing but her.

This was the man she'd always craved.

She twisted her hips, and he seemed to know exactly what she wanted because he shifted so that his weight covered her, heavy and erotic.

The hardness of his erection filled the cradle between her legs as if it belonged, the other half of her. Heat ignited. She leaned forward, kissed his cheek hungrily, following the line of his jaw to nuzzle behind his ear, heard him moan and let her lips open against his neck. He tasted salty, male. She licked him, eager to taste more.

His big, strong body shuddered against her. He moved against her, the hardness beneath his jeans sliding against the soft mound covered by her satin black pants.

She felt the zip give, then his hand was moving in wide sweeps and her pants and panties were gone. A rasp of a second zipper and his jeans and shirt followed suit. Their bare legs tangled, his male and muscled against the softness of her thighs.

Her legs jerked apart. Instantly he edged into the space. The maddening friction notched higher, driving her wilder and wilder, up and up, heat and want and a ceaseless pressure spiralling within her.

Restlessly she spread her legs wider still.

"You're hot for me."

She didn't speak, didn't respond to his harsh statement,

simply rotated her hips against him and tried to get closer, closer, so that he could touch the heart of her.

"You want me, don't you?"

Something in the insistence of his tone brought her down a little. Opening her eyes, she found his face above hers, his blue eyes boring into hers.

"Say it, Rebecca! Tell me how much you want me."

"I want you…."

"I want more. Tell me more."

More? She shook herself. What did he want?

His face was taut, sweat glowing on his cheekbones. There was no hint of softness. No tenderness. No l—

Surely Damon couldn't be waiting for her to tell him she loved him. Or could he? Could she expose herself to him? Give him that kind of power over her?

Dare she risk it?

She tilted her pelvis, firming the taut connection between them. He gasped, closed his eyes, threw his head back.

"God, what you do to me!"

Exhilarated, she moved again.

"Why, dammit? Why you?" The cry was filled with ecstasy and agony. And revealed a vulnerability that she knew he'd never have shown any other time. A vulnerability she was certain he'd regret revealing later.

Suddenly Rebecca knew what he wanted. Snaking her arms around his neck, she pulled his head down to hers. "It's mutual. I want you, too, Damon, more than I've ever wanted anyone," she whispered.

"Anyone?"

"Anyone," she vowed.

"Much more?"

"Much, much more," she affirmed, her arms tightening fiercely.

He gave a hissing sigh and sank into her.

Rebecca cried out.

She told herself he cared for her. He wouldn't be doing this if he didn't. Not like this. He wouldn't be so determined that it should be…more…than ever before if it meant nothing to him.

This was something he'd never felt before. She had to believe that. Otherwise…

He started to move. She shuddered, opened herself wider, forcing the junction of her thighs close to him, trying to become one with him.

He lowered his torso, the contact sensitising her breasts until she almost cried out again. She bit down hard on her bottom lip, wildly conscious of the heat rising deep within in her.

The pressure where their bodies joined was growing…growing…the heat rising higher. She could bear it no more. She ground herself against him, heard him gasp, felt his shudders.

"I can't hold back," he panted.

"Come," she whispered. "Come with me. Stay with me. Always." He opened his eyes. She read confusion. She moved, slow and sinuous, and the confusion vanished. There was passion and heat in the blue depths…and something deep and unfathomable.

And then all rational thought vanished and the shivers seized her. She fell through layers of sensation, felt his body freeze, then release into pulsing convulsions as he came deep within her.

Afterward they dozed for a while. When Rebecca woke, the red digital numbers on Damon's bedside clock revealed that it was after midnight.

"T.J." She leaped from the pile of scattered bedclothes.

Damon caught her hand. "He's still sleeping, I checked. Stay."

The heat in his eyes, the hoarseness in his voice told her what he intended.

"I can't." She looked away. And she felt herself weakening, but guilt ate at her.

"Rebecca, I want you." His admission caused her to melt. She turned to him. No words were necessary. Before she'd lain down, he fell on her. This time their loving was wild, uncontrolled. There were no barriers between them. No past. No future. Only the present.

Yet she knew that soon a new day would dawn. Tomorrow…tomorrow they would talk. She could delay no longer, she had to tell him the truth.

When the first pale strands of daylight slid into the room Rebecca rose and pulled on her clothes. Damon slept, his breathing deep and rhythmic. Standing beside him, she resisted the urge to kiss the shadowed groove under his jaw and touch the smooth curve of his shoulder. Instead she picked her pendant off his bedstand and, leaving her feet bare, padded to the door, sandals in hand, and quietly shut the door behind her.

Once in her room, she crossed to the adjacent dressing room. The dawn cast a soft pink glow across the walls. T.J. had tossed the bedclothes off and lay on his stomach, his face turned to the door. She bent and brushed a kiss on his brow, whispered "I love you," then pulled the blankets up to cover him.

She didn't go to bed immediately but stood at the open window of her room staring at the rosy streaks lightening the darkness, the pendant clutched in her hand. Something in Damon's eyes had told her that he didn't care for the pendant. She would not wear it again. It was time to say goodbye to Aaron, to think about the future.

And Damon.

Last night had been the most tender, the most passionate, the most incredible experience of her life.

She'd gone wild in Damon's arms. She feared she'd revealed too much. How would he react when he next saw her? Oh, God. How was she going to tell him what she knew she had to? He was going to hate her. After last night, she didn't know how she could go back to that half-life where he despised her.

She turned from the window. Carefully she placed the pendant in the jewel box on her dressing table and closed the lid. The rasp of the hasp sounded so final. Rebecca placed a kiss of her fingertips and let them linger for a moment on the carved lid.

After a brief sojourn to the bathroom, Rebecca donned her nightgown, aware of her body aching in unaccustomed places. A pleasurable ache. Her thoughts shifted to Damon. She could barely believe what had taken place between them.

The passion. The frenzy.

Yet there had been gentleness, too. She slipped between the Egyptian cotton sheets and let herself remember. The first time his touch had been so careful, tender even. So far removed from how he'd treated her in the past. Whether that tenderness would still be there after they talked, she was too scared to even think about.

Tomorrow would come soon enough.

Seven

The sound of screaming woke Rebecca.

Shrill, childish screams followed by a chilling silence. The door to T.J.'s room stood wide-open and her bedroom door was ajar onto the corridor. She leaped up, the thick mists of sleep falling rapidly away.

"T.J.?"

There was no answer. Fear galvanised her into action. She hurtled into his room. Trains lay scattered across the carpet. Thomas…Henry…Gordon. A wild glance took in T.J.'s favourites. But no T.J.

Terror released a wave of adrenaline, her knees turning to liquid. Rebecca burst out into the corridor, uncaring that she still wore nightclothes.

"T.J.!" Rebecca was yelling now, her voice hoarse with shock. She rushed down the stairs. At the bottom she paused. The large double-height lobby led to the solid carved front door and beyond that lay the road. To the right lay Soula's rooms, and in the opposite direction another corridor led to the entertainment rooms and the kitchen.

She heard shouts. An adult this time. Coming from outside. It sounded like…Johnny. A swift glance at her watch showed her that it was a little before seven.

She started to run.

A large male form brushed past her. A blur of flesh wearing only a pair of boxers and moving at breakneck speed.

Damon.

Then he was gone, tearing into the lounge as if all the hounds of hell were after him.

Rebecca had a brief recollection of billowing curtains, of the open ranch sliders, and a sick, swirling sense of horror filled her.

"Please, no. Oh, God. *T.J.*" She burst out onto the deck in time to see Damon disappear under the water, heard the resounding splash. Her shell-shocked gaze swept the deck, the pool.

Where was T.J.?

Johnny was also in the water. Incongruous in his sodden black blazer and limp tie, his thinning hair plastered to his scalp, his eyes worried.

So where was T.J.?

Someone was screaming, an unending, unearthly howl of grief. Johnny held up a hand, beckoning urgently. Only then did Rebecca realise it was her—she was screaming. Wailing. The scream died abruptly. She scurried to the water's edge.

"Wait," Johnny shouted. "Don't jump in. Call the ambulance. Call Dr. Campbell—his number is on the handset. The boss will get the youngster out."

Shaking with reaction, she ran blindly back to the lobby, snatched up the cordless phone and dialled 111 with fumbling fingers. "Hurry, hurry," she prayed, and dry sobs of relief racked her when the operator came on the line.

Rebecca gave the details and the location in a blur. Her fingers shook as she punched out the next number. Dr. Campbell's receptionist promised to send him immediately.

Rebecca rushed out onto the deck again, dropping the handset at the sight of Damon emerging from the water, T.J. struggling in his arms.

T.J. Her baby was alive! Her vision blurred. She scrubbed at her eyes and her hands came away wet. She tore across to where Damon was laying T.J. down on the terra-cotta pavers. T.J. was retching and then the screaming started—the most welcome sound Rebecca had ever heard.

"I'm here, baby." Rebecca fell to her knees. A tear plopped onto T.J.'s pale skin, mingling with rivulets of water from the pool. "Thank God."

"T.J. Oh, T.J., I am so sorry."

The ambulance and Dr. Campbell had been and gone. T.J. lay on the couch, asleep, exhausted from the toll the shock and the crying jag had taken on his system. Rebecca hunched over her son, her back tense and shaking, her anguish palpable. From time to time she stroked T.J. with hands that trembled, as if to assure herself he was alive.

Rebecca who never cried.

Coming to a decision, Damon strode to her. Without giving her an opportunity to resist, he swept her into his arms. Crossing to the sofa opposite the one T.J. occupied, he lowered himself, fitting Rebecca into his lap.

"Dr. Campbell says he's fine."

"I know, but I can't seem to stop. When I think what might have happened…God!" Her whole body started to shake.

Holding her, he rocked her. "Don't think. It achieves nothing."

She drew a deep, heaving breath and buried her face in his chest, into the black T-shirt he'd hurriedly shrugged on after Dr. Campbell had checked T.J. out.

He braced himself for more tears. "Hush, you'll make yourself ill."

No tears came, but the tremors grew worse. "You don't understand. I nearly lost him."

He did understand. How to tell her? He hated the helplessness that swamped him. Nothing he could say, do, would take away her pain. In silent sympathy he tightened his arms around her and said inadequately, "He'll be fine."

She sniffed against his chest. "It's my fault."

"No, it's mine. I should have thought about that door." Damon stared bleakly over her head. Last night he'd plotted the seduction of the woman he held in his arms. He'd been so intent on her, on his pleasure, that he'd forgotten about the blasted sliders. After he'd promised Rebecca they would remain locked at all times, he'd let her down. Rebecca's son had paid for his carelessness.

Nearly with his life.

"It should never have happened," she choked.

"It won't happen again." He went cold as he relived those horrible moments.

"I mean—" she lifted her woebegone face "—it wouldn't have happened if I'd been a better mother."

The immaculate mask had been torn away. Still clad in her nightie, her hair tangled, her eyes red-rimmed from crying, she had never looked more vulnerable nor more beautiful.

He brushed his lips across her smooth brow. "Don't blame yourself. If anyone is at fault, it's me for assuming that it would be simple to keep the sliders closed—after all, they latch automatically. I know better now. And I know that you couldn't possibly be a better mother."

She hiccupped. "I'm a terrible mother. I'm a total failure as a mother, I always knew I would be. I've failed—"

"Rebecca." He gave her a shake. "Listen to me! No one can doubt your commitment to T.J. You're patient, loving. What more could a child want?"

But instead of calming her, his praise simply made her sob, her dark eyes spilling tears that wrenched his heart.

"I don't deserve T.J."

"You know, if you'd asked me four years ago what kind of

mother I thought you'd be, I would have said appalling. Selfish. But I've watched you with T.J. You've astounded me. You've impressed me. I admire your patience. Even when he's being downright difficult, you always do the right thing."

"I'm not a natural mother."

"You could have fooled me." With a gentle hand, he stroked her hair.

But the gesture did little to calm her. Instead she only cried harder. "You don't understand!"

"Try me."

"No. I can't." She sat up in his lap, shaking her head wildly so that her long hair whipped around her tear-drenched face. "There are things…things I haven't told you. Things you should've known before we…before we slept together."

"Shush. Don't worry about that now."

"I must." Her teeth were clattering. "Ignoring it won't make it go away. I'm so scared—"

He yanked her back against his chest, so close that he could feel her hot breath against his chest. He scanned her uptilted features, concerned about the misery, the guilt he read there. "Stop this. You'll make yourself ill!"

Remorse flashed across her face, making her look even more wretched. "And then what good will I be to T.J.?"

"That can't be self-pity I hear, is it? Come on, buckle up."

She gave him a watery smile. "You mean buck up."

He shrugged. "Whatever."

Rebecca made a valiant effort to pull herself together. Pulling away, she perched on the edge of his lap and examined him. "*Whatever?* You're always so formal I sometimes forget that you only arrived here in New Zealand when you were—what—eight? Nine?"

"Ten," he corrected, looking surprised at the change of subject. "My father saw New Zealand as a land of opportunity. When I arrived, neither Savvas nor I could speak any English. Where were you when you were ten, Rebecca?"

"With the Austins. They were one of the better foster families I stayed with." But that was when she'd been parted from James. The Austins had two daughters and didn't want to foster boys. They hadn't minded taking two girls into care. The other girl had been Fliss. Poor shell-shocked Fliss who had recently lost her parents in a freak boating accident. Separated from James for the first time in her life, Rebecca had shared Fliss's bewildered sense of loss. It had been natural that the two of them had clung to each other.

"How many foster homes did you stay in?"

"Altogether? Four," she said bleakly.

He pulled her back into his arms. "You know, T.J. is very fortunate to have you for a mother."

"No, I'm the lucky one. It's easy to love him." She glanced up at him as she spoke and her eyes were luminous with profound emotion, and for an instant Damon felt a pang of envy at her bond of love with the child. He pushed it aside.

His voice rough with emotion, he said, "You're a wonderful mother. I've watched you. Never think you're a failure as a mother."

Wonder lit her eyes. "Thank you, Damon. That means a lot to me. More than you could ever know, because my mother abandoned James and me, and we never knew who fathered us."

"You're not your mother. You've done wonders. He's a son to be proud of." He brushed a kiss across the top of her head. It didn't matter who her parents were. But it explained her fierce determination to be independent. Every word he'd spoken was true. She *had* surprised him. At first he'd assumed the mothering thing was all an elaborate act. An empty charade. But slowly he'd seen the depth of her love for T.J., and for some reason the bond between them highlighted the emptiness of his own life. He'd enjoyed the trip to Goat Island, the visit to the zoo. Much to his astonishment, Damon found *he* wanted to be included in the intimate moments of warmth they shared, to be part of the unbreakable bond.

Rebecca stayed close to T.J. all day.

Damon had carried him upstairs to his room and he'd slept until well after midday. When T.J. finally awoke, he'd been tearful and told Rebecca emphatically that he never, ever wanted to swim ever again.

Hugging his shivering body, Rebecca hoped that it would be a temporary aversion and made a mental note to arrange him a course of swimming lessons after a little time had elapsed. Then they'd settled down to play with the brightly painted trains on the wooden tracks.

Several hours later a light rap at the door caused them both to raise their heads. The door swung open. Damon stood there looking oddly hesitant. "Dr. Campbell just rang. The hospital is discharging my mother tomorrow morning."

"You must be thrilled." Rebecca gave up trying to manoeuvre Gordon through the signal crossing and sat back on her heels. "Is she strong enough?"

He shrugged. "Dr. Campbell thinks she's fine. He also wanted to check on T.J. I told him that T.J. had eaten, that you were with him. You're welcome to phone him later if you're worried about anything." Damon's assessing glance flickered over T.J. "May I come in?"

"Want to play trains?" T.J. invited, blissfully unaware of the growing tension.

"May I?"

T.J. nodded enthusiastically. "The green train is Henry. The black engine is Diesel. He's being naughty today."

Damon squatted on the floor. "Naughty? Why? What did he do?"

Rebecca waited, heart pounding under her throat.

T.J. didn't look up. "He fell in the duck pond."

Damon went white. "T.J.—"

"He did it on purpose because he wanted to swim."

Rebecca drew a cautious breath. "Maybe Diesel needs a couple of swimming lessons?"

"No." T.J. was adamant. "Diesel never wants to swim again."

Damon shot Rebecca a helpless glance over T.J.'s head.

"Diesel loves to swim, just like you do. Lessons will help him swim better," Rebecca said calmly.

"What if he's scared?"

Damon pushed the Chinese Dragon along the track. "It's fine to be scared, T.J. Everyone gets scared sometimes."

"Not you—you're a man. A big growed-up man. You don't get scared," T.J. replied with childish logic.

Rebecca fought the smile that threatened to break out across her face at the observation. Damon *was* a man, every muscled inch of him.

"Even me," Damon said emphatically. "I get scared, too. I've been very scared because my mother has been ill. And I was scared this morning, too."

"I scared, too," T.J. said. Wide round eyes looked up at the man crouched beside him.

"Nothing wrong with that, son."

Rebecca sagged. Watching Damon with T.J., she couldn't believe how well he'd handled that. She'd been treading on eggshells all day, terrified of bringing up the subject, yet knowing that it would be healthier for T.J. to discuss it rather than let it fester.

Gratitude filled her—and something more. Something that made her throat thicken, a warm sweet feeling with a bitter edge that made tears threaten.

Dear God, how she loved this man.

The emotion she felt now was stronger than almost four years ago. More compelling than the fierce attraction that had drawn her to Damon all those years ago. Then she'd fallen madly in lust with him.

And thought it love until it had turned to pain.

Pain that had shattered her.

It wasn't the same as what she felt now. Then she'd only recognised Damon's sensual magnetism, glimpsed the passion beneath the tight control.

She'd accused him of judging her without getting to know her. Well, she hadn't known him, either. Not beyond the fierce pull he held over her body. She'd pursued him with headstrong recklessness—and paid the price.

The price had been his contempt.

Over the recent weeks she'd gotten to know him. Really know him. Not just the sexy, charismatic Greek male she'd been wildly infatuated with years before. But the real man under the corporate billionaire mask. Had grown to understand his fierce loyalty, the protective love with which he guarded his loved ones. This morning Damon had done everything in his power to rescue T.J.

T.J. was under his roof, so he felt responsible for what had happened. Even though they'd both been there. Not once had he blamed her for leaving the sliders open. Without a word he'd assumed the full mantle of guilt.

And now, watching him playing trains with T.J., their dark heads close together, she recognised the essence of his strength and his capacity to show care and tenderness to a child—a child of a woman for whom he'd had little respect in the past. A woman who was now his lover.

The woman who loved him with an intensity of feeling that scorched her. And this time it was more than lust. This love had the depth of an adult, confident woman. This was the love of a mother who trusted a strong, dominant male not to harm her child, to protect them both to the limits of his strength, with his life if necessary.

Damon was the man for her. So strong, so passionate, so gentle. A man that a woman would be proud to have beside her for all the years of her life. There would be no other man for her.

There never had been.

* * *

That night, once T.J. was sleeping, Damon insisted that Rebecca come downstairs for a break after spending the whole day closeted upstairs.

Damon had given Johnny time off to allow Rebecca some privacy and space to recover from the morning's trauma. Once Johnny vanished to his quarters, they were alone. Savvas and Demetra would only be back tomorrow afternoon, and Damon had decided against calling them. They would find out soon enough about T.J.'s brush with tragedy.

Now, as she sat curled up on the sofa opposite him, Damon saw that her eyes were bruised with tiredness. While he was tempted to sit down beside her and pull her into his arms he resisted the temptation lest she think he was prompted by lust. Sex was the last thing Rebecca needed right now.

"Are you okay?"

She glanced up at him and nodded. There were grooves of tension beside her mouth and her face was full of hollows. The long, tempestuous day had been hard on her.

He ached to kiss the strain away. All his preconceptions were under attack. The woman he'd once considered vain and selfish was a devoted mother. She was kind to his mother. Yet thinking back to the past, he could remember instances where she'd been fiercely protective of Felicity. To the point where she'd confronted him, pleaded with him not to marry Felicity. He'd been enraged when she'd accused him of coercing Felicity into a marriage that she'd regret. He'd dismissed Rebecca's pleas as machinations, an attempt to get what she wanted: *him.* But now he was no longer sure that it had been all about him. Perhaps—

"Damon…" Rebecca interrupted his thoughts.

"Yes?"

"It doesn't matter." She looked away, a vivid flush staining her pale skin.

"What is it?"

"Will you hold me?" The words came out in a rush and the eyes that met his were shadowed by uncertainty.

"Of course!" He moved to sit beside her. Looping an arm around her shoulders, he pulled her close. She nestled her head against his chest with a soft sigh. She smelled of talcum powder and something sweet. He had a strong urge to tilt her face up to his and kiss her breathless. He killed the impulse and pressed a tame, gentle kiss against her hair instead.

His thoughts drifted back to the past. Why had Rebecca been so set against his marriage? Why had Felicity left? Had Rebecca known something that he hadn't? Rebecca had been right about one thing: Felicity had not been happy married to him. She'd tried to hide it with demure smiles. And failed miserably.

It had frustrated him. He'd showered his bride with gifts. She'd accepted them, but he'd sensed a…sadness in her. He'd given her his attention, escorted her to plays, the finest restaurants, everything that a woman who had grown up poor should have revelled in. Everything except his love.

Had her unhappiness been his fault? At the time he hadn't considered that. Too soon she'd been gone. And he'd been furious, humiliated that his bride of six weeks had deserted him. He'd blamed Rebecca. Hated her for publicly emasculating him.

He'd wanted to go after her. But his mother had told him he needed time to get some perspective. Soula had argued that Felicity's desertion couldn't possibly be Rebecca's doing. He hadn't had the heart to disagree, but his resentment of Rebecca had grown like a cancer within him—and then Felicity had died.

Felicity's casket. Strewn with waxen white flowers.

He hadn't spoken to anyone except his family at the funeral. He hadn't stayed after the burial in case he'd taken Rebecca apart with his bare hands where she stood motionless beside the raw ochre earth at the cemetery, as immaculate as ever, only her red-rimmed eyes revealing that Felicity had meant anything to her at all.

By the next day he'd calmed down and she'd been gone. Vanished. Before he could mete out the accounting. It would've been easy enough to have his security agency locate her, to drag her back. Instead he'd let her go. Because he'd known that his fury was beyond tempering, that his reaction would've cost him more than he dared risk—the loss of his self-control.

He shook his head furiously to clear it of the stranglehold of the past. It was dead, dead, dead. Just like Felicity. It was time to move on. And Rebecca was very much alive, her body soft and warm in the curve of his arms. Damon rested his unshaven cheek against her head and rubbed it back and forth.

"Damon?"

"Mmm?" he murmured.

"Will you make love to me?"

"Now?" His body kicked into action despite his disbelief.

"If you don't mind."

"Mind? Of course I don't mind." He wished he could see her face. Already his body was reacting, hardening. "Are you sure that's what you want?"

"I've had the worst day of my life. I want to…to do something that will help me forget. To put some distance between this morning and tomorrow. Is it terrible to seek oblivion in your body?"

"No…" he croaked, then swallowed and found his voice. "No, it's not terrible at all." Pulling her into his lap, he said, "Tell me what I can do to make the pain go away."

"Just love me."

Rebecca sounded so despairing that he groaned and dipped his head to kiss her. Tonight he'd help her forget, Damon vowed. He'd wipe the shadows from her eyes and let passion replace her pain.

T.J.'s hold tightened on Rebecca's hand as they entered the house shortly before noon on Sunday. Rebecca couldn't help wondering if something of her own nervous excitement at the thought of seeing Damon again had communicated itself to T.J.

Last night's lovemaking had been slow, gentle and immensely satisfying. She'd fallen asleep wrapped in Damon's arms. By the time T.J.'s stirring had woken her this morning, Damon had already gone from her bed, the sound of splashing telling her he was swimming his daily laps. It didn't take Rebecca long to pull on a pair of crisp white shorts and a red tank top. With trainers on her feet and her hair loose about her shoulders, she and T.J. had gone down to breakfast. Damon had come into the dining room, his hair still towel-damp. His light kiss had been full of warm affection that had caused her stomach to flip-flop. After breakfast, her spirits high, she and T.J. had walked down to a nearby park while Damon went to the hospital to fetch Soula.

"It's okay," Rebecca reassured T.J. now as they crossed the airy lobby. "We're not going onto the deck or anywhere near the pool." T.J.'s steps slowed at the mention of the pool. Hurriedly Rebecca distracted him, "Remember I told you about Damon's mother?"

T.J. nodded.

"Well, you can come and meet her now. I can hear her voice. She's home from hospital." Rebecca hesitated. *Kyria Asteriades* was too much of a mouthful for a child of Damon's age. "You can call her *Kyria* Soula. Or maybe just *Kyria*."

T.J. baulked for an instant then followed Rebecca into the lounge. Damon was seated at a right angle to his mother, conversing in rapid Greek. His jagged profile stood out, harsh and barbaric amidst the immaculate, subdued decor of the room.

A pirate in civilised surroundings.

Her lover.

Flushing, Rebecca led T.J. further into the formal room. Damon broke off and rose to his feet. The smile he sent her was exquisitely warm. T.J. crept forward from where he'd huddled behind her legs.

"Come," Damon said and switched the warm, comforting smile to T.J.

Despite the horror of the previous day, a glow of something approaching happiness surrounded Rebecca. Giving T.J.'s hand a gentle squeeze, she walked forward.

"Soula, no, don't stand up." Rebecca let go of T.J.'s hand and waved Damon's mother back to the couch. She glanced at the teapot and the empty cups beside the plate of shortbread on the coffee table. "Can I pour you another cup of tea? How are you feeling?"

"No more tea for me. I'm much better for being home, *pethi*. I'm tired of lying, sitting. I need to stretch my legs." Damon's mother rose and embraced Rebecca.

Rebecca inhaled the elegant floral perfume Soula wore. Feminine, classy, slightly old-world. After a moment Soula stepped back to peer past Rebecca. "Where is your boy?"

With a sense of inevitability, Rebecca watched Soula's jaw drop.

"*The mou.* Those eyes! My God. He's the spitting image of—" Her shocked gaze met Rebecca's.

Rebecca stared back. Hoping, praying, that Soula would not let the cat out the bag, that she'd keep what she'd seen to herself.

Soula cast Damon a fleeting glance and flashed a calculating look at Rebecca. Then she swung around to her son, her arms outstretched. "*Ye mou*, you should have told me."

Damon looked thoroughly at sea. "Told you what, Mama?"

"That you and Rebecca have a child!"

Rebecca's own shock was nothing compared to that mirrored on Damon's face.

"*A child?* What are you talking about, Mama?"

Soula clasped a hand over her mouth. "You do not know?"

"Know? Know what?" But his gaze was already flickering between T.J., Rebecca and Soula. Rebecca could see him putting it all together in that lightning-swift brain.

"No." Rebecca stepped forward. "Soula, you have it—"

"I'm so happy!" Soula kissed Damon on the cheek and draped an arm around him. "This is what I have longed for. My grandchild. Rebecca, come." She motioned with her arm and hugged her close, including her in the circle. "You have made an old woman so happy. I have prayed for years you two would realise the terrible tension between you is not hatred."

Rebecca didn't dare look at Damon.

"The child is baptised?" Soula asked.

Rebecca nodded, trying to ignore the tension that vibrated in Damon's body beside her.

"But not in the Greek Orthodox faith," Soula stated. "We need to attend to that. You two will need to get married. I cannot have Iphegenia and the rest of my family gossiping."

Soula's words shocked Rebecca to the core. *Marriage? To Damon? For T.J.'s sake?* Never! She jerked herself out of the family circle, her heartbeat loud in her head. "No! Damon and I are not getting married. T.J. is *not* Damon's child and we should not be having this discussion in front of him."

Soula nodded, but her black eyes were sharp with curiosity as she bit back her questions.

"Mummy, can I have a biscuit?" To Rebecca's relief T.J. seemed oblivious to the mood.

"Yes, of course, sweetie. Let me get you a napkin." Rebecca hurried to the sideboard, where a stack of paper napkins stood, her hands shaking as she reached out.

Damon got there first. "What does my mother mean?" he muttered, his back to Soula. "Who is T.J. the spitting image of?"

"Well, certainly not you," she huffed under her breath.

"Not unless he was born by immaculate conception." Damon's tone was barbed. Something flashed in his eyes. "So whose child is T.J.? My brother's?"

Rebecca turned away. Inside the ache grew and grew as the icy coldness expanded.

In a low voice that only she could hear he said, "My mother desperately wants a grandchild."

Shaking her head, desperate to escape him, Rebecca huddled into herself.

"Stop whispering, you two," Soula's voice broke in. "Rebecca's right—now's not the time. Rebecca, dear, I've poured you a cup of tea. Come sit next to me. Damon, do you want a cup?"

Rebecca shot Damon a despairing glance. His face was pale under his tan. A pulse beat violently in the hollow of his throat.

"Not for me, thank you," he replied grimly, making for the sliding doors. And Rebecca, holding the napkin, walked to where Soula sat with T.J. munching on the couch beside her.

There are things...things I haven't told you. Things you should've known...before we...before we slept together.

The damning words buzzed inside Damon's head, driving him mad. He stood alone on the wooden deck, staring blindly at the flat water of the lap pool. Behind him, from inside the house he could hear his mother's voice offering T.J. a shortbread biscuit, could hear Rebecca's cool, composed reply telling her son it was the last one. Blowing out hard, Damon swung around and slid the ranch slider closed to block out all sound of her.

But inside his head her words continued to echo. *There are things...things I haven't told you.* What had Rebecca meant? Was it possible...?

Yes, goddammit, it was possible! The boy could well have been fathered by Savvas. *His brother.* She'd dated his brother. Despite his orders that she stay away from Savvas.

She's a very beautiful woman. She was kind to me. We had some good times.

Savvas himself had admitted he'd been attracted to Rebecca. What man wouldn't be? His brother could easily be T.J.'s father. His mother had spotted the resemblance immediately. She'd taken one look at the boy's eyes and known he was an Asteriades.

How the hell had he missed it? Damon's knuckles whitened. Blood rushed in his ears. Hot, unsteady rage. He wanted to hit the wall. Anything. He restrained himself. He was losing it. That in itself was dangerous. He prided himself on his fierce, unrelenting control.

Yet he'd already lost every vestige of his control in passion. An image of Rebecca lying beneath him making hoarse little sounds as he drove into her welcoming body flashed in front of him, and he suppressed it ruthlessly. A tight, fist-curling anger threatened.

Rebecca…and Savvas.

God!

When had it happened? Another image, this time the memory of Savvas and Rebecca dancing at his wedding. Rebecca laughing up at Savvas. Had it happened on his wedding night? During his honeymoon? Was that when T.J. had been conceived? While he, Damon, was congratulating himself on finding the perfect bride? While he forced himself to be tender, to meet china-blue eyes, while he struggled to forget the unsuitable witch with slanted dark eyes? The curse of Rebecca—her devastating effect on the Asteriades men. His stomach turned.

Was this why she had agreed to come back to Auckland? Had money alone not been the only enticement? Or was it the hope of a fortune beyond her dreams, child support from Savvas Asteriades? No. He shook his head. That wasn't right. She'd had years to sue Savvas for child support. Yet she'd never claimed a cent. Why not? The money was legally due her, and she'd always been savvy when it came to money. So why had she walked away from the child maintenance claim?

He forced himself to take a deep breath. Trying to think right now was hard after the bombshell that had exploded in his face. Yes, he was furious with Rebecca. She hadn't told him the truth. But then, to be fair, when had he ever given her the opportunity?

There are things...things I haven't told you. The refrain whirled in his head. When had he ever indicated he'd listen calmly, rationally, to what she wanted discuss?

Hell, in the past he'd made it clear that he despised her. That would hardly have invited her to confide in him. Lately he'd had his own agenda: to court her, to get her into bed. Hardly a good time for her to confess that she'd borne his brother's child.

He raked hard fingers through his hair. T.J. was a great little kid. Angry as he was with Rebecca, he couldn't find it in himself to be angry that the kid existed. He only wished... Hell, he didn't want to think about that. *T.J. was not his son.*

But even though T.J. was his brother's child, there was no way in hell he intended to let Rebecca escape his grasp. He intended to keep her in his bed. He turned on his heel and reached for the handle on the ranch sliders. Through the glass he could see T.J. seated beside his mother, holding a cup. Rebecca stood beside them both.

What if Savvas broke off with Demetra when he found out about T.J.? What if Savvas decided that he wanted Rebecca *and* his son? He could not—would not—allow that to happen.

As the ranch sliders scraped open, Rebecca glanced up. His face must've given his state of mind away, because her expression grew apprehensive. She leaned forward, murmured something to his mother and disappeared out the opposite door.

Again anger surged in him. She was running away. But this time she would not escape.

Rebecca was his.

No matter who had fathered her child.

Eight

"I am correct, am I not?" Breathing hard, Damon caught up with Rebecca at her bedroom door. "T.J. is Savvas's child. That's what my mother saw, his resemblance to my brother. Isn't it?"

Rebecca tried to shut her bedroom door in Damon's angry face, but he stuck his foot into the gap and forced it open. Her hands clenched, her eyes smouldering in her unnaturally pale face, Rebecca stared at him, trying to think of something smart and cutting to say. But nothing came to mind.

Dammit. This was exactly why she'd retreated to her room with a feeble excuse to Soula that she needed a tissue. The last thing she wanted right now was a confrontation with Damon. She wanted a reprieve, time to think, to gather her defences. That scene downstairs had shattered her. Damon actually believed she'd slept with Savvas. It made her want to gag.

"Isn't it?" he repeated, coming closer. "Answer me, damn you!"

Outrage came off him in waves. She scuttled backward.

"Will you stop asking me about T.J.'s parentage. It has nothing, *nothing*, to do with you."

He followed her into the heart of the room. "Of course it does. It was Savvas! My brother was your lover. Savvas is T.J.'s father."

She edged back until the side of the bed pressed against the back of her knees. Trapped, she glared at him. "Savvas is *not* T.J.'s father."

"When was the child born?"

Now he wanted evidence? Absolutely fine. The pressure of the bed against the back of her knees increased. She resisted the urge to sit down.

"T.J." She paused meaningfully, "His name is T.J., remember?"

"Okay, when was T.J. born?"

Her heart pounding, she told him. And then told herself it didn't matter. There were no inferences he could draw because T.J. had been a couple of weeks premature—although the obstetrician had said it was no cause to worry, joking that if he hadn't known better, he would have sworn T.J. was *overdue* by a couple of weeks.

"Don't play me for a fool. I can add. It all fits together. You dated my brother after my wedding, had his baby and kept it from him…and from me. What kind of woman are you?"

She wanted to scream, to pound her fists against his chest. *How could he get it all so wrong?* Instead she counted to five, then spoke in a slow voice, the way she did when T.J. was being particularly contrary. "You're jumping to conclusions—"

"So what else is there? That you were sleeping with other—"

"No!" She put her hands over her ears and bowed her head.

Damon grasped her arms and pulled them away from her face. He wanted to see her eyes. "Listen to me." This time Rebecca was going to listen to him, she wasn't going to block him out. This close he could feel the soft, moist breath from her ragged breaths, smell the exotic, feminine scent of her body.

Her wrists were slim in his large hands. With a sense of shock he became aware of her fragility, how much stronger he was. Strange, because she'd always challenged him, never given an inch, so he'd never been aware that this more delicate side of her existed. The last time he'd been this close to her, last night, he'd been so overwhelmed by forbidden emotions, so busy fighting a losing battle. Making love to her…

"No." With one sharp movement she twisted her wrists out his grasp.

She was hotly furious, he realised and drew a deep, calming breath. "Rebecca, I could not let my mother discover the truth. It might upset her. In her medical state, it could trigger a heart attack. It could even kill her."

"Truth?" She laughed, a hard, angry sound. "You wouldn't recognise the truth if it hit you in a bar fight."

"I prefer not to brawl in bars," he said with a calmness he was far from feeling.

Rebecca looked mad enough to hit him. No hint of fragility remained. With her fisted hands, her chin pushed pugnaciously forward and her long hair dishevelled, she looked beautiful. Desire twisted inside him. Even now he wanted her.

She uncurled her fingers, sighed and pushed her hair behind her ears. "I wish I'd never come back, never gotten involved with you. I know I'm not blameless." She paused, looking oddly hesitant after her burst of fury. She opened her mouth. "Look, I owe you an—"

"Tell me," he cut across her, unaccountably hurt by the words she'd thrown at him. "What are you going to tell Savvas? What do you think this will do to Demetra?"

"Listen to me, Damon. I like Demetra, dammit!"

"You claimed to love Felicity like a sister. She was your best friend, yet you did your damnedest to break us up."

"Because I knew you were wrong for each other. Because I thought she—"

He snorted. "Because you thought you were right for me?"

"No! Yes. Oh—"

"See? You can't even answer a simple question truthfully."

She flinched, the last colour draining from her lily-white skin until she looked waxen. And just like that the fragility, her vulnerability, knocked the heart out of Damon's anger and frustration, leaving remorse in the vacuum that remained. With shock he realised that he was in danger of becoming twisted around her long, elegant fingers. Panic ignited in his brain, scattering his thoughts. He was no different from her wretched husband.

He gulped in air and rallied what remained of his tattered shreds of sense together, but the alarm and fear refused to go. "After last night was I supposed to fall for your tricks? Declare undying love, like Grainger—"

"Leave Aaron out of this! You know nothing—"

"That's what you keep telling me—I know nothing. Nothing about Felicity. Nothing about Grainger. Nothing about you. But, you forget, I *do* know you." He pressed his body up against hers, vividly aware of the bed that waited behind her. She was soft against him, her lush breasts full against his chest. He inhaled sharply. Her scent was fresh and incredibly sexy. He nudged closer still. Resenting her. But turned on, too.

"Stop it, damn you."

"Make me." He wedged a thigh between hers, intensely conscious of the brevity of her shorts, the softness of her bare legs. He was breathing hard. "No more winding me around your little finger—"

A broken laugh escaped her. "You? Around *my* little finger?"

"Yes," he murmured, caught in her spell. "That's what you do, isn't it? Isn't it?" He pressed his hips up against hers.

She toppled onto the bed with a cry.

He dropped down beside her.

He intended to kiss her. A hard kiss. A punishing kiss for making him want her this much, for confusing him, for turning his life inside out.

But that was before he read the stark bewilderment in her eyes. This close the hurt in her dark, slanting eyes dominated his vision. They seemed to drill down into his heart. God knew what she saw there. The thought killed all desire stone cold. Instead he felt weary, tired and very uncertain.

Yet under the exhaustion, the confusion, he desperately wanted to salvage something. He didn't want to lose her. Not again. Not when he'd only just found her.

"So what happens now?" he asked.

"God!" There was annoyance in her voice. "You are such a bastard."

He tried to smile. "Don't say that to my mother."

"This is not funny, damn you."

"No, it's not." At once it all came rushing back. *Rebecca. Savvas. T.J.* With a sigh he sat up, slung his legs over the edge of the bed and dropped his head in his hands. "What a mess!"

Frustration closed around him like a suffocating red mist. He fought it. He banged a fist on the bedside table. The lamp rattled. Her purse slid off, fell with a thud onto the floor. Behind him he heard her breath catch.

He turned. Her eyes were wide.

Remorse filled him. "Rebecca, I would never hurt you—"

"I know that." She blew out hard. "The sound gave me a fright."

He knew it was more than that. She was on edge. And he wasn't helping matters. He was losing control, frightening her. Frightening himself. A sigh tore from his throat. "I'm sorry."

"It's okay."

Her eyes were velvety again. She'd forgiven him. Their eyes held. Her tongue tip appeared. Pink. Provocative. It flicked across her bottom lip. His heart started to pound. Without thinking, he bent toward her. Her breathing quickened. She wasn't going to rebuff him. Much as he probably deserved it.

Then her eyes glazed over and the pink tongue disappeared. "Damon, this is not a good idea. We need to talk."

She was right. They needed to talk. And he needed to pull himself together; he was too far under her spell for his peace of mind. Damon pulled away, stood and bent to pick up the purse he'd knocked off the bedstand. It had fallen open. Inside a photo of a handsome dark-haired man confronted Damon. The stranger faced the camera, his hands tucked into the pockets of faded jeans; he wore a reckless smile and the devil glinted in his eye.

"So who is he?" He held up her purse. "Another foolish lover?"

"Stop it!"

"Why? We both know how attractive you are to my sex."

Rebecca simply looked confused.

"Oh, please." He'd been aware of her ripe, taunting sensuality the first time they had met. Was it possible that she had no idea of the sexuality she projected? She had to be aware of it. Or perhaps not. He sighed. "Perhaps you don't deliberately lure them to you, perhaps it is just the unusual chemistry of beauty and that subtle challenge your very existence offers."

"So I'm no longer a little scheming bitch then?"

He paused, detecting hurt, a hint of aggression as if he'd wronged her in some way. He'd never called her that. Or had he? He tilted his head, trying to remember. "Let's just say you're not slow to take advantage of the qualities nature endowed you with."

She glared at him from the bed.

"But you haven't answered my question. Who the hell is he?" The burning curiosity astounded him. Damon wanted to find the stranger, tear him to pieces. How dare she carry another man's photo in her purse when she made love to him like a wicked angel? "What's his name?"

"James."

"And where is he now?" he was driven to ask.

"Dead."

The answer jolted him. Rebecca no longer glared at him.

Her face wore a faraway expression, remote, and her eyes were lifeless. He wanted to shake her, kiss her, tell her to focus on him, that he lived.

"I'm sorry." But he wasn't at all sorry that the man she'd cared for was dead. He didn't need that kind of competition. And then he realised what he'd thought….

Competition. He stalked to the window and stared blindly into the falling dusk. When had it all become a competition? When had it become so important that Rebecca's attention be taken up with him and only him?

And why did anyone else matter? He had her now. What did James…Aaron…even Savvas matter? Now there was only him. And he had no intention of letting her forget that.

"Forget James." He swung back. In two long strides he was back on the bed beside her. He pushed her flat and followed her down. He didn't dare name the dark, hot emotion that coursed through him, making him determined to eradicate the memory of the other man, this James.

He kissed her with dark, sexual purpose. She jerked as his mouth took hers. His mouth softened at once. And it all changed. She gave a mewing groan and responded. No holds barred.

There!

Fierce triumph filled him. He reared up and stared into her aroused face, flushed with passion. "Did James kiss you like that? Did you feel that same wild abandonment that you feel with me?"

"Get away from me!"

"Admit it's good." He leaned to kiss her again. She pummelled his chest.

"Get off me."

He let her go and sat up. "Oh, for heaven's sake!" Her red top had ridden up, revealing the creamy skin of her midriff. He forced his gaze away before his thoughts scattered. "He couldn't have meant anything to yo—"

"Why? Because I devour men like some black widow?

Twist them around my little finger like trophies in some cruel game? Because I'm incapable of love?"

"Hell." He couldn't meet the reproachful challenge in her gaze. Something tugged inside him at the thought of her loving this James. He didn't want her loving anyone…except him, he realised bleakly. He wanted her to save all that passion, all her smouldering ardour, for him and him alone. No man should mean anything to her, not while she made love with him with such sweetness.

He was jealous.

But before he could examine how in God's name that had happened, he saw the tears spill onto her cheeks, and his heart tightened.

Rebecca who never cried.

Who had now cried twice in as many days.

Rebecca who gave as good as she got was sobbing her heart out…

She had loved this man, this James.

The realisation devastated him. He turned away, needing to think about how he was going to deal with this latest discovery.

"I'm sorry," he repeated. This time it was true. He didn't want to see her pain.

"Why? Because I loved someone? Or are you sorry for James? Maybe I drove him to suicide, too? Is that what you believe?"

He flinched at the acid words.

"Well, let me tell you this. He didn't commit suicide. James was ill, terminally ill. But the funny thing is that he died in a car accident. A merciful release, everyone told me. But you know what? It doesn't make it any easier. I miss him." And she started to cry again, great wrenching sobs that make his heart tear.

"Shh." Damon was beside her in a flash. Pulling her into his arms, he leaned back against the padded headboard, cradling her.

"Aaron, James—both dead."

She sounded utterly desolate.

"Hush," he repeated, at a loss of how to resolve this. How could it be that a wealthy man, a man responsible for the livelihoods of thousands, a man who prided himself on his control and who was admired as a business leader, a negotiator, a solution maker, didn't know how to deal with the grief of the woman in his arms?

"Aaron, then James and then Fliss, too. Everyone I love dies." She shuddered. His body vibrated with the force of it. "Yesterday T.J. nearly died, too."

She wanted him to believe she'd loved Aaron? And James? Perhaps in her own fashion she had. And what about Savvas? Perhaps she wasn't a woman who could only have one great love, as his mother had.

He tried to tell himself none of it mattered. But it did. It mattered very much. He desired her—wanted her with an endless yearning—even if he had to slay the shadows of a whole slew of ghosts in her past. Rebecca was the woman she was today precisely because of the relationships that had shaped her. Relationships with other men. They were part of her. If he wanted to keep her, he'd have to live with that, accept it, or he'd have no peace. He'd be torn apart every time he held her, made love to her.

She was still weeping, great tearing sobs that pierced him to the soul. He held her tightly. Tried to think of something to say that might help her deal with the loss of this…James. The loss of her husband.

Suddenly he found it. "When my father died, I was furious with him for leaving us so suddenly. It hurt so much, too. I didn't know what was worse—the pain or the rage." It was true. He'd felt deserted by his father. The father who'd been like a god to him. All-powerful. Above death. Damon stroked Rebecca's hair. "But the pain passes. And for you it will, too. You're strong, the strongest woman I've ever known."

This time it was Rebecca who pulled away. He tried to hold her, but she wriggled until she'd put distance between them. Turning, she met his gaze, and he flinched at the bleak despair he saw there.

"James wasn't my lover. He was my brother."

The revelation struck him like a blow. His breath caught. "I didn't know you had a brother." But instantly the pressure that had been building inside him deflated.

James was not her lover.

"We were put in foster care but not together, not since I was ten. But we kept in touch. James grew wild, a real rebel. He went off the tracks for a while. Then later there was a girl…"

"There always is," he said wryly.

"They fell in love. But she was scared, scared of the wildness in him. Insecurity and fear drove her away. James was devastated. He pulled himself together. They found each other. But then…he felt ill, tired. We thought he had the flu." She fell silent and shot him an odd glance. Then she swallowed. "James was diagnosed with cancer."

Damon had a funny feeling that hadn't been what she had been about to say. But he wasn't about to challenge her, not now. Not while her renewed pain was so fresh.

"Come. Let me hold you."

She snuggled against him. "This is so weird. All my life I'd been the strong one. The rock Fliss clung to, the person who fought to get James help, the one who held them when they cried, hugged them when they got lonely. But there was no one to hug me."

"What about Felicity?"

She shrugged. "Fliss was needy. I'm not going to say more. I loved her. She loved me."

"But she was draining, too," he said slowly.

"Yes."

"What about James—he was your brother. Didn't he look after you?"

She sighed. "I told you, we were separated. And he got in with the wrong crowd."

Damon shook his head, wishing he was hearing something different.

"Drugs." Rebecca sighed. "He got into drugs. He was in a downward spiral."

"So he was needy, too."

"Kind of. But his foster parents had a younger teen. They didn't want him influenced by James."

"And so…?" he prompted.

"I convinced his foster parents to get him help. It took two years, quite a bit of money—some of which I had to pay—and he cleaned up his act. I was working by then, for Aaron."

She stared past him with unseeing eyes, the sorrow reflecting only the ghosts of the past. Damon's throat tightened. He pressed a kiss meant to comfort on top of her head.

"So that's how you met."

She nodded. "He asked me out. I said no. After all, what would a wealthy guy like him want with me except for the obvious? I was young, not stupid."

Damon couldn't believe she'd placed such a low value on herself. But given her upbringing, he imagined her self-esteem would have been rock-bottom. "No, never only that. Aaron Grainger was a wise man." Far wiser than he had been. "He saw a woman who was intelligent, funny, smart."

She looked up at him, doubt in her face. "You think so?"

"I know so." He swallowed. "Now tell me about Grainger."

"Aaron wouldn't take no for an answer. He kept asking."

Of course Grainger had kept asking—she was beautiful…and young. How young? he wondered. "How old were you?"

"Eighteen."

Eighteen. Grainger deserved to be shot; he'd been at least fifteen years older. "And then…?"

"Fliss wanted to become a chef. She'd done a couple of local cooking courses, but she wanted to train in France. And

James was in trouble again—this was before he got his life back together."

Damon closed his eyes, suspecting what was coming. He remembered how proud he'd been of his wife's talents, her Cordon Bleu skills. Never had he realised how they'd been financed. And he'd had the gall to tell Rebecca on one occasion that she should take a leaf out of Fliss's book, to stop trying to be the world's greatest entrepreneur and get some skills. As Fliss had.

God, how arrogant he'd been!

He wished he could take every thoughtless, cruel comment back.

Rebecca hadn't uttered a word in her own defence. Hadn't pointed out she'd been getting things done while those around her clung to her for support. He couldn't help wondering what else she'd failed to tell him.

"Okay, so you asked Grainger for the money to pay for all that, and he demanded you marry him in return," he said flatly and he held her tight in his arms.

"No, no." She gave him another of those strange, unfathomable looks. "I asked Aaron for a loan to pay for Fliss's plane ticket and Cordon Bleu course. I found a fabulous therapist for James to see. Aaron was fantastic, refused to accept interest on the loan, said I worked hard. I started staying later each day to make up for the interest-free bit. He insisted on taking me to dinner a couple of times. I discovered I liked him."

"I'm sure you did." Damon remembered how personable Grainger had been and found himself resenting the manipulation the other man had used. What eighteen-year-old could have resisted that? Let alone one who was starved of attention. Rebecca would've had no social life, only debt to work off. She'd have been a pushover.

"It was so nice to have someone else to lean on for a change. I told him about my dream. I wanted to be independent. One day I wanted to start a business of my own. He encouraged me, offered me a loan."

"Interest-free again?" Damon found he couldn't keep the edge out of his voice.

"No, this time the loan was done through the bank. But he arranged me a good deal with a low interest rate. The day I left his employ and started Dream Occasions he took me out to dinner, ordered champagne—the real French stuff—told me he'd already referred me to a whole lot of friends and colleagues." She smiled. "I was a little horrified. Then he told me he loved me and asked me if I would marry him."

She had felt obligated! The man had played Svengali to her Trilby.

"You didn't have to marry him."

"I know. But I was nineteen by then." She shrugged, matter-of-fact. "What do you know at nineteen? I'd always wanted security and Aaron handed it to me. I thought my dreams had come true. It all happened so fast."

And just as fast she'd been the manhunter of the year, snaring one of Auckland's most elusive bachelors, establishing a successful business.

The piranhas had been circling.

"There were rumours," he said slowly.

"About my lover? The drug addict? That was James."

It made sense.

"And the others?"

"Others?"

"The other lovers?"

She stared at him, her dark eyes flat and unfathomable. "What about them?"

"Tell me about them." His chest contracted at his demand.

Her face had lost all animation. "I've told you before. I don't kiss and tell."

"But what about my brother?" Pain like a knife twisted in Damon's chest. "Surely I deserve to know about him?"

She struggled out of his arms. "I told you—he never was

my lover." Rebecca sat on the edge of the bed, her back to him, her hands hanging loose between her knees.

Damn, he didn't want her so far away. He wanted her back in his arms. "When? When did you me tell that?"

She turned to look at him. "When you threw it at me that he was T.J.'s father."

"No," he said slowly, trying to remember back to the exact words she'd used. "You denied that he was T.J.'s father—you never denied sleeping with him."

"Oh."

He could see her thinking about it, myriad thoughts crossing her delicate face.

"Well, I haven't," she said finally.

Could he trust her on this?

His heart wanted to. Straightening, Damon caught her chin in his hand and searched her eyes. They were dark, filled with secrets. But she met his gaze without flinching. At last he released her chin.

"You believe me?"

He did. No, he was confused. Hell, he didn't know what to think anymore.

And there was still the boy. "So who the devil is T.J.'s father?"

"Does it matter?"

Her secrets ate at him. She consumed him. He wanted to know everything about her. Of course it mattered! "I don't want to one day walk into a room and be faced with the man who fathered your child. Not without warning."

"Trust me," she said. "That will never happen."

Trust her.

Trust her? Just like that?

Damon couldn't believe how badly he wanted to do just that. It was curiously liberating.

Nine

"Okay." Rebecca drew a deep, shuddering breath. "Look, maybe it's time to tell you something else about T.J. Something I've waited too long to tell you. But I was afraid—" She broke off.

"Afraid?" Damon prompted, coming closer.

Rebecca forced herself to continue, not to run a million miles away. She stared at thc strong features she loved so much. "Not long ago you said I'm the strongest woman you've ever known. But I must be the most fearful, too."

He brushed a strand of hair from her face. "So tell me," he invited. "What are you afraid of?"

Damon was so confident, so sure of himself. Why had she ever thought that the truth she'd hidden so carefully might hurt him? "Well, there are lots of things. I'm afraid of losing those I love. You know that."

His gaze softened. Wordlessly he covered her hand with his. His touch was warm and comforting. It gave her the courage to carry on. She took a deep breath. "I'm afraid of hurting people, most of all I'm afraid of hurting you."

"Don't worry about that. You couldn't hurt me. I'm tough." But his eyes turned a shade darker as wariness crept in. "So why don't you just spit out this big dark secret of yours?"

"Okay." She squeezed her eyes shut, murmured a prayer and clutched his hand like a lifeline. "T.J. is Fliss's son. Not mine. I adopted him."

The silence was total.

Nothing moved. But his hand grew stiff in hers. Rebecca opened her eyes.

Damon dropped her hand and rose slowly to his feet, his face white. Finally his mouth moved. "T.J. is my son?"

"No."

"I heard you, Rebecca," Damon accused. Every last vestige of humour had fled. "You said he was Fliss's son. You kept this from me?"

"I—"

"You what exactly?"

"I wanted to tell you that he's Fliss's son."

"When?"

"I was trying to tell you…" She drew a quick, fortifying breath. "I wanted to tell you before—"

Before we made love. But she couldn't speak of love. Not while he stood there so pale and angry. Rebecca shut her eyes in frustration.

"You—" He broke off. She flinched and opened her eyes, waiting for the invective to follow. "You robbed me of my son."

"Stop it!" she yelled. "T.J. is not your son."

"What?" The bones of his face stood out sharply under his tan. "What do you mean he's not my son?" He was grappling, searching for words. "But I heard you…you said he was Fliss's son." But the massive self-confidence had dwindled. He looked shaken.

"I didn't want to ever have to tell you this."

"Tell me what?"

"Fliss..." Her voice trailed off.

"What? What about Felicity? Talk, dammit."

"Fliss was in love with my brother. He asked her to marry him."

"James." His voice was colourless. "Your brother. He'd recovered from his addiction, hadn't he? So why the hell didn't she marry him if everything was so damned perfect in Eden?"

"Because she was insecure. You have to understand. Fliss lost her parents when she was nine. She was terrified of change. She wanted security above all else. James's cancer horrified her. She couldn't stand beside him and watch him die. And then she met you."

He folded his arms, closing himself off from her. "You're telling me I was her meal ticket?"

"Oh, no, no. It went much deeper than that. You're more than simply a rich billionaire." Was she getting through to him? Or was she wasting her time? "You're strong, confident, respected. Fliss craved all that. Nothing was ever going to go wrong with you around."

"But it did. She left me after barely six weeks of marriage. Without a word of explanation she upped and left with you. No sooner was the honeymoon over and the bride fled."

He'd hated that, Rebecca realised. He must have thought himself the laughingstock of the city.

He was glaring down at her now. "Did you and Fliss laugh yourselves silly when you read the papers? Did you see what they said about me? They wondered what kind of monster I turned into after dark."

"No," she said slowly. "I didn't know. We didn't read the papers. James...the cancer was spreading. Losing Fliss had jolted him. He'd decided to try radiation. I came to tell Fliss. The only reason Fliss left you was because James wanted to see her before the radiation. He was terrified of the treatment. I think Fliss grew up very quickly right then. She couldn't bury her head in the sand anymore. He loved her, he needed her."

Damon had grown fuzzy in front of her. The whole room blurred. Rebecca blinked. A hot tear splashed down her cheek. Impatiently she smeared it away.

"And she went?"

"Yes. I only meant her to go for a day. James was here, in Auckland, for a final consultation before the treatment started. But once she saw him—" Rebecca broke off. How could she explain how Fliss had felt?

Fliss had felt terrible about abandoning James, about betraying him by marrying another man while she still loved him. There'd been guilt, too, that she hadn't stood by James while he came to terms with his diagnosis. Fliss had faced the fact that she could no longer run, that she wanted to spend whatever time he had left at his side. Yes, James had cancer, but there was a slim chance that he might survive. This time she'd chosen to betray Damon and her marriage vows.

"In the days before the treatment she stayed with James in my apartment. After the radiation—" Rebecca swallowed "—they discovered she was pregnant. It was like a miracle."

"But she was still *my* wife," Damon growled.

"That was the only thing that put a damper on their happiness. They'd have to wait the legally required two years before Fliss could divorce you. James was scared he'd be dead by then. So they decided to live each day to the fullest. James was convinced the baby was a sign that he would make it. But six months later the cancer was back. This time the doctors weren't as optimistic. But James and Fliss wouldn't accept it. They thought James would pull through."

Except they had both died. James had been having a good week. The baby was due soon. He'd agreed to attend a party in his honour, celebrating his temporary reprieve and their baby's imminent birth. Fliss had been blooming and James had so desperately wanted to live. For Fliss. For the baby.

No one had foreseen a car accident. James had been killed instantly. Fliss had held on long enough to speak to Rebecca, to sign a will and an application for a birth certificate…to hold her baby and name him Tyler James. There had been a lot of blood loss, shock, multiple transfusions before she passed away.

Rebecca had walked away with a huge lump of a bruise where the seat belt had restrained her and a massive case of survivor's guilt.

She started when Damon put his hands on her shoulders.

"And while she was pursuing her future happiness with your brother, she didn't think to tell me why she'd left? To call? She owed me an explanation."

She shrugged his hands away and stood. "Your wife was scared you'd be angry. She thought you'd come after her—she planned to tell you then."

"I don't think so," he drawled. "I suspect she hoped you would explain it all for her when I finally turned up. Except I didn't."

"No, you served her with a separation agreement instead and washed your hands of her."

"And gave her a healthy payoff. What happened to that?"

Rebecca raised her chin as a wave of anger swept her. "It formed part of Fliss's estate. I invested it for T.J. He'll get it when he turns twenty-five. Sue him then."

"Laws of prescription aside, I wouldn't do that to the boy. I don't need that money." He considered her, his head tipped to one side, inspecting her as though she were an unfamiliar species. "What really interests me is why Felicity thought she could marry me while she loved someone else."

Rebecca sighed. "I've wondered that myself too many times to count. She didn't think she and James would work out. Not with James refusing even to talk about his cancer, refusing to discuss radiation and pretending it didn't exist. Fliss was terrified of being abandoned after his death, I think. I honestly believe she hoped she'd grow to love you." Rebecca had clung to that hope. That Damon and Fliss's marriage would work. Only that would make the pain she'd suffered worth it.

"And you?" He was curious, she saw. "What did you think about all this?"

She glanced away. "It wasn't my decision to make."

"But you didn't approve."

It was a statement, not a question. Surprised, she stared at him. He'd anticipated her reaction. "No. I told her she shouldn't marry you."

"You told me that, too." His mouth twisted. "What else did you tell her?"

"That it wasn't fair on you, that she was cheating you. But I couldn't tell you that. Her relationship with my brother wasn't my secret. So I tried to convince her that both of you would suffer if she didn't break it off." Did he finally believe her? It was hard to gauge.

"Pity that neither of us took your advice. Arrogant fool that I was, I thought your motives were suspect. Quite simply I thought you wanted me for yourself. How utterly conceited. I should've noticed that the moment I started courting Felicity you never once flirted with me again."

"Not quite true." She gave him a sad smile. "Remember the rehearsal, the night before the wedding?"

"When you begged me not to marry Fliss, told me she'd regret it? And when I refused to listen, you threw yourself at me, kissed me. How could I ever forget?"

It had been a life-defining moment for her. She'd told Damon that he couldn't marry Fliss. He'd stared at her down his impressive nose without deigning to respond, looking at her as if she were trash. Something inside her had snapped. The next thing she knew, her arms had been wrapped around his neck, her body plastered against his. She'd stared at his beautiful, sensuous mouth. Then she'd kissed him. Open-mouthed, with all the passion she could muster. She'd put everything she felt for him into that kiss.

"You did kiss me back," she said at last.

"Ah, God, how could I not? You were pure sin, pure delight. I couldn't stop myself. I should have seen sense then. Instead I thought I'd gone mad, tempted by a woman—"

"You despised."

"Yes," he said very quietly. "But I lied to myself. Self-preservation. You terrified me."

"So you pushed me away and told me never to come near Fliss again after the wedding."

"I seem to remember I called you some vile names. Some of the anger you bore the brunt of was directed at myself. I couldn't believe I'd kissed you back, that I'd been weak enough to betray Fliss. I'd always considered myself a man of principle."

And for a heart-stopping second Rebecca wondered if he'd ever be able to forgive himself for that breach of honour. He'd hated the passion, the emotion she aroused in him. Now she could see his abhorrence for what he considered his weakness of character. Would that reckless kiss the night before his wedding come between them now, almost four years later, and drive them apart?

"You were arrogant. She was my best friend and I knew she would do whatever you wanted. I felt betrayed by both of you. You broke my heart. So I flirted with you shamelessly on the dance floor the next day."

His face became sombre. "I'd wounded you, called you names, treated you like dirt. I deserved everything you dished out. But my question still stands. Apart from those two occasions, you never flirted with me after Fliss and I started to date. Nor were you ever hostile to her." He paused. "Why was that?"

"I can't say I didn't hope that Fliss would come to her senses and remember James. Fliss was like a sister to me. I loved her. My brother loved her, too. How could I hate her or flirt with the man who was interested in her?"

"Even though she snaffled the man you desired? She did it under false pretences, yet you still loved her?"

"Yes, I still loved her." Rebecca met his frowning gaze squarely. "Even though she married you when she should've known better."

"I admire your loyalty. It's a pity Felicity didn't show you the same loyalty."

"I don't think she realised…quite what I felt for you." It was painful to admit.

Damon looked disbelieving.

Rebecca flushed. "I was painfully obvious, wasn't I? Must've been very amusing to you. But I'd never felt that kind of…response to any man. After Aaron, I never thought I'd marry again. Then *poof*—" she snapped her fingers "—there was this out-of-control yearning." Her voice shook. "You and me, I thought it was meant to be."

"I'm sorry." He touched her cheek. "I was cruel."

"Yes." She ducked her head away.

His hand fell to his side. "I judged you."

"Yes."

"You didn't defend yourself."

"If it had been meant to be, I wouldn't have needed to defend myself."

A silence followed her words.

He'd turned white under his tan again. "I deserved that. I listened to the rumour mongering of fools. I heard only what I wanted—" He broke off.

"I wasn't prepared to stoop to counter the rumours." Rebecca held her head high. "Some of them tried it on with me—"

"And you told them to go to hell?"

"Something like that."

"So they destroyed your reputation."

"More like they didn't want the rest of the boys to think they were the only ones who didn't get lucky." Her mouth twisted. "The stories of my…accomplishments…grew in the telling."

"God!" He raked fingers through his long hair, pushing it back. "A lot has happened in the past couple of days…today. There's a lot I need to think about, Rebecca. I need time."

She bit her lip. Here it was—the kiss of death. She'd known that what they had now would not survive the long shadow of the past.

"Do you want me and T.J. to go?"

"No." His blue eyes looked weary. "No. Never that. But I need time to think this through. I've discovered that a lot of what I believed is false, I've learned some things that have made me not particularly like myself. I need time to come to terms with it all."

This was all because of his twisted sense of honour. He couldn't forgive himself for kissing her when he'd pledged himself to another. He couldn't forgive himself for the hurt he'd caused her. All because of what he saw as his own weakness. Every time he looked at her he'd remember how he'd failed himself.

And what was the point of arguing? He said he wanted time. Rebecca suspected he wanted to inveigle himself out of a dead-end situation. Because of the past, they had no future. What future was there with a woman who every day of his life would remind him of the humiliation of the past? So what if he desired her—had even come to like her? There was no point in fooling herself that he'd ever love her the way she wanted to be loved.

Rebecca raised her chin. "I understand."

"I don't think you do." He gave a sigh of frustration. "Look, I'm flying—"

"Rebecca, we're home." Demetra's voice floated through the house.

Damon swore.

A moment later the door burst open. "Oops, sorry." Demetra's hand flew to her mouth.

Damon snarled something in Greek, leaped from the bed

and barged out the room, leaving Demetra staring wide-eyed at Rebecca.

"Wow. What did I interrupt? What have I missed? Tell me everything!"

Rebecca had just watched T.J. drift off to sleep when a knock sounded on her bedroom door. She hurried across before the sound could rouse T.J. and yanked the door open.

Damon stood there, his knuckles poised to rap again, his eyes guarded. "I came to say goodbye."

For an instant her heart stopped and she felt winded.

He must have seen the shock in her eyes, because he pushed his hands into his hair. "I'm leaving to go to L.A. tomorrow, remember? For two weeks?"

The business trip. Of course. Why had she been so shaken? Perhaps because "goodbye" was her worse nightmare? Because he'd said he needed time, and deep down she feared that meant it was over? "Come in." Rebecca stood aside.

Something—desire?—flashed in Damon's eyes. But he didn't move. "No, I'm not coming in. I wanted to give you a cheque."

Rebecca frowned. "A cheque? For what?"

"For the time and work you've spent on the wedding so far—to tide you over until I get back."

"I can't take it." She backed away from the cheque he was thrusting at her.

"Don't be ridiculous. You've earned it. That's why you came back to Auckland originally. Take it."

"That's *not* why I came back to Auckland." Her heart tore and her temper snapped. "You are so blind!"

His head snapped back. "Okay, so why did you agree to do the wedding then?"

She looked away. "Because your mother was sick and you were worried about her." Her voice was low, even to her own ears.

"Spare me! I can't talk now." He thrust it at her and started to walk away.

Without looking at the face of the cheque, she tore it across. "I can't accept it. It's in breach of my contract."

That stopped him in his tracks. He swung around, his eyes narrow slits in that barbarian face. "What contract?"

"The contract selling Dream Occasions. I have a restraining clause."

"But you sold the business nearly four years ago. It would be unreasonable that you couldn't work as a wedding planner in the city after two years."

"I had a clause restraining me from contacting old clients for five years. That's not up yet."

"My mother was never your client."

"But you were."

And she saw the memory hit him. When he'd thrown the cheque at her the night before his wedding to Fliss, told her to take it as payment for the work she'd done for him and Fliss. Defiantly she'd taken it, holding the gaze that was full of contempt. At first she'd kept it as a reminder of her stupidity for falling for a man who hated her.

And later, when he'd served the separation agreement on Fliss, she'd endorsed the cheque and given it to Fliss. When Fliss died, the proceeds of Fliss's estate together with the payout from Fliss's life insurance policy had all been invested. T.J. would inherit a tidy sum when he was twenty-five.

"So, I'm sorry, I can't accept that payment." She held Damon's narrowed gaze, refusing to drop her own.

"Why?"

She pretended to misunderstand him. "I told you—the contract."

"No." He made an impatient gesture. "Why did you agree to help with the wedding?"

She gave a little huff of impatience. "Don't you listen to anything I say? I told you that, too. Because your mother was ill. And you were worried about her. How could I turn my back on you both then? When you were suffering? How could I walk away when your mother might be dying?"

He flinched. "It was the one thing guaranteed to change your mind, wasn't it? After all the losses you have suffered, you couldn't leave me to face the chance that my mother might die alone. And I never even realised. Stupid!" He banged his palm against his forehead. "But you should still have told me you couldn't accept payment."

"I did. I kept repeating it. But you wouldn't listen!"

"I thought that you agreed to do the wedding because I doubled my offer. I thought it was the money. And when you told me your mother had deserted you and James, that you didn't know who your father was, I started to understand why you were driven to be so self-sufficient. I realised why money is so important to you and for the first time it stopped maddening me that I'd had to pay you a damned fortune to get you back to Auckland. But, as usual, I screwed up." His eyes were a dark, pained blue. "I don't know anything about what goes on in that beautiful head, do I? God, what a mess." He sank his hands into his face. When he finally raised his head, Damon looked haggard. "It never changes, does it?"

"It really doesn't matter," she said.

Damon watched her with an expression she could not read. The silence was unnerving. At last he exhaled and said flatly, "It matters." Then he turned on his heel and walked away.

The knowledge that Damon had jetted out to L.A. made the house feel as if the heart had been ripped out. Rebecca found it hard to settle down on Monday morning to make the calls she needed to. Nothing filled the hollowness within her. Finally she made a deal with herself. She would go back to Tohunga for a few days, maybe a week. But only after she'd completed the list of tasks she'd set herself for the week—that would give her a goal. And she'd start with finalising the seating arrangements for the wedding with Soula, which Demetra—typically—wanted no part in.

She found Soula in the lounge.

"Rebecca, *pethi*, don't hover in the doorway. Come sit down. I've been wanting to speak to you, child." Soula set aside the piece of tapestry she'd been working on. "Has T.J. gone with Demetra?"

Rebecca nodded. "He loves helping Demetra. Personally I think it's the joy of making mud. But today is a special treat. T.J.'s going to watch the landscapers transplanting giant full-grown palms into Demetra's front garden. He can't wait to see the crane."

"We must be grateful. He's recovered well from a nasty experience."

Rebecca crossed the room and sank down beside Soula. "Dr. Campbell told me it would take a while before he feels completely secure, that he'll need a lot of attention and love until he comes to terms with it." Rebecca hesitated. "Soula, there is something I need to tell you."

Oh, where to begin? Rebecca fidgeted with her fingers.

"What is it, *pethi?*" Soula's eyes were sombre. "Ah, don't tell me you can't arrange Savvas and Demetra's wedding? That you are leaving?"

How had Soula known?

Rebecca looked up. "I need a break for a few days. I want to go to Tohunga and check that everything is okay with my business and my house. But, don't worry, I will be back to finish arranging the wedding."

"Pah." Soula flapped an arm. "I'm not worried about the wedding. I'm more worried that once you leave you may never return."

"I'll be back," Rebecca promised.

"When will you go?"

"I thought I'd leave at noon on Friday. That way I can reach Tohunga by late afternoon."

Soula slid her a sideways look. "Does Damon know about this?"

She shook her head. "But he's going to be away for two weeks. I'm only going for a week—I'll be back by the time he returns."

Soula gave an impatient puff. "Well, what can I say? If you need to check on your business, then you must do so, my child. Now tell me about T.J."

"T.J.?" Rebecca could feel the blood draining from her face. "What do you want to know?"

"When do you intend to tell me that he is not your son?"

"Is it so obvious?" Shaken, she stared at Damon's mother. "How did you know?"

"Oh, Rebecca, Rebecca." Soula shook her head sadly. "Except for the dark hair and the eyes, he is the spitting image of Fliss. The curls, the heart-shaped face, the dimples are all Fliss."

She'd already had this discussion with Damon. It was good to have it all out in the open. She was so tired of living a lie.

"So why did you pretend yesterday that you thought he was *my* son? Mine and Damon's?"

"I wanted to give that son of mine a shove in a direction he should have taken a long time ago." Soula gave a weak but wicked smile. "That way everything works out. You keep T.J., whom you obviously adore, and T.J. gets to have the love of a mother and his blood father."

"Wait a moment." This was going to be hard. But she'd committed to the truth, so there was no other way. Rebecca picked her words carefully. "Soula, T.J. is not Damon's son."

"Of course he is. He has the Asteriades eyes."

"No, those are Fliss's eyes—"

"Yes, they are blue, and I grant that they are the same shape as his mother's. But the colour is pure Asteriades. My husband had those eyes, too."

Rebecca was shaking her head. "No, you're wrong." She

moved closer, took Soula's hands in hers. "Look, this is going to come as a shock, but Fliss didn't love Damon. She loved someone else—"

"Oh, I know all that." Soula gave a dismissive wave of her hand.

"You know?" Rebecca stared. "But *how?*"

"I'm a mother. I knew that Fliss didn't love my son. But neither did he love her. Each had their own agenda for marrying—and, no, it wasn't love. I didn't approve. I was very disappointed with my eldest son's choice."

"T.J. is the son of—"

"Hush," said Soula. "Don't say anything that you will later regret. T.J. is Damon's son, and when you marry that will be final."

"No, we're not getting married." Rebecca shook her head at Soula's obstinacy but couldn't help feeling flattered that Soula wanted her in the family. "Thank you, Soula. But it won't work."

Soula sagged back on the sofa, her wrinkles deeper, looking every one of her years. "You know, I told that stubborn son of mine not to come back to Auckland without you. For once in his life he did what I asked. I think he was scared I was going to die. I wanted him to see you again and fall in love with you. I want grandchildren."

So Soula had been scheming. She hadn't been well, but she'd seen an opportunity to manipulate. A true Asteriades. The ends always justified the means. But Rebecca couldn't stir up any anger. Instead she gave the older woman a wan smile. "You are a truly wicked woman, but I wish you hadn't meddled."

"I wasn't well. I didn't lie about that." Soula tried to look righteous. Then she spoiled it by shooting Rebecca a guilty look. "There's something else I shouldn't have done, so I'm not even going to tell you about it, because it has the potential to make everything so much worse. I should've left everything well enough alone, never tried to get you two back together again."

"But then I wouldn't have gotten to see you again."

"Oh, Rebecca." Silver tears glistened in the corners of Soula's eyes. "You are the daughter I wish I had. So gracious, so loving."

Rebecca's own throat closed up. "You know, I don't really remember my mother. But in my dreams, she's you. But sometimes no amount of forcing will make something work if it's not meant to be." She bent and planted a kiss on Soula's forehead. "Damon and I, well, there is something between us, but we've agreed to give each other a little time and space. I'm going to miss you while I'm in Tohunga. But I will be back and I want you to promise not to interfere again. This is something that Damon and I must sort out, not a fairy godmother's wand."

"I won't meddle again. I promise. But that stubborn son of mine is headstrong. An idiot. And sometimes he needs a good old-fashioned kick up the pants."

Despite her misery, Rebecca couldn't help herself. She laughed.

It was Friday evening in Los Angeles—Saturday in Auckland. Instead of planning the coming week, as was his norm, Damon stood on the balcony of a hotel suite overlooking Santa Monica Bay, ten minutes away from the flurry of LAX. The continuous drone of planes over the Pacific held Damon transfixed. T.J. would've loved it. He stared west over the endless Pacific. Beyond Hawaii to the south lay New Zealand…and Rebecca.

What were Rebecca and T.J. doing? He couldn't stop thinking about Rebecca. The shock and fear that had flashed in her eyes when he'd said goodbye bothered him. She'd thought that he was leaving, telling her it was over. Was that what she expected? Did she think he'd make love to her like there was no tomorrow, then walk away at the first opportunity?

Perhaps she did.

When had he ever given her reason to think differently? She'd probably read his request for time as the precursor to his leaving. What had he ever done to deserve her trust?

The pain that had been kindling ignited into a burst of anguish. Four years ago he'd made a massive mistake. He'd picked the bride his brain told him he wanted. In his arrogance, he'd refused to see what Rebecca was. Even his mother had known.

He'd compounded his error in judgment by letting Rebecca slip through his fingers. Not because she was unsuitable, outrageous, manipulative. Despite all the things he'd told himself, he'd still wanted her, burned for her. And he'd driven her away with cold glares and cruel barbs.

Because of fear.

She terrified him. He shifted, uncomfortable with what he was forcing himself to admit.

He feared losing control of his inner self, of putting his heart and soul into the hands of a woman he couldn't bring himself to trust.

So he had run and married Rebecca's best friend to give his mother the grandchildren she craved. He married the wrong woman, for all the wrong reasons. And Fliss had married him for the wrong reasons, too. Both of them had done Rebecca a terrible injustice.

At Fliss's funeral he'd stared across the grave at Rebecca, humiliation scorching him. Yet despite the consuming fury there'd been a kind of relief.

His marriage had been wrong.

Fliss's death had freed him.

But it had been too soon for him to admit the enormity of his mistake—not that his arrogance would've let him. He'd allowed his mother to convince him to let Rebecca go, without taking revenge. Because deep down he'd known. He was the one who had screwed up.

Not Rebecca.

And he'd needed to come to terms with that.

Now he had. It had taken him all week to realise how brave people conquered fear. Rebecca's great overriding fear was losing a loved one. It was a real fear.

Damon balled his fists.

Rebecca had lost her parents. *Theos,* she'd never even had a chance to know her father. He uncurled two fingers and stared at them. Her brother and her best friend. Another two fingers unfurled. Aaron Grainger had committed suicide. He stared down at the five outstretched fingers of his right hand.

Five people. The five closest to her. Did her fear of loss stop her loving T.J.?

Of course not. She loved him. Recklessly. Incandescently. Tenderly. Without restraint or fear, Rebecca had raised her dead friend's baby. The child of the woman who had betrayed her. All Rebecca had done was give and give and give. No one gave her anything back.

She was so strong. She was even prepared to risk becoming his lover when she suspected that there was nothing down the road for her except rejection.

He was the coward. He'd never even told her how she made him feel. He'd told her that he needed time. Damon unrolled the index finger on his left hand and stared at his hands. Yes, Rebecca believed she'd lost him, too. If he wanted to be part of Rebecca's life, part of the family Rebecca had recreated, he had to act and overcome his fear.

Damon wheeled around and hurried into his suite.

His cell phone lay on the table in the sitting room. But Rebecca was not home. Demetra told him that she'd gone to Tohunga to check up on her business and she wasn't sure when Rebecca would be back. Damon disconnected and checked his watch. Rebecca would be at Chocolatique now. It would be better to say what needed to be said face-to-face.

The printout of his diary lay on the coffee table. The pages showed that the next month was hell. He frowned. He had to get through the next week here in L.A. But after that…

Picking up a fat gold pen, he slashed through his commitments for the last fortnight of the month. Everything would have to be rescheduled because he was taking two weeks off to invest in his future.

The next move was his.

Ten

It was Monday morning, eleven days after she had departed, that Rebecca drove back into the elegantly curved drive of the Asteriades mansion. For the last time, she promised herself.

T.J. was bubbling with excitement in the car seat behind her, his oblivious joy underscoring Rebecca's dread.

It had taken Rebecca two whole days to compose herself after the phone call she'd received from Soula on Friday evening. She still could hardly believe what Soula had told her. Yet she'd begged Soula to let her be the one to break the news to Damon. He deserved that much. Friday night had passed in a blur of tears. As the pale dawn had broken on Saturday, she'd decided what she had to do.

Yesterday had been heartbreaking. She'd taken T.J. down to their favourite rock pool at the beach. He'd paddled, knee-deep in the water, his fear slowly receding as he'd splashed around. With her digital camera she'd taken hundreds of photos. As if that would ever be enough.

In the afternoon they'd sat in the shade of the pohutukawa

tree in the front garden, and Rebecca had known that when the tree burst into flame-red flowers this Christmas she would not have the heart to sit beneath it. She would be struggling to put together the broken shards of her life.

The time had come to sell the house. She'd buy another, start afresh. Perhaps closer to Auckland. Chocolatique would have to go, too. Miranda and her sister had expressed interest in taking over the business. She'd start looking out for a new business opportunity. It would give her something to do to keep her mind off—

Soula opened the front door, interrupting her fragmented plans. Deep lines scored the older woman's cheeks. She'd aged. Rebecca saw from her face that Soula, too, knew this was the end. Wordlessly Rebecca walked into Soula's arms. They clutched each other and Soula's shoulders shook.

At last Rebecca stepped away. "Is Damon here?"

"His flight landed an hour ago. He should be home any minute." Soula's voice broke. "Come to my suite. I'll give you the report."

"Will you keep T.J. entertained until I've spoken to Damon?"

Soula nodded, her eyes wet with unshed tears.

When Damon strode into the lounge, Rebecca was waiting for him, outwardly composed but inwardly shaking. He'd already shed his jacket and pulled his tie loose and was in the act of unbuttoning the top buttons of his silk shirt when he saw her. A range of emotions flashed across his face. Rebecca thought she saw a glimpse of wonder and then it was gone and only astonishment remained.

"I thought you were in Tohunga?"

Rebecca rose to her quaking feet. "I've come to return your son."

"My son?" A frown creased his brow. "What do you mean?"

"T.J. is your son. Your mother had a DNA test done. She posted off samples of your hair and T.J.'s to some company in Australia a while ago—without my knowledge. However reprehensible her actions might've been, the results are pretty much conclusive. Here's the report." She thrust it into his hands. "He's your son. Yours and Fliss's."

Her eyes were filling with tears. Dear God, she wished she'd stop blubbering. "Damon, I swear I never knew." She stopped, swallowed, fighting to compose herself. "You'll find T.J.'s birth certificate in the envelope, too. Just before she died Fliss signed the application and stated in the declaration that James was the father."

Damon pulled the document out. "Tyler James. My son's name is Tyler James. Fliss always did say she wanted to call our son Tyler." His eyes were blank, shocked.

Remorse streamed into the empty hole in her heart. "I'm so sorry. I can't imagine how you must feel. I feel so *guilty.* The day after he was born I signed a declaration as James's kin confirming that he was James's son. I believed it. James believed it. But I can't forgive myself—because of me, you've lost out on time with your son, time you will never recover."

He didn't answer. He was still staring at the paper he held, the paper that listed her brother as T.J.'s father. What was he thinking? God, he must hate her. Unending questions spun through her mind. Had Fliss ever believed James to be her baby's father? Or had she known she was already pregnant, bearing Damon's child? Rebecca remembered the doctor saying after the birth that he would have said the baby was full-term—not premature at all. But she didn't even want to think about it. She'd never know for certain anyway.

"I'm sure you'll be able to get T.J.'s second name changed. And the father's name corrected," she babbled. "A court order will be easy enough to obtain with the DNA evidence."

What would her baby's name be? Not T.J. anymore. Damon would drop the James. He wouldn't want any reminders. Maybe he'd keep Tyler.

She didn't know what more she could do to make it right.

What would ever be enough? "I'll sign any documents you need me sign to relinquish my rights to Tyler."

"Relinquish your rights to Tyler?" Those startling blue eyes focused on her. "What are you talking about?"

"I'm talking about the fact that I adopted him. Maybe you'll want to change both his names on the certificate." Inside her heart ached with savage grief. "I'll do whatever I can to make it right, even though I can never give you back the missing years." With trembling fingers she wiped the fresh tears out her eyes. "All his stuff is upstairs, in the room I was using. He's going to need you. It will be difficult at first." Then she added in a rush, "I'd like to see him sometimes."

"What the hell do you mean?"

She could understand Damon's never wanting to set eyes on her again, not wanting her in T.J.'s life. But she needed that—she couldn't let T.J. go completely. She drew a deep breath. "I'm selling my house in Tohunga—and Chocolatique. I'll find something in Auckland, somewhere closer to—" *you and T.J.* "—T.J."

"You can stay here."

She went still. "I can't stay, Damon. He's your child."

He shook his head, looking stupefied. "But you're his mother."

She shook her head wildly. "No, I'm not. Fliss is his mother."

"You're his mother in every way that counts."

The pain nearly shattered her. "But you're his father, his real father. His place is with you." She'd have the memories of the years with T.J. as a baby, the memories of Damon's lovemaking to carry her through the rest of her life. Hopefully Damon would agree to visits, too. She'd see them maybe once a month. That would have to be enough.

He took a hesitant step toward her, then stopped. "You would do that? You'd give up the person you love more than your own life to me?"

"You belong together."

"You belong with us, too."

Her heart skipped. "What do you mean?"

"T.J. is your child." He moved quickly. Before she could blink, he had her in a rough bear hug. "I'm not letting you go. I love you," he whispered against her neck. "You're not going anywhere. I'm going to do what I should've done four years ago if I hadn't been so blind. I'm going to marry you."

She started to tremble. "You love me? You want to marry me?"

"Yes." He held her tighter, his arms hard bands around her ribs.

His throat was very smooth, very tanned, and she watched his Adam's apple move convulsively. "You don't even know if I love you," she murmured.

"You love me. If I wanted proof, you just gave it. You were prepared to leave T.J. with me, sign him over to me completely and go away. But I'm not letting you go. Never again."

"You're right, I love you." Rebecca pressed her lips against the hollow of his throat and then she whispered, "So what are you going to do about it?"

They tore off their clothes and fell on top of Damon's wide bed. Damon pulled Rebecca onto him, moaning as her naked skin slid across his torso.

She placed her lips over his, swallowing his next moan, and licked the slick heat of his mouth. The salty taste of her tears on his skin made her wipe the back of her hand across her face.

"Let me," he whispered, the sound husky in the silent room. His thumbs stroked across her eyes, closing them, the pads soft against her eyelids.

When she opened her eyes again, she stared down into his and asked, "Do you forgive me?"

"What for?" His expression held bewilderment.

"For keeping your son from you."

He stilled. "You didn't know he was my son. And you

raised him with love, lots of love, without holding back and never hesitated risking your heart. You kept him safe. How can I ever hold that against you?"

"Thank heavens." Relief washed through her, turning her knees weak. "When Soula, called I was so afraid—"

"Don't." He pulled her close. "I don't want you to ever be afraid again. We have so much for which to be grateful. I must have done something good in my life to have got this… you…right."

She made a sound that was half laugh, half choke. "I'm far from perfect, you know."

"You're perfect for me." His hand smoothed over the back of her thigh, over the curve of her buttock. She murmured something incomprehensible as his fingers traced up the groove of her spine. Shivered.

Then his hands laced into her hair. He held her fast. He pulled her down and opened his mouth as their lips met, his tongue surging into her mouth. The kiss was ravenous.

Rebecca scissored her legs against his, then let them part, falling on either side of his thighs, and she pressed herself against him.

He shuddered.

His hands loosened and he fell back against the pillows.

Rebecca wriggled a little, rubbed against his hardness and watched the blaze of heat light his eyes.

"Rebecca. Oh, Rebecca." His voice was throaty. "Never leave me."

"Never! I'll keep you close. Forever." She shot him a little grin. Shifted her lower body over a fraction. Felt his erection leap. Then she moved.

"Woman, what are you doing?"

But he knew.

His face was alight. She stared down at him. There was desire and passion in his face, but more than that, there was love. Naked, unashamed love.

For her.

It turned her on.

She raised her hips carefully, slowly, conscious of the length of him below her. Her body was already slick with arousal. His hand was moving downward.

"No."

He froze at her command.

"Keep still. Watch me. I want to love you."

His eyes never wavered from hers. "I love you more than I've loved any woman. Do you know that? I love everything about you. I wouldn't change anything about who you are, how you make me feel. I've never felt anything like this before."

Rebecca stared into the deep blue depths. The black streaks like dark, dangerous rocks in a tempestuous sea. "I believe you."

She paused for a heartbeat.

Then she sank down with one swift movement, sheathing him within her heat. There was a moment of sheer pleasure…and a warm glow of completion. She watched emotion explode in his eyes until the blue burned like silver. Wonder, pleasure and more love.

His arms wrapped around her shoulders, pulling her down against him. A moment later he began to rock his hips. Skin slid against skin. Slowly. So, so slowly. The pleasure that burst through her was incredible.

She gave herself up to the wildness, the heat.

When they finally gained track of time, Damon and Rebecca came downstairs to announce that they would be getting married. There was jubilation and Soula wept a little with joy.

Finally everyone settled down to dinner and Rebecca gazed around the faces at the table: Soula, Demetra, Savvas, T.J. *Her family*. Her own eyes prickled with tears of happiness. So many people, so much love. When her gaze came around to the man seated beside her, he gave her a slow, satisfied smile.

"So who gets to plan your wedding, Rebecca?" Demetra chimed in.

"I'll take care of that," Damon said firmly. "I think I know what the bride's fantasies are." His smile grew wide and Rebecca eyed the curve of that sexy lower lip with hunger. Beneath the table his hand moved in lazy circles against her thigh. Rebecca shot him a narrow glance.

Demetra started to laugh. "Well, this is one marriage no one needs to worry about. You two are so in tune it's positively scary."

"About time they realised it," Soula snorted.

"If Mummy marries Daddy, does that mean I get ducks?" T.J. piped, tugging at Damon's sleeve.

"Whatever you want—"

"Let's think about it, okay?" Rebecca interrupted Damon, rolling her eyes. "Ducks in the lap pool? I can see that you're going to take full advantage of the situation, young man."

T.J. gave a naughty grin. "But I've never had a Daddy."

Damon's eyes flared hot with emotion as he looked from T.J. to Rebecca. "I've never had a son. And soon I'll have a wife. What more could any man ask?"

Later, back in Damon's bed, their bodies a naked tangle under the covers, Damon murmured, "I meant every word."

Rebecca nestled closer. T.J. was fast asleep a couple of doors down in his new room, the room Rebecca had occupied before. Damon's hand stroked her shoulder, then disappeared under the covers to caress the smooth skin of her back. Heat followed where his fingers touched. She shifted.

His hand stilled. "Can you ever forgive me?"

She lifted her head, stared down at him. In the dim gold of the bedside light she saw that his face was relaxed, his mouth tender.

"Forgive you for what?"

"T.J. should have been your son."

She brushed back the lock that had fallen across his

forehead. "He is my son. In every way that matters." She kissed his cheek. "And how could I not forgive you? You forgave me for keeping T.J. away from you."

"You did that unknowingly."

"You believe me?"

He gave her a content, trusting smile. "Of course."

She settled down beside him. "I can't tell you what your belief means to me."

He turned his head on the pillow beside hers and met her eyes. "Why does it mean so much?"

"I feel like I'm always fighting what people believe." She paused. "It wasn't true, you know."

He hooked his arm around her, drew her close to his side until he felt her grow warm from his heat. "What wasn't true?"

"That Aaron left me a fortune and I squandered it. Aaron committed suicide because he'd been caught with his hand in the till, he'd defrauded the bank to the tune of millions. Naturally the bank didn't want the news to get out—bad publicity, the impact on the share prices and all that." Curling up in his arms, she said, "He didn't even tell me what he'd done. I knew something was wrong, but I never dreamed it was that."

Damon hugged her tightly. How could Grainger have messed it up? The man had had it all. Money. Success. And, above all, Rebecca. Damon knew he could afford to be gracious. "He was a good man. But his position must have offered temptations he was incapable of resisting. And once he was found out, well, he would never have wanted you to see him in trouble."

Damon suspected Aaron Grainger had liked the godlike status he'd achieved. He wouldn't have wanted a life without the patina wealth brought, without the status. The sneers during a trial, the snubs when he came out of prison would've destroyed Grainger.

"After his death—" Rebecca broke off and gave a shiver.

"It was months of hell. Aaron had opened heaven knows how many offshore accounts and siphoned the funds out the country. I gave the bank all the help I could. They repossessed fixed assets, liquidated everything. He should've told me. I would've stood by him."

Damon shook his head and stroked slow fingers down her back. He didn't doubt that Rebecca would've stood by her husband. Aaron Grainger had left his young bride to face the heat, and taken the coward's way out. And she still didn't denounce him.

What kind of woman was she? A saint?

Shame seeped through Damon. He'd heard the stories, been eager to believe them. Now he'd discovered the truth. She hadn't squandered Aaron's ill-gotten fortune, she hadn't driven him to suicide. She'd respected her dead husband's memory, had never sledged him off to anyone.

He kissed the top of her head. "I've told you before that Aaron recognised your worth. Infinitely precious."

Her head came up and she gave him a grateful smile. "Thank you for that. Aaron was very good to me."

He wasn't going to argue. The man was dead. No threat to what they shared. And he could never forget that Aaron Grainger had taken a chance on him and helped him when Stellar International had been in trouble. Aaron had played an important role in both their lives. He deserved to be remembered. Damon stared into the dark, slanting eyes that did such dangerous things to his equilibrium. He swallowed. "You must wear the pendant he chose for you. It suits you."

Her face lit up. "You wouldn't mind?"

He hesitated, then said firmly, "Of course not."

"This sounds awful, but I have to tell you—it's my favourite piece of jewellery."

Damn, he'd be reminded of Aaron Grainger every day of his life if she wore it. Then he pushed away the tiny sliver of resentment. Rebecca was the woman she was today because of her past. Earlier he'd told her he loved everything about her, that he wouldn't change anything about who she was. Every word had been true. She was complex, caring and much more woman than he deserved. If the pendant gave her happiness, he would never object to her wearing it. "It suits you. Grainger had good taste," he said gruffly.

"I used to wear it a lot."

"I remember."

"At first I wore it to remind me of Aaron." For an instant she looked apprehensive. Then she said in a rush, "After I met you, I wore it because the colour always reminded me of your eyes."

God. She never ceased to surprise him. But he was thankful he'd told her how much he loved her before this final bastion had fallen. Her arms crept around his neck and pulled him close. The kiss he placed on her mouth was long and lingering. Her lips parted and he deepened the kiss. Heat rose swiftly within him. After a few minutes, he raised his head and muttered hoarsely, "I don't deserve your love. I don't deserve a second chance."

"Watch it, you're talking about the man I love." She reared up on her elbow.

"When we first met, I looked at you, wanted you…but I was a coward. I saw all your passion, your intensity, and turned and ran instead of sweeping up the challenge you presented. I would've received riches beyond measure. Instead I retreated, threw Felicity in your face as the model for womanhood. You say I'm blind. I'm not. I'm stupid."

"You're not stupid. Fliss was a darling."

"Loyal to the last, aren't you?" He brushed her hair back from her face. "I married her for all the wrong reasons. Because my mother wanted grandchildren. Because she was biddable. Because she was so different from you, she didn't tie my head—or my heart—in knots. But I came to wish she had a little of your steel." As he admitted the truth, the shame started to recede.

"Fliss was weak. But it's not her fault. Not wholly. She had a hard time."

"She had you. Yet she married the man you wanted, left you to look after the man she loved—and still you defend her."

"I must. I loved her. And she gave me T.J."

"Our son."

"Yes, our son. Now I've got you. And you love me. What more could I want?" She smiled at him, a slow smile. A happy smile filled with promise.

Damon leaned forward and gave her a gentle kiss, thankful that he'd found her again. The woman who loved him more than he deserved. The woman who bewitched him. The woman who held his heart in her hands.

Two weeks later and a world away from the bustle of Auckland, a lone couple stood on the wide strip of golden sand. The woman's feet were bare and damp from the surf, and she was clad in a simple long white dress. A blue opal pendant hung from a gold chain that glinted in the late-afternoon sun. And she wore a brand-new set of matching earings and a bracelet that her bridegroom had given her as a wedding present. The groom wore a light-coloured suit fitting for the island's humidity, and the page boy wore a pair of floral board shorts and a dun-coloured shirt.

There were no bridal attendants, no guests, no hoopla. Only a bride, her groom and their son. As the celebrant walked toward them with two women who had agreed to act as witnesses, the groom leaned down. "Is a Pacific island close enough to your fantasy?"

The bride tipped her head up. "I don't need anything beside you—and our son."

"You're sure you don't feel cheated of the celebration, the guests, the presents?"

Rebecca laughed. "Believe me, there will be mountains of presents to open when we fly home—between your mother and Demetra, I don't doubt that. But I've had the best gifts already. You, the fact that T.J. swam today and that he laughed while doing it."

The groom cupped her face in both his hands and stared down at her with gleaming blue eyes, his touch warm and tender. She turned her head and kissed the arch of his thumb. Never had she been happier.

"I love you," Damon told her, his voice fierce. "Have I told you today?"

"Yes, but I'll never tire of hearing it."

"And I'll never tire of the wonder of finding you and my son" He bent to kiss her.

Rebecca's toes curled into the soft sand. The familiar flare of desire flickered within her. The celebrant gave a cough. For a moment Rebecca thought Damon was going to ignore the man. Then he murmured, "Later" against her lips and drew away. The wide white pirate smile he flashed her held a promise that made her tingle.

"Dearly beloved," the celebrant intoned. "We are gathered here today to celebrate a wedding, the love of two people for each other…"

Soula Asteriades smiled from ear to ear as she made her way to the deck where the sound of festivities could be heard.

Her eldest spinster sister, Iphegenia, was ensconced in a large comfortable chair with plenty of cushions supporting her. The younger, Athina, was playing *tavli* with Johnny. Soula's three brothers and their wives and children and grandchildren were scattered across the deck, some of the little ones playing in the peculiar long, skinny pool her son had built. Savvas and his bride-to-be shared a lounger, their heads close together like a pair of lovebirds.

"Look, a photo," Soula announced, holding up a cell phone. "The first photo of my eldest son, his new bride wearing a beautiful white dress—no sign of scarlet in sight—and their son, my first grandson. This is a miracle for which I claim no responsibility."

As the family surged forward, happiness swamped her. She tilted her face to the heavens and knew somewhere out there her beloved Ari was watching, celebrating with her.

* * * * *

Don't miss Tessa Radley's next release,
Rich Man's Revenge,
available in July from Desire™.

HIS VALENTINE BRIDE

CINDY KIRK

To Harlequin Editor – and fellow dog lover – Shana Smith, who I've had the pleasure of working with on this book. Thanks for all your help in making this story the best it could be!

From the time she was a little girl, **Cindy Kirk** thought everyone made up different endings to books, movies and television shows. Instead of counting sheep at night, she made up stories. She's now had over forty novels published. She enjoys writing emotionally satisfying stories with a little faith and humour tossed in. She encourages readers to connect with her on Facebook and Twitter, @cindykirkauthor, and via her website, www.cindykirk.com.

Chapter One

Elizabeth "Betsy" McGregor had been out of work for six weeks, three days and twelve hours. With Thanksgiving closing in, Betsy knew if she didn't get a job before the holiday season began, she might as well forget about finding one until after the first of the year. Her desperate straits had smacked her in the face last weekend when she'd put pen to paper and determined she only had enough money for one more rent payment. That was the *only* reason she'd agreed to interview for a position with Ryan Harcourt's law firm.

Okay, perhaps the medallion she'd dropped into the pocket of her suit jacket this morning had something to do with her decision. She'd been trying to decide if she should keep the interview or cancel when she found the octagon-shaped copper coin while cleaning out her great-aunt's home. After reading the accompanying note her recently deceased aunt had addressed to her, Betsy had been seized with a certainty that her luck was about to change.

No matter that the percentage of unemployed in Jackson Hole was on the rise or that the holidays were just around the corner. According to Aunt Agatha, the medallion would bring her not only good luck, but also love.

She snorted. It would take a lot for a tarnished metal coin engraved with ivy, a few hearts and some funny French words to send love her way. Luck, she could believe. But love?

Betsy had never been one to lie to herself. Not only was she rapidly approaching thirty, but she was also the epitome of the word *average*. Average height. Average weight. Average looks. Even her hair was average. Instead of being a rich chestnut-brown like that of her best friend, Adrianna Lee, the strands hanging down her back were a mousy shade of tan. It figured that her eyes couldn't be a vivid emerald green—like Adrianna's—but instead were a dusty blue. Not light enough to be interesting nor dark enough to be striking.

Her features were arranged nicely enough, although if she could wave a magic wand, the sprinkle of freckles across the bridge of her nose would be banished forever. The only good thing Betsy could say about her appearance was that she was so ordinary she could blend in anywhere.

She pulled the key from the ignition, accepting the truth but irritated by it nonetheless. She didn't want to be ordinary. Or to blend in. Just once she'd like to be the type of woman who turned heads when she walked down the street. The type of woman a man would see and immediately want by his side. The type of woman a man like Ryan Harcourt could love.

Heat flooded her face at the realization that she was still as foolish as she'd been at age ten when she'd secretly vowed to marry the slender dark-haired boy with the slate-gray eyes.

It hadn't mattered that he was five years older or that all the middle school girls drooled over him. Unlike most of her brother's friends, Ryan had always been nice to her. She vividly remembered the day he'd come across some boys taunting her, saying horrible things and making her cry. Ryan had not only run them off, but he'd also walked her home. That was the day she'd fallen in love with him.

That's why working for him made absolutely no sense. Seeing him every day would be a dream come true and her worst nightmare. He'd be nice to her. She didn't doubt that in the least. But to have someone see you as only an employee when you yearned for him to see you as a desirable woman, well, it was bound to be difficult.

Still, she'd had a lot of experience handling challenging situations. Hadn't she survived a childhood with an alcoholic mother and an absent father? The bottom line was she needed a job. She had to have money to pay her bills and to replace the red-tagged furnace at the house she'd inherited from her aunt.

While she hoped the medallion in her pocket would bring good fortune, she wasn't counting on it. That would be foolhardy. Betsy had always been a firm believer that God helped those who helped themselves. And that's just what she was doing by interviewing for this job—tossing a Hail Mary and hoping for a touchdown.

Squaring her shoulders, Betsy stepped from her parked car, then paused at the curb to straighten the cuffs of her best camel-colored suit. Because the temperature was a balmy forty-two degrees, she'd slipped on a tan all-weather coat instead of her thick fur-lined parka, the one her brother said made her look like an Eskimo.

The snow from the small storm two days ago had already begun to melt, turning the streets into a slushy mess.

Yet the sky was a vivid blue and Betsy reveled in the feel of the sun on her face.

She let her coat hang open and started down the sidewalk toward Ryan's office. Even though she tried to walk slowly, all too soon the frontage for his office came into view. She glanced at her watch and grimaced. Arriving ten minutes prior to an interview was appropriate. Twenty minutes early smacked of desperation.

While she might indeed be desperate, Betsy certainly didn't want to give that impression. Perhaps it'd be best if she relaxed in her car a little while longer.

She abruptly turned back in the direction of her vehicle, her mind consumed with the upcoming interview until her heel caught in a crack, plunging her forward.

A tiny cry sprang from her throat as the sidewalk rushed up to greet her. At the last second, a man reached out and grabbed her.

His hands were strong, pulling her to him, steadying her. The chest he held her against was broad. She lifted her head, the words of sincere thanks already formed on her lips. Then she saw his face. Suddenly Betsy found it difficult to think, much less speak. Finally she found her voice. "Ryan?"

He smiled. That boyish, slightly crooked grin was guaranteed to make a woman's heart skip a beat. It was hard to imagine she'd been in Jackson Hole all these months without their paths crossing. Actually that wasn't quite true. She'd seen him at a local sports bar a week or so ago, but he'd been too busy flirting with a couple of ski-bunny types to notice her.

Even from a distance, it had been apparent the years had been good to him. Despite being a regular on the rodeo circuit during his college days, Ryan was one of those guys who only got better with age. He was slender, just as she remembered, but now with a man's broad shoulders and lean hips. His dark hair brushed his collar and tiny laugh lines edged his eyes.

She let her gaze linger a second longer on the crush of her youth packaged in gray dress pants, a charcoal-colored shirt and dark topcoat. After a moment all she could see were those beautiful silver eyes that a girl, er, woman, could get lost in….

"Betsy?" Her name sounded like a husky caress on his lips.

She shivered but not from the cold. In fact, she felt positively warm. Okay, hot. His arms remained around her. Betsy couldn't remember the last time she'd been this close to him. It felt…nice.

"Are you okay?" His beautiful eyes were filled with concern.

She managed a nod and the lines of worry between his brows eased.

"I was on my way to the office," he said. "I saw your name on the interview list and didn't want to keep you waiting."

Even though prior to running into him she'd barely walked ten feet, her breath now came in short puffs. Every inch of her body sizzled.

"Until I received your application I didn't know you'd moved back." As if realizing he still held her in his arms, he stepped back and let them drop to his side.

Betsy resisted the urge to pull him close again. Instead she forced a smile. "I've been here almost three months. I was working at Dunlop and Sons, but they cut back on employees."

She saw no reason to mention that Chad Dunlop had wanted to fire her. Only some quick thinking and determination on her part had kept her work reputation intact.

Ryan tilted his head, confusion furrowing his brow. "Hearing that firm is downsizing surprises me. I thought they'd be adding personnel, not cutting back."

"It was a surprise to me, too." Betsy lifted a shoulder in a slight shrug.

He took her arm and they continued down the street in the direction of his office.

Despite the layers of clothing between them, Betsy's arm tingled beneath his touch. She found herself slowing her steps, wishing his office wasn't so close. She'd like to prolong this time for a few more minutes. But it seemed as if they'd barely started walking when they reached the glass storefront of his law practice.

To her surprise, Ryan kept walking.

She glanced back over her shoulder. "Wasn't that your office?"

"I thought I'd do the interview at Hill of Beans." He opened the wooden door, stepping aside and waving her ahead of him. "After your altercation with the sidewalk, I'm sure you need a hot chocolate or a latte to steady your nerves."

Betsy fought back a rush of pleasure. Going to Jackson's newest coffee shop with Ryan made this feel more like a date than an interview.

For a Tuesday, the coffee shop—known for its fabulous selection of beverages and bakery items—was surprisingly busy. Although Betsy insisted she wasn't hungry, Ryan got a large piece of coffee cake for them to share as well as two cups of hot cocoa.

Once they were settled in a booth by the window, Betsy expected him to start rattling off questions. She'd been through so many interviews in the past couple of months that she doubted there was anything he could ask that would catch her off guard.

"I was sorry to hear about your mom."

Okay, he'd surprised her. Betsy couldn't remember the last time anyone had mentioned her mother. When she was small, everyone was always commenting on the resemblance. Back then, Betsy had been proud to be compared to her beautiful mother.

It wasn't until she got a little older that she realized her mother wasn't pretty. Not on the inside anyway.

"She was drunk when she hit the telephone pole," Betsy said in the unemotional tone she'd cultivated over the years. "The police said she was going seventy. She barely missed a kid on a bike."

"She was your mother," he said softly. "Her death had to hurt."

Betsy didn't say anything.

"Is that why you moved back to Jackson?" His large hands encircled the tan coffee mug. "To settle her estate?"

"What estate?" Betsy gave a little laugh. "All she left was a bunch of bills."

She wondered what Ryan would think if she told him the reason she'd stayed in Kansas City until now was because she'd refused to move back to Jackson Hole as long as her mother was here. He *should* understand. After all, as a friend of her brother, Keenan, he'd witnessed Gloria's out-of-control drunken rages.

"I'd wanted to move back for some time," Betsy said in a matter-of-fact tone. "And Adrianna Lee has been encouraging me to 'return to my roots' for years."

Ryan's eyes took on a gleam she couldn't quite decipher. "That's right. I'd forgotten you and Adrianna were good friends."

"Since kindergarten." A smile lifted Betsy's lips, the way it always did when she thought of her oldest and dearest friend.

"It surprises me that some guy hasn't snatched her up by now."

"I guess she just hasn't found Mr. Right." Betsy kept her tone light. While Adrianna was beautiful and bright with a great job as an ob-gyn nurse-midwife, her friend had her own demons that made it difficult to trust men.

"I've seen her at Wally's Place," he said, referring to the popular sports bar that was at the top of everyone's list. "Rarely with the same guy twice."

"I wouldn't know." Of course she knew, but Betsy was beginning to get a little irritated. She had the feeling Ryan was more interested in talking about everything *but* his open position.

A sudden thought struck her. Could this be a *pity* interview? She sat down her cup of cocoa, finding it difficult to breathe. She needed this job. And she'd thought she had a real shot at it. But—

"Enough about her." Ryan waved a dismissive hand. "Let's talk about you. How did you like Kansas City?"

His gaze settled on Betsy, as if she was the only woman in the world. Or, at least, the only one who mattered. Even though it was a heady feeling to be the object of such focus, she knew this was simply Ryan's way. The guy was a natural-born charmer, and she'd do well to keep that fact front and center in her head.

"I liked Kansas," she said. "But Wyoming has always been home."

"Your résumé said you graduated from KU with a degree in Political Science." He smiled and a teasing glint filled his eyes. "Looks like you were planning to go to law school. Am I right?"

"I considered it," Betsy admitted. "But I really love being a paralegal."

Betsy went on to tell Ryan that after high school, she'd

moved to Lawrence to live with a cousin. She'd worked for a year as a waitress, then decided to give higher education a shot. "After graduating from KU I moved to Kansas City and completed a paralegal program in Overland Park."

"I bet you're a dynamite legal assistant," he said with such sincerity that tears stung the back of her eyes.

"My past employers all seemed to think so." With the exception of Chad Dunlop, of course.

"Now you're back in Jackson Hole to stay."

Betsy nodded. "Shortly after my mother died, my great-aunt passed away and left me her house. Once the furnace is repaired and the city says it's safe for me to occupy, I'll move in."

"The place sounds like a real gem."

Another woman might have taken offense, but Betsy simply laughed. "It's definitely a fixer-upper, that's for sure."

Having a place to stay rent free—at least once she could move in—was a big plus. But to survive in Jackson Hole, Betsy needed a job. Lately she'd considered practicing saying "Do you want fries with that?" but she enjoyed being a legal assistant and was darn good at her job. Before she gave up on the hope of getting a position in her field, she had to know she'd left no stone unturned.

"You got a great recommendation from the Kansas firm." Ryan offered an encouraging smile. "Tell me about your duties there."

"They were a large, diverse practice. Initially I worked for one of the older partners who primarily practiced family law. He had a stroke and was out of the office for an extended period. During that time I helped several of the other partners, which gave me a wide range of experiences."

Betsy described her duties in greater depths. There were

so many interesting stories that she was halfway through the third example when she realized he was smiling at her.

She stopped and raised a hand to her face, praying she didn't have a hot cocoa mustache or something equally horrifying. "Do I have something on my face? In my teeth?"

"No. Why?"

"You were looking at me so strangely."

He cocked his head. "Was I?"

"You know you were." If this was a regular interview, she'd never have challenged him. But this was Ryan.

"I'm just impressed by the breadth of your experience."

Was that honest-to-goodness admiration she saw reflected in those gorgeous eyes? Before she could respond, a gruff voice filled the air.

"Who let you in the front door?"

Betsy looked up into the grinning face of Cole Lassiter. The owner of the Hill of Beans coffee empire and another of Ryan's many friends from high school had a devilish gleam in his eyes.

"Don't think I didn't notice the timing, Lassiter," Ryan shot back. "You wait until I pay and *then* you show up."

Cole chuckled, grabbed a chair from a nearby table and sat down at the edge of the booth. He gave Betsy a curious glance. Since moving back, she'd seen Cole, his wife, Margaret, and son, Charlie, in church, but only from a distance.

He was a handsome man with thick dark hair and vivid blue eyes. He and Ryan looked a lot alike—so much so that back in high school, those who didn't know them well would often mistake one for the other.

"Aren't you going to introduce me?" Cole's gaze lingered on Betsy.

"Are you blind?" The look on Ryan's face would have been laughable at any other time. "It's Betsy McGregor, Keenan's little sister."

Cole shook his head and gave a low whistle. "You were a girl the last time I saw you. Now look at you, all grown up and beautiful."

Was that a scowl on Ryan's face? Betsy simply laughed. All her brother's friends had been blessed with an abundance of charm.

"Congratulations on marrying Margaret Fisher," Betsy said. "I knew her younger sister better than I did her, but Margaret was always nice to me when I stopped over."

"I'm a lucky man." The look on Cole's face told her he meant every word.

"She might not remember me, but be sure and tell her I said hello."

"Oh, she'll remember," Cole said gallantly. His gaze shifted from Ryan to her, then back to Ryan again. "Are you…dating?"

"Goodness, no." Betsy spoke quickly before Ryan had a chance to respond. Or heaven forbid, *laugh*. "I'm interviewing to be his legal assistant."

Cole shifted his gaze to Ryan. "What happened to Caroline?"

"Her husband got a promotion. They're leaving for Texas tomorrow."

"Good for them," Cole said pointedly. "Bad for you."

"I was bummed." Ryan shifted his gaze to her and smiled. "Until I received Betsy's application."

Was he saying… Betsy's fingers stole to the medallion in her pocket.

Ryan saw the look of bald hope on her face. "The position is yours. If you want it."

"Just like that?" Betsy's voice shook with emotion. And were those *tears* in her eyes? "Aren't you even going to check my references?"

She was a funny sort, all wide-eyed and serious. Ryan

had never realized what pretty eyes she had, large and a curious shade of blue with specks of gold. Until she'd stumbled earlier and he'd pulled her close, he'd never realized she had such delectable curves either.

Of course, to him she'd always be Keenan's little sister. The one who'd toddled after them and messed up their toy soldiers. The one who'd bravely stood up to those bullies who'd taunted her, asking if she was a whore and a drunk like her mother.

He leaned forward resting his arms on the table. "Just tell me you don't have any deep dark secrets and we're good."

"Nope." She shot him a blinding smile. "What you see is what you get."

Beside him, Cole started to chuckle. Ryan kicked him before Betsy noticed.

What you see is what you get?

Ryan knew Cole's mind had gone totally in the wrong direction. Betsy was his new legal assistant, not a potential lover. And perhaps, a friend. A guy couldn't have too many friends.

He smiled and nodded. Yep, from what he'd seen so far, Betsy was the type of woman who'd make a great buddy.

Chapter Two

When Friday night rolled around, Ryan already had his evening planned. Meet some friends at Wally's Place, toss back a few cold ones and play a game or two of darts. Then he overheard Betsy talking on the phone to Adrianna and learned there was a party at Michelle Kerns's house that evening.

Ryan knew the young ob-gyn but not well enough to merit an invitation to her home. When he heard Adrianna was going to be there, his plans for the evening did a one-eighty. Somehow, someway, he would attend that party.

He made a few calls and within a matter of minutes, Mitzi Sanchez reluctantly agreed he could go with her. Mitzi was an orthopedic surgeon he'd dated a few times. As much as he enjoyed the feisty Latina's company, the chemistry wasn't there. Now they were simply good friends. Okay, that might be stretching it a bit.

Still, they were good-enough friends that he could tag

along with her. Mitzi had made it clear that once they got to the party, he was on his own.

"Would you quit primping?" Mitzi said in a disgusted tone as they made their way up the walk to Michelle's townhome. "I swear you're worse than any girl."

He finished adjusting the cuffs of his sweater. "I love you, too."

She made a retching noise and rolled her eyes.

"Seriously, thanks for making me your plus-one tonight." He glanced down at his black jeans and cowboy boots. While the sweater under his jacket dressed up his party attire, he hoped he hadn't gone too casual. Adrianna was a hard woman to impress, and he'd already blown several opportunities.

"You're not my plus-one," she said. "You're some guy I'm dragging along because I didn't have the sense to say no."

That's what Ryan liked about Mitzi. She told it as she saw it. It was a shame there was no chemistry between them, because not only was she a beautiful woman, she could also sing karaoke like a pro.

"I don't know you," he said as they reached the stoop. "Once you get me through the front door, that is."

"You'll owe me, Harcourt." She brushed back a strand of brown hair that looked as if it had been streaked with peanut butter. Although part Argentinean and part Mexican, with her light hair and blue eyes Mitzi looked more Irish than Latina.

"The first time you get slapped with a malpractice suit, I'm your man."

"What a pleasant thought." She reached out to press the doorbell, but he gently pushed her arm down.

"Allow me."

"Such a gentleman," came the sarcastic reply.

"I aim to please," he said just as the door opened.

Before she could object, Ryan placed an arm loosely around her shoulders. He half expected Mitzi to shrug it off or punch him in the side. Instead she gave a long-suffering sigh. "Michelle, I believe you know Ryan Harcourt."

"Of course." The hostess clasped his hand firmly in greeting. She was tall, with honey-colored hair and big blue eyes. "Welcome. We have wine and beer and snacks. Help yourself to whatever you want."

Ryan wondered if that meant he could help himself to Adrianna.

He felt Mitzi's eyes on him as he placed his coat in Michelle's outstretched hand. For an uncanny moment he had the feeling he could read her mind.

"The answer is no," Mitzi said as the hostess stepped away, leaving them alone.

"You don't even know the question," he protested.

"I have my suspicions."

"Ryan," a familiar voice behind him gasped. "Why didn't you mention you were coming tonight?"

He turned to see Betsy standing in the hallway near what was obviously the kitchen, holding a glass of white wine. Like the hostess and most of the other women in the room, she wore jeans and a sweater suitable for the ski slopes.

She'd done something different with her hair. He narrowed his gaze. "You look nice."

"You like it?" Pleasure ran through her words. She raised a hand to her hair that had been long and sleek during the day and now stopped at her shoulders and had a bunch of layers. "I got it cut after work."

The new style emphasized her large eyes and made her cheekbones more pronounced. He realized suddenly that his friend's sister—and his new employee—was a very attractive woman. "I do like it."

Even if he hadn't, the blinding smile she shot him would have been worth any lie. But it was the truth and he was glad he'd said it. Even after only three days in the office, he'd discovered Betsy responded best to positive reinforcement.

"Are you and Mitzi dating?" she asked, twisting the toe of her shoe into the hardwood.

Ryan glanced across the room where his "date" stood chatting with Benedict Campbell, one of the physicians in her practice. Even though Mitzi claimed to hate the man, she'd protested so much that Ryan suspected there were some red-hot sparks beneath that animosity.

"Nah," he said. "She just didn't want to come to the party alone, so I agreed to come with her."

He glanced around the room. Smooth jazz was playing low in the background and the wine was being served in crystal glasses. Although everyone was dressed casually—practically a given in Jackson Hole—Ryan instantly knew that this wasn't his kind of party. Although he'd gone back East for law school and had attended many elegant events, he was a country boy at heart. Give him a can of beer, a bowl of chips and football on the flat screen and he was happy.

"Who did you come with?" he asked Betsy politely. Not because he was particularly interested in who she was dating, but rather to pass the time while he searched the room for the woman he'd come to see.

"Oh, look, there's Adrianna," Betsy said.

Like a hunting dog that had just gotten a whiff of a delectable scent, Ryan stiffened. He forced a casual smile to his lips. "I haven't seen Adrianna in months. I bet I wouldn't even recognize her."

Even as he said the words, Ryan had to stifle a smile. As if he'd ever forget even the minutest detail about anything to do with Adrianna.

"Oh, I'm sure you would," Betsy said with great earnestness. "She looks the same. The stylist tried to get her to do something different, but you know Adrianna. She dug in those heels and refused to let him touch her hair."

"Her hair is beautiful," Ryan said without thinking. "It would have been a shame to cut it."

"Ryan agrees with you," Betsy said and he shifted his gaze to see Adrianna standing there.

"Really." Adrianna's cool green eyes settled on him. "About what?"

"About cutting your hair," Betsy said, seemingly oblivious to the sudden tension in the air. "He said why fool with perfection?"

Ryan didn't remember saying those exact words, but it was a true sentiment nonetheless.

Adrianna didn't appear impressed. In fact she was looking at him as if he was the lowest form of worm. Surely she wasn't holding that one little prank all those years ago against him?

"Ryan is the best boss, Anna," Betsy said, the words laden with sincerity. "I'm so glad I returned to Jackson Hole."

"I'm certainly happy you're back, Bets." A warmth filled Adrianna's voice and when she glanced at Ryan, some of the coolness in her eyes thawed. Apparently the nurse-midwife appreciated him more because he'd been good to her friend.

Ryan wondered if telling Adrianna that he'd given Betsy the afternoon off would give him extra points or make him look like a suck-up. He decided not to chance it. "I couldn't believe it when Betsy showed up to interview, but I'm sure glad she did."

From the continued thawing in Adrianna's eyes, he was onto something here.

"Can I get you something to drink?" he asked, smiling at her. He would have included Betsy, but she already had a drink in her hand.

"I'm good." Instead of meeting his gaze and letting him drown in those emerald-green depths, she glanced around the room. "There's Travis and Mary Karen Fisher. I need to pop over and say hello."

Ryan's heart dropped as she started to walk away, her high-heeled boots clicking on the hardwood, her cute little derriere swaying in those tight-fitting jeans. But at the last minute, she glanced over her shoulder and flashed him a brilliant smile.

"You take care of Betsy," she said in a low husky voice that conjured up images of rumpled sheets and entwined limbs. "See that she has a good time."

"Anna," Betsy moaned, but Ryan scarcely noticed.

How long had it been since Adrianna had smiled at him with such warmth? Years, he thought to himself, too many to count. She was clearly softening to him, which meant if he played his cards right, it wouldn't be long until she was his.

Betsy stared at her friend's retreating back and felt heat rise up her neck. The next time she got Adrianna alone, she was going to read her the riot act. Why, she'd practically thrown her at Ryan.

Not that he'd protested, she thought, looking for the silver lining. In fact he seemed in a remarkably good mood.

"Do you want to scope out the appetizers?" she asked. "Not that you have to go with me. Adrianna was just kidding. I don't need anyone taking care of me."

She was on the verge of saying more when she snapped her mouth shut. Men hated women who babbled, and right now she was poised to babble with the best of them.

"I'd like to check out the food." Her heart skipped a beat when he held out his arm. "If I remember correctly the only thing you need to avoid is anything with shrimp."

Betsy groaned. Honest to goodness groaned. "Of all the things to remember, you had to recall that?"

"It's not every day I get to see a person covered in hives," he said with a little too much enthusiasm for her liking. "You even had them on your—"

"Scalp," she said. "Yes, I remember."

"Keenan put that pink stuff all over your skin," he said, warming to the memory. "It looked like Pepto-Bismol."

"Don't remind me." She remembered that night well. Her mother had been out running around God knew where and Betsy had been hungry. She'd eaten some old shrimp rollups they'd had in the freezer. That's when the hives had broken out. She'd been terrified, then relieved when Keenan had come home early.

But when she saw whom he was with, her terror had turned to horror. The last person she'd wanted to see her with those big red welts covering her skin was Ryan. But he hadn't laughed or made fun of her. Instead he'd called his parents to find out what they should do.

While Keenan had helped smear the Caladryl lotion on her hard-to-reach places, Ryan had run to the corner store and gotten an antihistamine for her to take. By the time her mother finally dragged herself through the front door at 3:00 a.m., the hives had already started to fade.

"Hey." He leaned closer, a teasing glint in his eyes. "How many men can say they've seen you at your worst?"

"Ha, ha." Betsy was thankful her voice came out all casual and offhand, which was a real feat considering her knees had gone boneless and she was having difficulty thinking with him so near.

He sat back and his gaze zeroed in on a large buffet table at the back of the great room. A pristine white linen cloth with scalloped edges covered the oak top, but it appeared to be the food which had captured Ryan's attention.

"Is that—" he turned to her, his eyes wide and guileless "—shrimp cocktail? I could get you one. Maybe you're not allergic anymore."

Betsy jabbed him in the ribs, forgetting he was the man she'd loved—and lusted after—for years. "Settle down, or I'm going to tell everyone the story of when Keenan locked you out of the locker room in your boxers—"

"You're right. Stay clear of the shrimp."

She couldn't help it. Betsy laughed with sheer joy. This was the Ryan she wanted. Not the perfectly behaved gentleman lawyer who hadn't cracked one joke all week. But the Ryan who made her laugh and with whom she shared a common history.

If only she could figure out a way to capture this moment. And better yet, find a way to translate friendship into love.

In the past ninety minutes Adrianna had talked to everyone but him. Yet Ryan wasn't discouraged. He'd already accomplished a lot for one evening. When the hostess suggested a rousing game of charades, he knew it was time to leave on a high note.

Ryan glanced at the woman by his side, delicately picking a piece of chicken meat from the bone. Her brows were pulled together and she was studying the tiny piece of meat as if it were a complex legal case she was researching. He got the feeling Betsy was bored, too.

Actually, he realized, she was what had saved this party

from being a total washout. They'd roamed the room like a couple of old friends, laughing and talking to others they knew and some they'd just met. The buffet table had drawn their attention several times and they'd picked and chosen from its sumptuous bounty.

Betsy was fun, with a quick wit and a sly sense of humor in sync with his own. They talked about the old days and he'd just finished reliving his high school prom debacle when Betsy had decided she desperately needed more wings.

"It's no wonder you had to lasso a few more," he said to her. "There isn't enough meat on one to feed an ant."

A becoming shade of pink rose up her neck, but she lifted her chin. "I didn't eat supper. So I'm not quite the porker I appear to be."

"Porker?" He dropped his gaze and slowly surveyed her lean but curvy body. "Not hardly."

The pink on her cheeks deepened to red. "You don't need to make nice," she said with a dismissive wave. "I love to eat. In fact several times during my childhood I was sorely tempted to cut the candy heart out of my Raggedy Ann."

"You played with dolls?"

"I did when I was a little girl."

"You just never seemed the doll-playing type to me," he said. "I don't recall seeing any lying around your house."

"That's because I hardly had any." Betsy dropped the chicken wing to her plate, then wiped her fingers on a linen napkin. "Keenan bought Raggedy Ann for me with his paper-route money. She was my first and only doll. He was ten and I was five."

"Keenan bought a doll with his paper-route money." Ryan could barely fathom that the rough-and-tumble friend from his youth would do something like that, even if it was for his little sister.

The realization that perhaps he hadn't known Keenan as well as he thought he did hadn't even had time to settle in when Betsy grabbed the front of his sweater in her hand and pulled him close. "Don't you say one word to him about it either." Her eyes grew piercing. "Understand?"

Ryan considered teasing her a bit more, but something in her eyes made him simply nod. Growing up in the McGregor household hadn't been easy for either Keenan or Betsy. If his friend had found a way to make it easier on his little sister, well, Ryan would give him a break on the doll thing.

Betsy's gaze drifted to the groups already forming for the game. She wrinkled her nose. "I hate charades."

"That makes two of us," Ryan said. "Want to sneak out?"

A look he couldn't quite decipher skittered across Betsy's face. Then she sighed. "You came with Mitzi, remember?"

Mitzi? Heck, he hadn't seen the brunette since he'd walked through the door behind her. And that was just the way they both wanted it. "We drove separately."

Ryan thought for a minute. He hadn't seen Betsy with anyone all night, with the exception of him, of course. But that didn't mean she hadn't come with someone. "What about you?"

"I'm on my own." The words came out on a little sigh.

"Good."

She cocked her head. "Why good?"

He smiled. "Because you and I are going to do some serious partying and now there's nothing standing in our way."

Chapter Three

Betsy glanced at the glass of wine in her hand. Could someone have slipped something in her drink? That was the only explanation. She had to be hallucinating. There was no way on God's green earth that Ryan Harcourt would ask *her* to party with him.

She glanced up and into those eyes that reminded her of liquid silver. "Pardon?"

"Good. I knew you'd be up for it." He disappeared into a bedroom and returned with two coats—her Eskimo-inspired parka and his stylish but rugged L.L.Bean coat.

"How did you know this one was mine?" she asked, slipping her arm into one sleeve.

"You've worn it to the office every day this week."

Yes, but it had also been safely tucked into the coat closet by the time he arrived. While it was warm, Betsy was well aware it wasn't the most fashionable of outerwear. Obviously all her stealth had been for nothing.

The man was observant. Too observant. Alarm bells began ringing in her head. He'd noticed her coat. What would be next? Would he one day look in her eyes and see what she tried so hard to hide?

He can't know I love him. I won't allow that to happen.

"Nothing gets past you," she said with a halfhearted chuckle.

"Thanks for the compliment," he said, sounding pleased.

Before Betsy knew what was happening, he'd hauled her off to the hostess, and they'd said their goodbyes to everyone, including Adrianna, who seemed oddly pleased to see her best friend leaving the party early.

Because Betsy and Ryan both lived not far from downtown Jackson, she dropped her car at her home and they took his truck from there. She wasn't sure it was a good idea. What if she wanted to leave the bar before Ryan was ready to go? But he assured her that he would leave whenever she said the word.

It made sense, she supposed, to ride together. After all, parking was at a premium in downtown Jackson, especially on a weekend night. Luckily a big Ram 4x4 was just pulling out of a spot on the street when they drew close.

Ryan shot a smile at her and stopped to wait. "Looks like this is our lucky day."

Our lucky day. Not his lucky day. Not her lucky day. But *ours*.

Even though Betsy liked the sound of that—liked it a lot—it didn't mean she'd lost all power of rational thought. She knew she'd simply been in the right place at the right time. Ryan had wanted to ditch the party and it looked better to be leaving with her than to leave alone. Still, "our lucky day" did have a nice ring.

"I'm going to leave my coat in the car," Betsy said as he

pulled into the vacated parking spot. She unfastened her seat belt, then reached for the zipper to her parka.

"Let me help you with that." Ryan leaned over and assisted her with slipping the jacket from her shoulders.

She looked up and their eyes met. Electricity filled the air. Betsy held her breath.

But when he stepped from the truck without saying another word, she decided it must have been only her own overactive imagination conjuring up something that wasn't there.

"I'm glad we found a close spot," Betsy said over her shoulder. She'd started hurrying along the sidewalk the second her boots hit the pavement. Although she knew it would be toasty warm inside the crowded bar, outside the wind held a bone-chilling bite.

Despite her rush, Ryan still reached the door to the bar first. Like a proper gentleman, he pulled it open, then stepped aside, motioning her inside.

Betsy slipped past him, taking one deep breath of his spicy cologne before the pleasing scent was lost in the smell of sawdust, French fried potatoes and peanuts.

Ryan leaned close, shouting in her ear, "It's packed tonight."

She nodded, unable to keep the smile from her face. She couldn't remember the last time she'd been so happy. Okay, it had been Tuesday when Ryan had told her the job was hers. And again that day, when she'd learned that the salary was considerably higher than what she'd been making at her previous position.

But this, well, this was different. This was a fantasy come to life. A night out with Ryan. She felt as if she was at a craps table in Vegas rolling sevens.

"Ryan, ohmigod, someone said you weren't coming tonight."

The sexy, breathless voice belonged to one of the blondes Betsy had seen him with last week. Her hair was tousled around her pretty face, but it wasn't her bright smile that seemed to capture Ryan's attention. It was her chambray shirt with pearl buttons hanging open, showing an amazing amount of cleavage. Even Betsy was impressed.

Snake eyes, she could almost hear the craps dealer call out. Her luck had come to an end.

"Who's she?" The young blonde's brows furrowed as she finally noticed the former bull rider wasn't alone.

"This is Betsy," Ryan crooked a companionable arm around her shoulders. "She's an old friend."

Old friend. Hmm. Better than saying she was his employee.

The blonde looked her up and down, clearly not liking where Ryan's arm was positioned. "I bet you don't play darts."

Before Betsy could answer, the woman jerked a thumb toward Ryan. "Me and him are a winning combination."

"Actually I've tossed quite a few in my time." *Quite a few* may have been a bit of an exaggeration, but Keenan had taught her how to hold and toss a dart. At one time she'd been pretty good at it, too, but that had been years ago.

"I don't think so." The girl sniffed.

Betsy felt the hair on the back of her neck stand up. She narrowed her gaze. "Are you calling me a liar?"

"Ladies, ladies." Ryan may have spoken to both of them, but it was Betsy who found herself on the end of his conciliatory smile. "There's no shame in not playing."

He thought she was lying, too. Betsy pressed her lips together and counted to ten. When she finally found her voice, she pinned the young blonde with her gaze. "Let's play a game. Then you can offer me an apology."

A momentary indecision filled the girl's gaze. She shot a glance in Ryan's direction.

Someone handed him a beer and he smiled benignly at the two women. "Sounds like a good solution to me," he said, taking a sip.

Suspicion filled the blonde's eyes. She glanced from Ryan to Betsy. "Is this some kind of setup?"

"A setup?" Betsy asked, puzzled.

Ryan simply grinned and took another drink.

"It is." The blonde tossed her head, sending her hair cascading down her back. "Well, you can forget it. I'm not playing along."

She turned abruptly and sashayed her way across the bar, her head held high.

"What's up with her?" Betsy asked.

"Heidi doesn't—"

"Her name is Heidi?" Betsy bit back a giggle, the name conjuring up an image of a mountain girl frolicking with goats.

Ryan began to nod, then paused. "At least I *think* that's her name."

"She looks more like a Bambi to me." The second the words left her mouth, Betsy wished she could pull them back. Even though the girl's attitude rubbed her wrong, there was no need to stoop to her level.

"Maybe that is her name," Ryan said, her comment appearing to have gone straight over his head. "I don't remember."

The fact that he wasn't really on a first-name basis with the curvaceous blonde buoyed Betsy's spirits. She couldn't keep a smile from her lips.

"Can I get you something to drink?" he asked.

"Club soda with a twist of lime, please."

"Ah, so you've decided to be a little wild and crazy tonight," he said teasingly. "I like it."

He'd barely left for the bar when Betsy saw her former employer, Chad Dunlop, making his way through the crowd. Dressed in jeans and a navy long-sleeved cotton shirt, he looked different than he did in the office. There he always wore a hand-tailored suit and shiny Italian shoes with names she couldn't begin to pronounce.

She supposed she could have moved or looked away, but she didn't. When she'd walked out of his family's law offices all those weeks ago, Betsy had vowed that she wouldn't let anyone make her feel like a victim. If anyone should feel awkward about their paths crossing again, it should be him.

He saw her and changed course, making his trajectory one that would intersect with her. It figured that he wasn't smart enough to leave well enough alone.

Betsy wasn't sure of his motives, but there was one thing of which she was certain. She wasn't going to run or back down. If Chad was foolish enough to cause a scene, the only loser tonight was going to be him.

While Ryan waited at the bar for Betsy's club soda—with a hint of lime—he flirted with a few of the waitstaff. Out of the corner of one eye, he kept watch on Betsy. Although he'd expected her to snag a table, she stood in the same spot he'd left her.

The only difference was her back was now ramrod straight. As he watched, she lifted her chin.

"Hurry up, Wally," he said to the bartender without moving his gaze from Betsy. "The lady is really thirsty."

Of course it wasn't true, but Betsy was Keenan's little sister and nothing was going to happen to her on Ryan's watch. For some reason, he had a feeling she needed him.

"Here you go." The plump, bald-headed owner of the establishment set the drink on the bar. "Can I get you a draw?"

"Not now." Without shifting his gaze from Betsy, Ryan curved his fingers around her glass of soda.

He started through the crowd, smiling when someone called out a greeting or slapped him on the shoulder but not slowing his steps. Ryan was almost to Betsy when he saw him.

Chad Dunlop had been a senior at Jackson Hole High School when Ryan was a sophomore. They'd been on the football team at the same time. Ryan had no use for the man. As a boy, he'd had a mean streak. As a man, there was something about him Ryan didn't trust.

From the defiant way she was standing, Betsy didn't like the guy any more than he did. Even though Chad had given her a glowing letter of recommendation, Ryan wondered if there was more to the story of her departure than a simple downsizing.

No time like the present to find out. He reached his friend's little sister at the same time as the attorney.

"Chad," Ryan said in a hearty tone. "Didn't expect to see you here tonight."

Ryan turned to Betsy and handed her the club soda. "Sorry it took so long."

Chad's gaze turned sharp and assessing. "You're together?"

"Betsy and I are old friends," Ryan said. "I understand she worked for you for a while."

For a second, the man's smooth facade slipped and the bully Ryan remembered from all those years ago stood before him.

"Yeah, what of it? We had to downsize." Chad's pale

blue eyes settled on Betsy. "Whatever else she told you is a lie."

Anger rolled off Betsy in waves. If looks could kill, Chad would be six feet under.

"She didn't tell me anything." Ryan kept his gaze fixed on the tall blond man. "But sounds as if there's something to tell."

Chad shot Betsy a warning glance, then turned to Ryan. "Lynnette is waiting for me at home. We're taking the kids over to the grandparents' tonight."

If Chad was trying to convince Ryan he was a committed family man, he might as well have saved his breath. Ryan had seen the way the guy flirted with the waitstaff.

"Jerk," Betsy muttered as Chad spun on his heel and walked away.

"You got that right," Ryan said.

Betsy looked surprised. "You know about him?"

"I know he's got a wife and kids, but he's no family man." Ryan met her gaze. "I don't know what he did to you."

Betsy averted her gaze and took a sip of her club soda. Her hand shook slightly. "Who said he did anything?"

"You did." Ryan put a hand on her arm and steered her to a table that a couple had just vacated. It was away from the karaoke stage and far from the three-piece band playing country classics. A quiet spot. Or at least as quiet as it got in Wally's Place.

"I did not."

"You said, and I quote, 'You know about him?'"

"That didn't mean anything."

"It did, but you don't have to tell me about it if you don't want to." Even though Ryan wanted to know what Chad had done to put the anger in her eyes, he was determined not to press. Until he saw tears forming.

She blinked rapidly and immediately lowered her gaze to her drink, as if hoping he hadn't noticed.

But he'd noticed all right. He placed a hand on her arm. "You can trust me."

She looked up and met his gaze. Something in the liquid blue depths told Ryan he wasn't going to like what she had to say.

"This has to stay here," she said finally. "Just between us."

Ryan nodded. "Understood."

"Chad attacked me in the boardroom."

"He what?" Ryan shouted. He rose from his seat, but Betsy grabbed his hand and pulled him down.

"Keep your voice down," Betsy ordered. "This is between us, not everyone else in the bar."

"Tell me," Ryan demanded. "And don't leave anything out."

Although he'd been in his share of fights, Ryan wasn't a violent man. But this was his friend's sister and Keenan was, well, he wasn't here. Betsy had no one to protect her. No one but him.

"We were working late on a case." Betsy's voice shook slightly.

Ryan tightened his fingers around the edge of the table. *Let her talk,* he told himself, *don't interrupt.*

Betsy glanced down at her club soda and took a deep breath. She lifted her gaze to meet his eyes. "He made remarks about my—" she paused and chewed on her lower lip, then glanced down at her chest "—breasts. Apparently he likes women who have, uh, who are generously endowed."

Ryan wasn't quite sure how to respond. Everyone in town knew that in looks she'd taken after her Las Vegas showgirl mother. He hadn't really paid attention to her curvaceous figure—she was Keenan's sister, for crying out loud—but had no doubt other men had noticed.

"I told him that kind of talk wasn't appropriate. That he was my employer." A bleakness filled her eyes for a second, then disappeared. "He laughed and said if it bothered me, I'd have said something long before then."

Ryan chose his words carefully. "Had he made other overtures?"

Betsy gave a jerky nod. "The first day I started, he made some comment about how my dress flattered my figure. It wasn't so much what he said as how he said it. I didn't like the way his gaze lingered on my chest, but I told myself I was simply being overly sensitive."

"Then what happened?" Ryan forced a conversational tone at odds with the anger sluicing through his veins.

"The comments continued, becoming more blatant, more…crude." Betsy's eyes took on a distant look. "I started searching for another job, but there was nothing. And he was very careful to be perfectly respectful when we were around other people."

"How did you end up alone with him?"

Thankfully she didn't appear to take offense at the question. "One of the other attorneys was with us, but she got a call that her child was sick and had to suddenly leave. We were almost through, so I thought it would be okay."

"What happened?" Ryan asked through gritted teeth.

"He started talking about how I wanted it, how I wanted him. I tried to laugh it off, but he was, well, he was acting crazy. He lunged at me, tore my silk blouse. I'm not sure how far he would have taken it. I used one of the self-defense moves Keenan had taught me and I got away."

"You should have called the police, charged him with attempted rape."

"It would have been my word against his…and we both

know that his family's reputation in the community is so much better than mine."

"Still—"

She placed a hand on his arm. "He wanted to fire me, but I told him he would give me a good reference and say I was downsized. If he didn't, I'd go to the police."

"The authorities need to know what he did." His lips were stiff and the words sounded as if they were coming from far away.

"Ryan." Her tone took on an urgency. "Listen to me. You don't know what it's like coming from a family like mine. I want to put all that behind me. I don't want to go to court and feel like a victim and then have people look at me and whisper and wonder what I did to encourage him."

Ryan clenched his hands into fists. "I hate the thought of his getting away with this."

"As do I," she said in a sad little voice. "But that's how it has to be."

"I suppose…" Ryan fought to keep a lid on the anger rising inside him. The thought of Chad talking to Betsy in that manner, of touching her, made him want to go over to his house and punch him in the nose.

"You promised me," she reminded him.

"I won't do anything."

"Or say anything."

"Or say anything," Ryan reluctantly agreed, not liking this arrangement at all and already trying to think of a way around it. Must be the lawyer in him.

"Thank you." Her hand reached over and covered his, giving it a squeeze. Then, as if realizing what she'd done, she pulled it back. "You know, I vowed to never tell anyone about the incident."

"Why?"

"I felt stupid, almost as if I was the guilty one."

"That's how predators like Chad want you to feel."

"I know," she said with a sigh.

"You didn't tell anyone?" A thought struck him. "Not even Adrianna?"

Betsy shook her head.

"Yet you told me."

"Maybe because you were available." She gave a little laugh. "Maybe it was time to get it off my chest."

He winced at the pun and she chuckled.

"Seriously, I feel better."

"I'm glad you do. But I'm mad as hell." If Chad had been standing in front of him now, Ryan would have decked the guy.

"I shouldn't have said anything."

"No, I'm glad you did," he said, realizing it was true. He'd known Betsy as long as he'd known Keenan. He'd watched her struggle to grow up in that difficult home life. She had every reason to be proud of her success in breaking free of her mother's world. "That's what friends are for."

Tears filled her eyes. "Do you really mean that?"

"Absolutely." Ryan looked into her soft blue eyes and made a vow. While Keenan was away, he would be Betsy's champion, her protector and her friend.

As long as he was around, no man was going to even look at her wrong. If they did, they'd answer to him.

Chapter Four

"That pond-sucking scum." Adrianna's green eyes flashed and she placed the dress back on the rack with extra force.

Betsy had just finished telling her friend the same story she'd told Ryan last night. The way she figured, she couldn't tell him about Chad and keep her best friend in the dark.

When Adrianna had called Saturday morning and mentioned doing some shopping, Betsy had been seriously tempted to beg off. After recounting the tale of that night in the boardroom with Chad, she'd had difficulty sleeping.

But she'd decided nothing would be accomplished by moping in her apartment. And she wasn't in the mood to go over to Aunt Agatha's home—with no heat—and clean.

"Let's not talk about Chad anymore," Betsy said. "He's so not worth the time."

Adrianna met her gaze. "You should file charges."

"That's what Ryan said," Betsy said with a sigh.

"You told Ryan Harcourt the story?" Adrianna's eyes widened with disbelief. "Before you told *me?*"

Betsy briefly explained about running into Chad at Wally's Place. "I have to admit I felt better getting it off my chest."

"Why didn't you tell me when it happened?" Hurt underscored Adrianna's words. "You had to know I'd be there for you."

"I was embarrassed," Betsy began, then paused when the clerk, who'd been hovering just out of earshot, moved closer.

"Is there anything I can help you ladies find?" the woman asked.

Adrianna flashed her trademark smile at the plump grandmotherly type. "Thank you, but we're just looking."

After making them promise to let her know if they needed anything, the woman bustled off to help a customer at the cash register.

"Let's talk about something more pleasant," Betsy said. "Delivered any babies lately?"

It was a question guaranteed to change the subject. Her friend loved her job as a nurse-midwife and could talk about it anytime, anywhere.

Adrianna laughed. "All I'm saying is that nine months ago must have been an extremely busy time. It's been crazy lately."

"Maybe one of these days it'll be you or me having a little one." The second the words left her lips, Betsy wished she could pull them back. With Adrianna being so commitment-phobic and her being so, well, it wasn't as if men were beating down her door, the odds that either one of them would end up with a home and family of her own were decreasing every day.

"Perhaps." Adrianna gave a little shrug, her eyes giving nothing away. "By the way, did I mention that I got a text from Tripp Randall the other day?"

Betsy thought for a moment. "Tall, sandy-haired guy? His dad had cattle?"

"That's the one."

"Does he still live in Jackson Hole?" She hadn't heard the name since she moved back.

"His parents do, but he's been living back East since he got out of college."

Betsy wasn't surprised. A lot of the people who grew up in Jackson Hole and left for college didn't come back. But one thing did surprise her. "Why did he text you?"

"His wife, Gayle Doyle, and I were friends." Adrianna put down the gold sweater she'd picked up only moments before. Her hands fluttered to her hair, nervously pushing a long strand of chestnut hair back from her face. "We played on the volleyball team together. She was a wing spiker. You could always count on Gayle to make the big play."

If it were anyone else, Betsy would have labeled the talk nervous chatter. But Adrianna *never* chattered.

"You remember Gayle, Bets." Adrianna's eyes were a little too bright. "She was a senior when we were freshmen."

Betsy thought harder and an image of a vivacious brunette came into focus. Betsy never realized she and Anna were friends.

Acquaintances, yes. But friends? Gayle had been so much older. Not to mention popular.

"So Gayle and Tripp married and now he's texting you." Betsy picked up a tan cardigan. Adrianna shook her head ever so slightly and Betsy dropped the sweater back on the stack. "My question is, what does Gayle think of his contacting you?"

Sudden sadness filled Adrianna's eyes. "Gayle died during childbirth several years ago."

Betsy gasped. "I didn't think that kind of thing happened anymore."

"It doesn't. Not often anyway." Adrianna expelled a heavy sigh. "It's always so sad when it does."

"What went wrong?"

"The placenta separated from the uterine wall. There was massive bleeding. Both she and the baby died."

Betsy thought of Gayle with her laughing dark eyes and big smile. She'd always seemed so full of life. Now she was dead. "Did they have other children?"

Adrianna shook her head. "That baby was their first."

"You still didn't say why he contacted you."

"I think he's lonely. He texts me every now and again."

Okay, so the guy was lonely. Betsy noticed her friend hadn't really answered her question. "Sounds to me like he might be on the hunt for a new wife."

Adrianna took extra time inspecting what looked to be a snag in a pair of silk pants. She spoke without lifting her gaze. "Tripp lived down the road from me growing up. He was like a big brother. Sort of like you and Ryan. Same kind of relationship."

Betsy inhaled sharply. She'd often thought that Adrianna suspected she liked Ryan a whole lot more than she let on. Now she was unsure whether the comment meant that Adrianna liked Tripp, as in *really* liked him, or if they were simply friends. She put a hand to her head. This was getting so confusing.

Adrianna placed the pants back on the rack. "Tripp wanted to tell me he was—"

A shrill, pulsating sound filled the air, drowning out the rest of Adrianna's words.

"I'm sorry, ladies." The clerk reappeared, but this time

her friendly smile seemed forced and there were lines of strain around her eyes. “I’m afraid I’m going to have to ask you to vacate the building.”

“Is there a fire?” Betsy sniffed the air. She didn’t smell smoke or see any flames.

“A fire hasn’t been identified.” The woman herded them in the direction of the front door as she spoke. “We’ve had some electrical problems the past few days. I’m sure this is part of that issue. Still, we can’t take any chances.”

“Of course not,” Adrianna murmured.

Once they were out on the sidewalk, Betsy turned toward her friend, eager to hear more. “Tell me—”

Adrianna raised a hand and slipped her cell phone out of her pocket. With the sirens of fire trucks filling the air, Betsy hadn’t even heard it ring.

Her friend listened for several seconds, asked a few questions, then told the person she was speaking with that she’d be right there.

“What’s up?” Betsy asked.

“Baby on the way.” Adrianna reached into her bag for her car keys. “Sorry to cut short our shopping trip.”

Betsy glanced at the firemen hustling into the boutique. It didn’t look as though she and Adrianna would have been returning to that store anytime soon. “No worries.”

“I’ll call you later and we’ll set up another time,” Adrianna said.

“Then you can tell me all about Tripp,” Betsy said pointedly.

“Nothing to tell,” Adrianna said over her shoulder as she started down the sidewalk. “Old friend. No big deal.”

Betsy opened her bag and took out her keys, pondering the words. *Old friends*. She thought about Ryan. Thought about Adrianna’s blasé attitude. Thankfully Tripp lived far away. If he lived close, Betsy might have to warn Adrianna that a girl needed to watch out for old friends. They could be dangerous, very dangerous, to a woman's heart.

The next couple of weeks passed quickly. Betsy and Adrianna talked on the phone but never did find another time to get together. At work, Betsy settled into a comfortable relationship with Ryan.

He treated her like a good friend.

She fell more deeply in love.

Even though she tried to hide her feelings, she wondered if he was starting to see through her. Several times in the past few days she'd caught him eyeing her curiously when he didn't think she was looking.

Today she'd made a concerted effort to keep her distance.

"In the mood for a cappuccino?" he asked unexpectedly as the end of the day loomed.

Betsy would die for a shot of espresso, but it wouldn't be wise to encourage such closeness. *Just say no,* she told herself.

"Absolutely," she said instead. "Do you want me to finish up these documents first?"

"They'll still be here tomorrow." He grabbed her parka from the closet and handed it to her. "You'll need this. The temperature has dropped at least twenty degrees since this morning."

"I haven't been outside," Betsy admitted, then swallowed a groan. Ryan had made it clear when she started working for him that she needed to take a lunch break.

But he didn't appear to make the connection. Instead, his eyes took on a distant, faraway look.

"I met Cole for lunch," Ryan murmured, his mind drifting back to their conversation. Talking with his friend about old football plays had gotten Ryan thinking that an offense-driven approach would be more productive than waiting around.

It was then that he'd begun to formulate his game plan. He wasn't sure how Betsy would react to his declaration, but he certainly wasn't making any progress with his current strategy. He could have said something to her in the office, but because it was a personal issue, he wanted to do it in a nonwork setting.

Because it was the Tuesday before Thanksgiving and midafternoon, Hill of Beans should be fairly deserted. After helping Betsy on with her coat—obviously made to withstand a subarctic blast—he shrugged on his own jacket, then opened the door and waited for her to pass.

As she slipped out the door, he caught a whiff of vanilla and smiled. After almost two weeks he'd finally made the connection: Betsy smelled like his mother's kitchen on baking day.

A pleasant scent for a pleasant coworker. Having Betsy in the office had worked out better than he ever imagined. She was prompt, efficient and managed to somehow anticipate his every need. They were like a well-oiled machine. He hoped today's conversation wouldn't affect that happy balance.

The wind was brisk, but thankfully the coffee shop sat just around the corner. Before long, they were inside the warm shop with cups of frothy cappuccino before them.

"Got big plans for the Thanksgiving weekend?" he asked.

"Adrianna is having a few people over on Thursday." Betsy took a sip of her drink. "I'm helping."

"I bet you're an excellent cook."

Red crept up her neck, although his comment seemed to please her. "I could be awful."

"You're too competent at everything you do to be awful."

She frowned slightly and took a sip of her drink.

Even though he'd meant it as a compliment, for some reason that's not how she'd appeared to have taken it. Since when wasn't "competent" a good thing?

"You're right," she said, finally. "I'm very good in the kitchen. In fact, my pumpkin strudel pie is to die for."

"I'd like to try it sometime."

Betsy merely smiled and took another sip of her cappuccino. "What are you doing for the holiday?"

"My plans are up in the air." In fact he'd deliberately turned down Cole and Meg's invitation as well as a Thanksgiving invite from Travis and Mary Karen Fisher. All because he wanted to be available should this conversation go the way he'd hoped. "Betsy, there's something I need to tell you."

Her dusty blue eyes met his. For a second, all he could think of was how pretty she looked in her pink fluffy sweater. And how her lips looked like plump ripe strawberries. Ryan shook his head to clear the thoughts.

"You're scaring me." Two lines of worry furrowed her brow. "Is it something with my work? If I'm doing anything wrong, just tell me and I'll correct it."

"It's nothing work-related." He offered her a reassuring smile. "You're doing an awesome job. In fact, I don't know what I'd do without you."

She expelled a breath. "Good."

"This is something personal."

Her fingers stilled on the large cup sitting in front of her. "Really?"

While Betsy hadn't given him permission to stray into the personal realm, she hadn't shut the door either. Ryan decided to plunge through the slight opening he'd been given. “I’ve never had any trouble getting dates. Or talking to women. But when the woman is special to you and she doesn’t know she is, finding the right words can be hard.”

Betsy simply stared.

“Do you know what it’s like to want someone but not be sure if they want you?”

Her eyes never left his face. She nodded slowly.

“To wonder if they only think of you as a friend or if their feelings run as deep as yours but they’re afraid to say anything for fear of looking foolish?”

“I—” Betsy cleared her throat before continuing “—I can relate.”

“Can you?” Ryan reached forward and took her hands. “It’s difficult having such intense feelings but having to keep them hidden.”

“A person shouldn’t keep feelings like that under wraps.” Her voice shook with emotion. “You should always say what you feel.”

“Even if I’m not sure the other person feels the same way?”

“How do you know unless you ask?” Two bright spots of pink dotted her cheeks.

Ryan wondered if she’d guessed his secret. “You’re right,” he said. “I’m going to just blurt it out.”

He realized with a start that he was still clutching Betsy’s hands as if he were a drowning sailor and they were a life raft. But when he started to pull away, she tightened her hold.

“Tell me, Ryan,” she urged. “Tell me what you’re feeling.”

He took a deep breath. “I’m in love with Adrianna Lee, but I’m not sure how she feels about me.”

A shutter fell across Betsy’s eyes. Even when she blinked the shutters remained firmly closed, hiding her thoughts, her reaction from his view. She released his hands and sat back, which he took to be a very bad sign.

"You and Adrianna?" Betsy stumbled over the name. "I thought that you, that we—"

She clamped her mouth shut.

Ryan tilted his head. "Did you think I was talking about you and me?"

Was that pity in his eyes?

Betsy's heart fluttered like a thousand tiny hummingbirds in her chest. Dear God, this was her worst nightmare come to life. Somehow she had to find a way to salvage this situation. And while she was doing that, save her pride.

"You and me?" She somehow managed a respectable-sounding laugh. "Pssh. We're just friends."

By the look in his eyes, Betsy knew she hadn't quite allayed his suspicions. How uncomfortable would it be for them to work in the same office day after day if he thought she was pining over him? She had to make him think there was someone else. But who? They knew most of the same people.

"Actually, as long as we're sharing confessions, I have my own secret crush. That's why I could so easily relate to what you were saying."

The muscles in his shoulders relaxed and the suspicion that had colored his gaze all but disappeared. "Who is he?"

If she refused to tell him, he'd think she was lying. But she couldn't pick anyone currently living in Jackson Hole. That would be way too uncomfortable. And she wouldn't put it past Ryan to spill the beans.

Think, she told herself, *think of a name.*

"Tripp Randall."

"The Tripp Randall who used to live here?"

"He lives back East now." Betsy relaxed against the

chair, feeling comfortable enough to take a sip of her now-lukewarm drink. "He was married, but—"

"His wife died."

At first Betsy was surprised. How did he know that Tripp's wife had passed away? Then she reminded herself that this was Jackson Hole. It was hard to keep any kind of secret in this town.

"Even though he's now single, I don't think there's any chance of our getting together," Betsy said. "I mean, he's in Connecticut and I'm here."

"Not for much longer."

"What do you mean? I don't have any plans to move."

"You haven't heard?"

"Heard what?"

"I just got a call from him this morning," Ryan said. "Tripp is moving back to Jackson Hole."

Chapter Five

Betsy dressed for work the next morning, still thinking about her conversation with Ryan in the coffee shop.

She hadn't known what to say when he announced he was in love with Adrianna. It made perfect sense. Heck, if she was a guy she'd pick Adrianna, too. The woman was smart and beautiful. And she had a kind heart.

His announcement had shaken Betsy to the core. Even though she'd never admit this to anyone, there had been a few wonderful seconds where she'd been convinced he was going to declare his love for her. When he said her friend's name instead, she'd wanted to cry. But she hadn't. She'd kept her pride.

So what if he now thought she was interested in a man she could barely remember? There were worse things, such as his knowing her true feelings.

No, it hadn't been a good day. But if she hadn't thought quickly, it could have been so much worse.

By the time she arrived at work she had her emotions firmly under control. Only eight hours to get through and then she'd have four days away from Ryan. Four days to lick her wounds. Four days to figure out how she was going to deal with working for a man she loved who had the hots for her best friend.

Ryan was in court all morning. Adrianna had asked Betsy to meet her for lunch. Although she didn't like lying to her friend, her emotions were too raw and she made up an excuse about having too much work to do.

Actually it wasn't far from the truth. She was hoping to bc able tu gel her tasks done so she could leave early and minimize the time spent with Ryan.

The clock had just chimed one when Ryan appeared. Betsy smiled and said hello as he walked through the back door, knowing it would have looked odd to do anything else. Then she immediately returned her attention to the papers on her desk, hoping he'd go straight into his adjoining office and shut the door.

Instead he crossed the room and stood by her desk giving her no choice but to look up. "Is there something you need?"

He shifted from one foot to the other. "About our conversation yesterday—"

"All forgotten." She spoke quickly before he could continue.

Ryan dropped into the chair next to her desk. The spicy scent of his cologne teased her nostrils. "I did a lot of thinking last night."

Every muscle in Betsy's body tensed. She had no idea what he was going to say, but she had the feeling she wasn't going to like it.

"I've come up with something that might just solve both

of our problems." His voice said he was quite pleased with himself.

"I don't have a problem." Betsy picked up the promissory note she was working on for one of Ryan's clients, but the words swam before her eyes.

"You like Tripp. You want to be with him. And now he's moving back to Jackson." He smiled expectantly as if he'd just given her all the information she needed tied up in a neat little bow.

The truth was she didn't have a clue what he was trying to say. And she wished he would take his enticing smile and his delicious-smelling cologne and leave her alone. "While I might like Tripp, he doesn't know I exist."

"You realize this man you like is a good friend of mine."

The man I like is you, you idiot, she wanted to say. But Betsy bit her tongue.

"And you and I share a common issue," Ryan continued. "Like Tripp, Adrianna doesn't know I exist."

He seemed to expect her to say something, so Betsy obliged. "Adrianna is a good friend of mine."

"Exactly." Ryan slapped his hand on the table as if she'd just answered the million-dollar question.

Except…she didn't know the question. "I don't understand."

The look he shot her seemed to say, *You're smarter than this.* But, of course, that wasn't true. Because if she was the least bit intelligent, she'd have stopped herself from falling in love with him.

"Are you familiar with the principle of 'you scratch my back, I'll scratch yours'?"

Betsy slowly nodded.

"Well, you help get me in front of Adrianna," he said with a little smile, "and I get you in front of Tripp. Then we let nature take its course."

"Get in front of…" Betsy dropped the promissory note to the desk. This conversation required her full concentration. "What does that mean exactly?"

"For example, you help me spend time with Adrianna. That way she'll have the opportunity to get to know me better. After all, to know me is to love me."

Betsy couldn't even manage a smile. "You mean, like I'd take you with me to Adrianna's house for Thanksgiving?"

"Yes." Ryan practically jumped out of his chair in his enthusiasm. "That's exactly the type of intervention I'm talking about. But I want to make it very clear that this wouldn't be one-sided."

"It wouldn't?"

"Absolutely not. Once Tripp is back and settled in, I'll definitely return the favor."

Betsy felt a knot in the pit of her stomach. The fact was, she might need an introduction to the man. Even though he'd been a friend of Ryan, she didn't remember Tripp all that well. And unlike Adrianna, she hadn't thought about him since high school. Even back then, he hadn't made a big impression. "I don't know…"

"What's not to know? To get someone to fall in love with you, they have to be around you, spend time with you."

The flicker of hope that one day Ryan might wake up and realize he was in love with her had been all but snuffed out when he'd announced he was in love with Adrianna. Still, she realized now that a tiny spark remained. Which meant she was either a hopeless romantic or the dumbest woman on the face of the earth. Betsy suspected both were true.

Because now, gazing into those beautiful gray eyes, she found herself wondering if maybe, just maybe, they spent more time together, Ryan would see that it wasn't Adrianna he loved, but her instead.

You're going to get your heart broken, a tiny voice of reason in her head whispered. But she ignored it. The way Betsy saw it, love wasn't for wusses.

"What would make the most sense would be for the two of us to start hanging out together." Betsy forced a slightly bored tone. "We make it clear to everyone that we're just old friends. That way Adrianna and—"

Panic rose inside Betsy. Who was it she was supposed to be in love with? For a split second his name fled her mind.

"Tripp." Ryan filled in the blank.

"Yes, Tripp." She quickly repeated the name ten times in her head so she wouldn't forget it again. "Because we don't want them to think we're a couple or anything…"

"No, we don't want that." Ryan spoke a little too quickly for her liking.

"Anyway, it would seem less suspicious. I know that Adrianna—" Betsy paused for effect "—wouldn't think it strange at all if you started coming around with me."

Betsy vowed in that moment if Ryan and Adrianna discovered that they were soul mates, she'd be happy for them. And even while her heart was breaking, she'd never let it show on her face.

Ryan's expression turned thoughtful. As he drummed his fingers on the table, she could almost see him considering the pros and cons of what she'd suggested. "I think it would work," he said finally. "Tripp would be less suspicious, too."

Her gaze met his. "Please know that if we give it our best shot and he doesn't return my feelings, I'm not the type to cling or to be where I'm not wanted."

The words flowed from her heart and they were as much for her sake as for the attorney sitting beside her. It wasn't Tripp who needed to know this about her, it was Ryan.

Betsy jumped when his hand closed over hers. "You're a wonderful woman. He'd be crazy not to want you."

Her skin turned hot beneath his touch and she pulled the words close to her heart. But she wondered, if she was so wonderful, why didn't Ryan want her for himself? She slipped her hand out from beneath his. "Sounds like we have a deal."

Ryan rubbed his chin. "When should we start?"

"Adrianna is having a few friends over for Thanksgiving dinner tomorrow. I'll tell her to set the table for one more. Unless you're busy—"

"I'll be there," he said immediately. "What time shall I pick you up?"

"Five o'clock would be fine."

"I've got a good feeling about this," Ryan said.

Well, Betsy thought, *that makes one of us.*

The next morning, while making a sweet-potato casserole, Betsy made her own pro-con list in her head. She still hadn't told Adrianna that Ryan was coming because she wasn't sure she was going through with their agreement. Food wouldn't be a problem if she did decide to go along with his scheme and let him come. There was plenty to eat.

Even after she'd finished with the food preparation, she still wasn't certain the pros outweighed the cons. But later that afternoon, she realized she had no choice. Not unless she wanted Ryan to know it was him she liked, not Tripp.

She called Adrianna and told her she'd like to bring Ryan with her. Just as she thought, Adrianna hadn't minded. In fact she'd been rather enthusiastic. Even though Betsy had stressed that Ryan was simply a friend, she got the feeling Adrianna didn't believe her. It was at that point Betsy thought about coming clean and telling her friend about the crazy scheme Ryan had concocted.

Several things stopped her. She'd given Ryan her word to keep this arrangement just between them. In this day of easy promises, she liked to think that her word meant something. And then there was a more practical matter. If she went back on her promise, what would stop Ryan from going back on his word? If he told Tripp Randall that she was interested in him, she'd be mortified.

And—she glanced at the medallion lying on the dresser—this would be her chance to get to know Ryan better and for him to get to know her in a nonwork setting. Perhaps she'd discover he wasn't her one true love. Then she could move on with her life. Find the man she was meant to be with.

But say she didn't get tired of him. She'd give this odd arrangement until the holidays were over. If he hadn't fallen for her by then, he never would. Then she would make every effort to do as she'd promised and steer Adrianna his way. Until then, she was giving herself the best shot.

The ringing of her doorbell pulled her from her reverie. She glanced at the clock on the wall, surprised to find it was time. Taking one last quick look in the mirror, she was pleased to see that for an average person, she looked a little above average today.

She paired a soft red sweater with a black tweed skirt and boots. Even if she had to say it herself, she looked pretty darn good.

The doorbell rang again, and Betsy swiped on another layer of lip gloss. She shut Puffy, her Pomeranian, in the bedroom before hurrying to the door.

Betsy's breath caught in her throat as the door swung open. Above average was today's ugly duckling. Next to Ryan she was a brown moth with nothing to recommend her.

For the casual dinner this evening Ryan was once again

dressed all in black. Black sweater. Black pants. Black boots. Few guys could pull off such a look, but on him, with his broad shoulders, lean hips and classically handsome features, it worked. His hair was tousled and still slightly damp from the shower. He looked, well, way out of her league.

"Happy Thanksgiving." He leaned forward and brushed a kiss across her cheek.

Betsy went absolutely still, resisting—but barely—the urge to touch the tingling spot where his lips had just been. "What—what was that for?"

His eyes widened ever so slightly. "It's a holiday and you looked so nice." Concern filled his eyes. "Was I out of line?"

Mutely, she shook her head.

"Really, if you think I was even the least little bit, just slug me." He leaned over, sticking out his chin.

Betsy raised her hand, but instead of clenching it into a fist, she cupped his face and kissed him right on the lips, like she'd been longing to do for years.

For a second he responded. His lips were warm and firm, and he tasted faintly like chewing gum. When she pulled back, a tiny smile tugged at his lips. "What was that for?"

Betsy shrugged and reached for her coat. "You looked so nice," she said mimicking his response to her, "and it is, after all, a holiday."

The rest of the tension left his face. He grinned. "And I'm starving."

"You and me both, buckeroo."

He helped her on with her parka. His fingers brushed her neck, and a curious thrumming filled her veins. She wasn't sure what had gotten into her, but she was happy she'd taken advantage of the opportunity. Because when this was all over, she didn't want to have any regrets. And right now she didn't have a one.

Somehow Betsy ended up across the table from Ryan at dinner while Adrianna sat directly to his right. He wasn't sure how much Betsy had to do with the seating arrangement, but he owed her big time for this.

The beautiful brunette had smiled a welcome when he'd walked through the door with Betsy, thanking him warmly when he'd handed her a bottle of wine. It had to be the fact that he was here as a guest of her best friend that made the difference. Whatever it was, he appreciated Betsy's efforts. And once Tripp was in town and settled, he would definitely return the favor.

Betsy was telling a hilarious story about the time she and her brother had gotten lost at Yellowstone. He wondered if she knew how pretty she looked when she smiled. He had the feeling he wouldn't have to do much pushing to get Tripp to notice her.

Although Ryan liked Tripp, he was surprised Betsy had a thing for him. He just didn't seem her type. Ryan pulled his brows together and stabbed a piece of, ugh, purple asparagus.

"Does the asparagus taste okay?" Adrianna whispered to him. "I made it myself."

Her perfume was sultry, a sexy fragrance he usually loved. But tonight he found himself wondering if she'd ever considered wearing something different, lighter, say a vanilla scent. For some reason that fragrance held more appeal.

"Everything is…wonderful," he said, looking into her beautiful green eyes. Had he ever known a more beautiful woman? He didn't think so. "My favorite is the sweet-potato casserole."

"Betsy made it." Adrianna smiled proudly.

"How?" he asked. "We didn't bring any food with us."

We? Us? Using words like that made it seem that he and Betsy were a couple. Hardly the impression he wanted to give to Adrianna. Thankfully she didn't appear to notice.

"Betsy is a fabulous cook." Adrianna's long slender fingers curved around the wineglass as she lifted it to her full lips and took a sip. "She came over this morning and helped me get the dinner together. Left to my own talents, this feast would not have been nearly so delightful."

Ryan's admiration for Adrianna inched up another notch. Not many women would be so generous with their praise. He had the feeling she cooked much better than she was admitting.

"Betsy is a special woman." Adrianna smiled in her friend's direction.

"She's a good friend." Ryan put extra emphasis on the last word, not wanting there to be any misunderstanding.

"It's been hard on her, being estranged from her mother and having Keenan…gone." The corners of Adrianna's lips lifted when Betsy laughed at something Benedict Campbell said. "I like seeing her happy."

Ryan absently nodded, his entire attention suddenly drawn to Betsy. He didn't like the way Ben was looking at her. The prominent Jackson Hole orthopedic surgeon was known for being a love-'em-and-leave-'em kind of guy. He wondered if Betsy was aware of that fact. Perhaps he'd have to find a way to bring it to her attention on the drive home. It was a good thing she was interested in Tripp. He wouldn't want her falling for Benedict.

"When Betsy called, I sensed she was concerned that I might not want you here."

Ryan reluctantly jerked his attention back to Adrianna. It almost looked as if Ben had placed his hand on Betsy's knee. But that wasn't his concern. He was here to make a good impression on Adrianna and to mend that long-ago rift. His hostess had just given him the perfect opportunity to discuss that incident. He needed to take advantage of it and not worry so much about Betsy. Still, he kept one eye focused in her direction.

"I'm sorry about the high school incident," he said to Adrianna. The regret in his voice was real. He hadn't known she'd be in the middle of changing her clothes when he'd led the charge into the locker room. "Truly if I knew you—"

"Didn't have any clothes on—"

"—I never would have entered the locker room." His voice was low, for her ears only. "Please accept my apology."

Her gaze narrowed. She searched his eyes. Then a smile lifted her lips. "Accepted."

Ryan reached over and took her hand, lifting it to his lips. "Thank you."

Satisfaction flowed through him when she didn't pull away. Her skin was warm and smooth beneath his lips. But he found he couldn't fully enjoy the moment.

Not with Benedict holding Betsy's hand, right across the table from him, with that familiar predatory gleam in his eyes.

Chapter Six

"She accepted my apology." Ryan handed Betsy a glass of wine and sank into her sofa. He ignored the Pomeranian's growl of displeasure.

After they'd left Adrianna's, Betsy invited him to her apartment for a recap of the evening. Outside, snow had begun to fall in earnest, but Ryan scarcely noticed. Betsy's apartment was warm and inviting. Unlike most of the women he knew, her place had a homey, rather than a designer, feel.

There were rag rugs on the hardwood floors, and the furniture had that comfortable, lived-in look and feel. Her coffee table was rugged with various nicks and stains. When he asked if she had a coaster before he set down his beer can, she'd waved a hand and told him not to worry.

She'd flipped on a couple of table lamps that cast a golden glow over the room, making confidences come more easily. He'd just relayed his conversation with Adrianna. Ryan couldn't wait to hear what she had to say about Benedict. He lifted the can of beer to his lips but didn't take a sip. "So what was going on with you and Benedict?"

"He's a nice guy. We were just talking." She waved a dismissive hand. "Did you like the dinner?"

"It was good. Adrianna said you made most of it."

"I helped," Betsy said modestly. "Cooking is a passion of mine."

"My favorite was the sweet-potato casserole."

Betsy paused. Were they really going to sit here and talk about the food? When there were so many more important things to discuss?

She swallowed past the lump in her throat. "I saw you kiss Adrianna's hand."

He took a sip of beer before speaking. "Do you think it was too much?"

Was he really asking her for dating advice? She, who hadn't been out on a date in almost a year? She was willing to help him out, but not now. Not this way. Not until she'd given herself a fair chance.

"Trust me, you don't want to rush Adrianna."

"Okay. I'll keep that in mind."

To her surprise Ryan didn't seem all that upset. He was a strange one. Like tonight. Unless it was just her overactive imagination, she could have sworn that he'd spent more of the evening watching her than flirting with Adrianna.

"Do you want to play Monopoly?"

Betsy jerked her thoughts back to the present. "What?"

"Monopoly. I haven't played in years. I see it on your shelf."

Betsy followed his gaze. There was a bookcase against the wall filled with games and puzzles. She didn't know what surprised her most—that Ryan had wanted to come in her apartment in the first place or that he appeared to be in no hurry to leave. But she wasn't complaining. Hadn't she just this morning made a vow to get to know him better? And let him get to know her?

"Sure," she said, rising to her feet. "But I've got to tell you one thing first."

"What is that?"

Her lips curved up in broad smile. "I play to win."

Two hours later, Ryan landed on Park Place. He let out a groan that could be heard around the world. The rent for the four hotels Betsy had placed on the expensive property took the rest of his money. He leaned back against the soft fabric sofa. "You're one tough businesswoman, Ms. McGregor."

Betsy scooped up the paper bills. "It's a pleasure taking your cash, Mr. Harcourt."

"Shyster," he said beneath his breath.

"What did you say?"

"I said I'd be happy to help you pick up."

"Yeah, it sounded like that."

They worked together to put all the pieces of the game back together. Ryan couldn't believe how relaxed he had been all evening. Even though they'd eaten a big dinner, Betsy had brought out some homemade snickerdoodle cookies, and they'd munched on those while playing the game. She hadn't even objected when he'd asked if they could have the football game on in the background.

To his surprise she was as much of a football fanatic as he was. Yes, he decided, it had been a good evening. Unfortunately now he was going to have to brave the cold and the icy streets and head home alone.

At least he'd had only two beers and those were hours ago. After finishing the one Betsy had given him when he arrived, he'd switched to milk, which went better with cookies anyway.

Betsy scrambled to her feet and put the game away.

He stood, oddly reluctant to have the evening end. "I can't remember a nicer Thanksgiving. Thanks for inviting me."

She retrieved his coat from the hall closet. "I had a good time, too."

He wanted to ask her what she was doing this weekend but thought better of it. Besides, it shouldn't really be her plans he should be inquiring about; it should be Adrianna's. "Is it okay if I give you a call tomorrow?"

Betsy nodded. "I'll be around."

Ryan shrugged on his coat, making sure the zipper was all the way up. When he walked out of Betsy's front door, he'd be outside. No enclosed hallway or common foyer for this apartment complex. Certainly no covered parking. While Ryan hadn't looked outside lately, he had no doubt the weather had worsened.

He reached for the knob but stopped when he felt her hand on his sleeve.

"Drive safe," she said, her eyes dark and unreadable. "The roads are bound to be snow-packed by now."

Ryan turned the knob and reluctantly pulled the inner door toward him, then pushed open the storm door. The wind immediately tore the door from his hands, flinging it against the siding. Snow filled the air, whipping against his face, making it difficult to see. With Herculean effort he finally got both doors shut, then paused to wipe the ice particles from his face. "I thought the forecasters said we were only getting a dusting. It's a blizzard out there."

Betsy's brows pulled together in a worried frown. "You can't drive home in that."

"I don't see that I have another option." He pulled the

gloves from his pockets, praying he'd put the scraper back in his truck's cab.

"You're not going anywhere." Betsy lifted her chin. "I won't allow it."

"Why, Miss Betsy," Ryan said in an exaggerated Southern drawl, "are you inviting me to spend the night?"

"I'm not inviting," she said in a matter-of-fact tone, "I'm telling. You're staying here with me where you'll be safe."

An image flashed through his head. Him and Betsy, cuddled under the mounds of quilts he'd seen on her bed when he'd used the bathroom earlier.

"I'm not sleeping in your bed." Sleeping with Betsy would make no sense on so many counts that it would be difficult to name them all. If he was going to get naked with anyone, it would be Adrianna.

"I don't recall offering that option." Betsy jerked her head in the direction of the sofa. "It's a sleeper, so you should be comfortable. I know this place isn't as big or as nice—"

He put two fingers over her lips, silencing her words. "I like it here. I feel comfortable. As long as you keep the little red fluffball away from me."

"Puffy is going through a difficult time. Aunt Agatha was her whole world. She simply needs a little TLC and time to adjust."

From several things Betsy had said during the game, Ryan knew she hadn't planned on having a dog. Not only because of the expense, but also because she wasn't home all that often. Despite those issues, she'd taken the ten-year-old dog into her home and into her heart because it was the right thing to do.

According to Betsy, her great-aunt had loved Puffy as if the dog were her own child. There was no way Betsy was letting her go to the pound or to a stranger. Ryan doubted any of the women he'd dated would make such a sacrifice.

Even Adrianna.

It didn't take long before they were both ready for bed. Betsy gave him a pair of pajamas she'd bought in case Keenan was ever able to visit. When she pushed them into his hands, Ryan accepted, knowing his friend wasn't likely to use them.

She went into her bedroom to change. When she came out, he did a double take. Flannel pajamas with feet? "I haven't seen a pair of those since I was four years old."

Her cheeks turned bright pink. "They keep my feet warm."

"You're not going to impress anyone wearing that getup to bed."

She lifted her chin in a defiant tilt. "You're the only one I see here now, and I'm certainly not trying to impress you."

Despite her bravado, he could see that he'd hurt her feelings, which wasn't his intent at all. The truth was, seeing her in such a getup made his fingers itch to take it off her, to see the creamy flesh beneath, to touch her, to kiss her all over….

He pulled his thoughts up short. Seeing Adrianna and having such a pleasant conversation with her this evening must have sent his hormones surging.

"I was just thinking of you and Tripp," Ryan said. "Most guys like silky, sheer stuff."

"I appreciate your advice." Her tone said she didn't appreciate it at all. "But I think I can be trusted to handle my own love life. Good night, Ryan."

He sat on the top of the blankets she'd given him for his makeshift bed. "Don't I get a good-night kiss?"

Ryan expected her to say no. Possibly in a not-so-very-nice tone. Instead she crossed the room and kissed him on the lips, like she'd done earlier. Only this time she let her lips linger for an extra heartbeat. "Sleep tight."

"You, too," he called out as she flicked off the lights and headed to her room.

He crawled under the covers and pulled them up to his chin. Betsy might look like a sweet innocent, but she sure knew how to kiss.

Tripp Randall, he thought to himself, better prepare to be dazzled.

Even though they'd been up late the night before, Puffy was ready to go outside at 7:00 a.m. Betsy tiptoed into the living room, holding the dog in her arms, hoping she wouldn't wake Ryan.

She cast a glance at the couch when she slipped past it. His hair was all mussed and stubble graced his lean cheeks. His eyes were shut and he was breathing easily. From the position of the covers, it looked as though he hadn't moved a muscle all night.

He was still sleeping by the time Betsy brought Puffy inside. She quickly fed the dog, then brought her back to bed. Once under the quilts, Puffy quickly fell back asleep. Betsy wasn't so lucky.

All she could think of was Ryan lying in the other room. When they'd begun the evening, she hadn't been sure she'd get to see him today. Now here he was. In her apartment. Sleeping. With her.

Well, not technically with her. He'd just happened to get stranded at her place. They'd had a good time last night. And she'd learned a lot.

As they played the game, they'd started talking about the people they'd dated in the past. She hadn't realized before then just how many women Ryan had dated and how many times he'd fancied himself in love. While he talked, her mind began counting up the women who at one time or another seemed like "the one" to him. It was a staggering number.

In one way it was reassuring. Was he really in love with Adrianna? Or simply in love with being in love?

It was also worrisome. What if he did fall in love with her? Would she always have to worry that he'd fall out of love as quickly as he fell into it?

"We're not even close to being at that point." Betsy stroked Puffy's soft fur. "There's no need worrying about it…right?"

The Pomeranian opened her eyes, stared at Betsy for a long moment, then licked her chin.

Tears sprang to Betsy's eyes. She couldn't help it. Sometimes she felt so alone. Other than Adrianna, how long had it been since she'd had someone in her life? Someone she truly cared about?

Keenan. But he was in prison.

Aunt Agatha. She was dead.

Ryan. Who considered her simply a means to an end.

But she was going to change that, right? She was going to make him fall in love with her. Which wasn't going to happen if he spent the rest of the morning in bed.

"Time to get up," she called out. "We're going to—"

The words died in her throat when she saw Ryan, all tall, dark and handsome, standing in the doorway to her bedroom, still in Keenan's pajamas.

"What are we going to do?" He stifled a yawn.

Betsy's heart fluttered in her chest. "I thought I'd make breakfast. Later, maybe we could build a snowman."

It had been an impulsive thought, and the second the words left Betsy's mouth she wished she could pull them back. Even though her parka and mittens would keep her toasty warm no matter what the temperature, her cheeks would get chapped and her nose would turn a red that would rival Rudolph's. Hardly a way to make an impression. She should take a clue from Adrianna. Her friend wouldn't be caught dead playing in the snow.

"Snowman?"

"Of course if you can't stay or aren't interested I completely understand," she said quickly.

"No, I'm interested."

Her heart nearly stopped when he crossed the room and sat on the bed. He rubbed his arms up and down with his hands. "Jeesh, it's cold in here."

"I keep the temperature at fifty-eight," Betsy admitted. "Saves on heating costs."

"I bet it does."

Before she knew what was happening he'd flung aside the covers and slipped into bed beside her. Puffy growled but moved over to make room for him.

"What—what are you doing?" Betsy stammered.

"What does it look like?" Ryan said. "I'm preventing myself from getting frostbite while we discuss our plans for the day."

"Oh." Betsy forced herself to breathe. While a tad awkward, this was no different than sitting across the table from him talking over a cup of coffee. Right? *Wrong*. The desire to fling her leg over his and plant an openmouthed kiss on his neck told Betsy that much.

"What shall we have for breakfast?" he asked in a husky voice that did strange things to her insides. "Cereal?"

Betsy made a face. "I was thinking more along the lines of eggs, bacon and brioche French toast."

"Sounds good to me," Ryan said. "Then what?"

"Nothing," Betty stammered, finding it difficult to think

with him so near. She'd be lucky if he thought she had a single brain cell in her head.

"You said something about building a snowman," he prompted, proving despite that sleepy look he'd been listening.

"I haven't done it in years," she admitted. "It's not much fun building them alone."

Sheesh, Bets. Why not just paint a big L *on your forehead?*

"I think we should build one," he said. "And you know what else?"

Betsy shook her head, unable to keep from staring at those luscious lips of his.

"We should call Adrianna and ask her to join us."

Chapter Seven

Betsy felt as if she'd been punched in the stomach. She hadn't seen that one coming. Still, she didn't think Ryan noticed her surprise. Because of her mother's shocking behavior, she'd had years of practice schooling her features.

"What a good idea," she said brightly. "I'll give Adrianna a call right now."

Pushing the sheets and comforter aside, Betsy hopped out of bed, not even minding the coolness of the air. All she knew was she had to put some distance between her and Ryan. Give herself a few seconds to compose her thoughts and her emotions.

This is what you agreed to, she told herself as she scurried from the room to get her phone. *You're supposed to be fixing him up with her.* Last night they were two buddies hanging out. When he'd slid into bed with her this morning, her hopes had risen, but he'd only wanted to stay warm. He hadn't given her a second thought. How could he when his thoughts were so firmly focused on Adrianna?

Betsy located her phone in its usual spot, next to the coffeepot on the counter. She took several deep breaths while she unplugged it from the charger, then speed-dialed Adrianna.

Her friend answered on the first ring. They chatted for a few minutes before the conversation ended.

"Did you reach Adrianna?" Ryan asked from the kitchen doorway, Puffy standing beside him.

"She can't come." Betsy tried not to let her relief show. She wasn't surprised. Adrianna hated driving on snow-packed roads. If a baby was on the way, she went out. Otherwise, she stayed at home. "She has the day off and wants to relax and enjoy it, not play in the white stuff."

A startled look crossed Ryan's face. "She said that?"

"Those were her exact words." Betsy grabbed a sack of coffee from the cupboard and held it up. "Care for a jump start? I have to warn you, I drink the extra-strong cowboy blend."

Ryan grinned. "A woman after my own heart. Bring it on, baby."

For someone supposedly in love, the attorney didn't seem all that upset that Adrianna wasn't joining them. He whistled as he crossed the room with Puffy trotting alongside him. But when he reached the table, he paused. "Should I get dressed first?"

Betsy dumped some dry dog food into a bowl with tiny bones around the perimeter. Not until she'd placed it on the floor did she realize she'd already fed Puffy. Flustered, she glanced at Ryan. "What do you mean?"

"My mother. She was very strict with us boys." Ryan's lips lifted in a rueful smile. "No food until we were fully dressed."

Betsy thought of her own mom. It had been the same in her house, except she and Keenan didn't get food unless they made it themselves. "Well, I'm not your mother—"

"Thank God—"

"And I've been known to spend the whole day in my pj's.

His eyes lit up. "Watching football?"

"When the Broncos are playing." Betsy started the coffee and almost instantly a rich aroma filled the air. "Usually I read."

"Do you have any big plans for today?"

"Not until later." She held up a mug. "Black or with cream or sugar?"

"Black, please."

She filled the cup, then placed it before him. "With all the sales, I probably should be shopping, but it's not like I have anyone to buy for. Except Adrianna and I already know what I'm getting her."

"What about me?" He took a sip of the steaming brew.

Betsy added a dollop of cream to her coffee, then took a seat at the table across from him. "Are you asking if you should get Adrianna a gift?"

"Actually I was asking if you were going to get *me* a gift."

"Dream on, boss man. You make a heck of a lot more money than I do."

Ryan grinned and wrapped his hands around the mug. "Can't blame a guy for wanting something under the tree."

Betsy laughed. Ryan had parents, brothers and a boatload of friends. She seriously doubted the guy had to worry about not getting any presents. "Well, if you end up with no gifts, I'll bring one to put under your tree."

"First I have to have one."

"You've lost me."

"A tree." He straightened in his chair so quickly that

coffee spilled over the top of his cup. "That's what we should do today. Pick out a Christmas tree. One for your place and one for mine."

She handed him a napkin. "I don't put up a tree."

"Why not?" He looked up from the spill, his eyes wide, as if she'd said something horrifying like she didn't eat meat or didn't know how to ski.

The truth was, Betsy didn't feel like telling him the holidays had never been a particularly happy time for her. The last time they'd had a tree, she'd been seven. Her mother had come home drunk and fallen into it. "Who'd see it?"

Ryan sat back in his chair, an expression of faux shock on his face. "A scrooge. That's what you are, Betsy McGregor. A modern-day scroogette."

Even though he was clearly teasing, something in his tone must have hit Puffy wrong. The Pomeranian lifted her head from the food bowl and growled.

"It's okay, Puffball," Ryan said. "Just keeping it real."

After a moment the dog resumed eating.

"You call me a scrooge simply because I don't put up a Christmas tree?" Betsy laughed. "That's reaching, Harcourt."

"There was a distinct scroogelike quality to your voice," Ryan insisted, all serious. It was the twinkle in his eyes that gave him away.

"Hey, I'm a romantic. A woman who loves doggies and kitties and small children. I even carry around a coin with hearts on it in my purse."

Ryan leaned back in his chair, a smirk on his face. "You're bluffing."

"Oh, ye of little faith." She grabbed her bag from beside the counter and reached inside. Her fingers quickly located the medallion in the small inner pocket where she'd put it for safekeeping. She pulled it out and tossed it to him.

He caught it easily, flipping it over, then holding it up to the light. "This is a love token."

"You're making that up."

"I'm not. My father found one in an antiques store and bought it for my mother for Valentine's Day a couple years back."

"What's a love token?"

"They were popular in the eighteenth and nineteenth centuries. It was a coin a man personalized for the woman he loved."

"This one has writing on it, too," Betsy pointed out. "But it's not English."

"It's French," he said. "If those years of college French were worth anything, I should be able to translate."

Betsy got up and rounded the table, peering over his shoulder. "What does it say?"

"Vous et nul Autre," he murmured. "You and No Other."

"What?"

"That's what it says, 'You and No Other.'" His eyes softened. "Whoever had this engraved was obviously very much in love."

Betsy loved the sentiment. "You think it's stupid."

To her surprise the smile left his lips. He shook his head, suddenly serious. "Not at all. Actually I hope to feel that way about my wife. And I hope she'll feel that same way about me."

Even though he didn't say her name, from the look in his eyes Betsy knew Ryan was thinking about Adrianna.

That feeling of closeness that had begun to build, disappeared. "Ready for breakfast?"

"You still need a tree."

"So you say."

Ryan met her gaze. "I'm not giving up."

Betsy steeled her resolve. "I'm not either."

But as she got out the skillet, Betsy knew she wasn't talking about a tree. Rather, she was talking about the man sitting across the table, the one she loved.

You and no other.

Give up? Not on her life. Not as long as there was a chance he could love her, too.

Ryan had known a lot of women over the past fifteen years. None of them like Betsy. Most of them barely knew what a kitchen was, much less their way around it. Adrianna had been right, Betsy was a fabulous cook. The breakfast she'd made had been the best he'd ever tasted.

Each egg had been a perfect sunny-side up, the bacon crisp without being brittle and the brioche French toast, well, even though he was full, his mouth watered just thinking of it now. But her talents didn't end in the kitchen.

She had a keen eye. After she'd showered and he'd cleaned up the kitchen, they'd driven to a Christmas-tree farm not far from Jackson. With it being Black Friday, there weren't many searching for a tree.

Ryan found one almost immediately, but Betsy had shaken her head and pronounced it too tall. Then he'd found a tree that was beautifully shaped, wide and full. She'd dismissed it as too short.

For someone who hadn't even wanted a tree, she was being awfully picky.

"I've found it," he heard her call out.

He quickened his steps, which wasn't easy because of the snow on the ground. Yet it was beautiful outside. The day was clear and the breeze, while cool, had that crisp bite he'd always liked. Overhead the sun shone brightly in a blue sky.

Ryan followed the sound of her voice, grabbing on to a tree branch to help him make his way up a steep slope, wondering how she'd made it. Ryan could see by her tracks that she'd slipped and inched her way up the incline while he was checking out trees farther down. But she hadn't complained or called to him for help.

He finally made it close enough to get a good view of the tree that had met with her approval. It was a Douglas fir, thick without being stubby, tall but not straggly. A perfect specimen. Sort of like the woman who stood beside it with her head cocked.

"This one has it all," she said with a decisive nod.

"It will do."

Betsy nodded again. "Now we have to find one for you."

Ryan frowned. "I thought this would be mine."

Betsy's lips twitched. "Nope."

She looked a bit too self-satisfied for his liking.

"Because it's yours..." Ryan grabbed a handful of snow, packed it slightly, then let it fly.

It sailed past Betsy's head and splatted against the tree.

Betsy whirled. "Hey, what do you think you're doing?"

"Testing how your perfect tree handles snow load."

"Well, stop it."

"Not yet." Without pausing, Ryan quickly made another snowball. This one clipped the top of the tree.

He smiled. How long had it been since he'd made a snowball, much less thrown one? He really should get—

Snow hit his chest.

Giggles filled the air.

He fixed his gaze on Betsy. "Did you deliberately hit me with that snowball?"

She shook her head, while doubling over with laughter.

"You know what that means...." He scooped another handful of snow and carefully packed it, his gaze never leaving hers.

Her laughter ceased. She straightened and her eyes flashed a warning. "You wouldn't dare."

His smile widened. "You started it."

He released his snowball the instant she released hers. He aimed for her chest. Hers hit him right in the face.

From that second it was game on. The balls flew fast and furious. Ryan bobbed and weaved, but Betsy had a deadly aim. After several minutes, even with gloves, his hands felt frozen and his cheeks stung from where she'd nailed him. Three times. But he was having so much fun he didn't want it to end.

"Stop this right now." The portly owner of the Christmas tree farm huffed and puffed his way up the hill, giving a little yelp as Betsy's last snowball barely missed him. "What the heck is going on here?"

"She's got a wicked arm," Ryan said, only half joking. Because he had the snowball in his hand, it seemed a shame to waste it. He let it fly.

"That was unfair, Harcourt," Betsy called out. "He'd said to stop."

"Good to know you're a woman who follows the rules." He knew he shouldn't push his luck, but he couldn't help it.

"I'm going to—" She reached over to grab some snow, but the owner held up his hand.

"If I see one more snowball flying through the air, I'm not letting either of you have a tree."

Ryan thought of how long it had taken them to find even one acceptable specimen. "Truce."

"I'm the winner," Betsy announced.

"You two can discuss that later," the owner said. "Did you find a tree you wanted? Or were you too busy hitting each other with snowballs?"

Betsy caught Ryan's eye and they burst out laughing.

The old man looked at them as if they'd lost their mind.

Twenty minutes later, the tree had been cut and placed in the back of Ryan's pickup. When he saw Betsy shivering, Ryan nixed looking for a second tree.

"One's enough," he told her. "For today. Besides I'd like to get out of these wet clothes. I imagine you would, too."

"I am a bit chilled." Betsy hunched her shoulders against the wind.

"I'll drop you and the tree off at your place, then I'll go home, shower and come back. We can hang the ornaments tonight."

"Uh, actually, Adrianna and I are getting together this evening." Betsy glanced at the blue sky. "Because the weather is better, I'm sure she'll be coming over."

Ryan thought about suggesting that the three of them put up the tree, but he decided not to force the issue. "Do you two have big plans for the evening?"

Betsy lifted one shoulder in a slight shrug. "I'm not sure."

"Because it's Friday night, I'll be at Wally's Place. At least for a little while." Ryan kept his tone casual and offhand. "If you're out you should stop by."

Betsy made a noncommittal noise and changed the subject. They chatted easily on the way to her house. He hadn't realized she was such a rodeo fan.

"Do you miss it?" Betsy asked.

"I miss the adrenaline rush," he admitted. "There's nothing like being on the back of a two-thousand-pound bull and making it a full eight seconds."

"Why did you quit?" From the look in her eye, she was truly interested.

"It's hard on your body," he conceded. "I was fortunate that I'd never been seriously injured. But it was only a matter of time. Besides, I was ready to move on to something else, to the next phase of my life."

"You're a good attorney," Betsy said. "You care about your clients and about seeing justice served."

"My professional life is solid."

"So what's next?"

"Hopefully marriage and a family," Ryan said.

"That's what I want, too."

"That's why we're working together," he reminded her. "To help each other get that special person."

"Adrianna."

"Don't forget Tripp," Ryan said. "On that front, I have some good news."

She glanced out the window.

"I got a text from him while we were looking for a tree. He should be back in Jackson Hole any day. Good news, huh?"

"I guess."

Was that a sigh? "You don't sound very excited."

"I'm realistic," Betsy said. "He won't like me."

Up ahead the light changed to red and Ryan pulled the truck to a stop. "What are you saying? He's going to love you. You're the kind of woman any man would want."

"I'm not that kind of woman," Betsy said, almost sounding angry. "I'm a buddy. A friend. Someone they can tell their troubles to and then go back to their girlfriend feeling better."

Ryan thought how enticing she'd looked on that hill with her cheeks red with the cold, her eyes as blue as the sky. He wasn't even her boyfriend and it had been all he could do to keep from kissing her.

"Trust me," he said, "Tripp is going to take one look at you…and it'll be all over."

And if Tripp couldn't see what a gem Betsy was, well, he didn't deserve her.

Chapter Eight

After ordering at the Perfect Pizza front counter, Betsy and Adrianna found a small table by the window and sat down with their drinks.

"I'm glad it quit snowing." Adrianna barely glanced at the outdoor winter wonderland that resembled the front of a Christmas card. Snow clung to bare tree branches while strings of brightly colored lights decorated the nearby storefronts. "I don't like driving when the roads are slick, but I hated the thought of missing our girls' night out."

"What did you do all day?" Betsy asked.

"Slept late, did my nails, read a couple issues of *Maternal-Fetal Medicine* that I hadn't gotten to yet."

"Wild day."

Adrianna's cherry-red lips tilted upward. "I'm betting yours wasn't much more exciting."

"Actually it was." Betsy took a sip of her soda, then

filled Adrianna in on everything that had happened since they'd last spoken.

Her friend's green eyes widened. "You let him spend the night?"

"He didn't sleep in my bed, if that's what you're intimating." Betsy had conveniently left out the part when he'd crawled under the covers with her that morning. "What was I to do? Throw him out into a blizzard when I have a perfectly nice sofa bed?"

"I suppose not," Adrianna grudgingly admitted.

"We played Monopoly."

"I know that smile. You won, didn't you?" Her friend leaned forward, resting her elbows on the table. "You bought a bunch of properties and put hotels on all of them. He landed on them one too many times and went bankrupt."

Betsy lifted one shoulder and batted her eyelashes. "Perhaps."

Adrianna chuckled. "I'm surprised he's still speaking to you."

"He took it like a gentleman." Betsy realized with a start that Ryan hadn't been at all threatened by her success. "In fact I think he admired my business acumen."

"You need to hold on to him, Bets," her friend said, suddenly serious. "You should consider making him your boyfriend instead of simply your friend."

Oh, if it were only that easy. "He's not interested in me in that way."

"He wouldn't be spending so much time with you if that was true. I've seen how he looks at you."

"Well, I've seen how he looks at *you,*" Betsy blurted out.

"Small, thin crust, green and black olives." The college student who'd appeared out of nowhere held out the pizza.

"That's ours." Betsy welcomed the interruption. Hopefully by the time they started eating Adrianna would forget all about their Ryan conversation.

But from the speculative gleam in her friend's eyes, Betsy had a sinking feeling that was simply wishful thinking.

Adrianna delicately forked off a bite of the pizza. "Are you saying you think Ryan likes *me?*"

"You're his type, Anna. You've got the look he goes for. Perfect hair. Immaculate makeup. Stylish clothes." She couldn't say more without betraying Ryan's confidence.

"And that's really gone well for him, hasn't it?"

"What do you mean?"

"He's dated a lot of women since he's been back in Jackson Hole, but none of them have stuck." Adrianna swept her hair off her face with the back of her hand. A group of men in a nearby booth cast admiring glances her way, but her friend didn't appear to notice. "What does that tell you?"

"Um, that he just hasn't found the one?"

"Or that he's looking for love in all the wrong places," Adrianna said.

Betsy couldn't help but smile. "Do you *really* have to use the lyrics from a country song to make your point?"

"You have to admit it fits."

While they ate, Betsy wondered if perhaps Adrianna was right. Was Ryan setting his sights on unattainable women? Not that the handsome cowboy-turned-lawyer wasn't a worthy catch himself, but it seemed as though the women he chose weren't a good match for him.

Adrianna was a perfect example. Ryan was an outdoorsy type who loved winter sports. Once snow started flying, Adrianna considered being outdoors as going from a building to her car. Not only that, Ryan was a meat-and-potatoes guy. Adrianna refused to eat anything with a face. The reality was, the two had little in common and Ryan didn't even know it.

This led Betsy to the logical conclusion that Ryan didn't *love* Adrianna but was merely mesmerized by her beauty. Not that her friend wasn't a wonderful woman. She just wasn't the right woman for him. And if Ryan had been around Adrianna for any period of time, he'd have discovered that for himself.

Which meant Betsy didn't need to fear the two being together. In fact she should be encouraging interaction.

Contemplating that idea, Betsy took a big bite of her slice of pizza and washed it down with a sip of soda. "Ryan told me Tripp should be back in Jackson next week."

"That's what he told me, too," Adrianna said in an offhand tone.

Intrigued, Betsy lifted a brow.

"Tripp called this morning and mentioned he was relocating. Because I know Jackson Hole so well, he wanted my help and thoughts on various rental possibilities."

"Why would he need your help?" Betsy pulled her brows together. "The guy grew up here."

A deep red inched its way up Adrianna's neck.

"It's been a long time since he's been home," Adrianna responded, then promptly changed the subject. "What shall we do tonight? Do you have any thoughts?"

"A movie?"

"We could." Adrianna expelled a sigh. "But there's not anything good playing right now."

Wally's Place was an option. Until this moment Betsy had planned to keep Adrianna away from the popular sports bar because she knew Ryan would be there. But perhaps she needed to rethink her strategy. As long as Ryan thought he was in love with Adrianna, any feelings he might be developing for Betsy wouldn't stand a chance.

He needed to be around Adrianna so he could see just how incompatible they were....

Risky. But deep in her heart, Betsy believed she stood a chance. A good chance. When they were slinging snowballs and insults at each other today, she'd felt a connection. The look she'd seen in his eyes told her he'd felt it, too.

"We could check out Wally's Place." Betsy's casual tone was at odds with her racing heart. "They have a live band tonight."

Adrianna took another bite of pizza, thought for a moment, then nodded. "Sounds like fun."

"Would it make you uncomfortable if Ryan were there?" Betsy had to ask. Adrianna didn't appreciate surprises.

"What makes you think he'll be there?"

"From what he's said, he usually goes there on the weekends."

"Ah, now I understand." A knowing look filled Adrianna's eyes. "This is all part of some grand plan, isn't it?"

Betsy simply smiled and let her beautiful friend draw her own conclusions, praying this "grand plan" wouldn't blow up in her face.

"Sure you don't want to come with me?" Betsy asked with a smile so appealing that Ryan was almost tempted to agree. Emphasis on the word *almost.* He didn't like Benedict Campbell enough to go three feet, much less push his way through a crowded room simply to greet the guy.

He lifted his glass of beer. "I'm a little busy."

Betsy rolled her eyes and pushed back her chair. "I guess that means I go by myself."

She pretended to be irritated with Adrianna, who'd also refused her request. But Ryan wasn't fooled. It was obvious she'd set it up so that he and her friend could have some time alone together.

He cast a sideways glance. As always, Adrianna looked stunning. Tonight she wore a green sweater and jeans that hugged her slender curves and made her legs look as though they went on forever. The overhead light played off the auburn highlights in her hair. Her cherry-colored lipstick emphasized her full lips.

The strange thing was, Ryan felt no urge to kiss her. It must be because they were in a bar. He'd never been into public displays of affection.

"How's the baby business?" he asked when she continued to sit there sipping her martini. If it had been Betsy, she'd have been talking a mile a minute by now. Ryan had to admit that it had taken him a while to get used to the nonstop chatter, but now it felt odd to be sitting in silence.

"It's been surprisingly busy lately." Adrianna turned in her chair to face him. "More women are choosing to have their babies at home. It's a great way for other family members to be a part of the birth. After all, it's a completely natural experience."

Ryan's smile froze on his face. Was she saying that the kids were there for the birth? He couldn't imagine if his mother had wanted him in the room when his little sister was born. He might have had to run away from home. "How nice."

She returned her attention to her martini.

He shifted his gaze to Betsy, who now stood next to the prominent surgeon. Like Adrianna, Betsy wore jeans and a sweater. Unlike her friend, Betsy had a girl-next-door prettiness that made the whole room light up. She was laughing and talking with the doctor as if they were old friends.

"She's really coming out of her shell." Adrianna leaned closer.

Her perfume seemed almost cloying tonight. He sat back. And he didn't appreciate her comment.

"I didn't know Betsy was ever in a shell," he said, rising to her defense. He would have said more but a hand slapped him on the back.

"Why did I know I'd find you here?"

Ryan recognized the voice immediately. He turned in his seat, rising as he did. "I thought you weren't getting into town until next week."

Tripp Randall laughed. "Can't a guy be spontaneous?"

His friend's blond hair was covered by a ball cap. A hint of a scruff dotted his chin. He cast a curious glance in Adrianna's direction. "Aren't you going to say hello?"

Adrianna rose in one smooth movement, stepped forward and gave their new guest a big hug. "Welcome back to Jackson."

Tripp looped an arm around her neck in a friendly gesture. "Now, that's more like it."

Ryan shot him a pointed glance. "If you're expecting a hug from me, you can forget it."

"Mind if I sit?" Before Ryan could answer, Tripp pulled out Betsy's chair and plopped down.

"That spot is taken, but I guess you can sit there for now." Ryan slanted a sideways glance at Adrianna. "Unless you prefer it be just you and me?"

Her eyes widened and she looked shocked.

"Just kidding," Ryan told her.

Tripp stared at him and Adrianna. "Are you two a couple?"

"Us? No," Adrianna said, a little too quickly for Ryan's liking, despite the fact that issuing a quick disclaimer had been the first thing that had come to his lips, too.

"Actually, I'm here with Betsy." Ryan pointed to where she stood with her hand on the doctor's arm. "She's the one in the blue sweater. And I'm also with Adrianna."

"Two women. You're moving up in the world, boy,"

Tripp said with an easy smile. "I don't believe I know Betsy."

"Keenan McGregor's sister," Ryan said. "I recently hired her as my legal assistant."

"Betsy's a sweetheart," Adrianna said loyally.

For some reason, Ryan didn't want to talk about Betsy with Tripp. He knew his reluctance made no sense. After all, he'd promised Betsy he'd try to get the two of them together. Of course, he reasoned, first he had to make sure his friend was worthy of her. That might take some time.

"How long are you in town?" Ryan asked.

"Depends. Through the holidays, for sure." Tripp's expression turned serious. "Hopefully longer if the job I want comes through. My dad isn't doing well. Because I'm here, I'd like to spend as much time with him and my mom as possible."

"I remember you saying he'd been diagnosed with cancer." Ryan cocked his head. "I thought he'd beaten it."

"That's what we all thought." Tripp pushed back his chair and stood.

"You're leaving?" Adrianna said, sounding panicked.

"Just getting a draw. The waitress looks swamped. Who knows how long it will take her to get to our table." Tripp glanced at Ryan and Adrianna. "Can I get you anything?"

"Another apple martini?" Adrianna said with a smile that Tripp didn't appear to notice.

"I'm okay," Ryan said.

"I'll be back," Tripp said, but instead of turning in the direction of the bar, he headed across the room toward Betsy, who'd finally left Benedict's side.

Ryan narrowed his gaze as Tripp approached her. Betsy's tentative smile widened when Tripp pointed in the direction of him and Adrianna. She probably thought he sent the guy to her. As Ryan watched, Tripp crooked his arm. She slid hers through it and sauntered with him toward the bar.

"She doesn't even know him," Ryan said to no one in particular.

"Like I said, our little Betsy is coming into her own." Adrianna laughed. "I knew it would happen."

"What are you talking about?"

"Betsy hasn't always been popular with men," Adrianna said. "But lately guys are finally seeing what a great girl she is."

"What guys?" Ryan demanded. Betsy hadn't said one word about other men in her life.

Adrianna shoved her chair back, still managing to look graceful in the process. "I'm going to check out the ladies' room. I'll be back."

Just like that Ryan found himself alone. No Adrianna. No Tripp. And most important, no Betsy.

Betsy found it easy to converse with Tripp. Perhaps because she didn't care what he thought of her.

He looked different than she remembered, taller, more manly. While he didn't make her heart beat even a little faster, with his thick blond hair, vivid blue eyes and strong features, he was an attractive man. Even the scruff on his chin looked good on him.

The tattered jeans and well-worn henley shirt weren't much to speak of, but perhaps he'd fallen on hard times. She could certainly empathize.

"What brings you back to Jackson Hole?" she asked when they reached the bar.

"I'm out of one job and looking for another." He motioned the bartender over and quickly gave his order. "I have a promising lead here, so I'm back for an interview."

"I hope you get the position." Betsy covered his hand

that was resting on the bar with hers. "I know how it feels to be out of work and out of money. It's no fun."

He searched her eyes, then a tiny smile lifted the corners of his lips. "But you have a job now."

"I do." She glanced over her shoulder at Ryan, who was now sitting alone at the table, and waved. "I'm Ryan's legal assistant."

The bartender set down the drinks and Tripp pulled a twenty from his pocket.

"No." She pushed his crumpled twenty back at him and took one of her own from her purse. She held it out to the portly bald-headed gentleman behind the bar, who watched the interchange with an amused smile. "My treat."

The bartender took the money and turned away, already busy with another order.

Tripp tried to push the twenty-dollar bill into her hand, but she clenched her fist and shook her head.

"You might not get this job." Betsy hated to be blunt, but Tripp had to be realistic. "I mean, I hope you do, but if you don't, you're going to need every penny to just survive."

His gaze searched her face. His cool blue eyes softened. "Thank you. You're very kind."

"Once you land your job," she said, "you can buy me a drink."

"It's a deal." Tripp slanted a look back at the table. Adrianna had returned, and she and Ryan were talking. "He's really obsessed with her."

"Obsessed? What are you talking about?"

"Adrianna. Ryan told me a couple of weeks ago that she was 'the one.'" His eyes darkened and Betsy couldn't tell if Tripp was happy about that or not. Perhaps he wanted Adrianna for himself. Or maybe he agreed with her and didn't think the two were a good match.

Betsy swallowed past the lump that had appeared without warning in her throat. "She's as pretty on the inside as she is on the outside."

"How do you feel about her and Harcourt hooking up?"

I hate it, Betsy wanted to cry out, *because he's mine.*

But he wasn't hers. Not yet anyway. "If Adrianna and Ryan become a couple, I'll be happy for them."

"Really?" He lifted a brow. "Something in the way you look at him made me think there might be more between you."

"We're friends," Betsy said firmly, hoping to put an end to his fishing expedition.

"Good."

"Why good?"

She felt him rest his hand lightly against her back as thcy made their way to the table.

"Because I like you, Betsy McGregor," he said. "And when I land this new position, I'm going to call and ask you to celebrate with me."

Betsy smiled, knowing he was only teasing. But she played along anyway. "Then I'll keep my fingers crossed you get the job."

Chapter Nine

Across the room, Ryan's gaze settled on Betsy laughing with Tripp at the bar. A knife twisted in his gut. It had been a long time since he'd felt the sensation flowing through his veins, but he recognized it immediately. *Jealousy.*

Surprisingly, it wasn't Adrianna engendering the response, but Betsy. Betsy. With her mile-a-minute mouth just made for kissing. With her snowball-throwing arm and fabulous cooking skills. With her kind heart and killer Monopoly instinct.

He'd watched Adrianna picking her way through the crowd. Seen the admiring glances sent her way. Until recently Ryan had been one of those guys. Even though she was a nice woman, he realized now that his attraction had been superficial, not deep. Certainly not the lasting kind.

When Betsy and Tripp returned to the table, he flashed an easy smile, settling his gaze on Betsy. "What kept you away so long, sweetheart?"

The endearment felt right on Ryan's tongue.

Even in the dim light, he could see Betsy's cheeks pink.

After staring curiously at Ryan, Tripp handed the drink to Adrianna with a flourish. "Your apple martini, ma'am."

The smile that had been missing from the pretty brunette's lips for most of the evening returned. "I'm not sure about the ma'am part, but thank you, Tripp."

Ryan stood and gestured for Betsy to take his seat, then grabbed a chair from a nearby table and slid it next to hers. When she smiled her thanks, Ryan felt a surge of satisfaction. She hadn't looked at Tripp once since she'd reached the table. Which made him wonder if Betsy liked Tripp as she'd said. No matter. When he got his friend alone, Ryan was going to have to make it clear that Betsy was off-limits. Tripp would understand. A real friend never poached on another man's woman.

"You're up to something," Betsy said in a low tone just loud enough for his ears. "I recognize that look in your eyes."

"Ever thought of riding a bull?" Okay, so it wasn't a great way to change the direction of the conversation, but it was the first thing that popped into his head.

Betsy knew it was noisy in the bar, but had he really asked if she'd ridden a bull? "Ah, no. I lead a rather boring life."

"Our lives are only as boring as we make them." Ryan jumped to his feet and held out his hand. "No time like the present to kick things up a notch."

Betsy accepted his hand and slowly rose to her feet. "Kick what up a notch?"

"Life," Ryan said. "I suspect we've both been sitting on the sidelines playing it safe. It's time to reach out and grab what we want."

Betsy cast a sideways glance at Adrianna, who appeared engrossed in a conversation with Tripp.

"This isn't about her," Ryan leaned close and whispered in her ear. "This is about you."

He stood so near that it seemed a shame not to slide her arm around his waist. She looked into his eyes, not caring what he might see in hers.

Whatever he saw must have pleased him because a slow smile spread across his face. "Are you ready?"

She'd been ready for him for years, but she'd like to hear exactly what he had in mind. She trailed a finger down his shirtfront. If he wanted to live dangerously, she was definitely in the mood. "For what?"

"I'll show you."

Riding a mechanical bull wasn't exactly what Betsy had in mind. In fact, simply sitting on the back of the black-and-white monstrosity scared her spitless.

"This isn't what I thought *living dangerously* meant," she muttered.

Ryan's hand ran down her leg as he checked her seat. "What did you say, sweetheart?"

She didn't know why he'd started calling her his sweetheart, but she liked it. It made her feel connected to him in a very personal way.

"Hey, Ryan." Heidi—or whatever her name was—suddenly appeared holding a bottle of beer loosely between her fingers. "What's up with this? You can't possibly think she's going to stay on."

Betsy lifted her chin. "I can make it eight seconds."

Heidi's peal of laughter felt like a swift slap. "Honey bunny, I hate to break it to you, but this isn't a real bull. Fifteen seconds is what most people do on this one. You'll be lucky to make it two."

"Don't listen to her." Ryan's voice took on a hard edge

and his gray eyes were cold as steel. "We're a little busy here."

The woman's gaze drifted from Ryan to Betsy, then back to Ryan. "So that's how it is."

"Yes," Ryan said firmly, "that's how it is."

Flipping a strand of long blond hair over her shoulder, Heidi flounced off.

"I'm going to embarrass you," Betsy said, suddenly miserable.

Surprise flickered in Ryan's eyes.

"Hey, Harcourt." The bored voice of the ride operator interrupted. "This ain't no pony ride. Let me turn it on or get 'er off."

"Shut up, Hank." Ryan didn't even look in the burly man's direction. Instead his gaze remained on Betsy. "Do you want to do this?"

Betsy didn't want to be on the bull. Didn't like having all these people staring at her. But what Ryan said had struck a chord. *Our lives are only as boring as we make them.*

It was as if her life flashed before her and she realized she'd been living in shades of brown. A careful, well-ordered life designed to not draw attention to herself lest anyone compare her with her mother.

But her mother was dead and she was alive. And Betsy suddenly realized she didn't want to be brown. She wanted to be red and purple and the vibrant orange that sometimes colored the skies over the Tetons.

"Betsy—" Ryan's hand closed over hers "—it's your decision. What do you want to do?"

"Turn it on."

Ryan started having second thoughts when he saw Betsy's legs shaking. This was supposed to be fun. "Are you sure?"

"I'm ready." Betsy gave a decisive nod.

The resolve in her voice reassured him. And her legs had almost stopped shaking. He rested his hand on her shoulder. "Let me give you a couple of pointers."

Ryan went on to explain the importance of squeezing with her thighs, of using her leg muscles to "root" her to the bull. Then he checked her grip and nodded his approval.

"Try to relax your upper body." Even as he said the words, a shiver of unease traveled up his spine. He knew that most riders got rolled off when the ride operator had the bull bow down in front and the rear tipped up. "When the bull leans forward you lean back. Use your free hand for balance. Move with the bull instead of against it."

He almost made her get off. The fear that she would be hurt hit him with the force of a sledgehammer. But she looked so determined, so brave, he couldn't take the chance away from her.

"I can do this," Betsy vowed, tiny beads of perspiration dotting her brow.

"I know you can." He leaned over and kissed her. Not a peck on the cheek either, but one designed to make her toes curl.

"What was that for?" she asked, her eyes wide and oh so beautiful.

"For luck." He winked. "Turn 'er on, Hank."

At first, being on the bull reminded Betsy of riding one of those horses they used to have sitting outside the supermarket. If you put in a quarter, it would go up and down with a gentle rocking motion.

For a second, she felt confident enough to smile. *This isn't so bad.*

Then the front of the bull took a nosedive. Thankfully Betsy had her legs pressed tightly against the sides of the mechanical animal or she'd have been tossed onto the cushioned mat right then. She remembered what Ryan had said and leaned back, waving her hand in the air for balance.

Had that "Yeehaw" really come from *her* throat?

Just as quickly as the bull lunged forward it rocked back. Betsy kept her upper body fluid and her lower legs tightly gripped.

Calls of "Ride 'em, Betsy" filled the air. Exhilaration fought with fear as the bull gave it everything he had to buck her off.

It was the wildest ride she'd ever been on, but thanks to Ryan's tips, she was prepared. When the fifteen seconds was up, Betsy was almost disappointed her time in the spotlight was over.

As the crowd roared its approval, a cowboy she didn't recognize plopped his black Stetson on her head. "Congratulations, cowgirl."

Betsy smiled, feeling as if she'd just been crowned Miss America.

Ryan pulled her into his arms and, with everyone watching, gave her a big kiss. "That's my girl."

Out of the corner of her eye, Betsy saw Heidi turn and meld into the crowd, a sour look on her face.

"You did good, babe." Ryan's eyes looked like liquid silver in the light. "Full fifteen seconds."

"I had fun." Betsy's breath came in short puffs. "I can see why you liked riding bulls. What a rush."

He slung an arm around her shoulders and the crowd parted before them.

Betsy couldn't believe all the congratulations she received, most from people she'd never met. "Adrianna is going to tell me I was crazy to do it," she said, her words running together in excitement. "She doesn't like anything connected with rodeo."

But when they reached the table, it was just Tripp waiting there, a worried expression on his face.

"Where's Adrianna?" Betsy asked, glancing around.

"She didn't feel well," he said. "She ran to the restroom right after you left to ride the bull. She hasn't come back."

Betsy glanced at Ryan.

He smiled reassuringly. "I'm sure she's fine."

"I'm going to check on her anyway."

"If you need anything—" Ryan began, but Betsy had already disappeared.

As Ryan dropped into the chair, he realized his heart had finally settled into a normal rhythm. All those years he'd rode bulls, his mother had rarely come to watch. She'd told him it was too hard for her to sit there and worry. He'd never understood. Until tonight.

Watching Betsy on the back of the mechanical bull had been almost painful. Intellectually he knew if it tossed her she wouldn't be hurt. Wally's cushioned floor surrounding the bull would see to that. But it wasn't his head that had been stressed seeing her rockin' and a rollin'; it was his heart.

While he'd wanted her to stay on so she could experience that thrill, it had taken everything he had not to pull her off and hold her close, hating to take even the slightest chance that she could be hurt.

It hadn't been his legal assistant on the back of that bull. It hadn't been his childhood friend's sister. It had been the woman he loved.

Ryan sat back as the realization washed over him. Even though it sounded corny, he knew Betsy was the one he'd been waiting for his whole life.

"You know, even if the hospital doesn't offer me the job, meeting Betsy made coming back to Jackson worth the trip," Tripp said.

His friend's words and who Tripp was referring to suddenly registered. It almost sounded as if he was smitten with…Betsy. But that couldn't be true.

"I understand you and Adrianna have kept in touch."

"Adrianna and Gayle kept in touch through the years," Tripp said in an offhand tone. "She's merely a friend."

"Well, Betsy is more than a friend to me." Ryan met the other man's gaze.

Ryan's irritation soared when Tripp laughed. "Don't tell me she's your new flavor of the day? Last time we talked it was Adrianna. Make up your mind, man."

"Betsy is the one—"

Ryan stopped as Betsy and Adrianna walked up. The tall brunette's eyes were watery and her skin unusually pale.

"Adrianna isn't feeling well," Betsy began.

"The stomach flu has been going around the office," Adrianna said with a weak smile. "I'm sorry if I exposed you."

"Do you need help?" Ryan started to rise from his seat.

Betsy waved him back down. "We'll be fine."

She took off the cowboy hat still on her head and handed it to Ryan. "If you could return this to the proper owner, I'd appreciate it."

Ryan took the hat. There were so many things he wanted to say to her, but now wasn't the time or the place. "I'll call you tomorrow."

"It was nice meeting you, Betsy," Tripp said, then shifted his gaze to Adrianna. "Take care of yourself."

"We better go, Betsy." Adrianna's pale complexion now looked almost green.

As the two hurried off, Ryan watched them go. The statuesque brunette and her solicitous friend. The woman he'd thought was "the one" and the woman he loved.

* * *

After taking her friend home, Betsy had barely opened the door to her apartment when the same bug hit her.

She spent that night and most of Saturday alternating between the bedroom and the bathroom. Puffy watched her from the hall with worried eyes. But when Betsy awakened Sunday morning to the ringing of her phone, she realized that for the first time in almost thirty-six hours her stomach felt normal.

She fumbled for the phone she'd flung onto the bedside stand sometime yesterday. "Hello."

"I'm picking you up for church in forty-five minutes."

Betsy pulled the phone from her ear and stared at it. "Who is this?"

"Who do you think it is? Ryan."

"Good morning, Ryan." He'd called several times yesterday but she'd been in no shape to talk to anyone.

"Why didn't you return my calls?"

"I was, uh, incapacitated with the same bug that hit Adrianna." Betsy plumped up several pillows and sat up in bed. "I'm better now."

"You should have told me." Concern filled his voice. "I'd have brought you over some chicken soup or something."

"Trust me, you wouldn't have wanted to be here."

"I could have taken care of you," he insisted. "Or at the least kept Puffy out of your hair."

Betsy glanced at the small red Pomeranian. Other than demanding to be fed and taken outside on schedule, the dog hadn't been much trouble. "Puffy was no problem."

"Well, consider this fair warning. Next time you don't answer my calls, I'm coming over," he said. "I don't like it that you were home all alone and sick."

Her heart rose to her throat. "Well, I'm better now."

"Good. I'll have the truck nice and warm for you."

Where had he said he wanted to take her? Ah, yes, to church.

"I don't attend Sunday services." Betsy had gone a couple of times with friends when she'd been small. But once she realized God really didn't answer prayers, she hadn't been back.

"It'll be fun." He spoke with such enthusiasm that she found herself believing him. "It's casual, so you don't need to dress up. Afterward we'll go with everyone for breakfast at The Coffeepot. They have bland things—like oatmeal—on the menu, too, so you should be able to find something to eat."

Betsy was familiar with the café in downtown Jackson. It was known for its hearty country-style breakfast fare. But who was Ryan referring to when he said "everyone"? She knew church wasn't on Adrianna's agenda. "Will Tripp be there?"

Silence filled the other end of the line. "Probably not. Does that make the difference?"

"No," she said, surprised by the edge to his voice. "I was simply curious who 'everyone' was."

"It varies from week to week," Ryan informed her. "Usually Lexi and Nick Delacourt, David and July Wahl, Travis and Mary Karen Fisher, and Cole and Meg. If they're in town, Derek and Rachel Rossi usually show up, too, as well as a few others."

Although Betsy was acquainted with everyone Ryan mentioned, she didn't run in their social circle. Of course, there was no reason she couldn't get to know them better. And perhaps get to know Ryan better in the process? After all, hadn't someone once said that to know a man, you just need look at his friends? "How long do I have to get ready?"

"Forty minutes."

Betsy swung her legs to the side of the bed and stood, already eyeing her closet. "Okay. And, Ryan?"

"Yes?"

"Thanks."

"For what?"

"For caring that I was sick and offering to come over." She kept her thanks simple, not wanting to be maudlin. "I haven't had anyone who cared for a long time."

"Well," he said, "get used to it. Now you do."

Chapter Ten

Sitting beside Ryan in church felt oddly intimate. When he opened the book in his hand for the next song, Betsy smiled. After the opening hymn, she'd discovered Ryan had a surprisingly good voice and that their voices blended together as if they'd been singing harmony their whole lives.

She wasn't so much conscious of the words as she was the beautiful melody. Life was certainly strange. When Betsy had tumbled into bed last night, she'd never thought she'd be sitting in a church this morning.

As they sat down, Ryan took the book from her hand, his fingers brushing against hers, lingering for an extra beat. Electricity traveled up her arm. He must have felt it, too, because his eyes met hers. For a second she thought he might kiss her right then and there. If that wasn't shocking enough, she had a feeling she'd have let him.

Someone read some scripture, but Betsy scarcely noticed. It was as if there was a bubble around her and Ryan and they were the only two in the room. When he reached over and took her hand, she curled her fingers through his and expelled a happy sigh.

Betsy knew she should ask why he hadn't mentioned inviting Adrianna, but she didn't want to spoil her fantasy. For just this morning she wanted to pretend that Ryan wanted her and no one else.

"Grace is something needed but not deserved," the minister intoned.

The sermon this morning appeared to be centered around forgiveness. It was a topic Betsy preferred not to think about. Those who didn't know her relationship with her mother, who didn't know all she'd endured growing up, often spouted the forgiveness talk. But Betsy was having none of it today.

She'd heard all about forgiveness setting you free, but she already felt free. And how could she forgive a woman who'd never asked for her forgiveness? Who'd gone her merry way through life, hurting all those around her? Who'd even at the time of her death been in a destructive mode?

Betsy hated that the preacher had a voice that was hard to ignore. But she did her best, concentrating on the feel of her hand in Ryan's, on his muscular thigh pressed up against her in the packed pew.

Dress casually, Ryan had said. Thankfully she hadn't tossed on a pair of jeans like she'd considered when she'd hopped out of her superquick shower. Instead she'd chosen a wraparound tweed dress with brown boots and tights. Ryan had whistled when he'd seen her. For a second she'd felt beautiful.

Actually he was the one who was beautiful in his dark pants and gray sweater. And the way he smelled…so good she couldn't stop thinking of that time he'd crawled under her covers. If she had him there now, she'd make sure they did a whole lot more than just talk.

"Time to stand." Ryan tugged her to her feet.

She rose, her heart pumping hard and fast, unable to let go of the image of him in her bed, a visual that seemed stuck in her consciousness.

The minister offered a benediction. When he quit speaking Betsy realized she'd sat through her first church service in over five years. Other than the forgiveness part, it had been bearable. Ryan kept hold of her hand as they exited the pew. It was then that the horde descended.

Okay, so maybe it wasn't a *horde.* But close. Ryan's friends seemed to come out from the woodwork.

"When did you and Ryan start dating?" Mary Karen Fisher had pulled her blond hair back in a bouncy ponytail, making her look more like a college student than a mother.

Betsy had always liked Mary Karen. She was as upbeat and friendly now as she'd been back in high school. Which was amazing considering she had five small children at home, four of them boys.

"We're not actually—" Betsy began.

"Just started," Ryan said before she could finish.

Betsy inhaled sharply.

"You're a good match for him." Lexi Delacourt, a prominent social worker in Jackson Hole, nodded her approval.

"What makes you think that?" Betsy asked.

"Call me for drinks sometime—" Lexi winked "—and I'll tell you why."

"Lexi," Meg Lassister called out, "we're heading over to The Coffeepot to get a table."

"You guys are coming, aren't you?" Mary Karen asked.

Ryan placed a hand on Betsy's shoulder. "We'll be there."

The two of them slowly strolled out of church. The sky was a bright blue and the sun shone warm against her face. Ryan was telling her a story about when Lexi's husband came to Jackson Hole, got caught in an avalanche while skiing the backcountry and lost his memory.

The tale was so unbelievable that she wondered if Ryan made it up. Or maybe this was *all* a dream. It felt like one. Ryan calling her for a date. Being so attentive.

She looped her arm through his. If this was a dream, she was going to enjoy every minute of it.

"Oh, no," Betsy said when they drew close to The Coffeepot. "There's a line."

"No worries." Ryan smiled and edged his way through the crowd, then led her through the maze of tables to a large one in the back. "See? Cole and Meg got the table."

Betsy recognized another one of the couples already seated. Joel Dennes was a prominent contractor in town. His wife, Kate, was a pediatrician. She was also one of Ryan's former girlfriends.

Awkward, Betsy thought to herself as Ryan held out her chair, seating her next to the couple. After introducing her to Joel and Kate, he smiled. "I hear congratulations are in order."

Betsy tilted her head.

"We're having a baby." Kate slipped her hand through her husband's arm.

"Congrats from me, too," Betsy said. "When are you due?"

"The middle of June." Kate's face lit up like a Christmas tree. "Our daughter, Chloe, is thrilled. She said she doesn't need any other presents. Knowing she'll soon have a brother or sister is present enough."

"But we know when it comes time to unwrap gifts,

she'll want something more under the tree," Joel said with an indulgent smile.

Once it got going, the conversation flowed easily. Betsy had seen Kate around, but she'd always seemed a bit standoffish. Today she discovered that Kate was as nice as she was pretty with her dark brown hair, big hazel eyes and a curvy yet lithe figure. Betsy felt like an ugly country mouse sitting next to a pretty city one.

Ryan was in his element, laughing and joking with his friends. Although everyone was friendly, Betsy held back, not sure of her place in this group, not wanting to be too bold.

But the man at her side would have none of it. Ryan skillfully drew her into the conversation, first by making them aware that she was Keenan's sister, then telling all her secrets. From her bull-riding talent to her skill with snowballs.

"You should come out to our house sometime." Kate paused for a moment as the waitress placed plates of food—and her bowl of oatmeal—on the table. "We could build a fort or have a snowball fight. Chloe would love it."

"Count us in." Mary Karen leaned across the table. "As long as we can bring the boys."

Mary Karen's oldest set of twins made Dennis the Menace look like a choirboy.

"If we play, we get Betsy on our team," her husband, Travis, announced.

"What about me?" Ryan pretended to be outraged.

"You already said how good she was," Mary Karen said in a matter-of-fact tone. "Naturally we took that to mean she can take you out."

"Yep," he said, bringing her hand to his lips and kissing it. "She can take me out anywhere, anytime."

Betsy looked him in the eyes and wondered if he'd say

the same thing if Adrianna was sitting beside him. She prayed he was sincere. If he wasn't, she was in trouble. Because she was falling more deeply in love with him by the second.

"Have you slept with him yet?"

"Adrianna, shush," Betsy hissed. "Someone might hear you."

The following weekend, the two women spent the morning checking out the current exhibit at the National Museum of Wildlife Art, then stayed to grab some lunch at the Red Sage Café, located inside the building.

Adrianna glanced around the empty café. "There's no one here. Everyone is out Christmas shopping or skiing."

"I don't feel comfortable discussing my personal life in such a public venue." Betsy kept her voice low.

Although Jackson Hole held almost twenty thousand people, it was also a close-knit community. The last thing she wanted to do was to get some gossip going about her and Ryan.

"Okay, how about if I speak in a whisper?" Adrianna grinned, her voice as loud as before. "Then will you tell me your secrets?"

"There's nothing to tell," Betsy said. "We're only friends."

Adrianna took a bite of her tuna pita. "You really expect me to believe that? I saw the way he looked at you last Friday at Wally's."

"And I've seen the way he looks at *you*." Betsy took a sip of her iced tea, hoping Adrianna would drop this line of questioning but knowing she wouldn't.

Adrianna waved away the comment. She chewed thoughtfully. "Perhaps he doesn't want to push you."

Or maybe he's in love with you.

The thought rose unbidden from the deepest recesses of Betsy's subconscious. Ryan had made it clear he liked being with her, yet he *had* originally enlisted her to help him win over Adrianna. He'd also told Tripp that it was Adrianna he wanted.

Was spending time with her part of a plan to make Adrianna jealous? Or had he simply decided to settle for second best?

Betsy sighed. "Ryan and I are friends, Anna. I've told you that many times."

"Still not believing it."

That's because so far Betsy knew she hadn't been all that convincing. "I think Tripp is going to ask me out."

Adrianna's eyes widened and she straightened in her seat. "Are you going to go?"

"Of course," Betsy said with what she hoped was a convincing smile. "Why wouldn't I?"

Betsy picked up her purse, ready to head out the door when Ryan called to her from his office. She sighed and set down her bag on her desk, hoping this wouldn't be another invitation to stay late.

All week Ryan had been consumed by a case scheduled for court next week. Every night he'd asked her to work late. The first time it had happened she'd thought he had something more personal in mind. But when he'd pulled out his case notes and started to talk, her hopes of a more intimate evening sank like a lead balloon. It had been the same story every night since.

By the time they finished it was usually close to ten and she'd gone home exhausted. Too tired to even trim her Christmas tree. It still sat in her living room, in water, begging for decorations. She'd thought about asking Ryan if he wanted to come over this weekend to help, but decided against it.

She'd started to wonder if the connection she'd felt between them had been all in her head. That's why when Tripp had called, told her he'd gotten the job and offered to take her out to dinner to celebrate, she'd said yes.

"You need something?" Betsy asked, stopping in the doorway to Ryan's adjoining office.

He looked up and she saw the lines of fatigue around his eyes. Putting down his mouse, he sat back in the leather-and-cowhide desk chair. "We've both put in a lot of hours this week. I'd like to take you out for dinner as a token of my appreciation."

A token of his appreciation. The sentiment was sweet, but it hit Betsy wrong. Like he felt forced to take her out.

"Thanks for the kind offer," she said in as pleasant of a tone as she could muster through gritted teeth, "but I already have plans for dinner."

"Oh, are you and Adrianna getting together?"

Now he was really starting to get on her nerves. Granted, some of her less-than-good mood was probably because she was tired, but did he really think she didn't have any other options than dinner with a girlfriend?

"Actually, no. Tripp is taking me out to dinner."

Ryan pushed back his chair and stood. His brows pulled together. "Tripp Randall asked you out?"

Anger shot up Ryan's spine. After that night at Wally's Place, he'd told Tripp he was interested in Betsy and to back off. Of course, come to think of it, Tripp hadn't agreed. His friend had just laughed and asked if Betsy was Ryan's flavor of the day.

When he'd asked Tripp what he meant by that crack, Tripp had said they both knew his infatuation with Betsy wouldn't last. After all, barely two weeks ago he'd told Tripp he was sure Adrianna was "the one."

It pissed Ryan off to know that Tripp was right about him, or rather former Ryan. Even though he knew his friend hadn't meant to hit a nerve, he had. For a few seconds all Ryan could think was he sounded a whole lot like his uncle Jed.

Uncle Jed had three ex-wives and a girlfriend young enough to be his daughter. That wasn't the kind of life Ryan wanted for himself.

Regardless of what Tripp implied, Betsy was different from the others, and he could see them having a future.

But you thought Adrianna was different, too, a little voice whispered in his head. He immediately silenced it and focused on the conversation at hand.

"Is there anything else?" Betsy asked.

She hadn't really answered his question, but from the look on her face, it wouldn't be safe to ask again. But he'd be damned if he'd let Tripp monopolize her weekend.

"Joel called and asked if we wanted to come out for some fun in the snow at their place tomorrow."

"You mean he called and invited *you.*"

"Yes, but he specifically mentioned wanting you to come." Ryan had planned on talking to her about those plans over dinner tonight. But that wasn't happening.

Because she was having dinner with Tripp.

Ryan took a deep breath and forced a smile. "It should be fun. Afterward I thought we might decorate your tree, if you haven't already decorated it, that is."

"When would I have time to trim the tree?" Her expression softened. "My boss is a real slave driver and I spend all my time at work."

Hope rose in his chest. "So you'll do it?"

"Sure," she said. "Sounds like fun."

"I can pick you—"

"Call me tomorrow," she said before he could finish. "I've got to run."

"Okay," he said. "I'll call you in the morning."

"Not too early," she said as she headed toward the front door. "I may be out late."

Chapter Eleven

By the time Ryan called her the next morning at ten and told her they were expected for lunch at noon, Betsy had to scramble to get ready.

She'd had fun with Tripp. He'd taken her to the Spring Gulch Country Club for a night of dinner and dancing. When he'd told her to dress up, she thought he'd been kidding. But just in case, she'd pulled on a little black dress she'd bought last year on clearance.

When he'd shown up wearing a suit and tie, she was glad she'd taken the time. Yet she worried about the cost of the meal and the price of the bottle of wine he'd ordered after he'd announced he was the new hospital administrator at Jackson Hole Memorial. Apparently Mr. Stromburg was retiring and they'd picked Tripp to fill his shoes. He'd come to Jackson Hole to meet with the hospital board before they confirmed the offer.

She'd told him that while it was good that he had gotten

a job, there could still be cash-flow problems while waiting for that first check. He'd simply smiled.

They'd laughed and talked and danced. But when he put his arms around her while they were dancing, she couldn't help but wish it were Ryan holding her tight.

The doorbell rang as Betsy was tying her snow boots. If she and Ryan were going to play in the snow, she was prepared. Flannel-lined pants, ski sweater with silk underwear, Eskimo parka and pink plaid aviator hat.

She'd told Tripp last night about her plans. When she'd mentioned she was planning on wearing her aviator cap with the fur inside, he'd laughed. He'd told her if he could wrangle an invitation he'd go simply to see her in that hat.

The doorbell rang again.

"Coming," she called out.

Puffy ran ahead barking her own greeting.

Betsy hurried to the door and flung it open. Her heart flip-flopped when she saw Ryan. "Good morning."

His navy ski coat made his eyes look more blue than gray and the smile on his face was enough to melt her heart. He held out an insulated paper cup to her.

"What's this?" She took the cup from his hands and waved him inside.

"Cappuccino. I know it's your favorite, and I thought it'd get your Saturday morning off to a good start."

Betsy tilted her head when she saw his hands were now empty. "You didn't get one for yourself?"

"I had some coffee on the way over."

Betsy took a sip. "It's delicious."

"That good, eh?"

"Here." She held out the cup to him. "Try it."

He glanced down where her lips had once been and she immediately regretted her impulsive gesture.

"I'm so sorry. Take off the lid—"

His lips closed on the same spot where hers had been only moments before. “It *is* good.” His gaze never left hers. “And I don’t mind drinking after you. After all, we’ve kissed. How is this so different?”

“We kissed a long time ago.” Betsy stopped herself from admitting that she knew exactly how many days it had been since he’d last kissed her. “It scarcely counts.”

“I can remedy that.”

Before she knew what was happening, he’d placed the cup on the side table near the front door and tugged her to him. Betsy told herself not to fall under his spell, but an invisible web had already begun to weave around her, pulling her in.

He tilted her chin up with a curved finger before his mouth closed over hers. His kiss was sweet and slow, exquisitely gentle and achingly tender.

The momentary thought that she should pull away vanished as she gave in to the moment, to the delicious sensations streaming through her body.

His tongue swept across her lips, and she opened her mouth to him. A smoldering heat flared through her, a sensation she didn’t bother to fight.

“Oh, Bets.” His voice was a husky caress.

His hand slid under her sweater, beneath the silky undergarment. Red flags popped up in her head. She ignored them.

His long fingers lifted and supported her yielding flesh as his thumbs brushed across the tight points of her nipples. All the while he continued to kiss her.

Then a knock sounded at her door.

She stiffened.

“Ignore it,” he murmured.

When three more quick knocks sounded at the door, Betsy knew the unexpected visitor wasn’t going away. “It’s

Mr. Marstand from next door. That's his signal. He knows I'm home."

With obvious reluctance, Ryan dropped his hands to his sides and took a step back.

Betsy adjusted her sweater and hurried to open the door. Her elderly neighbor stood shivering in a light jacket.

Stepping aside, Betsy motioned him in. "Mr. Marstand, you need a heavier coat."

The older gentleman wasn't much taller than Betsy with a mop of unruly white hair and skin pulled taut over his bones. His mustache needed trimming. But his dark eyes were bright and missed nothing.

"I'm only shivering because it took you so long to open the door." Ralph Marstand's eyes settled on Ryan.

After pushing the front door shut, Betsy turned and hurried to the sofa. She grabbed a cotton throw and wrapped it around the man, then gestured to the sofa. "Take a seat," she said. "I'll brew you up a nice cup of tea."

Ryan was all for being hospitable, but they were expected at Cole and Meg's for lunch. He tried to catch Betsy's eye, but she was too focused on the old man.

He dropped into a chair opposite the man and Puffy immediately jumped into his lap. Ryan thought about pushing the Pom off, but Mr. Marstand was staring.

"How long have you known Betsy?" the old man asked.

It had been years since Ryan had dated a girl, rather than a woman. But he remembered being back in high school and having to be interviewed by their father before his date could leave the house. "Pretty much all her life. I'm a friend of her brother, Keenan."

"The one who's in prison?"

"I'm sure Betsy's told you that Keenan is innocent." Without realizing what he was doing, Ryan stroked Puffy's soft fur. To his surprise, instead of growling or baring her teeth, the puffball licked his hand.

"You spent the night."

"What?"

"You heard me." The older man's eyes were filled with disapproval.

"I just got here." Ryan paused. Had Betsy had an overnight guest? Could Tripp have… Nah, Betsy was too smart to succumb to Tripp's charm. But then she *had* sounded sleepy when he'd called, as though he'd awakened her. The question was, who else had he awakened?

"Did you see a car parked over here last night?" Ryan fought to keep his tone casual and offhand.

But before the old man could answer, Betsy swept into the room with a tray in her hand and three cups of steaming tea. She smiled at the two men and placed the tray on the coffee table. "I heard you chatting in the kitchen. What were you talking about?"

"He wanted to know if the guy who picked you up last night—the tall blond one—spent the night." Mr. Marstand picked up one of the mugs and took a sip.

"What?" Betsy's eyes narrowed. "How dare you!"

Puffy hopped off his lap as if it were a sinking ship.

"Nonono," Ryan said. "You misunderstand. He was interrogating me—"

"I asked you a few simple questions," Mr. Marstand said with great indignation. "Since when is it a crime to be friendly?"

"He was the one who asked if I'd spent the night."

"I don't recall that part." The old man tapped his head with a forefinger. "But then my memory isn't what it used to be."

Betsy gave Marstand an understanding smile.

Ryan wanted to slug him.

"Did you ask Mr. Marstand if Tripp spent the night?" Betsy pinned him with her gaze.

"I did not," Ryan said.

"You asked if there was a car parked here overnight," Mr. Marstand said pointedly.

Great. The old guy chose now to regain his memory.

Betsy met Ryan's gaze. "Is that true?"

A trickle of sweat trailed down Ryan's back. Asking that question hadn't been one of his finer moments, but lying would only make it worse. "Marstand, er Mr. Marstand, implied I'd spent the night. I knew I hadn't, so I asked him if there'd been a car parked here overnight."

Betsy shifted her gaze to the old man.

The white-haired man shrugged. "Could have happened that way."

To Ryan's surprise, Betsy laughed. "What am I going to do with you two?"

"Tell us about your date last night," the old man said.

Ryan sloshed a bit of tea onto his hand. Just when he was starting to think the geezer wasn't so bad, he went and did this. But then Ryan realized perhaps the man had done him a favor. After all, it would have been tacky for him to pump Betsy about details of her date with Tripp. This way he wouldn't have to; the old guy would do it for him.

He shot Mr. Marstand an encouraging smile.

Betsy picked up her cup of tea. "His name is Tripp Randall," she said, taking a sip. "Like Ryan, he was a high school friend of my brother."

"Randall?" Mr. Marstand rubbed the gray stubble on his chin. "Is he related to Franklin Randall who owns Spring Gulch Land and Cattle?"

"Isn't that the big cutting horse and cattle ranch south of Jackson?" Betsy asked.

"That's his dad's place," Ryan confirmed.

Betsy pulled her brows together as if trying to sort everything out. "Tripp is rich?"

A lump the size of a large boulder settled in the pit of Ryan's stomach. To someone from Betsy's background, heck to almost anyone, Tripp's wealth would be very appealing.

"You don't look very happy, punkin'." Mr. Marstand's worried gaze settled on Betsy. "Something troubling you?"

"Yes, something's wrong," Betsy said. "I paid for Tripp's drink at the bar last weekend because I thought he was in dire straits. I chastised him for buying a bottle of wine last night. I feel like a fool. That man definitely owes me an explanation."

The minute she arrived with Ryan at Joel and Kate's new home in the mountains surrounding Jackson, Betsy knew her day was going to get even more interesting. Standing inside the foyer, nursing a tall glass of hot apple cider was Tripp Randall.

He lifted a hand in a semblance of a greeting and cast a pointed glance at her head.

Betsy held up her aviator hat, but when he motioned for her to put it on, she shook her head. She was still angry about his deception.

"We have a buffet table set up in the great room," Kate said with a welcoming smile. "Help yourself."

Joel held out his hand and Betsy couldn't think of any reason not to give him her coat. Except she had on pants with flannel lining that made her butt look big, and her ski sweater had a stripe across the chest—'nuff said.

With Ryan's help, she shrugged out of her bulky parka, placing it in Joel's outstretched hands. The second Ryan handed Joel his coat, he placed his hand against the small of Betsy's back.

"Tripp." Ryan's smile didn't quite reach his eyes. "I didn't expect to see you here today."

Betsy had forgotten that Ryan thought she had the hots for the rich hospital administrator. Had he made sure Tripp was invited today? But was that before or after he'd kissed her so ardently?

Tripp's gaze settled on Betsy and his lips lifted in a slight smile. "I heard there was a party and invited myself."

"Don't let him feed you a line," Joel said after hanging up the coats. "Any son of Franklin Randall is always welcome in my home."

"You know Frank?" Ryan asked.

It seemed a valid question to Betsy, because Joel had moved to Jackson Hole only several years earlier from Montana.

"Building another guesthouse on his property was my first big job when I expanded my business to Jackson Hole," Joel said as they walked down the hall to the great room at the back of the large log home.

Joel glanced at Betsy and Ryan. "I understand you're all old friends."

"Ryan and I go back to high school days," Tripp said. "Betsy and I are relatively new friends. Of course, I've known her brother, Keenan, all my life."

"Does your brother live in Jackson Hole?" Joel asked.

"He lives in Rawlins." It wasn't as if it was a big secret that Keenan was in prison, but Betsy didn't feel like answering a lot of questions right now.

"Betsy and I went to the Spring Gulch Country Club for dinner last night," Tripp said. "I'd forgotten how good the food is there."

She breathed a sigh of relief when the conversation moved to the newly revised menu at the country club and off her brother. She didn't have much to add. Last night had been her first visit to the country club. Before her eyes had been opened to the possibilities, she'd considered upscale dining to be dinner at Perfect Pizza, where you ordered at the counter but they brought the food to your table.

The doorbell rang and Joel smiled. "Help yourselves to some food," he said. "I think you probably know almost everyone here. If not, introduce yourselves. Once everyone has eaten, we'll head outside."

Betsy stared at the group of people, many the same as she'd met in church. Some familiar. Some not at all. Children were everywhere, preteens to toddlers. The room buzzed with conversation and laughter.

Even though Betsy considered herself to be fairly outgoing, she was suddenly overcome with the realization that she didn't belong here. These were the beautiful people of Jackson Hole, the doctors, the lawyers, the elite. She was a legal assistant. A woman whose mother had been a showgirl in Las Vegas before turning to the bottle.

Her breath came short and shallow as panic edged its fingers up her spine. "I'm going to run to the restroom and wash my hands," she said to no one in particular, although both Ryan and Tripp were nearby. "I'll be back."

She asked directions from a friendly blonde woman who introduced herself as Rachel Rossi and the curly-haired adolescent beside her as her daughter Mickie, then headed off the way they pointed.

Betsy hadn't gone far when she ran into Kate, looking as though she could have stepped off a cover of an outdoor-fun spread in a magazine. Her classic black ski pants looked like they had been made for her and the cable-knit sweater in a burned-orange didn't look at all bulky.

"It's good to see you again," Kate said with a warmth that surprised her.

Betsy shifted from one foot to the other as a large peal of laughter sounded from the other room.

"If my ears aren't deceiving me that's Mary Karen Fisher." Kate smiled. "I swear the woman has never met a stranger. I wish I were more like her."

Betsy tilted her head, not sure she'd heard correctly. "But you're very social."

"Thank you for that," Kate said. "But the truth is I'm actually quite shy. The first time I went for breakfast with Joel at The Coffeepot and saw everyone sitting there, I wanted to turn on my heel and walk the other way… quickly."

Remarkably, Betsy felt some of the tenseness in her shoulders ease. She chuckled. "I had the same feeling when I walked into your living room. I told Ryan and Tripp that I wanted to go wash my hands, but it was an excuse. I needed to collect my thoughts."

"A few deep breaths doesn't hurt either." Kate smiled. "How about I walk in with you? It'll make it easier for both of us."

"Sounds good." But when Kate started to turn in the direction of the great room, Betsy placed a hand on her arm. "Can I ask you something first?"

"Of course. You can ask me anything."

"You and Ryan dated."

"We did." A hint of wariness crept into Kate's gaze. "Right before Joel and I got together."

"What happened?" Betsy asked before it hit her that it might be too personal of a question. "If you don't mind my asking that is…"

"Ryan is a nice guy." Kate's fondness for the attorney was evident in her gaze. "We had fun together. I still consider him a good friend. But the spark, the sizzle, for whatever reason it just wasn't there. Then I met Joel and I knew it was him. He was the one for me."

"Tripp told me that Ryan tends to run hot then cold with women."

"And I bet he told you that when things go south, you should think of him."

"I told him that Ryan and I are simply friends."

"Oh, sweetie, I'm sure he didn't believe that any more than I do." Kate's eyes softened. "I've seen the way you look at him."

"Oh, God, is it that obvious?" Betsy brought her hands to her suddenly hot face.

"No, of course not," Kate said reassuringly. "But you do like Ryan."

Betsy settled for a nod.

"If he wants to date you, then I'd give it a shot." Kate smiled. "Think of it this way—what's the worst that could happen?"

He could break my heart, Betsy thought to herself, *shatter it into a million little pieces and I'd never be able to put it together again.*

"You're right," Betsy said. "I don't have anything to lose."

Chapter Twelve

Betsy didn't see Ryan when she and Kate returned to the great room, but Tripp was hanging out by a tall ficus tree decorated in bright orange lights.

"Oh, my," Betsy said.

"I know they're garish, but Chloe loves them," Kate said.

"It's not that," Betsy mumbled.

"Then what is…" Kate stopped, then smiled. "Looks like you have your pick of men this evening."

"When it rains it pours." Betsy could feel the medallion in the pocket of her pants. She wasn't sure why she'd brought it. Courage, perhaps?

"Look, if you want, we can hang out—"

"Thank you, but as the hostess I know you have a lot to do." Betsy offered a reassuring smile. "I'll be just fine."

Kate searched her eyes. "Sure?"

"Positive." Betsy laid a hand on Kate's arm. "I feel so

much better after talking to you. Like I'm in the home of a friend."

"That's because you are," Kate said. "I hope you and I can become good friends."

"Mo-om." A thin preteen girl who was a younger version of Kate motioned to her. "You're needed in the kitchen."

"Go," Betsy said. "I'm fine."

Kate gave Betsy's arm a companionable squeeze. "Well, if you need me, you know where to find me."

What I need, Betsy thought, *is a good stiff drink. Or perhaps a bubble bath.* She'd always done some of her best thinking when up to her neck in fragrant suds.

"Glass of wine, my dear?"

Betsy looked up to find Tripp standing beside her, a glass of white wine in one hand and a glass of red in the other.

"Which one is for me?" she asked.

"Whichever one you like," he said, shooting her a smile that showed off a mouthful of straight, white teeth. "I hedged my bets by getting one of each."

"Aren't you the clever one?" She took the burgundy and glanced around the room. "Where's Ryan?"

"Does it matte—"

"Of course it matters." Ryan suddenly appeared beside her. "I was looking for you."

Betsy knew it was crazy, but she felt better just having him there. "I ran into Kate and we got to talking."

"I think you two could be really good friends," he said.

"You would know," Tripp said. "You dated her for—"

"It's been great seeing you, Tripp, but Betsy and I have some things we need to discuss. In private." Ryan's gaze met Tripp's. There was something in his stance, in the tilt of his jaw, that said the topic wasn't up for discussion.

"See you later, Betsy," Tripp said pointedly before he walked away.

Ryan held out his hand. "Take a walk with me."

Betsy glanced around. "Won't it be rude to take off? We just got here."

Ryan chuckled. "I don't mean leave, just walk around the house with me."

"Oh." Betsy attempted a laugh. "You must think I'm stupid."

She knew it was because she was nervous. Oh, who was she kidding? It was Ryan. Whenever he was near he made her feel like an awkward schoolgirl who barely knew her own name.

"There are a lot of things I think when I look at you." He tucked a strand of hair behind her ear. "Never stupid."

She didn't know what to say, so she glanced around the room. "Look, Benedict Campbell is here."

Ryan muttered something. It almost sounded like a curse, but that couldn't be right. She noticed Ben was standing by himself. "Maybe we should go over and say hello."

"Later," Ryan said. "Much later."

He took her arm and steered her toward the stairs. "Have you seen the upstairs?"

"We can't go upstairs," Betsy hissed, digging in her heels.

"Joel," Ryan called out as their host walked past. "I want to show Betsy the upstairs. Do you mind?"

Something unspoken passed between the two men. Joel smiled. "Not at all."

"I won't touch anything," Betsy said.

"No worries," Joel said.

"C'mon." Out of the corner of one eye, Ryan saw Benedict headed their way. It had been hard enough to get Betsy away from Tripp. Ben wouldn't be so easily dismissed.

Ryan tugged on Betsy's hand. This time she came willingly. They climbed the stairs together and stopped. At the far end of the hall was an alcove with a love seat. "This way."

When they reached the love seat, he sat and pulled her down next to him. He took the wineglass she held clutched in one hand and set it on the side table next to the small sofa.

"What's going on, Ryan?" Betsy's brows were pulled together and her eyes were clearly puzzled. "Why did you bring me up here? Were you, are you ashamed of me?"

Ashamed of her? "What are you talking about?"

"You brought me up here, away from everyone." She chewed on her lower lip. "I admit that I'm not exactly dressed the best. But that's because I didn't think it was going to be this grand affair. I thought we were coming to build a snowman and maybe have a snowball fight."

She looked so miserable that anger rose inside him. Betsy was a wonderful, beautiful woman. He'd like to get his hands on the man or men who had caused this insecurity. "You look lovely. And I brought you up here because I wanted to be alone with you. Not with you and Tripp. Or you and Benedict."

"You wanted to be alone with me? That's why we're here?"

"Do you mind?" Without realizing what he was doing, Ryan held his breath.

"I like being with you." She smiled and ducked her head as if she'd said something intensely personal.

But maybe she had…

Unless it was simply his reading too much into the situation, it sounded as if she'd said she didn't mind his pulling her away from Tripp and Benedict. As if she wanted to be alone with him as much as he wanted to be alone with her. The thought gave him courage.

"I like being with you, too. That's what I wanted to talk to you about." Ryan took a deep breath. "I want us to date for real. Not this pretend stuff."

Betsy inhaled sharply, but her expression gave nothing away. "Really?"

This was her reaction? *Really.* A response that told him absolutely nothing. He comforted himself that at least she hadn't said no.

"I realize you like Tripp, but I get the feeling you like me, too." He forced himself to breathe past the tightness in his chest. "I'd like to give us a chance."

As she sat there, saying nothing, he realized that in his perfect world, she'd have flung her arms around his neck and cried out yes, yes, yes. But it didn't look as if that was going to happen. He waited a few more seconds—which seemed an eternity—then spoke. "What are you thinking?"

"What about Adrianna?"

"What about her?"

"You liked her. You thought she was—" Betsy paused and swallowed hard "—the one."

"I was mistaken." Ryan couldn't believe he'd ever thought he and Adrianna would be a good match, but he couldn't say that to Betsy. She was her friend and might think he was dissing the woman.

"Would you date me? For real?"

"Yes," she said. "I'd—I'd like that."

"You would?" Dear God, was that a quiver in his voice?

She jerked her head downward, a short quick nod.

He wrapped his arms around her and pulled her close. "That makes me happy."

"It makes me happy, too," she said, her breath warm against her neck.

He kissed her gently, sweetly, with all the love in his heart.

"This is so unreal," she murmured, arching her neck back, giving him access to the sensitive skin behind her ear. "I've never—"

She moaned as he sucked on her earlobe and he missed whatever she had said. He could have let it go, but he was curious.

"You've never what?" he asked.

"I've never dated two men at once before."

Ryan jerked back as the words registered. "Two men? What are you talking about?"

"You and Tripp." Betsy snuggled against him. "Before it would have just been him who was *really* interested. You and I were just pretending."

Ryan inhaled sharply. Surely she didn't still want Tripp?

"Tripp isn't interested." He couldn't be, Ryan thought. He'd made it clear to his friend that he needed to back off.

Betsy pushed away his hands and sat up, a strange look on her face. "What do you mean by that?"

Take a second, Ryan's rational part urged. *Think before you speak.* But he didn't. He couldn't let Betsy think of Tripp as a viable candidate for her affections. In the long run Tripp would only hurt her, and he couldn't let that happen.

"Tripp may seem nice," Ryan said, "but he's a player. Before he was married he dated a lot of women."

Betsy cocked her head. "Other than the married part, we could be talking about you."

Ryan paused. "It's different."

"Is it because you don't think he could be seriously interested in me?"

Even though he wanted nothing more than to say yes, to tell her Tripp wasn't serious, thank goodness for common sense popping up a red flag. Even without a warning, there was a vulnerability in her eyes that made him want to wrap his arms around her and never let her go. A protective urge that told him he would walk over hot coals rather than say something that would hurt her. Plus, he feared Tripp *was* serious. And that's what worried him.

"I don't have any doubts. You're a beautiful, desirable woman. The only thing I don't understand is why some guy didn't snap you up a long time ago."

The tenseness on her face eased and a warmth filled her blue bedroom eyes. Her lips curved up in a smile. "Perhaps that's because I was waiting for the right one."

She hadn't said that man was him, but she didn't have to, because she was the woman he'd been waiting for, the one he was meant to be with forever. All he needed was the time—and opportunity—to make her fall in love with him.

Ryan was discussing a legal precedent with Lexi's husband, Nick, when Kate appeared.

She smiled at Nick. "Mind if I steal Ryan for a few minutes?"

"Of course not," Nick said easily, taking a sip of wine. "I was just about to search for my wife anyway."

The second the attorney stepped away, Kate wasted no time. She slipped her arm through Ryan's and pulled him to a private area by the fireplace.

"Why, Kate, darlin'," Ryan said with a teasing grin, "I didn't know you cared."

"I do care." The smile left her lips, her expression serious. "About you. And about Betsy."

"Betsy." Alarm raced up Ryan's spine. It skyrocketed

when he glanced around the room and didn't see her. "Is she okay?"

"She's fine." Kate rested a hand on his arm. "I just need to know what your intentions are toward her."

Ryan had a whole repertoire of pithy one-liners on the tip of his tongue. Then he saw the look on Kate's face and realized this was serious. "Why do you ask?"

"Betsy and I talked. I think she's confused. I just want to make sure you're as serious about her as I think you are."

"I adore Betsy," he said.

Kate exhaled the breath she must have been holding. "Good. That's what I thought."

Last year Ryan had dated the woman at his side. Now they were what they'd been meant to be—good friends. "I understand about Joel. For the longest time, I didn't."

A tiny smile lifted the corners of Kate's lips. "I know you didn't."

"In fact when it came out that you were Chloe's birth mom, I found myself thinking it was awfully convenient that you'd fallen in love with her adoptive father."

"Joel initially thought it was a little convenient, too," Kate said with a sigh. "He accused me of using my relationship with him to get to Chloe."

"But he finally realized that wasn't true." Ryan liked the happy ending Kate had found. It made him think that same happiness was possible in his life, too.

"Yes, he did."

"Betsy isn't going to believe I love her." Ryan turned and planted his hands on the windowsill. He gazed unseeing into the darkness.

Kate placed a hand on his shoulder. "Why wouldn't she believe you?"

"I'm the boy who cried wolf." He whirled, frustration

surging through his veins. The knowledge that he had only himself to blame fueled the anger.

"I'd convinced myself that what I'd felt for those other women was love." Ryan gave a humorless laugh. He'd been such a fool. "What I feel for Betsy is so very different."

"That's how it was for me with Joel." Kate's eyes were filled with kindness rather than censure. He realized again how lucky he was to have her as a friend. "Anything I'd ever felt before paled in comparison."

Ryan shook his head in wonder. "All I want is her to know my feelings are real and aren't going to change. I don't want her to have any doubts."

"Words alone won't do it. She's going to be scared that you'll change your mind."

"I can't imagine life without her, Kate. I like hanging out with her. I like working with her on cases. We have fun together. She gets me. And you know what a challenge that is."

Kate's chuckle lightened the mood.

"She's the only one I want. The only one I'll ever want." He thought of the love token Betsy showed him. *You and No Other.* That pretty much summed up his feelings.

"You're going to have to be patient, Ry. Show her by your words *and* your actions how much you care." Kate's eyes met his. "In time she'll come to realize you're sincere."

"She has to, Kate," Ryan said. "I don't know what I'd do if I lost her."

Chapter Thirteen

Betsy hid behind a large boulder in Joel and Kate's backyard, snowball in hand. For a while she thought that the promise of a snowball fight had been forgotten. Then after lunch the kids were sent outside to make a snow fort and to mark off the camp of the attacking army.

Once that was done, Kate took the two different flags her daughter had attached to broom handles and everyone counted off. Through the luck of the draw, or perhaps the unluck, she and Tripp were on the attacking team while Ryan was a defender of the fort.

"Cover me," Tripp whispered from next to her.

He had their patrol's flag in hand and this was their last chance to breach the fort and thus win the game. All of their other comrades had gotten hit and were now out of the game. Of course the other side had lost many soldiers, too. As far as Betsy knew, Ryan was still playing.

"I've got five or six snowballs made up," she said to

Tripp. "But I'm not sure I'll be able to throw them fast enough to protect you."

"No guts, no glory." Tripp shot her a devilish smile. "If I go down, grab the flag and make a run for it."

Betsy smiled. "Deal."

"On the count of three," Tripp said, his voice filled with determination. Betsy wondered what the hospital board would think now if they could see their new administrator with his eyes blazing and snowball in hand. "One, two, three—"

Betsy rose and began flinging snowballs.

She got Joel in the shoulder, Mary Karen in the belly. Her oldest boy, Connor, came out from nowhere with snowball in hand.

He howled with frustration when her snowball caught him in the leg.

Tripp was almost at the fort, all of his snowballs gone, flag in hand when Ryan stepped out. He stood there, with no protection, waiting for a sure shot at Tripp.

Betsy stumbled forward, one last snowball in hand. She didn't know if Ryan discounted her or if he was too focused on Tripp to give her a second thought. But she released her ball just as he raised his arm, giving her a perfect shot to the abdomen.

He looked up in surprise as Tripp planted the flag, signaling the game was over and the blue team had won.

She didn't have a chance to say anything to Ryan, who was looking at her with disbelief in his eyes, because her team mobbed her, jumping up and down in the snow, chanting her name.

Betsy couldn't remember ever having quite as wonderful a day.

By the time they went inside and warmed up, the sun

had already set. Tripp left, but not before giving Betsy a congratulatory hug and promising to call her.

Ryan seemed strangely silent. Of course, it could be only her imagination. She hoped he wasn't disappointed in her. After all, she couldn't throw the game just because she didn't want to hit him with the snowball.

It wasn't until they were in his truck that they had the opportunity to talk privately. "About the snowball—"

He raised one hand, then turned on the highway leading back into Jackson. "I have something to say first."

A chill of dread slid down Betsy's spine. Over and over she'd heard girls say that guys don't like it if you beat them at sports. Or that you shouldn't flaunt how smart you were if you wanted to get dates. It had seemed silly to her. Of course she hadn't had that many dates either.

"I'm proud of you, Bets."

Betsy blinked. "For what?"

"For being such a competitor."

Had he forgotten her team had won? "If I hadn't hit you with that snowball, the red team would have won. You'd have been the hero, not—"

Betsy stopped herself. To say more would feel like bragging.

"You." Ryan smiled and took her hand, bringing it to his lips for a kiss. "That's why I'm so proud. You gave maximum effort. You didn't let anything stop you."

"You don't mind that I took you out?"

"I wish I'd played smarter and God knows I hate to lose, but it wouldn't have meant anything if I knew you'd handed me the win."

A warmth ran through Betsy's veins, and she was reminded again just why she'd fallen in love with this guy.

"But the Tripp thing," he said, keeping his eyes firmly focused on the road. "I have to admit that bothers me."

"You mean that he planted the flag in your fort?"

"Forget the fort." Ryan's hand cut a dismissive swath through the air. "That was a game. I'm talking real life. I'm talking about you wanting to date him and me at the same time."

I don't really want to date him, Betsy yearned to say, *I only want you.* But she kept her mouth shut.

He slanted a sideways glance. "You can date him if you want, but I'm not going to date anyone else. I don't want anyone else."

"What if Adrianna came and begged you to take her out?" The question popped out of Betsy's mouth before she could stop it.

"I'd say no." Ryan met her gaze. "Even if she got down on her hands and knees."

Betsy slipped her arm through his and moved as close to him as the seat belt would allow, resting her head on his shoulder. She heaved a contented sigh. "I like being with you."

Ryan's body relaxed. He took one hand off the wheel, then slipped it around her shoulder. "When we get to your house, invite me in?"

"Of course you can come in." Betsy lifted her head slightly. "Though I don't know what I have to offer you. The fridge is pretty bare."

He pulled up to a stop light, then glanced her way, his gaze dark with desire.

A fire ignited in Betsy's belly. The air became charged with electricity. Desire flowed through her veins like hot lava. She wasn't sure how she managed to keep from self-combusting before they reached her apartment. She looked for Mr. Marstand's car when they pulled into the parking lot, then remembered that he was spending the day—and hopefully the night—with his sister in Idaho Falls.

The only other obstacle to a romantic evening was Puffy. The dog ran to greet her when she opened the door, then turned and unexpectedly bared her teeth to Ryan.

"Hey, Puffball," he said, looking startled.

The dog began to bark.

"I don't know what to do with her," Betsy said, feeling the mood slip away with each yip.

"I have an idea." Ryan reached into his pocket and pulled out a small green-colored bone. "I picked this up for her. My parents' dog used to love these."

"What is it?"

"It's a Greenie. They're good for dogs."

"Puffy can be somewhat picky…."

Ryan leaned down, the bone dangling from his fingers. The Pomeranian paused midyap, swiveled her head and snatched it from his hand.

Betsy smiled as the animal ran across the room to sit on the rag rug in front of the sofa with her new acquisition. "I think she likes it."

"And I like you." He kissed Betsy's nose.

"Want a tour of the house?"

He cocked his head, his gaze puzzled. "I think I've been in every room."

"What about the bedroom?"

The light of understanding flashed in his eyes. "I'd like to check that room out again."

Betsy reached over and cranked up the thermostat as they walked by. Once they reached her bedroom, Betsy's courage began to falter. She'd never been good at this kind of stuff….

He must have sensed her distress because he moved to her side. "I know you're probably ready to start flinging off clothes, but I'd like to just talk for a while."

She narrowed her gaze. "Are you teasing me?"

He took her hand and tugged her to the bed. When she sat down, he took the place beside her, his fingers still laced with hers. “How about we kick off our shoes and see who can make them go the farthest?”

“They’ll hit the wall.”

“We could see whose shoes can hit the wall at the highest point.”

“Are you crazy? I don’t want marks on my—” She chuckled. “Okay, we’ll take off our shoes, but we’re not kicking them anywhere. Understand?”

Ryan slipped off one boot and then the other. “I guess I’ll have to think of another game to play.”

Betsy unlaced her shoes, trying to figure out what Ryan had up his sleeve.

“Is that a music box?” He pointed to a trinket box with a blue base covered with brightly colored horses.

Betsy leaned forward and grabbed the box. When she opened the top the horses began to revolve while the “Carousel Waltz” played. “My mother gave me this on my seventh birthday. I think it was because she knew I loved carousels.”

“A thoughtful gift.”

“Yes, it was.” Even though in recent years it seemed she could only recall the bad times, there had been some good, too.

“I’ve got an idea for a game,” Ryan said. “Have you ever played Pass the Parcel?”

“Is that sort of like hot potato where you pass something around and if you have it in your hand when the music stops, you’re out?”

“Yes, except we would pass the music box back and forth and when the music stops whoever has it will take off an item of clothing and share something about themselves.”

“Are you serious?”

"What's the matter? No spirit of adventure?"

Betsy thought for a second. She'd been lucky today. If her luck continued just a little while longer, Ryan would soon be naked and so would she. It was a heady thought. "I'm game."

For the first few minutes, the clothing came off slowly. A sock here. A sock there. She learned that Ryan hated asparagus but loved tuna. She shared her fear of spiders and love of anything chocolate. But now, they'd made it to the point where a shirt or pants would have to come off.

The music box moved carefully between them, the sound of the tinny waltz filling the air. Ryan had just passed it to her when the sound stopped.

"Share, then strip." A devilish gleam shone in his eyes. "This time something about family."

Betsy already knew her sweater was coming off. Thankfully she had the silky long underwear beneath the sweater. Sharing something about her family wasn't that easy. She'd spent a lifetime not talking about her mother.

"How about your favorite family trip?"

Betsy started to say they'd never gone on any trips until she remembered that summer between fourth and fifth grade. "When I was ten we got in the car and drove to Devil's Tower. It wasn't much to see, but we sang songs and played games as we drove. Mom stopped at this old gas station, and we all had bottles of orange Nehi soda pop. Keenan and I thought she might buy a beer, but she didn't."

The memory was disturbing. Had her mother quit drinking that summer and she hadn't noticed? Of course, even if she had, she hadn't stayed sober.

"Sounds like a fun trip." Ryan's eyes glittered in the dim light. "Now the piece of clothing."

"I'll take off my sweater."

"Good choice."

Betsy took her time peeling the garment over her head in a slow strip tease. When Ryan's smile faded Betsy knew he'd seen the silky long underwear.

"No wonder you weren't cold when we were throwing snowballs," he grumbled. "You're dressed for twenty below."

But she lost the next two rounds and found herself sitting before a fully clothed Ryan in only her bra and panties.

"I really like this game." His gaze remained focused on her chest.

Beneath the heat of his gaze, her breasts began to strain against the lace fabric holding them in. "I'm feeling decidedly underdressed."

"And I'd like to keep it that way."

He lost the next round and took off his sweater, leaving him with a short-sleeved T-shirt.

Betsy knew she would win the upcoming round. While he'd been busy ogling her, she'd been memorizing the tune so she would know just when to hand it off to him.

He placed it in her hands and she counted the beats slowly in her head. She was ready to move it to his hand when he gasped.

"Is that a spider on the dresser?"

Betsy whirled, music box in her hands. She barely noticed that the tune had quit. Her gaze frantically searched the top of the dresser. "Wherc?"

"I was mistaken," Ryan said with an expression that was way too innocent. "Must have had something in my eye."

She realized suddenly what he'd done. "You—you cad. You did that deliberately."

"Did what?"

"You knew I was about to give you the music box, and you deliberately distracted me."

"Betsy, Betsy, you're so suspicious." But the flash of a

dimple in his left cheek told the story. "Before you take something off, tell me how many lovers you've had."

"What?"

"We both know that after you strip this time, there's not going to be much talking going on." He gentled his tone. "I want to be prepared."

"Two," Betsy mumbled. "Just two."

"When?"

"One my first year in college." She'd been so lonely then. "The other was back in Kansas City. He was another paralegal in the same firm."

"It's been a while."

Betsy felt her face grow hot. "There's nothing wrong with that."

"No, there's nothing wrong with that," he said. "It's been a while for me, too."

"But you and Kate..."

"Kate and I were never lovers."

She thought of the blonde ski bunnies at the bar. "What about the girls, the blondes at Wally's Place?"

"You think I slept with them?"

"You flirted with them."

"You flirted with Tripp, but you didn't sleep with him."

"No," she said. "That would have been wrong."

He waited.

"Because," she said, "I don't care about him enough."

"But you'll sleep with me."

"Yes."

A warmth coursed through Ryan that had nothing to do with the fire burning in his belly. Betsy might say she wanted to date Tripp, but it was him that she liked, him that she trusted with her body and her heart. That's when Ryan knew everything was going to be okay.

He would win her over, show her that his love was sincere. Starting now.

Chapter Fourteen

Ryan stared at her for a long moment. The second his eyes met hers, something inside Betsy seemed to lock into place and she couldn't look away.

Then his lips curved upward in a smile that pierced her skin and traveled straight to her soul. She stood absolutely still as he reached out and touched her cheek, one finger trailing slowly along her skin until it reached the line of her jaw.

She stopped breathing when he leaned closer, brushing his lips across hers. The friction sent shivers and tingles spiraling through her body.

Betsy finally found her voice. She spoke his name, then paused, not sure what she wanted to say.

"Let me make love to you."

His request, spoken in a husky voice, sent blood flowing like warm honey through her veins. He moved his arm so her hand slid down to his and he gently locked their fingers together.

Betsy's heart fluttered. A thousand butterflies lodged in her throat. Her body quivered with anticipation. It had been a long time, but she felt sure that with Ryan it would be different. Better. Magical even.

She gazed into his eyes. Could he hear her heart pounding?

"Please," she said, not sure what she was asking for but knowing she wanted it all. Ryan was a smart guy. She was confident he'd figure out a way to meet her unspoken desires.

Before she could blink, his clothes landed in a heap somewhere behind him. Like a game of follow the leader, Betsy took a deep breath and tossed what remained of hers on the floor next to his.

When she'd been a child, teachers had told Betsy it was impolite to stare. But she was no longer a child and she couldn't help herself. Broad shoulders. Flat abdomen. Muscular legs. And—she swallowed past the sudden dryness in her throat—indisputable evidence of his desire for her.

Heat flooded her face, yet she didn't look away.

"Do I meet with your approval?" Even though a slight smile teased the corners of his lips, his eyes were dark and serious.

"You'll do," she said, then belied the lighthearted tone by blushing. "What about me?"

The second the question left her lips, Betsy wished she could pull it back. There was no way she could measure up to the previous women in his life unless she dropped ten pounds, worked out for a month straight and gained a cup size.

Instead of a quick comeback, his gaze lingered. Then his eyes lifted to meet hers. "You're beautiful."

Hating that she'd put him in the position to feel obligated to offer up a sentiment, she ducked her head and shrugged.

"Hey." He moved closer and lifted her chin with his fingers, his eyes like molten steel. "I mean it."

Betsy shook her head slowly from side to side.

"If you won't take my word, I guess I'm going to have to show you." His voice was heavy with resignation, but the gleam in his eyes told her showing was going to be a good thing.

For both of them.

Ryan took her hand and urged her to lie on the bed, then slid in beside her. Betsy's mind barely had time to register they were naked and on her bed—ohmigod—when he pulled her close. He smelled of soap and a familiar male scent that made something tighten low in her abdomen.

"You are *incredibly* beautiful." His breath was warm as he spoke softly into her ear right before he took the lobe between his teeth and nibbled. "And you're all mine."

Shivers of desire rippled across her skin as anticipation coursed up her spine.

"That vanilla scent of yours drives me wild." He planted kisses down her neck while his hand lightly stroked her belly. "I want to be inside of you. I want to fill you completely until your pleasure makes you scream."

Scream? Betsy had never screamed in her life. Unless she counted the time Keenan dropped a spider down the front of her dress. Still, she was open to the possibility.

She closed her eyes and reveled in the feel of his hands on her skin. Each sensuous stroke fueled the fire building inside her. When his hand slid upward from her stomach, Betsy forgot how to breathe.

"I think," he said in a low, husky tone, "your breast will fit perfectly in my palm."

Betsy opened her eyes just in time to see Ryan's hand

cup her breast. But he didn't stop there. He circled the peak with his finger. Her blood began to boil. He touched the tip of his tongue to the tip of her left breast. Her need became a stark carnal hunger she hadn't known she was capable of feeling.

Thankfully he didn't stop there. Or she'd have had to beg. He circled the nipple, then drew it fully into his mouth. Shock waves coursed through her body.

The gentle sucking soon had her arching against him. He couldn't seem to get enough of her breasts, kissing and licking each pink peak thoroughly, dragging his teeth across the sensitive skin. And she couldn't get enough of his touch.

Betsy squirmed in frustration. She pushed her hips against him, rubbing his erection. She wanted… She needed…

Even if she wasn't sure exactly what she needed, Ryan knew. His hand dipped south, slipping through her curls and between her legs.

Her breath caught in her throat as he rubbed against her slick center. No man had ever touched her like this. No man had ever made her ache like this. When his fingers found her sweet spot, she nearly rose off the bed.

"Don't stop," she begged.

"Not on your life." He kissed her and slipped two fingers inside.

Her muscles automatically tightened around them. Betsy inhaled sharply.

Ryan's lips lifted in satisfaction. "You're wet."

Was there any doubt? Betsy wanted to ask. Instead she opened her legs wider, moving sensuously against his hand, letting him know in every way possible that she wanted more of this, more of him.

With gray eyes so dark they almost looked black, he

shifted so that he knelt between her legs and began kissing his way down her belly. Part of her suspected what he was going to do while the rest of her couldn't believe it was really happening. She'd heard talk…she'd read about it in books…but no other guy had ever…

Leaning forward, he pressed his open mouth against the sensitive skin of her inner thigh. The sight of his dark head between her legs, the brush of his tongue dampening her flesh, was the most erotic experience of her life.

She rocked her hips, brazenly struggling to get the friction she needed to feed the incredible need building inside her. Her breathing came in fast pants. As the rising tension gripped her and wouldn't let go, she dug her heels into the mattress and clutched the sheets with her hands.

While fighting to catch her breath, it happened. One moment she was tossing her head from side to side, every nerve ending on fire. The next she was coming apart in his arms, exploding in an orgasm that dragged a scream from her that she didn't recognize as her own.

Her body shook, and she gave in to the waves of pleasure coursing through her. Once she could breathe again, Betsy opened her eyes to a world that looked different from the one she'd left moments before. It was as if she'd spent her life in darkness and someone had thrown a light switch, bathing her world in a golden glow.

A silly grin lifted her lips. "That was—"

"Unbelievably good." He kissed her mouth, gently brushing her hair back from her face.

"I've never felt anything like that," she stammered, feeling like a neophyte who'd gotten her first glimpse of the Promised Land.

"That was only the beginning. There's so much more." His eyes seemed to glitter in the dim light. "Make love with me."

Betsy thought that's what they'd been doing. But apparently what she'd experienced had been simply a fantastically fabulous appetizer, a prequel to the main course, which Ryan appeared eager to serve up.

"Bring it on, cowboy," Betsy said, then ruined the effect by blushing.

Ryan chuckled, but Betsy didn't feel like laughing when he began kissing her, branding her as his with hot moist imprints upon her skin. Sweet tension mixed with raw need.

Suddenly ravenous, Betsy couldn't wait any longer. She reached between them and guided him inside her. He was large and hard and stretched her in the best way possible. She wrapped her legs around his hips, urging him deeper.

"More," she breathed as he withdrew only to fill her again in a rhythm as old as time.

I love you. I love you. I love you. The sentiment ran over and over in her head with each thrust until she could no longer think.

"I—I—" she breathed as her body stiffened before convulsing into release a second time.

He thrust again and again until the shudders faded. She felt him plunge deep, calling out her name before burying his face against her neck.

Still intimately joined, Betsy clung to him as a languid drowsiness stole over her and his choppy breathing slowed. She knew she was grinning, but she couldn't get her lips to do anything else.

Ryan kissed her hair, her lips, her neck, a matching smile on his mouth. Even when he rolled off her, he pulled her close. In between kisses and sweet caresses they talked about anything and everything and nothing at all. Each time she thought about getting up, he kissed her again.

"I'd never—" Betsy lifted her head from his chest. Perhaps this wasn't proper post-lovemaking protocol, but she really had to know. "I never experienced anything like this before. Were those other two guys total duds? Or was it me?"

Ryan almost told her it was love that made the difference. He stopped himself just in time. Because while he knew he loved her, he wasn't sure those feelings were reciprocated. "It's the caring and the trust that made it special."

"Whatever the reason, I liked it." Betsy's well-kissed lips turned up in a satisfied smile. "I want to do it again. Now."

Her boldness delighted Ryan. "Can you at least give me a few more minutes to recover? You took me on a wild ride, cowgirl."

Betsy's hand stole under the sheets and closed around him. She grinned. "Feels to me like you're fully recovered."

Her smile faded. "Unless you don't want—"

"I want you," he said, the words a solemn vow. He wanted her not just in his bed, but also in his life. He'd never wanted anyone more.

"Ah, yes." She cocked her head. "The question is, for how long?"

Her tone was teasing, but the look in her eyes troubled him.

"Forever," Ryan said. "That's how long."

Betsy stared at him, then pulled him on top of her, kicking aside the sheet. "Let's start with tonight."

"That will do," he said. "For now."

Seconds after Ryan's truck pulled out of her driveway the next morning, Betsy was on the phone with Adrianna. "We have to talk. Can you meet for lunch?"

"I wish I could." Regret filled Adrianna's voice. "But my day is jam-packed. I'm just going to grab a yogurt and eat at my desk."

"How about if I bring lunch to you?" Betsy was not going to take no for an answer. "We could eat in your office."

"Sure," Adrianna said. "But I only have a half hour to spare."

After confirming the best time to stop over, Betsy hung up. Because Ryan would be in court until at least noon, he'd given her the morning off. She had to speak with Adrianna before she saw him again.

Ryan hadn't wanted to leave this morning. The way he kept kissing her and untying the chenille belt on her robe told her that much. But as much as she wanted him to stay, he'd turned her world upside down. She needed time and distance to get her thoughts together and gain some perspective.

Betsy pulled on a pair of tweed pants with a silk blouse and camel-colored cardigan before looking in the mirror. A new woman stared back at her. Her eyes looked darker and more mysterious. If she didn't know better she'd say her lips were swollen from his kisses.

The change wasn't simply on the inside. Her body felt different, as if it had been asleep for a long time and had finally awakened. In the span of twenty-four short hours her life had been forever changed. She and Ryan had forged a new path.

That meant, even if they wanted to, they'd never be able to go back to the way it was before.

Betsy placed the sandwiches and drinks on Adrianna's desk and waited while her friend closed the door.

"What's going on?" Adrianna settled into her leather chair and unscrewed the top of her soda. "You sounded strange on the phone this morning."

"Ryan spent the night." Betsy tried but wasn't able to keep the goofy smile from her lips.

"What?" Adrianna plopped the bottle on her desk without taking a drink.

"We went to a party at Joel and Kate's yesterday and had a fabulous time." Betsy took a sip of her cherry soda. "Then he took me home and stayed over."

Adrianna's eyes narrowed. "I thought you two were just friends."

Was that disapproval she heard in her friend's voice? Had Adrianna been secretly pining for Ryan? Betsy's heart sank. Her smile faded. "Are *you* interested in him?"

Adrianna's eyes widened. "Oh, my gosh, no."

"You told me you thought he was cute."

"I do think he's cute." Adrianna's expression gave nothing away. "That doesn't mean I want to date him or see a future with him. What about you, Bets? Do you see yourself having a future with him?"

"I'd like to." Betsy paused, wanting to be completely honest with her friend. "I love him, Anna. I know he cares about me, too. But I'm scared. How long will those feelings last? I worry that in time he'll get tired of me like he's done with the others before me."

"Did he ask…to see you again?"

Something in the way her friend asked the question told Betsy she wasn't confident of the answer she'd receive. That wasn't a good sign.

Betsy nodded. "He wants to date me. Exclusively."

"So you're a couple."

"Er, not exactly." When Betsy recalled her conversation with Ryan at Kate's house, she felt her cheeks warm. It hadn't been her finest hour.

Adrianna leaned forward, her eyes snapping with curiosity. "This sounds interesting."

"I told Ryan that Tripp wants to date me, too."

Adrianna froze. "Why would you say that?"

"Because it's true." Betsy sighed. "And because I wanted to make sure Ryan knew that another man finds me attractive. Childish, huh?"

Adrianna bit into her sandwich and chewed for several seconds. "Are you thinking that Tripp will be your backup when Ryan dumps you?"

"*If* he dumps me," Betsy protested. "Not *when*. We don't know *for sure* he's going to get tired of me. I could be 'the one.' The woman Ryan has been waiting for his whole life."

Her voice began to tremble. Horrified by how much she'd revealed, Betsy clamped her mouth shut.

Adrianna leaned forward and took Betsy's hand. "You're right. You don't know. That's why you need to tell Tripp to take a hike. You can't date him right now. You need to put your whole heart into this relationship with Ryan. Jump in with both feet. Don't sit on the edge dipping in one toe at a time."

"I don't want to be hurt."

"If he walks away from you, you'll hurt anyway." Adrianna gazed into her eyes. "Isn't that right?"

Betsy slowly nodded.

"Give this relationship your best shot. If he does walk away, it'll be his loss. But at least you won't be left forever wondering if things would have turned out differently if only you'd opened your heart fully."

What Adrianna said made sense. That didn't mean the thought of putting her suggestion into action wasn't scary as hell. "How did you get to be so smart?"

"I've made my share of mistakes." Adrianna's eyes turned dark. "I'd hate to see you make the same ones."

It sounded so simple. Give Ryan her whole heart and

hope for the best. Well, she'd already given him her body and soul in addition to her heart. That meant all that was left was to hope for the best.

Chapter Fifteen

Fully focused was how Ryan normally spent the workday. Not today. This morning, all he'd been able to think of was *Betsy.*

To make matters even more complicated, he'd run into Tripp at the courthouse. Ryan wasn't sure why the guy was there, and he hadn't asked. He was still pissed that Tripp had asked Betsy out after he'd told him to back off. Yet Betsy could have said no. When he boiled it down, that's what bothered him the most.

Ryan pressed his lips together as he strode down the cavernous halls of the courthouse.

"Watch where you're going," a man snarled.

Ryan had felt his briefcase bump against something but hadn't realized it had been a person. He glanced up. "Chad."

The tall attorney narrowed his gaze. "You need to keep better control of that briefcase, Harcourt."

Ryan shrugged. The case had merely smacked against the attorney's leg, he hadn't swung it against the guy's head. Even though after how Chad had treated Betsy, he deserved a good wallop to the head…and then some. But Ryan had promised Betsy he wouldn't hurt the guy, and he was a man of his word.

Still, Chad's unwarranted irritation said something was up. And that made Ryan curious. "What brings you to the courthouse?"

"What do you think?" Chad snapped. "I had business here."

He'd hit a nerve. Good.

"I heard you hired a new paralegal," he said as they both headed for the door. "How's she working out?"

"She's not with the firm anymore." A muscle jumped in Chad's jaw. "And I'm not answering any more of your questions."

Yep. He'd definitely hit a nerve. Ryan smiled.

They were outside now, in the cool crisp air. The walks had been scooped, but patches of ice remained. Chad moved with long purposeful strides down the steps as if he couldn't get away quickly enough. Until his Italian loafers connected with a patch of ice. The attorney waved his hands trying to regain his balance but instead did an alley-oop straight onto his backside.

Ryan's smile widened. He approached while Chad was bent over gathering the papers he'd been holding in his hand before the fall. A better man might have stopped to help. But when Ryan thought about how Chad had treated Betsy, he walked past without a second glance.

After one quick stop on the way, Ryan strode into his office at two o'clock and paused by Betsy's desk. Her eyes were glued to the computer screen. When she looked up and smiled, his heart tripped over itself.

He'd hated to leave her this morning. Last night had been a major turning point in their relationship. If Betsy needed reassurance, he'd wanted to be there to give it to her. He didn't want her having any second thoughts or worrying.

Heck, who was he kidding? He wanted the reassurance. Wanted to know that he'd satisfied her. Wanted her to tell him that she loved him as much as he loved her.

She cocked her head. "What's in your hand?"

He lifted his right arm and stared at the colors of yellow, red, white and orange in a mass of greenery as if seeing them for the first time. "I believe they're Peruvian lilies."

"They're gorgeous." Betsy breathed the words, her gaze never wavering from the bouquet.

"They reminded me of you." He handed the flowers to her. "Only not near as lovely."

A familiar rosy glow crept up her neck. "You bought them for me? Really?"

He smiled indulgently, pleased by her reaction. "You act as if a man has never bought you flowers before."

She buried her face in the bouquet and inhaled deeply before answering. "These are my first."

Men were fools. He'd been a fool. Such beauty. Such intelligence. And that sweet but-oh-so-sexy smile…

Ryan leaned close and kissed her on the cheek. "They won't be your last."

"Thank you." Without warning, she rose and her arms wrapped around his neck, the flowers gripped tightly in one fist. "I love…them."

For a second he thought she was going to say she loved *him*. Ryan tried hard not to be disappointed. A declaration would come in time. For now, her loving the flowers he'd given her was enough.

While Ryan had always believed in keeping personal relationships out of the work setting, he couldn't resist stealing one quick kiss.

She tasted like cherry soda, one of his favorite drinks. At least it was now. Her mouth opened and Ryan deepened the kiss. Desire, hot and insistent, surged. He cupped her breast through her silk shirt, teasing the nipple with the side of his thumb. Locking the office door never crossed his mind. Until the sound of clapping filled the air.

Betsy jerked back, the flowers falling from her fingers.

Ryan whirled, wanting to see who'd had the audacity to walk to his back offices without pressing the buzzer.

Chad Dunlop stood in the doorway, a smirk on his face. "I got to hand it to you, Harcourt. You succeeded where I failed."

Two long strides was all it took for Ryan to reach Chad. He grabbed the front of the attorney's coat and slammed him into the door frame. He'd already drawn back his fist, ready to wipe that smirk off Chad's face and shut his filthy mouth, when Betsy grabbed his arm, pulling him back.

"Don't, Ryan," she begged. "He's not worth it."

It wasn't her entreaty that stopped him from throwing the punch but something he saw in Chad's eyes. Something that told him there was more going on here. Something that said he'd be playing right into Chad's hands if he hit him.

"Get out." He dropped his fists. "Don't come back."

Chad just chuckled, turned on his heel and sauntered from the office without another word.

Ryan followed him to the front office and locked the door behind him. By the time Ryan returned to Betsy, she was picking up the last of the flowers from the floor.

She straightened, her face pale. "What do you think he wanted?"

"No idea." Ryan thought for a moment. "But you were right. It was as if he wanted me to hit him."

Even knowing that, Ryan found himself wishing he'd smacked the guy. Just once. Okay, maybe twice. The thought of Chad trying to force himself on Betsy still made him see red.

Even though he didn't say it aloud, he vowed he'd make sure Chad Dunlop got what was coming to him.

Ryan opened his arms to Betsy. "Come here."

Betsy shook her head, her jaw set in a stubborn tilt. "Not here. Not ever again."

The look in her eye told Ryan not to push the issue. "Can I get you a vase for the flowers?"

"You have one?"

"Several." He kept his tone light. "When Caroline worked for me, she got flowers all the time."

Betsy's eyes widened. "From you?"

"Of course not," he said. "From her husband."

"I'm sorry." A pained look crossed her face and the bleakness in her eyes tore at his heart. "I'm really making a mess of things."

"What are you talking about?" He moved close, rubbing his hands up and down her arms. Propriety be damned. This was the woman he loved and she was hurting. "It's me who can't keep my hands off you."

"The way Chad looked at me." She shivered. "I felt so dirty."

"He's an ass." Ryan clenched his jaw. "If he knows what's good for him, he won't come around here again."

"What are you going to do if he does?" she asked with a laugh that sounded suspiciously like a sob.

"He won't." Chad had gotten off easy today. And he'd

better keep his distance, otherwise Ryan might be forced to give him a lesson in old-fashioned cowboy justice.

The next few weeks passed quickly. Christmas came and went. Betsy couldn't remember ever being happier. Ryan's friends had become her friends. Best of all she felt as if they'd accepted her for herself, rather than just as Ryan's girlfriend.

Tripp called and asked her out, but she was always busy with Ryan. After a while he quit calling. Betsy began to believe the medallion's promise would be fulfilled, even if she couldn't find the blasted coin.

It had to be in her apartment somewhere. The medallion had disappeared around the time she and Ryan had made love for the first time. She hadn't seen it since. She'd even searched Puffy's bedding, but all she'd gotten for that effort was a long stare from the tiny Pom.

Tonight, the coin barely crossed her mind. The only thing she could think of was how handsome Ryan looked in a tux. When he'd invited her to attend the Jackson Hole Memorial Hospital's annual winter formal with him, she hadn't known what to say except, of course, yes.

Apparently the legal work he did for the hospital had landed him a spot on their much-coveted invitation list. Betsy was excited not only because it would the first dressy event they would attend together, but also because so many of their friends would be there.

She waited in the foyer of the Spring Gulch Country Club while Ryan checked their coats. Even though it was near freezing outside, Betsy had left her Eskimo parka at home. Adrianna had come through with a black velvet cape that was both warm and stylish.

The wrap was a perfect accompaniment to Betsy's new cocktail dress. Made of black satin, it clung to her curves in the most flattering way. She'd taken extra time with her hair and makeup and was confident she looked her best. Although Ryan had always been effusive in his compliments, if the look in his eyes was any indication, once they got home tonight, the dress wouldn't be on for long.

That was fine with Betsy because when she'd seen him in his tux, unbuttoning the pristine white shirt had been at the forefront of her mind.

After all these weeks she couldn't believe how well they meshed. Both in and out of bed. They enjoyed the same activities. Skiing. Riding bulls. Long walks under the stars when the air was so cold that Puffy had to wear a coat. Yet on nights when the snow fell heavily and the north wind howled, merely sitting by the fire watching a movie and holding hands was fun.

"Have I told you how beautiful you look this evening?"

Her handsome prince had returned.

"About a thousand times, but I wouldn't mind hearing it again."

"You are, without a doubt, the loveliest woman in the room tonight."

The sentiment was so over-the-top that Betsy had to smile. When she was with Ryan she felt beautiful.

He leaned close and lowered his voice. "After we go home, I'll *show* you just what I think of that beautiful bod of yours."

A delightful sense of anticipation skittered up her spine. Betsy placed her lips so close to his ear that it was all she could do not to nibble. "Show me yours and I'll show you mine."

"C'mon, you two, move it along."

Betsy straightened, immediately recognizing the deep voice with a hint of an East Coast accent. "Tripp."

"Doesn't someone look extrapretty this evening." Tripp's appreciative gaze lingered.

"Thank you," she said, cursing the blasted heat rising up her neck. She wasn't sure if it was his compliment or the fact that she'd blown him off that was making her blush.

Tripp gestured with his head toward Ryan. "This guy treating you right?"

Ryan's gray eyes flashed, a warning Tripp seemed determined to ignore.

Betsy looped her arm through Ryan's. "Extremely well."

The tension on Ryan's face eased.

"Well, if he doesn't," Tripp said, obviously joking but managing to sound completely serious, "you've got my number."

"Thank you, Tripp," Betsy said.

"She won't need it," Ryan said pointedly.

Tripp just winked at Betsy, slapped Ryan on the back and sauntered off.

"I don't know where he gets off—"

Betsy placed a finger over Ryan's lips. "He doesn't matter. I'm right where I want to be."

They stood at the entrance to the ballroom, which had been turned into a winter wonderland. Even the chandelier made out of antlers had white lights and greenery. Round linen-clad tables surrounded a large mahogany dance floor. Lights from flickering candles scattered throughout the room cast a romantic, golden glow.

A live band playing dance music brought men in tuxedos and women in fancy dresses to the floor. It was a world Betsy had never been exposed to, but surprisingly it didn't feel at all foreign. Probably because so many of the couples in attendance were friends.

Ryan held out his hand. "Dance with me."

"How can I refuse?" Betsy gazed up at him through

lowered lashes. "I've been looking for an excuse to put my arms around you since you picked me up."

Ryan led her to the edge of the mahogany floor, immediately pulling her to him. "Great minds obviously think alike."

Betsy wasn't sure how many songs they danced to, but it wasn't enough. Even though her dancing skills were minimal, she did fine simply following his lead. On the slower, more romantic songs, she rested her head against his chest and listened to his heart beat.

He'd told her, after one of their many lovemaking sessions, that his heart beat only for her. Those words could have come from her mouth. Even though she'd been convinced that she'd loved him for years, the past few weeks had made her realize that what she'd felt before had been simple infatuation.

It was different now. She'd spent time with him and had gotten to know the man he'd become. It was that man—not the boy of her youth—who she loved. A man she would always love.

"You and no other," she murmured against his shirtfront.

"What did you say?" Ryan leaned down and nuzzled her hair.

Betsy looked up, her mouth going dry at the passion in his eyes. "I, uh, the medallion is still missing."

"The love token?"

She nodded.

"It will show up."

"I've looked everywhere. I even checked Puffy's bedding."

Ryan's lips curved upward in an indulgent smile. "I'm betting the puffball didn't appreciate your messing with her stuff."

Even though Ryan acted as if he couldn't be bothered with the tiny scrap of a dog, she'd caught him feeding the Pomeranian bits of table food when she wasn't looking. Lately, Puffy had become his little shadow. He always acted put out, but Betsy could see a bond being forged between them.

Yes, Betsy decided, life was indeed good. She expelled a happy breath.

The announcement that dinner was about to be served caused Betsy to reluctantly lift her head from Ryan's chest. "I suppose we better find a table."

He shot her a wink. "Only if we want to eat."

"Betsy. Ryan," Cole called out, motioning them toward a table near the raised dais.

"We saved a place for you." His wife, Meg, smiled a warm welcome. Her gold dress was a perfect foil for her ivory complexion and auburn hair.

As Ryan pulled out her chair, Betsy returned greetings from the other couples at the table—Mary Karen and Travis Fisher, David and July Wahl, and Kate and Joel Dennes.

While they ate, conversation bounced around the table, comfortable and familiar. Even when Betsy spilled cocktail sauce on her dress, she felt more chagrined than embarrassed.

She pushed back her chair. "I'm going to run to the restroom to see if I can get this out."

"I'll go with you." Kate put down her fork and started to rise.

Betsy waved her back down. "Finish eating. I'll be back in a jiffy."

The restroom was deserted except for the attendant, who gave Betsy a washcloth when she pointed to the stain, and two women refreshing their makeup in front of a long row of ornate beveled mirrors. Betsy didn't recognize either of them.

While she worked on the spot, Betsy tried to tune out their private conversation, until she heard the name Chad Dunlop.

"The charges were filed today." The blonde in the sparkly blue dress didn't even bother to keep her voice low. "I feel sorry for Chad. It's obvious the woman is out to get him because he fired her."

"I can't believe such a respected attorney would rape anyone." The brunette widened her eyes and added more mascara to her already-long lashes. "I don't know him well, but I know his wife. They're a nice family."

"Prominent in the community."

"Who is the woman?" The brunette dropped the mascara in her bag, then pulled out a tube of lip gloss. She added a swipe of clear shine to the red already on her lips.

Before answering, the blonde spritzed the air with perfume, then leaned into the falling mist. "Her name hasn't been released, but I have it on good authority she recently worked for him as a legal assistant."

A chill traveled up Betsy's spine.

"If she's the one I'm thinking of, she has several kids. Never married." The blonde's tone was heavy with condemnation. "He gave her a chance and this is how she repays him."

"We better get back to the party." The brunette pushed back her chair and stood. "Our dates are going to come searching for us."

The two laughed and left the room.

Betsy gave up on the stain and sank into one of the chintz-covered chairs they'd just vacated. Her hands began to tremble and her head spun. She forced herself to breathe. In and out. Deep breaths.

"Are you okay, miss?" The gray-haired attendant stepped forward, her face lined with worry. "Shall I get someone?"

Betsy forced a smile. "I'm fine, thank you. Just a little light-headed."

Concern lingered in the woman's dark eyes. "May I get you a glass of water?"

"That would be wonderful. Thank you."

The woman bustled off, and once the door closed behind her, Betsy rested her head in her hands, blinking back tears. He'd done it. Attacked another woman. Only this time Chad had succeeded in forcing himself on her.

It's my fault.

If she'd had the guts to go to the police and report his assault on her, maybe Chad would have received the help he needed. Even worse, her lack of action probably perpetuated his belief that he was invincible.

But there was still time to do the right thing. She had to go to the police. Telling them what had happened to her couldn't help but add credence to his current accuser's story. But Betsy wasn't stupid. She knew the cost of such action. Chad and his family would seek to discredit her and everyone around her.

Thankfully the only family she had was Keenan. And her brother's reputation was already in the toilet.

Ryan.

A knife sliced into Betsy's chest, making breathing difficult. She recalled the puzzling satisfaction in Chad's eyes when he'd caught her in Ryan's arms. What had Chad said? Something about Ryan succeeding where he'd failed?

That would be his argument if she went to the police and told her story. He would say that she'd been after him, but he'd rebuffed her. Now she was carrying on an affair with her current employer. Betsy could see it now. Not only would her name be dragged through the mud, but Ryan's reputation would suffer, as well.

The gray-haired attendant returned, opening the door and pointing to Betsy. "There she is."

Ryan crossed the small room in two strides, his face tight with worry. If he was embarrassed to be in a women's restroom, it didn't show.

Betsy turned disbelieving eyes on the woman. "You went and got him?" Her voice rose, then broke. "Why did you do that?"

Ryan crouched by her chair, his eyes dark with concern. "I was waiting outside the restroom for you and saw her coming with a glass of water. When I asked if she'd seen a woman matching your description, she told me you were ill."

"I felt light-headed." She drew in a deep breath. "I should go home."

"Perhaps I should ask David to check you first. He's an E.R. physician—"

"No," Betsy said sharply, then softened the word with a slight smile. "I'm sure it's nothing. If I feel worse tomorrow I'll see a doctor."

"I'll get the car and our coats." His gaze shifted to the attendant. "Would you mind staying with her for a few minutes? I'd appreciate it."

"Of course." The woman smiled at him while handing Betsy the glass of water. "I'll take good care of her."

"Thank you." Ryan pressed a twenty into the attendant's hand, then turned back to Betsy. He met her gaze. "I'll be right back."

Still he hesitated, pausing to kiss her forehead and brush a strand of hair back from her face.

"He's a good man," the woman said when the door closed behind him.

Betsy nodded, tears welling up in her eyes. Ryan *was* a good man. The best. He didn't deserve the trouble she was about to bring into his life.

If she cared about him at all, she had to distance herself from him. And she needed to do it as soon as possible.

No, her heart cried out. *Tell him.*

End it now, the tiny voice in her head whispered. *For his sake.*

Rational thought warred with raw emotion on the drive home. By the time Ryan pulled to a stop in front of her apartment complex, Betsy was exhausted. He pressed to spend the night and take care of her, but she made him leave. She had a lot of hard thinking to do.

Once he left, she burrowed under the covers with Puffy at her side, conscious of only one thing: the time had come to say goodbye to Ryan. And here she'd thought they had a fighting chance at happiness.

Foolish woman. Foolish, foolish woman.

Chapter Sixteen

Monday was D-day. At the end of the day, Betsy would break up with Ryan and quit her job. Then she'd contact the county attorney and give her statement. Though she realized leaving two jobs in such a short amount of time would look suspicious, she saw no other option.

Thankfully she'd made enough money to pay for the replacement furnace at her aunt's house. Once the house sold, she'd leave the area.

Although she loved Jackson Hole and her friends here, she couldn't be in the same town as Ryan. Sooner or later he'd find someone new to love, and Betsy couldn't take the chance of running into him and his new girlfriend.

A sob rose to her throat, but she swallowed it, refusing to let the tears fall. Taking a couple of deep breaths, she forced her mind on business, on the stack of work waiting for her.

Betsy was so focused on her thoughts that she didn't

notice the older couple waiting outside the office until she reached the door. They looked familiar. Quickly she made the connection. "Mr. and Mrs. Harcourt?"

"I'm sorry." Ryan's mother tilted her head, her gray eyes clearly puzzled. "Have we met?"

Even though it had been ten years since Betsy had last seen her, Sylvia Harcourt didn't look a day older. Instead of brushing her shoulders, her dark hair now hung just past her ears in a trendy bob. She was still as stylish as ever in a tweed coat that put Betsy's parka to shame.

"I'm Betsy McGregor, Keenan's sister." She almost added "and your son's girlfriend," but she didn't. Not only because they probably already knew that, but because after today it would no longer be relevant.

"Oh, of course," Sylvia said a little too heartily, which told Betsy she didn't remember at all. "How are you, dear?"

"I'm doing well." Betsy unlocked the door and motioned them inside. "Ryan should be here shortly."

"I didn't know you were working for our boy." Frank Harcourt had to be close to sixty. Unlike his wife he looked every bit his age. Of course a bald head fringed with gray tended to do that to a man.

"It's a recent thing." Betsy flipped on the office lights. "About six weeks."

"He's lucky to have you." Sylvia unbuttoned her coat. "Good help is hard to find."

Betsy's smile froze. Ryan had talked to his parents since they'd become "involved," but it was becoming increasingly obvious he hadn't mentioned her in any of those conversations. "Ryan didn't tell me you'd be stopping by."

"It was a last-minute kind of thing." Frank shrugged out of his overcoat to reveal a pair of crisply pressed navy pants and a striped dress shirt. "We're headed to Salt Lake.

That's where Ryan's sister and her family live. But Ryan has been doing some legal work for us and—"

"Frank, I'm sure the girl doesn't want to hear our personal business," his wife chided.

A thin layer of ice slowly wrapped itself around Betsy's heart. "How about I make some coffee?"

"That would be nice, dear." Sylvia slipped off her coat and gave it to her husband. He hung it on the antique coat tree next to his, then wandered over to the photograph of Ryan receiving one of his bull-riding medals.

Betsy measured out the water for the coffee.

Frank shook his head. "I wish the boy would put the same amount of effort into finding a wife as he did riding those bulls."

"Ryan has dated a lot of women." Betsy wasn't sure why she'd jumped into the conversation with both feet. But once said, the words couldn't be taken back.

"He's like my brother," Frank said. "Just like him."

From the tone, Betsy surmised that wasn't a compliment. She added the packet of ground beans and turned on the coffeemaker.

"Our son is not like your brother," Sylvia protested. She straightened the picture, then stepped back, eyeing it as if to make sure it was level. "Jed is on his third marriage. Our son has yet to even walk down the aisle once."

"I'm not talking about marriages, Sylvia. The boy falls in and out of love so fast it makes my head spin. Just like Jed."

Betsy averted her eyes and pretended not to listen to the squabble.

"Oh, Frank, you know that's not—"

"What about that woman last year? Kate. All I can say about her is she lasted longer than most. Then it was Mary or Misty. No, Mitzi. That didn't last long at all. Then at Labor Day, it was Audrey."

"Is he still dating Audrey?" Sylvia asked Betsy.

Betsy thought about correcting her, but decided the name didn't matter. Adrianna or Audrey. She knew who Mrs. Harcourt meant.

"No," Betsy said in a voice that sounded hollow. "I don't believe he is."

"I tell you, Sylvia, the boy doesn't know what love is."

"Dad. Mom." Ryan stood in the doorway, a look of surprise on his face, a bag of scones in his hand.

Betsy knew the bag contained scones because every Monday, Ryan would pick them up on his way to the office. They'd enjoy them with their morning coffee. It had become a tradition. If you could call two weeks in a row a tradition.

"What are you doing here?" His gaze shifted from his parents to Betsy, then back.

"What does it look like?" his mother asked. "We're visiting with your secretary while waiting for you."

Betsy flinched. There was nothing wrong with being a secretary. There was just something about the way that his mother said the word. Dismissive. As if she didn't matter.

"So you've met Bet—"

"We don't have much time for small talk, son," Frank interrupted. "You mother and I need to go over those papers with you before we leave for Salt Lake."

"But I want you to get to know—"

"Honey." His mother put a hand on his sleeve. "Your father is right. We don't have much time. I apologize for simply popping in and expecting you to drop everything. But surely you can spare us a few minutes."

"Mr. Fitzgibbons is driving in this morning from Idaho

Falls to meet with you," Betsy reminded him. "He should be here any moment."

Ryan looked at Betsy. "Would you mind—"

"I'll take care of him," Betsy said. "And cover things out here."

"Are you sure?" His gaze searched hers.

She forced a smile. "Positive."

"Thank you." He handed her the bag. "I brought scones."

Betsy placed the sack on the desk for the last time. So often it was hard to know when a tradition ended. But after today there would be no more scones and no more intimate conversation and laughter between her and Ryan.

Her heart did a slow, painful roll.

"I'll see you when we're done?" he asked.

"Of course she will." His mother's comment spared Betsy the need of answering. "She works for you. Where else would she be?"

Where else indeed, Betsy thought as Ryan followed his parents out of the room.

The three had barely disappeared into his office when the phone rang. With the roads between Idaho Falls and Jackson snow-packed and more of the white stuff in the forecast, Mr. Fitzgibbons had decided against making the trip.

Betsy rescheduled the elderly man and wished him a good afternoon. Because they didn't have any other clients scheduled for the morning, she placed the bell on the counter and went to her office.

The door to Ryan's office wasn't shut completely. Betsy thought about closing it but decided that might be even more disruptive.

"Betsy isn't my secretary, Mom," Ryan said, his voice tight with frustration. "She's my legal assistant. More importantly, she's my girlfriend."

Betsy wasn't surprised he told them. The only thing that surprised her was he hadn't told them before. Of course, considering how his father had gone on about his past relationships, he'd probably learned to keep his mouth shut.

Betsy slid her chair closer to the door just in time to hear his mother laugh.

"Oh, honey, for a second I thought you said you were dating the girl."

"What happened to Audrey?" His father's voice boomed.

"Yes, Mother, that's what I said." Ryan's clipped tone spoke of his rising irritation. "Betsy and I are dating. And, Dad, I don't know anyone named Audrey."

Betsy wheeled her chair closer to the door. She glanced through the tiny opening just in time to see Frank's brows pull together in a frown.

"Of course you know her. The one you couldn't quit talking about over Labor Day. Audrey."

"Adrianna?"

"It doesn't matter now." His father waved a dismissive hand. "If you can't even remember her name, she's obviously ancient history."

"Betsy is the only woman who matters," Ryan insisted.

"Honey, you can't be serious. She's your employee." His mother sounded bewildered at his vehemence. "You barely know the woman. Last time we were in the office, Caroline was here."

"What does that have to do with anything? I never dated Caroline."

"I simply meant that Betsy is very new in your life."

"I love her, Mom."

Betsy's breath caught in her throat. Even though she'd seen it in his eyes, she'd never heard him say those three little words. Until now.

Betsy loved him, too. Enough to protect him from Chad. And the scandal.

"Give it time," Sylvia said in a gentle, if slightly patronizing, tone. "Don't rush into anything."

"I don't need to give it time." Ryan's jaw jutted out. "Try to understand. All those other women taught me what I don't want. Now I know what I want. I want Betsy. I want to marry her."

His parents exchanged a glance.

"All your mother is saying is to take it slow. Don't rush into anything."

"If it's true love, it will be there in six months." His mother reached across the desk and patted his hand. "If you marry in haste and discover in another couple months she's just another of your infatuations, it's not only you who will be hurt, but her, as well."

Ryan's brows slammed together like two dark thunderclouds. He shoved his chair back.

"I'm sure that Betsy is a lovely young woman," his mother continued, softening her tone. "She deserves a man who honestly and truly loves her. Until you're sure of your feelings, don't make any promises."

Ryan rose abruptly and Betsy scooted from the door, her heart pounding. Seconds later his office door closed.

Betsy knew she wasn't the kind of woman they wanted for their successful son. She wasn't a doctor like Kate and Mitzi or a nurse-midwife like Adrianna. She was the daughter of an alcoholic former showgirl. A legal assistant with a brother in prison.

In time Ryan would have seen that, too. Unfortunately he wasn't tired of her yet. Which meant he wouldn't be breaking up with her today.

She would have to do it. She would have to make him

believe that this had just been a brief fling for her. That *she* was tired of him and ready to move on.

Because if Ryan stayed with her, Chad would end up dragging him through the mud and ruining his reputation. Nobody was going to hurt the man Betsy loved. She would protect him…even if it meant breaking her own heart in the process.

Riding bulls had taught Ryan that he had to trust his gut. And right now his gut was signaling that something was wrong. Very wrong.

He tried telling himself it was simply a stressful morning for both of them. But the set to Betsy's shoulders, the shuttered look to her eyes and the way she was too busy to share a scone and talk once his parents left told the story.

Worse yet, the day turned busy with clients coming in and out, which meant there was no time for private conversation. But he consoled himself with the knowledge that after work they could go somewhere quiet, have a nice dinner and he could make things right. Once he knew what was wrong.

There wasn't anything they couldn't work out. He'd seen his parents do it time and again over the years. An issue would come between them, but they were always able to compromise, find common ground and a solution they could both live with. It would be the same with him and Betsy. If it was simply that she needed more reassurance that he cared, he would give it to her.

In fact, tonight might be the time to pull out the ring he'd been carrying around in his pocket, tell her he loved her and ask her to marry him. His lips curved up in a smile, thinking of the celebration sure to follow….

A knock sounded on his partially closed office door.

He lifted his head and widened his smile. Just the woman he wanted to see. "Since when do you knock?"

"I wasn't sure if you were off the phone or not."

Ryan ignored the fact that she hadn't returned his smile and motioned her inside. "With all the appointments done for the day, let's take off early and do something fun. What do you say?"

Still no smile.

She took the seat across the desk and folded her hands into her lap. "We need to talk."

Were there four more dreaded words in the English language? Unease slid its fingers up his spine, even as Ryan tried to tell himself this was no big deal. "What's on your mind?"

"This isn't working out."

He leaned forward, resting his arms on the table, trying to ignore his skyrocketing heart rate. *Don't assume,* he told himself. *Speculations are dangerous. Always work with facts.*

"Could you be a little more specific?" Somehow he managed to keep the smile on his lips and his voice even. "Exactly *what* isn't working out?"

"You and me."

His heart stopped. Honest to goodness stopped.

Ryan blinked and fought to find his voice. "Pardon?"

"Our relationship," she said. "It's not working."

"Since when?" His voice rose, then cracked.

"For a while." She pressed her lips together and gazed down at her hands.

"How can that be?" Ryan remembered the time he'd fallen off his dirt bike and had the air knocked out of him. He felt the same way now. "Everything has been good."

She lifted her head and met his gaze. "I just don't want to date you anymore."

Panic raced through his veins even as he kept his expression controlled. “Tell me what’s not working. What you don’t like. We’ll make it better. *I’ll* make it better.”

Compromise. They would compromise and everything would be as good as new, except she was saying it hadn’t been good. Not for her.

“There’s nothing you can do.” She met his gaze. “Just like all those other women you dated that you got tired of and didn’t want to date anymore. A person can’t change the way they feel.”

“But I love you.” The admission tumbled from his lips. This wasn’t the way he wanted to tell her. No, never like this. But it was important—very important—that she knew how much she meant to him.

Something flashed in her eyes. A look he couldn’t quite decipher but one that gave him hope. Hope that her leaving him wasn’t a done deal.

“It doesn’t matter,” she said. “And because we won’t be together anymore, it’d probably be best if I didn’t work for you.”

“Don’t I get a say in this?” he asked, on the verge of begging.

“No.”

“Don’t you love me? Or even like me? Just a little bit?”

For a second her tightly controlled features began to crumble, but then the mask returned. “It’s over, Ryan. There’s nothing you can say or do to change my mind.”

She rose then and turned toward the door.

“Why, Betsy?” he called out to her. “Why?”

“It’s for the best,” she said without turning as she walked out of his office and out of his life.

Ryan slumped back in his chair and realized his parents had left out one very important detail in their relationship advice.

Compromise only worked when both parties wanted a relationship to succeed.

Chapter Seventeen

Betsy kept her composure while meeting with the police and county attorney. She'd worried they might make her feel like a criminal, but everyone was respectful. They mentioned more than once that she'd done the right thing by coming forward. If only the action hadn't carried with it such a high price tag....

I love you. That's what Ryan had said. Betsy had wanted to tell him she loved him, too. Only the knowledge that he would be hurt by his association with her made her keep her mouth shut.

This was her battle, not his. And down the road when Chad's attorneys tried to discredit her by bringing up her relationship with Ryan, his clients would be reassured by the fact that she no longer worked for him. What she was doing might not make sense, but she had to protect Ryan. Somehow. Someway.

By the time Betsy reached her car in the courthouse

parking lot, she could no longer hold back the tears. And once she started to cry, she couldn't stop.

Damn Adrianna for telling her to jump into a relationship with both feet and her whole heart. Look where that had gotten her—desperately in love with a man who would never be hers.

"Betsy." A sharp rap sounded on the passenger-side window. "Are you okay?"

Betsy recognized Lexi's voice immediately. She hurriedly swiped at her eyes, then shifted to face her friend.

"I'm fine." Betsy's smile felt stiff on her lips. "Just getting ready to head home."

Lexi tried the door handle. When it didn't open, she frowned. "Let me in. I want to talk."

Talking was the last thing Betsy wanted to do, especially with a woman who was Ryan's friend.

She's your friend, too, Betsy reminded herself.

She'd barely clicked the door unlocked when Lexi slid into the passenger seat. Even though dressed in a black-and-gray-plaid coat that looked warm, her friend shivered. "It's cold out there."

Pulling a tissue from her coat pocket, Betsy surreptitiously swiped at her nose. Small talk. Definitely manageable. For a second Betsy considered asking what had brought Lexi to the courthouse but realized the social worker might then ask her the same question. "I heard on the radio it's supposed to dip below zero tonight."

Lexi's lingering gaze brought a warmth to Betsy's face.

"I'm not sure if there's snow in the forecast or not," Betsy added. "They say there's a band of moisture—"

With gentle fingers, Lexi took her hand, stopping the babbling. "We can discuss the weather for a few more minutes. Or you could go ahead and tell me what's wrong now."

Her soft voice invited confidences. Yet Betsy found herself reluctant to tell Lexi that she and Ryan were no longer a couple. Somehow, saying it aloud would make it seem so, well, final.

But it is final, she told herself. It had to be. Ryan had worked hard to build a respectable practice in Jackson Hole. She would not let his association with her ruin that for him.

Betsy took a deep breath and forced out the words. "Ryan and I, we're not together anymore."

"What happened?" Lexi released Betsy's hand and sat back, a stunned look on her face. "You two seemed perfect for each other. So happy."

Betsy could take the questions. It was the concern in Lexi's eyes that made keeping her composure difficult. But she had to pull this off. Ryan's reputation in the community was at stake. "He wasn't the man for me. I feel bad, but I had to call it quits. It's best for him."

The lies flowed surprisingly easily from her lips, but the speculative look in Lexi's eyes told Betsy the woman wasn't convinced.

"It's best for *him,*" Lexi repeated slowly. "An odd thing to say."

Darn. Darn. Darn.

"I meant," Betsy stammered, "that it's best for both of us. Best for him that he's not with someone who doesn't love—" Her voice broke. She took a deep breath and tried again. "Who doesn't love him. And best for me not to be with someone I, I don't love."

Lexi's gaze searched Betsy's face. She must have seen something that answered her question because her amber eyes softened. "I'm sure someone has told you the story about Nick and how he lost his memory."

Betsy nodded, the tension in her shoulders easing. Her

time on the hot seat was over. Even if Lexi wasn't *fully* convinced, it appeared she was ready to give her the benefit of the doubt. Betsy was grateful. Very grateful. "You fell in love with a man who didn't even know his own name."

"That's right. But what you probably don't know is that once we learned his true identity, we discovered he had a serious girlfriend back home." Lexi's eyes took on a faraway look. "By that time we were already deeply in love."

Lexi was right. This part she hadn't heard before. "What did you do?"

"Nick was certain it was me he loved, but at that point he could only recall bits and pieces of his former life in Texas. And nothing at all about the woman claiming to be his fiancée."

"Fiancée?" Betsy choked out the word. She couldn't imagine Nick with anyone but Lexi.

"Turned out Nick had never actually proposed, but I'm getting ahead of myself." Lexi shot Betsy a wry smile, then continued. "Nick and I talked, and we decided he should go to Dallas. We hoped that being back on his home turf would jog his memory. If he ended up wanting his old girlfriend, I told him I'd understand."

"But he didn't." Betsy already knew this story's ending. "He chose you."

"Yes." Lexi's lips lifted in a smile. "And happily his old girlfriend found her own true love, too."

The story was fascinating, but Betsy had a feeling there was a point to the tale she'd missed.

"Is there something about what happened with you and Nick that you think relates to Ryan and me?" Betsy cleared her throat. "Because the two situations couldn't be more different."

"Nick and I encountered an issue that could have torn us apart, but we faced it together. We discussed how we were going to handle it…together." There was a challenge in Lexi's eyes. "You and Ryan need to face whatever is going on in your life *together.*"

"He doesn't—" Betsy began, then stopped, remembering what he'd said to her. "I don't—"

"You don't what? Love him? Rubbish. I've seen how you look at him." Lexi chuckled. "And Ryan is in love with you."

"Stop it, Lexi," Betsy said, a hint of desperation in her tone.

She didn't want to talk about Ryan's love for her. All that did was remind her of how much she'd lost. And, if it was true, if Ryan *really* loved her, then she'd hurt him when she'd broken things off. For some reason that made her sacrifice seem almost selfish.

No. No. She'd done the right thing.

"I know I've never seen him like this with any other woman."

A chill traveled up Betsy's spine. The social worker speculating in the privacy of the car was one thing. If Lexi mentioned any of this to Ryan—

"This is not your business, Lex," Betsy said firmly. "Stay out of it."

The gorgeous brunette seemed more amused than offended by Betsy's blunt admonition.

"Sorry, I can't promise that." The words had barely left Lexi's lips when a car containing her husband and daughters drove up. The social worker opened the car door and stepped out but didn't immediately walk away. She leaned down and met Betsy's gaze head on. "I care about you. And I care about Ryan. If I find out there's something I can do to help this situation, I'm going to do it."

Betsy watched Lexi join her family, a sick feeling in her stomach. If Lexi discovered her motive for breaking up with Ryan and decided to tell him, her interference could cost Ryan his career. And then all of Betsy's sacrifices would be for naught.

The sun had set by the time Betsy arrived home. She hurried to the front door of her apartment, eager to be inside. The key turned easily in the lock. Perhaps a little too easily. Normally, it might have given Betsy pause, but right now all she wanted was to feed Puffy, then collapse in a chair.

She headed toward the kitchen, noticing she'd left on the light. When she reached the archway to the room, Puffy ran to greet her. Betsy picked the dog up, then stopped in her tracks.

"Dinner should be ready in five minutes." Ryan turned from the stove. "I hope you like Hamburger Helper. Potatoes Stroganoff is my signature dish."

Since she'd last seen him, Ryan had changed into jeans and a gray Denver Broncos sweatshirt. His smile was bright—too bright—and Betsy noticed the lines of tension around his eyes.

Her heart twisted. The last thing she'd wanted to do was hurt him. But she had. She'd hurt both of them. "How did you get in?"

"You gave me a key." He returned his attention to the skillet on the stove. "Remember?"

"I'm going to need that back." She held out her hand but he didn't look up. After a moment she dropped the hand back to her side.

Suddenly incredibly tired of the drama, Betsy sat down, hugging Puffy close. But it wasn't long before the Pom began to squirm. The second Betsy released her hold, the dog jumped to the floor and trotted to stand by Ryan.

It only figured Puffy would abandon her in her hour

of need. How many times had her mother bailed on her? Keenan? Even Aunt Agatha. She'd died without warning. Betsy didn't know whether to laugh or cry watching the little dog cozy up to Ryan.

He patted Puffy on the head, then stepped from the stove to the counter where a bottle and two wineglasses sat. With well-practiced ease he uncorked the bottle, then filled each glass halfway. "A full-bodied red should go nicely with the Stroganoff."

Ryan held out a glass to her.

Betsy shook her head even as she glanced longingly at the wine.

"Take it." His eyes softened. "You look like you could use a glass."

"I need to feed Puffy and take her outside." Betsy sighed. "She's been cooped up in the apartment all day—"

"Already done." Ryan placed the glass before her on the table.

"You shouldn't—"

"I shouldn't what?" His even tone took on a hard edge. "Care about you and Puffy?" He paused and gentled his tone. "Sorry, that's not possible."

"I think you should leave." Betsy tried, but there was no conviction in her voice.

"And I think you should lie down and rest," he said. "But because neither of those seem likely, let's have a nice meal with a glass of wine or two."

"But—"

"I'm your friend, Betsy. Give me at least some respect."

Betsy was too tired to argue, too tired to put up a stink and toss him out. The headache that had started when she'd been in the attorney's office and had grabbed hold when she'd cried in the car, now pounded just behind her left eye.

She rubbed her temples with the pads of her fingers. "I guess you can stay."

"You have a headache." The comment was made as an observation rather than as a question.

Betsy closed her eyes for a second. "Uh-huh."

Moments later he appeared at her side with a glass of cola and four tablets of ibuprofen.

She glanced down at the pills. "Four? And with a cola?"

"Four is eight hundred milligrams, which is prescription strength. And when you take them with a cola, it has a synergistic effect."

Betsy narrowed her gaze.

He smiled. "Hey, my sister used to get migraines, and if she caught them early enough by taking the ibuprofen and caffeine she didn't have to take her prescription meds."

Betsy popped the pills into her mouth and took a big drink of cola. At this point she'd give anything a try.

"Why don't you lie down?" He took the glass of cola she handed him without shifting his gaze from her face. "The food and wine will keep. And don't worry about Puffy, I'll keep her occupied."

Betsy wasn't worried about Puffy at all. She was concerned about Ryan being in her apartment, acting as if he belonged there. And about her still wishing he did.

But would a few minutes more really make that much difference? No, she decided, it wouldn't. She jerked to her feet and made it to her bedroom on autopilot. Slipping off her shoes, Betsy pulled back the covers and fell into her bed fully dressed.

When she opened her eyes, the clock on her bedside stand said an hour had passed. There were sounds of voices coming from her kitchen. That didn't surprise her as much as the fact that her headache had disappeared.

Betsy glanced down at her wrinkled clothes. She thought

about leaving them on. After all, she could change into something more comfortable after she kicked Ryan, and whoever it was he was talking with, out of her apartment.

But her closet doors were open and comfy clothes beckoned. She slipped on a pair of yoga pants and a long-sleeved T-shirt advertising a Kansas City 5K fun run.

Even though dressing nice usually gave her some measure of confidence, right now comfort mattered more. She stuck on a pair of bunny slippers that Adrianna had once given her as a gag gift and ambled into the kitchen.

Mr. Marstand looked up and smiled. He sat at the table with Ryan, an almost-empty plate of Stroganoff and a glass of wine before him. Ryan must have already eaten because he'd pushed his chair back and held Puffy in his lap.

When the dog saw Betsy, Puffy jumped down and ran to greet her. Betsy leaned over and patted her soft fur, her heart warmed by the welcome.

"Ryan said you were a bit under the weather." Concern filled Mr. Marstand's eyes. "Are you feeling better?"

Betsy nodded and dropped into a chair at the table. "I'm not sure if it was the nap or the ibuprofen-cola mix that made the difference, but my headache is gone."

"Good news." Ryan rose to his feet and squeezed her shoulder as he walked past. "We saved you some dinner. And a glass of wine."

"Ryan wanted to drink it all, but I told him because it was your place, a gentleman should save you at least one glass." The old man laughed as if he'd said something uproariously funny.

Betsy glanced at Ryan and they shared a smile before she realized that she shouldn't be sharing anything with him. Not a smile. Certainly not dinner. But how could she kick him out now? Not when he'd gone to all the trouble of making her a fine meal. And not with Mr. Marstand watching her every move.

"I am hungry," she said. "And wine sounds lovely."

In a matter of seconds the plate of food that had been warming in the oven was on the table and a glass of wine was sitting before her.

Betsy had just taken her first bite when Mr. Marstand squinted behind his spectacles. "Have you been crying?"

Betsy started to choke on the Stroganoff but quickly washed it down with a sip of wine. "I have a little headache, that's all."

Neither the older man nor the younger one looked convinced, but neither pursued the topic further. Instead they talked about the weather, the upcoming bowl games and Puffy's penchant for Greenies. Then silence descended over the table.

Oblivious to the undercurrent of tension, Mr. Marstand broke the silence first. "I hear you finally got the furnace installed in your aunt's house."

Betsy looked up from the absolutely delicious Stroganoff in surprise. "Where'd you hear that?"

"Well, actually we saw the billing statement on your counter." Ryan had the grace to look slightly abashed.

Mr. Marstand waved a hand. "It was sitting right there in plain sight."

Betsy didn't care. It wasn't as if the furnace was a big secret. "Yes, it's been installed. And the city inspector has been out and removed the red tag from the house. I'm going over there tomorrow to start cleaning."

"Don't you have to work?" Mr. Marstand asked.

Betsy shook her head, hoping Ryan hadn't said anything about her quitting. Even though her elderly neighbor liked to present a tough-as-nails image, if he knew she was unemployed, he'd worry.

Thankfully Ryan simply took another sip of his wine.

"What kind of cleaning will you be doing?" The old man sounded surprisingly interested.

"Aunt Agatha was something of a pack rat, so I had a Dumpster delivered today. I'm going to get there early tomorrow and start tossing things. Until I get all the junk out of there, it will be hard to clean."

And impossible to sell, she thought with a sigh.

At one time Betsy had envisioned her and Ryan working together to renovate the house. Even though the place was a mess right now, it had potential. In fact, since she and Ryan had become involved, each time Betsy had thought about the house, she'd pictured the two of them sitting together before the fireplace, eating breakfast in the little nook off the kitchen and making love in the large master bedroom.

Now she'd be getting the house ready to sell. Another couple or family would be the ones building memories in the home, not she and Ryan.

"Tomorrow? Well, this is your lucky day, missy," Mr. Marstand said. "I usually go to bingo on Tuesdays, but it got cancelled. Which means I'm available. What time do you want to start? I can be ready by six. Is that too late?"

Six? Was he kidding? "Er, I was thinking of starting around nine."

"That'll work." The older man shifted his gaze to Ryan. "What about you, son? Will that time work for you?"

Betsy tightened her hand around her wineglass. Nonono. This situation was rapidly getting out of control.

"I don't have any appointments tomorrow, so I'm available." Ryan kept his gaze focused on Mr. Marstand. "I'll have my truck if we need to haul any cleaning supplies, ladders, stuff like that."

"Good thinking." The older man nodded his approval before pushing back his chair and standing. "I hate to eat and run, but my favorite show will be on the tube in five minutes."

"I'll walk you out." Ryan stood. "I've got a few things I need to do yet this evening, too."

Mr. Marstand cocked his head. "Don't you want to stay and keep Betsy company while she eats?"

"I'd love to, but I have an, er, an appointment." Ryan edged toward the door.

"Ryan, honey," Betsy said in a sugary sweet tone. "Please stay. There are a couple things we need to discuss."

She needed to make it clear that while she appreciated his efforts tonight, this was not happening again. He was out of her life. It might not make sense now, but one day he would thank her for it.

"Sorry, can't." His hand curved around the doorknob. "My, er, my mom is expecting me."

"In that case you have to go," Mr. Marstand said before Betsy could say a word. "A man can't keep his mother waiting. Isn't that right, Betsy?"

Betsy tried to meet Ryan's eyes, to say in a glance what she couldn't say with Mr. Marstand standing there hanging on to every word. But Ryan looked everywhere except at her.

"I'll see you tomorrow." He opened the door and stepped aside to allow Mr. Marstand to pass, reaching out to steady the older man when he started to wobble.

Betsy rushed toward the door. The fact that he was out of her life had to be made clear before he got out of her sight.

"Ryan," she called out, her slippers' bunny ears flopping up and down with each step, "I want you—"

He reached out a hand and pulled her to him, his lips closing over hers. Her head told her not to respond. Her body had different ideas. By the time he broke off the kiss, she was swaying and her thoughts were a tangled mess.

Her head was still spinning when he headed down the steps. When he reached the bottom he turned and smiled. "I want you, too, sweetheart."

No, she wanted to call out, *I want you out of my life.* But she remained mute as he jumped into his truck and drove away.

She wanted him. That hadn't changed. But getting him out of her life? She touched her tingling lips. That was proving to be a far more difficult task.

Chapter Eighteen

Ryan drove slowly through downtown Jackson, encouraged but still frightened. Of course he'd never admit the frightened part to anyone. He'd ridden two-thousand-pound bulls and never once been afraid. Yet the thought of losing Betsy filled him with icy fear. Even though she'd kissed him as though she didn't want to let him go, he had the feeling she still planned to walk away. He just wasn't sure why.

Traffic was heavy, but Ryan didn't mind. Going home held little appeal, as did stopping at Wally's Place. Although it was Ladies' Night and the bar would be crawling with women, there was only one woman Ryan wanted, and she wouldn't be there.

As he slowed his truck for a turning car, he noticed that Hill of Beans was still open. Even though it didn't make sense to flood his system with caffeine this late at night, he turned into the parking lot.

Ryan pushed open the door to the coffee shop and

breathed in the rich aroma. White lights and brightly colored bulbs still decorated a large fir tree sitting in front of the plate-glass window. Garlands of coffee filters—hand-decorated by patrons—added a festive air to the exposed-brick walls and beamed ceilings. It was hard to believe twenty-four hours ago, Ryan had actually been excited for what the new year would bring.

This Valentine's Day would have been his and Betsy's first together, the first of many to come. Now it was looking like they might not make it there.

No. Ryan shoved the thought aside before it had a chance to fully form. Betsy and he would be together. Failure wasn't an option.

"Look what the cat dragged in." Cole's broad smile of welcome belied his words.

"I can't believe you're actually working, Lassiter," Ryan shot back. "I thought you'd be home counting your money."

Cole not only owned this store but was also head of the Hill of Beans empire. Last Ryan knew, his childhood friend had something like fifty or sixty stores in multiple states.

"There's a big holiday show at the high school tonight." Cole ignored the jibe. "I didn't want the kids who work here to miss it, so I volunteered to fill in."

"How are Meg and Charlie?"

"Charlie's growing like a weed," Cole said with a proud papa smile. "And Meg's just finished her first trimester, so she's starting to get her energy back."

A baby. Ryan fought a pang of envy. Before now he hadn't thought beyond the fact that he wanted kids. And that he wanted Betsy to be their mother.

Cole rested both hands on the counter, relaxed and confident, with an easy smile on his lips. After a dismal childhood, Ryan was glad his friend had finally found the happiness he'd long deserved. "What's your pleasure?"

"A small coffee should do it."

"I'll pour a cup for myself and join you." Cole lifted a brow. "If you feel like company, that is."

"Sure." The last thing Ryan wanted was to be alone with his thoughts.

Once Cole sat down, they talked sports for a few minutes. They'd just moved on to the upcoming Super Bowl game when the bells over the door jingled.

Both men turned in their seats.

Cole pushed his chair back, then lifted a hand in greeting to Nick and Lexi.

The two had been laughing about something when they'd walked through the door, and their laughter carried easily into the shop.

Another happy couple, Ryan thought with a trace of bitterness.

It had once seemed as if everyone had someone special in their life but him. Then Betsy had come along and he'd realized the wait had been worth it. Now, she said she didn't want him....

"What brings you out on such a cold night?" Cole asked.

Nick grinned. "If you could see the back of our SUV, you wouldn't have to ask. Lexi closed out three stores."

His wife punched him playfully in the side. "What my darling husband is trying to say is that we've been out hitting the post-holiday sales."

"And I've loved every minute." Nick looped an arm around her shoulders. "Coraline is keeping the girls overnight, so we're making the most of the evening."

The successful family law attorney shot his wife a look that said the night was far from over.

Ryan took a sip of coffee, relishing the heat on his tongue. A couple of days ago that could have been him and Betsy enjoying an evening out while anticipating a night of pleasure once they returned home.

Cole moved behind the counter and smiled at the couple. "What would you like? It's on the house."

After giving their orders, the two wandered over to where Ryan sat.

"May we join you?" Lexi asked.

"Of course we can, Lex." Nick pulled out a chair for her. "We'll be much better company than Cole."

"I heard that." Cole returned to the table with their drinks. "Just for that, a tip is mandatory."

Once they were all settled around the table, Ryan expected one of the three to ask about Betsy, but they ended up talking about some foster kids that Lexi had to place on an emergency basis that afternoon.

"I didn't leave the courthouse until after five-thirty. But I'm happy to report the children now have a safe place to stay," Lexi announced with a satisfied sigh.

"Did you happen to run into Chad Dunlop while you were there?" Cole asked.

Ryan stiffened at the name.

"I didn't." Lexi cast Cole a curious look. "Should I have?"

"Rumor is the county attorney is getting ready to charge Dunlop with first-degree sexual assault," Cole said in a matter-of-fact tone.

Ryan straightened in his chair. "Where did you hear that?"

Cole chuckled. "It's amazing what you learn when you stand behind that counter for an hour or two."

"I heard that same rumor earlier today," Nick admitted.

Lexi turned to her husband. "You never mentioned that to me."

"I didn't know you'd be interested." Nick shrugged. "We barely know the guy."

Ryan took a calming breath, determined to keep a conversational tone. "Either of you have details?"

"Only that a former legal assistant claims he sexually assaulted her when they were working late." Nick leaned back in his chair and shook his head. "Helluva thing."

A chill traveled through Ryan's body.

If Keenan hadn't taught Betsy how to defend herself…

If she hadn't gotten lucky and placed her knee in just the right spot…

Lexi's curious gaze settled on Ryan. "You don't seem surprised."

"I'm not." Ryan pressed his lips together, telling himself not to say anything more, but he couldn't help himself. "Dunlop is an animal."

"Didn't Betsy used to work at his firm?" Lexi asked in a voice that was a little too casual.

Ryan gave a short jerky nod.

"Did she have any trouble with him?" Nick asked, his gaze narrowing.

"I saw Betsy today in the courthouse parking lot," Lexi said when Ryan didn't immediately answer. "She was upset. I wonder if her tears had something to do with Chad."

"She was crying?" Ryan clamped down on the rage building inside him.

Lexi nodded. "She mentioned you and she were having… problems."

Ryan could read between the lines. She'd told Lexi they'd broken up. Which meant she was serious about her plan to push him out of her life. But why now? With all this stuff with Chad going on, you'd think she'd want him by her side for support. Unless…

The image of Chad in his office doorway, clapping, with that pleased expression on his face flashed before him. The puzzle pieces that had been floating around in Ryan's head began to lock into place. When he'd caught them together, Chad realized if Betsy ever came forward with her story, he could use her relationship with her current employer—him—to discredit them both.

Was breaking up with him a misguided attempt on Betsy's part to protect him? Surely not. Surely she realized he could protect himself. And her, too, if given the chance. Still, his possible explanation made more sense than her claiming out of the blue that she didn't care about him anymore.

Protecting him had to be the reason she'd walked away.

"What's going on, Ry?" Cole asked quietly.

Ryan ignored the concern in his friends' eyes. "Nothing I can't remedy."

"You don't have to do it alone," Cole said. "If there's anything Meg and I can do to help, just let us know."

"Same here," Nick said.

Lexi placed a hand on his arm. "You and Betsy have a lot of friends in this town. Remember that."

Ryan stood, his mind racing. "I appreciate the offers."

Tonight he'd plot a course of action.

Tomorrow he'd implement that plan.

She didn't know it yet, but soon Betsy would be back where she belonged. With him. They'd stand strong and face whatever Chad threw at them…together.

The day had dawned overcast and cold, but Ryan appeared in a particularly sunny mood when he stopped by Aunt Agatha's. Betsy had been awake most of the night coming up with just the right words.

She would make sure Ryan understood that he had to

leave and not come back. Betsy glanced out the living room window and watched him load blankets and clothing into his truck bed to take to the Good Samaritan Mission on Pearl Street.

Because the wind held an icy bite, Ryan had put on a blue stocking cap to keep his ears warm. Mr. Marstand was outside, too, hood up, wearing the extra coat the attorney had brought with him. Ryan had said the garment was too small and had offered it to Mr. Marstand.

The older gentleman had eagerly accepted. He was soon raving about the coat's thick lining and warm hood. That's when Betsy realized that her neighbor had worn those light jackets not out of choice, but out of necessity.

Shame flooded her. She'd been so focused on her own problems that she hadn't even noticed a neighbor in need.

Betsy had been prepared with her speech when Ryan had arrived, but when he'd presented the old man with the coat, she hadn't wanted to ruin Mr. Marstand's obvious pleasure with ugliness.

Her new plan was to wait for the two men to come inside. Then she'd send Mr. Marstand on an errand so she and Ryan could talk privately. While waiting, Betsy busied herself piling last year's newspapers into a metal shopping cart she'd found in the yard.

"My lordy, it's cold out there." Mr. Marstand pulled the front door shut against the brisk north wind, his wrinkled cheeks bright red.

If Betsy didn't know better she'd swear the man had bits of ice clinging to his mustache. "How's the coat?"

"Best I ever owned." Mr. Marstand lowered his voice to a confidential whisper. "I don't think it's ever been worn. I'm surprised the boy didn't take it back when he realized he'd gotten the wrong size."

"You know how it is." Betsy waved a hand. "You get

busy. Then all of a sudden too much time has passed for a return."

"Well, I sure do appreciate him thinking of me."

Betsy peered over his shoulder, as if expecting the attorney to open the door and magically appear. "Is Ryan still loading the truck?"

"He left."

Betsy inhaled sharply. She'd wanted Ryan to leave but not before she spoke with him. "Where did he go?"

Mr. Marstand shrugged. "Said he had some business that needed attention."

Betsy wasn't sure if the sensation coursing through her was relief or disappointment. Or maybe surprise that he'd left without saying goodbye. Of course, Ryan could have picked up on her coolness toward him and decided he'd had enough. A knot formed in the pit of her stomach. "Did he mention coming back?"

"Don't worry." Mr. Marstand patted her arm. "He'll be back. That boy likes being around you."

The words shouldn't have made her feel better, but they did.

Betsy changed the subject by pointing to a stack of magazines. "I have all this stuff I don't want while the one thing my aunt gave me that meant something has disappeared."

Mr. Marstand bent over and took an armful of the magazines, dropping them in the cart on top of the newspapers. "What's missing?"

"A love token." Betsy chewed on her lower lip, trying to decide the best way to describe it. "It looks like a coin. It has ivy and hearts and—"

"Stop right there." Mr. Marstand reached into his pocket. "Is this it?"

Betsy gave an excited shriek. "Where did you find it?"

"On the sidewalk in front of the apartment building

today. Didn't know who it belonged to." He flipped it to Betsy. "Do you know what the words mean?"

She slipped the medallion into the pocket of her jeans, pushing it way down so that there was no chance of losing it again. "You and no other."

Mr. Marstand thought for a moment, then smiled. "That's how your young man feels about you."

"Ryan isn't my young man." Betsy hardened her heart against the stabbing pain. "We broke up."

There. She'd told Mr. Marstand. Another step forward.

"You two don't look broke up to me." Mr. Marstand picked up the last of the stack of magazines and tossed them into the cart.

"That's because he won't go away," Betsy said more crossly than she'd intended.

"He loves you."

Betsy acted as if she hadn't heard the comment. "Is that all the magazines?"

"Yup." The old man lifted a misshapen plastic toy horse from a stack of junk and handed it to Betsy. "What's the story on this fella?"

Betsy swallowed a sigh. From one topic she didn't want to discuss to another.

"My mom stepped on it when she was drunk." Betsy kept her tone matter-of-fact. "Aunt Agatha tried to glue it back together. I don't know why she kept it. I told her to throw it away."

Betsy couldn't help caressing the palomino's nose. The horse had been precious to her. A birthday present from her aunt, the year her mom had forgotten the day entirely. "Mom never even apologized. Not about the horse or forgetting my birthday."

A look of understanding mixed with sadness filled the old man's gaze. "I had a daddy who liked the bottle. Like your mama he never apologized for nothin'. Mam said it was 'cause he didn't recall doin' it."

"My mom used to say horrible things to both me and Keenan."

"That was the alcohol talking." The lines on Mr. Marstand's face appeared to deepen. "Pap used to tell me I was more trouble than I was worth. My sis used to cry when he said that to her. Not me. I never cried."

"Keenan never cried either."

"I told everyone the words just bounced off me like one of them bouncing balls." Mr. Marstand gave a humorless chuckle. "It sounded good."

"My mom's words hurt," Betsy admitted. "But I tried not to let her actions—or her words—affect my life."

"Sometimes they still do, just in ways we can't see."

Even if Mr. Marstand hadn't been staring at her with that expectant look on his face, she'd have made the connection. "You think my past is affecting my relationship with Ryan."

"Isn't it?"

Even though she didn't owe her neighbor an explanation, Mr. Marstand was much more than simply the man next door. He was her friend. The grandfather she'd never had.

"No, it isn't. There are reasons Ryan and I can't be together," Betsy said. "Big, important ones."

"Have you shared those big important reasons with him?"

Betsy shook her head.

"Then I think it's about time, don't you?"

Chapter Nineteen

Ryan left the Teton County Courthouse with most of his questions answered. At first he'd encountered some resistance. Until he'd mentioned he was there representing Betsy's interests. Was it his fault they took that as saying he was her attorney?

After hearing the details of the case against Chad, Ryan knew why the prosecutors were so grateful Betsy had come forward. Although there was good forensic evidence, the legal assistant Chad had assaulted had a few things in her past that the defense would likely use to their advantage.

But with Betsy also reporting inappropriate actions, the chance that they would get a conviction had increased exponentially.

Ryan knew that surprises were never a good thing. He mentioned to the district attorney that Betsy now worked for him and that they were involved. He didn't stop there.

Ryan made it clear he expected Chad's legal team to use that fact to discredit her.

Had she coerced him into that relationship? the attorney had asked. When Ryan made it clear that Betsy was the woman he wanted to marry and confirmed her report that anything that had happened between them was consensual, he was told no worries.

All that was left was for Ryan to go to Betsy, explain what he'd done and tell her there was no obstacle to keep them from being together.

Only one thing worried him. What if this wasn't why Betsy had broken off their relationship? What if she simply didn't love him?

What was he going to do then?

Betsy took Mr. Marstand home, then returned to the house. The sun had set and the house that had been comfortable at fifty-two degrees while they'd been working had taken on a decided chill.

If she emptied more closets or cleaned out a few more cupboards, she might have been able to keep warm. But she was tired of working. Tired of wondering why Ryan hadn't returned.

Not that she wanted him to, but it was rude to promise to come back and then not call. Still, even if he did call, she wasn't in the mood to talk. Mr. Marstand had given her a lot to think about. Who knew the quirky octogenarian was such a sage?

Pulling a musty-smelling crocheted afghan from the table, Betsy wrapped it over her coat and leaned back in the chair. In the past when a childhood memory surfaced, she pushed it back.

For the first time, Betsy let the memories wash over her. Happy. And not-so-happy ones.

She recalled the drunken binges, the broken promises, the horrible things said in anger. To her surprise, she remembered a few happy times, too. Times when her mother's eyes had been clear and bright. Times when they'd laughed and sang songs. Times when her mother seemed genuinely glad to have a son and a daughter.

Her mother had never asked for her forgiveness. Now, because she was dead, that would never happen. What had that minister said? Something about grace being needed but not deserved?

Could she forgive her mother? Let go of the hurt? Put aside the anger?

She'd seen evidence of the rage that burned inside Keenan. Even though he was innocent of the charges that had sent him to prison, he'd been a short-fused bomb waiting to explode. It would have been only a matter of time until he'd really hurt someone or himself.

Betsy closed her eyes and summoned up an image of her mother and the trip to Devil's Tower. When they'd stopped for gas. When she'd returned to the car after paying and surprised Betsy and Keenan with the bottles of orange Nehi soda.

Another good moment, Betsy thought in surprise. Good times that she'd nearly forgotten.

"I forgive you," Betsy whispered. Then, because it seemed if you were going to forgive someone the words should be said with more certainty, with more gusto, Betsy took a deep breath and tried again. "I forgive you, Mother," she called loudly, her words echoing in the silent house. "For everything."

At first nothing happened. Then, like a warm summer rain that washes everything clean, the hurt and anger Betsy had been holding on to since she'd been a child let go of her heart and the tension in her chest eased.

Betsy glanced around the darkened living room. Nothing had changed on the outside. But on the inside, well, on the inside, the sun, which had been covered by clouds, was shining brightly.

Because the sidewalk leading up to her apartment was wet, Betsy carried Puffy from the car. She sniffed. "Puffball, I don't know if it's you or me, but one of us needs a bath."

Betsy figured it was probably both of them. Aunt Agatha's home had a musty, foul smell that made Betsy wrinkle her nose each time she walked through the door. Soon it would be clean. The hardwood floors would be resurfaced and waxed, and lace curtains would hang at bright and shiny windows.

She pictured Ryan and Puffy bursting through the door and her opening her arms to hug them both.

Stop it, she told herself. What Mr. Marstand had said was all well and good, but she refused to let Ryan be hurt because of her.

Puffy began squirming in her arms, making pulling the house key from her pocket even more difficult. Then her phone rang.

Betsy dropped the dog to the porch and gave her the hand signal for "Sit" while she pulled out the phone. "Hello."

She listened in disbelief as the district attorney told her the preliminary hearing on the charges against Chad had gotten moved up to tomorrow. Apparently Chad didn't want the "unpleasantness" hanging over him any longer than necessary. There was an opening on the docket and his attorney took it.

"Of course I can be there," Betsy said. The phone cut out for a few seconds. She thought he said something about having her attorney there for support, but she didn't have an attorney. "I'll see you at ten."

After retrieving the key from her purse, Betsy opened the door and found herself face-to-face with Ryan.

Puffy, the traitor dog, jumped up and down like an acrobat on a trampoline. Betsy had to admit, her own heart had given a little leap. But just one. Okay, maybe two.

Betsy shouldered past Ryan, inhaling the clean, fresh scent of him. Not only did he smell terrific, but he also looked even better. Black pants. Crisp white shirt with cuffs rolled up.

"You know breaking and entering is a crime," she said, acutely aware of her own disheveled appearance.

"I have a key." He smiled. "How many times do I have to remind you?"

"Yes, well—"

"What's that smell?" Ryan sniffed, then wrinkled his nose. "Is that foul odor coming from you?"

Betsy felt heat rise up her neck. "It's my aunt's house. The smell must have gotten in my clothes. Maybe even in my hair."

Before she knew what was happening, he'd unzipped her parka and slipped it off, holding it at arm's length. "I'll hang this on the back deck to air out," he said. "While you take a shower."

Who was he to order her around her own home? Although she had to admit, the smell was a bit overpowering. "Excuse me, this is—"

"No need to thank me," he said. "I'll feed Puffy, then take her outside. I don't think she smells."

He caught the dog midleap, then sniffed while Puffy tried to kiss him. "Nope. She's fine. It's just you.

"Go on," he said when she hesitated. "You don't want your apartment to start stinking."

With a little yelp, Betsy ran off down the hall. Once she was out of earshot, Ryan dropped his gaze to the small red dog staring up at him with a skeptical expression.

"You're right, Puffy, she didn't really smell all that bad. But when a guy asks a woman to marry him, I think she'd like to smell like vanilla, rather than musty old gym socks."

Betsy took her time in the shower, wanting to make sure no trace of that horrible odor remained on her skin or in her hair. Only when she was absolutely certain that it was all gone did she step from the shower. After slathering her skin with her favorite cherry-vanilla-scented lotion, she took a few minutes to dry her hair.

She heard pots clanging in the kitchen, which meant Ryan was making dinner again. Although she'd allowed it once, this time she was putting her foot down. But first she was dabbing on a little makeup and pulling out the flat iron.

Betsy strode into the kitchen about ten minutes later. Although she'd been tempted to put on her pajamas with feet, she decided that might send a mixed message. She settled for her favorite skinny jeans and an oversized turquoise sweater.

"You look fantastic." Ryan glanced up from a pizza crust he was decorating with her stash of olives, mushrooms and green peppers. He lifted his head and sniffed. "And you smell even better."

His grin was so infectious she couldn't help but return his smile. Until she remembered he must leave. And she needed to make him.

"I want you to go."

Ryan cocked his head and looked at her with a quizzical expression as if she'd spoken a language he didn't understand. "The pizza is almost ready to go into the oven," he said. "I saw some romaine in the fridge. Why don't you toss together a salad and I'll uncork the bottle of wine?"

"I'm not hungry." The comment might have been believable if her stomach hadn't growled.

He smiled and Betsy realized she wanted nothing more than to let him stay. She wanted to sit across the table and share her conversation with Mr. Marstand. She wanted to tell Ryan she'd forgiven her mother. She wanted to talk to him about the preliminary hearing tomorrow. Most of all, she wanted him to hold her in his strong arms and tell her everything would be okay.

But he had to leave. Or did he?

You and Ryan need to face whatever is going on in your life together, Lexi had urged.

Have you shared those big important reasons with Ryan? Mr. Marstand had asked.

After all the chaos she'd experienced growing up, Betsy prided herself on being a rational woman. One who looked at all sides of an issue and arrived at a logical conclusion.

That's what she thought she'd done with Ryan. She'd logically concluded that he—and his practice—would be badly hurt because of his involvement with her.

It didn't have anything to do with feeling she didn't deserve to be happy. She wasn't self-destructive, not the way Keenan had been.

She was doing this for Ryan. Walking away from the man she loved to protect him. The problem was he refused to let her walk away. He kept coming around. This was a complication she hadn't foreseen. It didn't make sense. He'd left all those other women without any fuss. Why was he being so stubborn now? Betsy raised a hand to her head, as if that could stop the spinning thoughts.

"Is your headache back?"

She glanced up to find him standing beside her, his eyes filled with concern.

"You would have eventually left me anyway, right?"

He didn't act as if he didn't know what she was talking about, didn't make a joke or brush the question aside. Instead he gazed into her eyes and said very simply, "I will never leave you."

Betsy wasn't sure how to feel about that answer. On one hand his loyalty thrilled her. On the other, it terrified her. How was she going to protect him if he wouldn't let her?

"I love you, Betsy." Ryan's voice deepened with emotion. "You're the woman I've been waiting for my whole life."

There was a part of Betsy that wanted to wrap the sweet words around her heart and hold them close. But the logical Betsy knew it didn't matter what he thought he wanted. She had to protect him.

"You've liked a lot of women," she said pointedly, trying to defuse his earlier words.

"Yes, Betsy, I've liked a lot of women. *Like* being the operative word." Ryan took her hand and led her to the sofa. He brushed the Pom off the sofa, ignoring Puffy's startled look, then pulled Betsy next to him as he sat down.

"We don't need to have a big conversation about your dating history." Betsy's voice sounded breathless, even to her ears. "I was simply making small talk. But I'm asking you again to leave. And this time don't come back."

The words were all there. The problem was her delivery lacked any real oomph. That was probably why Ryan merely blinked and shifted to face her rather than grabbing his coat and heading out the door.

"I'm not going anywhere." His hand slid down her arm, leaving goose bumps in its wake. "The reason you're having such difficulty making me leave is—"

"Because you're stubborn."

"No." He caressed the palm of her hand with his thumb, his stroking fingers sending shock waves of feeling through her body. "Because you don't really want me to go. And do you know why?"

It was difficult for her to think. How could such a simple touch be so sensual? She pulled her hand back. "No, but I'm sure you're going to tell me."

Time seemed to stretch and extend.

"Because you love me as much as I love you."

"You don't love me," she said automatically.

Ryan's expression didn't change. It was as if she hadn't even spoken. He stared at her for a long moment, his eyes boring into hers. "Do you love me?"

"What?"

"Answer the question," he said in a courtroom voice that left no wiggle room. "Do you love me?"

"Yes," Betsy blurted out, then instantly realized her mistake. "I mean no. I don't."

"Now that we've got that settled—" Ryan's mouth lifted in a slight smile, as if pleased by her response "—I'm going to tell you a story."

Somehow without her noticing, he'd moved closer. Too close. A smoldering heat flared through her. It took several erratic heartbeats for Betsy to find her voice. "Once you tell your story, will you leave?"

"When I finish, if you want me to go, I will." Despite his serious tone, there was a smile lurking in his eyes again.

"Okay." Betsy sat back and crossed her arms. "You may proceed."

"Once upon a time, there was a prince. He had a wonderful family, friends he respected and a career he enjoyed. But the prince was lonely. He wanted a princess to join him in his kingdom."

"First time I ever heard anyone refer to Jackson Hole as a kingdom," Betsy muttered.

He ignored the interruption. "There were lots of beautiful princesses for this handsome prince to choose from."

Betsy snorted.

Without warning Ryan bent his head and kissed her softly on the mouth.

"Hey, what—"

"Every time you interrupt, you get a kiss. Now, may I continue?"

Betsy nodded, resisting the urge to touch her lips.

"While there were lots of beautiful princesses, not just any princess would do. When the prince came upon Princess Betsy, he realized he'd found the one he'd been waiting for his whole life. But there was a problem."

His eyes seemed to glitter, suddenly looking more black than gray.

"Chad Dunlop." The name popped out before she could stop it.

His eyes dropped to her mouth. Leaning close, he kissed the base of her jaw, his breath warm against her neck as he spoke. "The problem was Princess Betsy didn't believe Prince Ryan loved her. She didn't trust him."

Betsy pulled her brows together. If he was telling a story, he should at least try to be factual. "I trust you."

He took the fingers of her hand and kissed them, featherlight. "Not enough to tell me about Chad and the upcoming hearing."

Betsy inhaled sharply, snatching her hand back. "You know?"

He nodded.

"So you understand why we can't be together."

"No." He shook his head. "I don't understand at all."

Ryan was a smart guy. The fact that he didn't seem concerned about the hearing only added to her worry. "You saw how Chad acted in the office the other day. He'll make it look like you're a fool taken in by my charms."

"I'm not sure about the fool part." He shot her a teasing grin. "But I have been taken in by your charms."

"Be serious. I won't let your association with me damage your reputation." Tears filled Betsy's eyes. "Please, Ryan, I'm not worth it."

His head jerked up.

Betsy didn't know which of them was more surprised. *Not worth it?* Did she really feel that way? Had Mr. Marstand been right? Had her past affected her more than she'd realized?

"You are worth it, Betsy. And don't worry about Chad's attorney. He might try to discredit us, but it won't work." Ryan slid his fingers through her hair. "We love each other. There's no shame in that."

"Your association with me could damage your reputation," she repeated, her voice cracking.

"If that happens, we'll deal with it." His gaze searched hers. "Being with you is all that matters to me."

Her heart swelled in her chest and she hugged the sentiment close. But Ryan wasn't being rational. He needed to look at what he'd be giving up, what he stood to lose if he was wrong. Having his good name and his reputation tainted by scandal was a real possibility. Chad was crafty and the attorney he'd hired was the best in the region.

Ryan's gaze scanned her face. The moment his eyes touched hers, something inside Betsy seemed to lock into place and she couldn't look away.

"I can survive losing my career." He cupped her face in his hand. The raw emotion in his eyes took her breath away. "I can't survive losing you."

Betsy's heart rose to her throat. Forgiving her mother

had been only the first step in throwing off the shackles of the past. Trusting in Ryan's love and feeling worthy of that love was the next step. Could she take that step? Was she ready?

"I love you," she murmured. Then, because something so important should be said with gusto, she said it again. Only this time louder and with all the passion in her heart. "I love you, Ryan. I don't want to live my life without you."

He let out a long breath but waited, as if sensing she wasn't finished. As if knowing there were still words welling up inside her that needed to be shared.

"From the time I was ten I was convinced I loved you. I realize now that it was mere girlish infatuation." Betsy fought the urge to drop her gaze to her hands. Instead she focused on his eyes, those beautiful gray eyes that held so much love. "Spending time with you has made me realize how superficial those feelings were. But my feelings for the man I've come to know are anything but superficial. They're deep and true. I'll never love anyone more than I love you."

"You and No Other." A sudden look of tenderness crossed his face. "That's what the coin says."

Betsy nodded.

"That's how I feel about you." His voice grew husky. "That's why I had those words inscribed inside the ring."

Before she knew what was happening, Ryan took her hand, then dropped to one knee. He reached into his pocket and pulled out a diamond ring. The large marquis-cut stone caught and scattered the light.

"Will you marry me, Betsy? Will you share your life and your heart with me?"

She leaned over and cupped his face in her hands and gently kissed his lips. "Yes."

He slipped the ring on her finger and suddenly she was

in his arms. Tears of happiness welled up and overflowed. As if on cue, Puffy jumped high in the air, barking and trying to kiss them both.

Moments later, dazed and breathing hard, Betsy stepped back from his embrace, lifting her hand to gaze at the brilliant stone. Its brightness was only surpassed by the love she had for the man who'd given it to her.

"You and no other," she murmured.

"Forever," he vowed.

"Forever," she repeated, ready to embrace the future with the man she loved, knowing there wasn't anything they couldn't face…together.

Epilogue

"I never thought it was possible to pull together a wedding in six weeks." Betsy gazed up at her husband of seven hours, then around the crowded ballroom.

The fact that the Spring Gulch Country Club was still decorated for Valentine's Day seemed appropriate because her wedding day three days after had been filled with passion. The promise of her and Ryan's love had been fulfilled when they'd said their vows this afternoon in a small ceremony in the mountains. Betsy smiled. "I can't believe so many people showed up."

"They wouldn't have missed it." Ryan's hand rested on her waist. "Just like the preliminary hearing. They make time for what's important."

When Betsy had arrived at the courthouse last month, she'd been stunned to find the place packed. Their friends had all turned out to show their support.

Chad and his attorney had been shocked. At first Betsy

thought he might waive the prelim, but both Betsy and the woman he'd violated had been allowed to testify. Despite the stress, Betsy had achieved a measure of peace by confronting her attacker in court.

When Chad's attorney had tried to bring Ryan into the picture, Betsy hadn't gotten defensive. She'd simply stuck to the facts and reiterated that anything that had gone on between she and her fiancé had been consensual.

Even though nothing had been decided, rumors around town were that Chad's attorney was proposing a plea agreement. That part of Betsy's life would soon be relegated to the past. But Betsy had already decided that once they got back from the honeymoon she was going to get involved with the Teton County Victim Services.

"You look a million miles away." Her husband leaned over, brushing his lips against her hair.

Betsy leaned into his embrace, resting her head against his shoulder. "I feel so blessed."

Puffy sat with a group of children, a shimmery white bow askew about her neck. The Pomeranian had been the consummate ring bearer, prancing down the red carpet of the small church.

Mr. Marstand, looking resplendent in the tux he'd worn when he'd walked Betsy down the aisle, was dancing with one of Aunt Agatha's bridge partners.

Scattered around the large room were friends and their families laughing, talking and dancing. Her gaze settled on Cole and Meg Lassiter's son, Charlie. Meg had mentioned that last year the little boy had been involved in Mutton Busting at the Little Buckeroo Rodeo in Pinedale.

Would Ryan want his son or daughter to be involved in rodeo activities? Betsy was curious but not concerned. She knew when the time came that she and Ryan would make that decision together.

"If you're worried about the love token," Ryan said in a low tone, "I'm confident it will show up."

The day after he'd asked her to marry him, the medallion had gone missing. Again.

Ryan chuckled and added, "It'll probably show up before some big occasion, like when we find out we're pregnant."

Betsy thought about the test she'd taken just that morning. Her lips curved upward.

"I can't believe it," Ryan said. "There it is."

"Where?"

"Stuck to the side of the cake." His voice was filled with disbelief. "How the heck did it get *there?*"

Betsy wound her arms around his neck. "You're so smart."

Ryan tilted his head. "Because I predicted that it would show up and it did?"

"Because—" she pressed a kiss against the edge of his lips "—you said it would show up when we find out we're pregnant."

"When we—" He froze. "Are you saying what I think you're saying?"

Betsy nodded. Her smile widened. "I did the test this morning. It was positive."

Ryan let out a whoop and spun her around until they were both laughing and out of breath. And as his lips closed over hers, Princess Betsy realized that life didn't get much better than being with Prince Ryan in the Kingdom of Jackson Hole.

* * * * *